Body of

a Crime

Michael C. Eberhardt

Body of
a Crime

A DUTTON BOOK

DUTTON

Published by the Penguin Group
Penguin Books USA Inc., 375 Hudson Street, New York, New York 10014, U.S.A.
Penguin Books Ltd, 27 Wrights Lane, London W8 5TZ, England
Penguin Books Australia Ltd, Ringwood, Victoria, Australia
Penguin Books Canada Ltd, 10 Alcorn Avenue, Toronto, Ontario, Canada M4V 3B2
Penguin Books (N.Z.) Ltd, 182–190 Wairau Road, Auckland 10, New Zealand

Penguin Books Ltd, Registered Offices:
Harmondsworth, Middlesex, England

First published by Dutton, an imprint of Dutton Signet
a division of Penguin Books USA Inc.
Distributed in Canada by McClelland & Stewart Inc.

First Printing, February, 1994
10 9 8 7 6 5 4 3 2 1

 REGISTERED TRADEMARK—MARCA REGISTRADA

Library of Congress Cataloging-in-Publication Data
Eberhardt, Michael C.
Body of a crime : novel / Michael C. Eberhardt.
p.   cm.
ISBN 0-525-93623-8
1. Trials (Murder)—California—Los Angeles—Fiction.   2. Lawyers—
California—Los Angeles—Fiction.   3. Los Angeles (Calif.)—
Fiction.   I. Title.
PS3555.B465B63   1994
813'.54—dc20   93-30902
                                                          CIP

Printed in the United States of America
Set in Janson and Helvetica Condensed

Designed by Steven N. Stathakis

ACKNOWLEDGMENTS

Thank you to my co-author and lifelong friend, John Tullius, who agreed to help me develop my story and then put it down on paper.

Additionally, my sincere appreciation to Sue Wilkerson, Cathy Darnold, Tammy Davenport, Lisa and Bob Marin, for their invaluable assistance in the writing of this manuscript.

For their patience and understanding, a special thanks to my family; Jolaine, Todd, Chad, and Paul Eberhardt, and to John's family, Shannon and Sommerset Tullius.

CORPUS DELICTI

The body of a crime: The body (material substance) upon which a crime has been committed, e.g., the corpse of a murdered man or woman, the charred remains of a house burned down. The corpus delicti of a crime is the body or substance of the crime, which ordinarily includes two elements: the act and the criminal agency of the act.

—BLACK'S LAW DICTIONARY

prologue

Todd brought all of his girls here—Newport Beach Lifeguard Tower 18. Until he got an apartment like his older brother with the sound-around stereo and king-size water bed and refrigerator packed with beer, this was the best place to take a girl at night. All the towers were huddled close to the long bluff along the beach where the cars parked single file, headlights pointing at the water. But Todd preferred number 18 because it was set in a depression in the shore, so the beams of the cars shot out over the tower, shining harmlessly into the dark of the sea beyond.

Each tower had a little glassed-in station room and a six-foot-wide balcony where the lifeguards perched all day, legs stretched out, hands clamped behind their heads, their white, sunblocked noses cocked toward the water. When the orange sun began to gutter on the horizon and the shadow of the tower stretched a hundred feet down the beach, the guards stowed the gray wood ladder in the shed below the balcony, along with their surfboards and floaties and spare shorts, and went home. Without that ladder, someone had to have the leaping ability of a slam-dunk champ to get up there. And why would anyone bother? There was nothing in the station to wreck or steal anyway.

The setup was just about perfect. Todd would bring along a short rope ladder and haul it up behind him along with the blankets and a little puff pillow to make the girl as comfortable as possible. That's all he needed. Except for the six-pack. And the girl, of course.

"Ready for another beer?" he asked Nicole. She was the new J.V. cheerleader, a bouncy blonde with hair halfway down her back and really nice jugs.

"Wait a sec," she said, lifting her bottle to eye level and swishing it around so she could see what was left. "Okay."

He opened a bottle and handed it to her by slipping his arm around her shoulder and holding it in front of her. She smiled and mischievously chugged down half of it. When she burped, she placed the tips of her fingers to her lips and giggled.

Todd leaned over and kissed her cheek softly. She swung right around and planted her lips against his. When he slid his tongue forward, she sucked it into her mouth. Thank God for Madonna, he thought. Her videos were like little sex-education classes.

When they embraced more deeply, their mouths wrestling furiously, he glided one hand under her blouse. She let his hand rest on her bra-encased breasts. After a few minutes, he slipped his other hand up behind her back, and in one quick move squeezed his thumb and forefinger together. The bra went limp on her chest.

While they made out, Todd kept one eye on the beach, watching for cops and rowdies and anybody else who could screw things up. When a white Mustang fishtailed onto the bluff above, his eyes lifted to watch it. It slid to a stop inches from the edge, its nose hanging over the barrier of foot-high boulders that lined the cliff.

A woman jumped out of the car before it had fully stopped, the skid dust billowing around her. She slammed the door angrily with both hands and stumbled down the cliff. When a big, long-armed man jumped out and started chasing her, Todd moved his lips to the side of Nicole's cheek so he could watch.

"Don't stop," she whispered. Then she opened her eyes and saw something in his face that didn't match the mood. "What is it?"

"Shhhhh."

The woman was running along the sand, heading right for the lifeguard tower. The man took the bluff in two steps and one long, athletic jump onto the sand. He rolled once when he hit, and without putting a hand down, he was on his feet chasing after her. Even though he sank up to his ankles with every step, he powered through the sand, big splashes of beach rooster-tailing up behind him. He caught up to her just as she got to the tower. When he grabbed her arm, she jerked to a stop in mid-stride.

They were both awash in the light affixed to the bottom of the tower's balcony, so Todd and Nicole could see them clearly. The woman was a blonde with long hair like Nicole, but a lot older. The age of the women his brother dated. The age when they didn't care what they did as long as the guy had a condo to do it in and a BMW to take them there.

She was a mess, though, her lipstick smeared across one cheek and her hair looking as if someone had been trying to yank it out by the roots. By the way she fought to keep her feet—wobbly-legged like a fighter who's taken one on the chin—Todd was pretty sure she was smashed. As the man held her, she spun around, slurring something about "kill" and flailing her red nails at him.

Todd and Nicole pushed up against the wall of the station house, as far from the edge of the balcony as they could. They could still see, though, when he grabbed her by the shoulders and started shaking her. He was very big—six-two or six-three—and muscular. When he shook the woman, her head and shoulders flopped around like a doll's. And she wasn't exactly little either. She was a tall woman built like a swimmer, with wide shoulders and well-shaped legs. Finally the man slapped her. His palm caught her flat across the cheek and even with the surf booming, Todd could hear the stinging *whap*.

That stopped her crying for a moment. She stood there stunned, trying to catch her breath like an infant before the first wail. Then she broke, collapsing into the man's arms and blubbering against his chest. He put his arm around her neck and pulled her tightly to him. She stopped crying after a minute, and as she looked up at the man, the tower light hit her face like a photographer's spot. Todd thought she was movie-star beautiful.

Todd and Nicole lay motionless above them, listening. The

ocean noise muffled their voices, however, so the teenagers could hear only wave-washed pieces here and there: the boom of the breaker, the rush of water to shore, the sea foam on sand, the backwash and then, as another wave silently gathered, their arguing voices rising in the momentary hush.

"Oh, God, Chad," the woman cried. "We're in trouble."

"What do you mean . . . ?" he yelled back as the lip of the next wave collapsed, washing away the rest of what he had to say.

"He's on to us" was the next thing they heard from the woman.

"Wait . . ." the big man said. "You're the . . . problem, Robin. We get rid of you, we get rid . . ."

A huge breaker shook the tower.

They yelled a few more unintelligible things back and forth. Then she pulled back and slapped him across the face and took off running again. He was right behind her. He caught her where the rocks of the jetty disappeared into the sand, tackling her by the shoulders and falling on top of her. She struggled but it didn't do much good. He easily held her down with one arm and struck her across the face with the other. And then he struck her again.

"He's beating the shit out of her," Nicole whispered.

The man stood up and yanked the woman to her feet by one arm. She broke loose again and this time disappeared beyond the jetty. He was right behind her, shouting as he ran her down.

Reaching over, Todd opened another bottle of beer and sat up against the wall of the station. The mood was broken, that was for sure. He'd spent an hour carefully coaxing Nicole, and then some gorilla slaps the hell out of a really awesome-looking girl right in front of them.

"We better go, Todd," Nicole said.

"One more beer?"

"I really have to go now. My mom gets home from work at nine."

"Yeah, right." He reached for his ladder and hung it over the side. It unrolled and hit the sand with a soft thump. He leaned against the planks of the balcony, then stopped. The man was coming back.

Todd crept back a foot or two and held his finger up to his lips to warn Nicole.

The man was carrying the woman now. Her arms and legs and

head spilled out of his arms like a beat-up beach blanket. Nicole and Todd held their breath as the man walked below them with his limp bundle. She looked unconscious, her neck stretched back impossibly and her glazed eyes and swollen lips hung open.

"She's dead!" Nicole whimpered between clenched teeth.

Todd held up his hand to keep her quiet, praying the big man wouldn't notice his ladder.

The man plowed through the sand and right up the embankment, slipping once or twice in the ice plant that covered the slope. Todd could see the woman's hair swinging and her arms bouncing as he hauled her up.

The man stepped onto the top of the cliff and then up over the boulders in one huge stride. He opened the door of the Mustang, threw open the seat, and tossed the woman in the back. Then he crawled in the driver's seat, slamming the door. A moment later, the car lights snapped on and hit the lifeguard tower. The Mustang had a cockeyed headlamp pointing almost directly at the ground, so when the car swung around, the misdirected beam spotlighted Nicole and Todd.

The teenagers dropped flat to the floor. The car backed up a few more feet, then stopped, and the man flashed his brights onto the tower.

"Jesus, he saw us!"

"Shut up, Nicole!"

"He killed her, Todd. He killed that woman!"

"Goddamn it! Shut up!"

The car door opened and the man got out with the motor still running, the headlights still illuminating the tower.

"Let's go!" cried Nicole.

Todd looked around. He knew there was nowhere to go. If they ran down the beach either way there was nothing but dark. He might be able to outrun the man, but he doubted it. This guy was a jock. He had former high school tight end written all over him.

No, their best bet was to pull the ladder back up, and if the guy tried to climb up after them, Todd would bean him with a beer bottle.

The man walked to the edge of the cliff and looked out at the beach lit up by his headlights. As Nicole lay flat on the balcony, the brown glass of a beer bottle cast an eerie shadow across her face.

Suddenly the man jumped over the boulders along the cliff. This is it, Todd thought, and he yanked the ladder up and reached for the beer bottle.

The man stopped halfway down the cliff, bent over, and picked something up.

"Her sweater," Nicole whispered. "It's her sweater."

"Yeah," he said and put the bottle down.

The man jumped back in his car and this time swung the Mustang around and drove away.

Todd looked at Nicole. She was shaking like someone who'd just gone for a night swim. He took her hand and helped her start down the ladder.

"She was dead, wasn't she?" she said, crying as they walked toward their car.

"Nah, just passed out drunk."

"She looked dead."

"Nah," Todd said, acting cool. Nicole was right, though. She had looked dead. Real dead.

chapter

one

Judge Sylvia Calebrese, a tiny woman with bony, blue-veined hands and a gaunt face, leaned over the bench and growled, "I'm warning you two *gentle-men*, if the two of you don't quit squabbling in my courtroom, I'll have to hold you both in contempt."

She looked down at Sean Barrett, a young defense lawyer, and then over at the witness, Detective Tom Gamboa, who felt uncomfortably lighter without his checked gun.

"Are we clear on that?" she warned again and then sank back into her chair. She knew these threats were mostly a waste of time. Barrett didn't have the experience of some of the bigger-name attorneys yet, but he was a brilliant and ferocious competitor. He always brought into court a towering stack of briefs and books marked with torn scraps from a yellow legal pad. And he could take command of a trial with a passionate opening or by the way he slapped down a hostile witness.

Gamboa, on the other hand, didn't give a damn about anything when he lost that famous temper of his.

"All right, Mr. Barrett. You may continue," the judge said.

Sean pulled out a huge sheaf of papers from his pregnant brief-case and dropped them loudly onto the lectern. He did it instead of coughing to quiet things. He was tall, bad-boyish looking, and in decent shape for a guy billing seventy-five hours a week. He had light brown hair that he still wore surfer-style, combed straight back so when he was out on his board he could get the saltwater and hair out of his eyes with a quick swipe of a hand. Of course, it was a lot shorter now that he was handling the criminal work for one of the best cor-porate firms in Southern California.

While he dug around in his briefcase for a pen, Sean raised an eyebrow and quickly surveyed the witness. Gamboa had a D.I.'s scowl, a bulldog's neck, and the clean, beat-up hands of a plumber. He never held a thing back. When Gamboa was mad, his face would flush crimson. Sean could read him as quickly as a Christmas card.

"All right, Sergeant, what time was it when you arrived at my client's home?" Sean nodded over at the counsel table, where Teddy Berger sat in a nervous clench. He was a dark, fidgety type in his late twenties who hyperventilated furiously at every court appearance.

Berger, an accountant trainee, was charged with the murder of an elderly security guard who had been working the night shift at the company that employed him. The guard had been shot in the head forty feet from his workstation only moments after he had logged out Berger. The prosecution's case against Berger was largely dependent upon a confession Berger allegedly made to Gamboa two days after the shooting. Sean was trying to get that confession suppressed.

"I got there about eleven p.m.," Gamboa answered.

"Did you have in your possession either an arrest or search war-rant at the time?"

"I didn't need a warrant, Counselor."

The old wood floor of the courtroom creaked as Sean paced slowly before the witness. It was a typical county courtroom, a high-ceilinged place with metal file cabinets along the side walls and nailed-up ash paneling that was supposed to match the judge's bench and the jury box. The counsel tables were a couple of odd pieces of darker lumber with two plastic signs stamped PLAINTIFF and DEFEN-DANT tacked to the front so the jury could identify the players.

"Oh, and why didn't you need a warrant?" Sean asked as if he didn't already know.

"I was just beginning my investigation and wasn't sure yet if Berger was involved in the murder. If he isn't a suspect, I don't need a warrant."

Turning around, Sean threw his pen and pad on the counsel table and smiled to himself. He wasn't buying any of this by-the-book routine. He knew Gamboa was the kind of cop who was interested in seeing justice done. Of course, if that meant a few innocent people had to go to jail or some slimy character suffered a few bumps and bruises, that was no concern of his.

"So my client wasn't a suspect at the time?" Sean asked, circling nearer to Gamboa.

"Like I've been trying to explain. We didn't have any suspects at the time. It was just a routine investigation. A guard at your client's office building was shot to death. I just wanted to see what Mr. Berger knew."

"So it's your testimony," Sean said and leafed quickly through a stapled document, "that, and let me quote you here, 'after I knocked on the front door, a minute or so went by before Mr. Berger opened the door.' "

Gamboa took a deep breath and said, "Right."

They both knew that Sean was building a pen around Gamboa, rail by rail, and there wasn't much the detective could do about it except try to wriggle free before Sean boxed him in.

"And Mr. Berger then stepped outside?"

"That's right."

"I see," Sean said and hesitated. He scratched his bottom lip with his thumbnail and tried to look confused. "But wasn't it raining at the time?"

"Like all hell," Gamboa said matter-of-factly.

"Well, then why wasn't Mr. Berger questioned inside?"

"I asked him if I could step inside, but he said no. Then he stepped outside and closed the door behind him."

"Where you proceeded to question him?"

"Correct."

"So you never went in the house."

"No."

Sean stopped there and looked up from the report. He was a bit over six feet, a few inches taller than the detective, but with Gamboa sitting in the elevated witness box, they were eye to eye.

"So you were standing in a driving rain, questioning Mr. Berger?"

"It was coming down."

Sean leaned against the jury box with his arms folded nonchalantly against his chest. "Who else was there?"

"Who else?" Gamboa said, stalling, wondering whether Barrett had a witness.

"Yes, you know, like your partner? Detective Knox, isn't it?"

"Yeah, that's right," Gamboa said warily. Had Barrett managed to wheedle something out of Knox? That's why this guy was so dangerous. Gamboa never knew what he was going to dig up. "Knox couldn't make it that night," he said. "He had some kind of family deal to go to."

"So you were alone?"

"Yes, Counselor, I was alone," he said, looking Sean over for some clue of what he was up to.

"Wasn't it a little late at night to be questioning someone who you say was only a routine witness?"

"A good detective doesn't work nine to five like a lawyer," Gamboa said.

"Unless he's got a family like Knox, huh?" Sean fired back. He knew the answer to that one. Gamboa's last two wives had walked out on him, and his kids didn't talk to him anymore. Without his police work, he'd have no life at all.

Gamboa frowned.

"Now, once my client stepped out onto the porch, what happened?" Sean asked.

"I told him I had a few questions about the shooting."

"And?"

"That we wanted to be sure he didn't see or hear anything."

"Anything else?" Sean asked, rattling off the questions. He wanted to get Gamboa going at full tilt so when he reached the cliff Sean was driving him toward, he'd have no choice but to jump.

"Well, yeah," Gamboa said. "I wanted to know why he happened to spend extra time at work on that particular night."

"And what was his response?"

"He said it wasn't that unusual for him to go to work for a few extra hours in the evening to catch up on his backlog."

"What did you say to that?"

"I told him that's not what I heard. I talked to his boss, and he told me he couldn't recall Mr. Berger ever coming into work after hours before."

"What did he respond to that?"

"He said his boss was wrong."

"All right. Now, in your direct testimony," Sean said, glancing down at the report again, "you said, quote, 'Mr. Berger blurted out, "I was there when he was shot. I was taking some documents I wasn't supposed to have, and the guard started chasing me. That's when this guy that was with us shot him." ' "

"That's right," Gamboa said.

"Just blurted it out?"

"Yeah."

"I see," Sean said. Backing away from Gamboa, he directed his voice at the judge. "I'm a little confused, Sergeant. You had information that my client was present at the time of the shooting, and yet your testimony is he still wasn't a suspect?" Sean threw his hands out wide in disbelief.

"That's right," the detective answered.

Sean turned abruptly, stepping close and raising his voice. "Why didn't you Mirandize my client?"

"Look, Counselor," Gamboa said, losing his temper. "It don't take a brain surgeon to see what you're trying to dig out of me." He had both hands on the railing of the stand as if he were about to vault over it. "Berger wasn't a suspect at the time, so I didn't have to Mirandize him! Besides, I never got a chance to question him. He dropped to his knees on the porch, covered his face with his hands, and started blurting out a confession. Hey, it surprised me too."

"I'll bet," Sean said. He didn't linger on the sarcasm, though. Gamboa was just about where he wanted him, so he pushed quickly on. "So then what did you do?"

"Read him his rights, asked him if he understood what I just told him, and when he nodded his head that he did, I handcuffed him."

"Sergeant Gamboa," Sean said, pausing. He came up close to the witness stand again and positioned himself so that the judge had an unobstructed view of the detective perjuring himself. "Did my client at any time that night tell you he wanted to talk to an attorney?"

"Not until after I Mirandized him."

"You're sure?"

"Positive," Gamboa said loudly, standing on the first syllable.

"Nothing further with this witness, Your Honor," Sean said, watching Gamboa closely to see how he would take the next bit of news. "But I would like to request that Mr. Gamboa remain while a Mrs. Anne Potter takes the stand."

The bailiff went into the hall and a minute later escorted a tastefully dressed woman into the courtroom. She was in her late forties, tall and slender in an expensive blue silk suit and matching suede high heels. She was the kind of pampered doll whose only occupation ever had been to look sensational. Her slackening looks had become by this point a full-time job—the deep winter tan, the gym-toned arms, the expensive blond hair.

"Mrs. Potter," Sean began after she'd been sworn in, "thank you so much for coming. I know it was a great deal of trouble for you to be here," he said as if he'd invited her to a fund-raiser. He was trying to calm her down. She was nervous as a sparrow, and exaggerated courtesy sometimes reassured these pampered types. He let her settle a little, rearrange her skirt, find a place for her purse. Then he started slowly to get her used to the sound of her own voice echoing in the cavernous chamber.

"Now, on the night of November 2 of this year, where did you reside?"

"One-four-six-six-seven Dover, Huntington Beach," she said softly.

"And do you know the defendant, Mr. Berger?"

"Yes, I do," she said. "He's my next door neighbor."

Sean put his hands in his pockets and began casually strolling toward her. He was using a walk-in-the-park tone as well. "How long have you known Mr. Berger?"

"Ever since we moved into the neighborhood three years ago."

"And who is 'we'?"

"My husband, John, and myself," she said.

She pulled an embroidered hankie from her handbag and coughed demurely into it. Sean thought it was a nice touch. Too bad it was wasted on a judge. The sentiment that gesture might have squeezed from a jury wouldn't mean a thing to Calebrese. Women crying, men weeping, little prison orphans in hysterics as their father was led off in forged restraints to do fifteen to twenty-five—a judge saw it every day.

"Would you consider Mr. Berger a friend?"

"Yes." Her eyes brightened as she looked over at the defendant, and a brave little smile fought its way to her lips. Berger hinted a smile back.

"Do you and your husband still live on Dover?" Sean asked.

"Well, no. I mean, I do," she said, a little unsure.

Sean nodded and half winked to nudge her on.

"My husband moved out last month," she said. "We separated."

"I see. What was the cause of the separation?"

"Well . . ." she started, then hesitated. Her eyes bounced around the room as if searching for the exit. If Sean could just get her past this question, he knew the rest would come more easily.

"My husband found out about Teddy and I," she whispered.

"I'm sorry, you'll have to speak up," Calebrese barked.

Mrs. Potter took a deep breath and looked right at Berger as if holding onto floating debris from a cruise ship that had been torpedoed.

"Teddy and I were having an affair," she said, her voice cracking.

The audience rippled with a few murmurs. Judge Calebrese eyed them. A revelation like that usually created a much bigger commotion, so she let the room settle without a gavel.

"Go on, Mr. Barrett" was all she said to quiet the gallery.

Sean turned back to the witness. He knew he had everyone's attention now. Gamboa suddenly sat forward in his chair, his meaty hands strangling the armrests.

"By Teddy, do you mean Mr. Berger?" Sean asked her.

"Yes," she said, again looking over at Berger tenderly. It was clear she was gone on the guy, but Sean couldn't understand why. Berger was twenty years younger with dark, brooding eyes and one of those spread-across-the-face Slavic mouths that might send the right message to a woman. But he was a struggling low-level executive at a small company, and his finances were a hop ahead of the bankruptcy courts.

"Now, on the night of November 2," Sean continued, "do you recall where you were?"

"I was at Teddy's—Mr. Berger's." She hesitated a second before adding, "My husband was out of town, so I spent the night."

The gallery stirred again. Calebrese gaveled once to head off any lengthy speculating.

"While you were at Mr. Berger's, did someone come to the front door?"

"Yes."

"And where were you and Mr. Berger at the time?"

"We were in bed," she sighed. Every revelation cut her dignity a little deeper. It would be months before they had gossiped themselves out at the Junior League and she could show her face again. It wasn't the affair that shocked them. They were all having affairs, usually with one another's husbands. But she had had the deplorably bad taste to get caught and, worse yet, to be embroiled in a murder scandal with someone like Berger.

She looked up and, gathering herself again, went on. "The bed is right next to the window on the side where I was lying, and Teddy leaned over me to see who was at the door."

"Did he say who he saw?"

"No. He said, 'Let's just ignore it.' But the pounding went on for several more minutes without letting up. It just got louder and louder," she said. "Then we heard a man's voice yell out, 'Berger, this is Sergeant Gamboa from the Sheriff's Department. I want to talk to you. I know you're up there. I saw a light go off.' "

Sean saw she was doing fine. He folded his hands behind his back and, with a few questions to guide her, let her tell her story. "What did Mr. Berger do then?"

"Well, it was late at night in a quiet neighborhood, and this man was announcing to the whole block that he was the police and he wanted to question Teddy. Teddy wanted to shut him up before the whole town knew. So he got out of bed, put on his robe, and went downstairs. I could hear him talking to the man at the door."

"Did you see who the man was?"

"Not at first, but after a few minutes he stepped back and I could see it was that man," she said, pointing at Gamboa.

"Just Sergeant Gamboa? Nobody else?"

"Not that I could see."

"Go on," Sean said.

"After a while I couldn't see the sergeant anymore because they'd switched positions."

"What do you mean, 'switched positions'?" Sean asked, circling his finger in front of him as if he were mixing a drink with it.

"Well, the sergeant was standing under the porch, and Teddy was out on the sidewalk now."

"So Mr. Berger was standing in a driving rain?"

"Yes."

Gamboa rolled his eyes.

"And you couldn't see the sergeant any longer?" Sean asked.

"Only his hand poking Teddy in the chest every so often."

Sean walked back to the lectern and glanced over at Gamboa, whose jowls were turning a violent purple. Sean now had the cop at Berger's late at night, forcing his client to stand in an icy downpour while he grilled him. And upstairs watching was a solid witness.

"All right, Mrs. Potter, what happened after the sergeant maneuvered Mr. Berger out into the rain?"

"Well, he started bullying Teddy," she said. "Yelling at him and using a lot of awful profanity."

"Could you give us a specific example, Mrs. Potter?"

"Can I say it in court?" she said and looked up at the judge.

"It's all right, Mrs. Potter," Calebrese said sympathetically. "There isn't an obscenity in English or several other languages that this court hasn't heard innumerable times before."

"The sergeant called Teddy a mother f'er," she said quickly.

Calebrese raised her eyebrows. Sean smiled, then went on quickly. "So the sergeant got rough with Mr. Berger?"

"Yes. He kept swearing at Teddy and yelling, 'We know you killed him. It'll go easier on you if you cooperate now.' "

"What did Mr. Berger respond?" Sean asked.

"He said many times, 'I'm not talking to you without my attorney.' "

"You're sure he said that?" Sean asked, thumping the jury box rail with his finger.

"Absolutely," she said. "He repeated it over and over. But Mr. Gamboa wouldn't let him go."

"He wouldn't let him go?" Sean's tone was appalled.

"No! Teddy was pleading with him, 'It's cold out here. I want to go in.' "

The next few responses should do it, Sean thought. He stepped closer to her. "And what did the sergeant say to that?"

"He said, 'Good, maybe it will make you think a little clearer,' " Mrs. Potter said firmly. Her voice was rising with every answer. " 'I'm not leaving until you tell me what I want to know.' "

"Those were his exact words?" Sean said and looked over at Gamboa. The detective sat with his hands clenched in double fists, his teeth grinding, his eyes pinned on Barrett.

"Yes, they were."

"I see. Then what happened?"

"Mr. Gamboa told Teddy that he had a witness who saw him shoot the guard, and Teddy better cooperate or he was going to the gas chamber, but if he talked now, he could help him."

"Sergeant Gamboa said he'd be able to help Mr. Berger if he confessed?" Sean asked, raising an eyebrow as if he could hardly believe it.

"Yes."

"What did Mr. Berger say to that?"

"He said he wanted to see his attorney and go back inside the house. This went on for at least a half hour. Mr. Gamboa kept yelling at Teddy, 'You killed him, didn't you? You killed him.' Over and over. Teddy kept pleading to let him go back in," Mrs. Potter said, then her eyes turned sad as if she'd just seen a puppy run over. "He just had a thin robe on, and he was soaked and shivering."

"Did Sergeant Gamboa ever let Mr. Berger back in the house?"

"Never," she said loudly but without a hint of unladylike shrillness. "Finally, there was a long silence and then I heard Teddy mumble, 'Yes.' Then, 'Yes,' again and then '. . . shot him.' "

"I see," Sean said. "Just 'shot him.' " He paused for a heartbeat or two on the brutal phrase, then went on. "Nothing else?"

"That's all I could hear," she said. "Except the sergeant kept saying, 'That-a-boy.' I remember it very distinctly. 'That-a-boy, now tell me who the others were that were with you.' It was so demeaning, like he was talking to some gutter bum or something. I wanted to go right down there and slap his impudent face," she said, sticking her chin out defiantly at the detective.

"And that was it?"

"Yes."

Sean backed away from the witness for a second, then returned to her again and spoke very slowly.

"Now think carefully, Mrs. Potter," he said with a suddenly urgent tone. He leaned right up next to her. "Did you ever hear Sergeant Gamboa tell Mr. Berger he had the right to consult an attorney?"

"Definitely not!" she answered. "Teddy kept telling him he wanted to talk to his attorney, and the sergeant wouldn't let him."

"So you did hear Mr. Berger request an attorney?"

"Many times."

"And that was before you heard Mr. Berger mumble the words 'shot him'?"

"Yes."

"Nothing further, Your Honor," he said and went back and sat down next to his client. Berger studied Sean's face and then asked, "How did she do?" Sean nodded in mild approval. But he was thinking that she'd buried the son of a bitch.

George Landes, the deputy district attorney, slowly got up to cross-examine. Landes had been around this shabby courthouse for twenty-five years, and it had worn him to a dull edge. But he was still capable of bludgeoning a witness when he thought it was worth the effort. Landes knew, however, that Barrett had pinned Gamboa into a tight corner. A jury would never hear that confession, no matter how long he battered Mrs. Potter. Calebrese wouldn't care if she'd diddled every young guy in Newport.

Landes asked a few quick questions and sat back down. After deliberating for less than a minute, Judge Calebrese gave her ruling.

"This court is granting Mr. Barrett's motion to suppress the statement allegedly made by Mr. Berger to Sergeant Gamboa. At the very least, based upon the information he had, Mr. Gamboa should have considered Mr. Berger a suspect and shouldn't have asked Mr. Berger anything about the murder without first advising him of his rights. In fact, I think Mr. Barrett has shown us sufficiently that Sergeant Gamboa probably coerced a confession out of Mr. Berger." Then she slammed the gavel on the bench. "Court adjourned!"

Sean started gathering his papers, raking them up with both

hands like a poker player sweeping in the chips after a big hand. "That was an important victory for us," he said to Berger while stuffing his briefcase.

"Now what?" Berger asked anxiously.

"Now we see if they still want to take it to trial," he said and nodded over at Landes.

"Do you think they will?"

"They've already got a very solid case for burglary, and they've got you at the scene of a murder. Yes, I'm pretty sure they'll go ahead with it. But without the confession they're down to circumstantial evidence. No gun, no witnesses, and what I'd call a shaky motive."

A bailiff had appeared on either side of Berger, who rose apprehensively to his feet. Each of them put a firm hand on either elbow, and Berger stood up straight in compliance. Berger didn't say anything. He always froze when the bailiffs came to take him away. It was the first time he'd seen the insides of a big-city jail. Suddenly he found himself doing lunch with the kind of guys who liked to party after they'd just beaten someone to death.

"Talk to you Tuesday," Sean said as the bailiffs led his client away.

Sean pulled the belt strap tight on his dilapidated briefcase. When he'd been accepted to law school, his father, just before he died, had borrowed money from his drinking buddies so he could buy it for him. It had been through a decade of battering duty, and it was completely shot. The top fasteners had long since stopped working, and the belt was the only thing keeping it together. But Sean refused to buy a new one. It was the last thing his father had given him, a final gesture that said, "Yeah, I thought law school was a pretty highfalutin idea at first, but I love you. Go kick some ass, son."

He put his briefcase under his arm like a football. The handle had fallen off last month, and he still hadn't gotten it fixed. But he kept writing reminders to himself to drop it by the leather shop in San Clemente.

Seelicke, the bailiff from Judge Macklin's court down the hall, stopped Sean as he came through the door of the courtroom.

"Got a message from Macklin, Barrett. He wants to see you, pronto."

"Did he say what it was about?" Sean asked.

"I think you've been elected to defend that 'no-body' case."

Sean knew immediately what Seelicke was talking about. Three weeks before, Chad Curtis, a former local high school hero, had been arrested for the murder of his old girlfriend, a beautiful young actress named Robin Penrose. The case was making headlines every day locally, and it had even spread to the national media because of its uniqueness. The young woman had been missing for six weeks and had been last seen fighting with Curtis on the beach. The D.A. had charged Curtis even though there was no direct evidence of her death. Robin Penrose's body had yet to be found.

"Macklin knows my firm won't let me take a court appointment," Sean said.

"The judge said he'd bet his ass you'll figure a way to take this one."

"What happened to Pelzer?" Sean asked, referring to the public defender who had been handling the defense.

"Conflicted out," Seelicke answered. "He almost cried when he told the judge."

Sean knew that the bailiff probably wasn't exaggerating much. A no-body case was the ultimate legal challenge for a criminal attorney, the quintessential test of one's abilities. Not only were no-body cases extremely rare, but the D.A.'s office would never file such a case unless the circumstantial evidence against the defendant was overwhelming. What attorney who still loved the law, loved hunting through all the reports for that one little clue that could unlock a case, loved the battle between two good lawyers who'd done their homework, what attorney wouldn't want this case? And now it appeared it was going to be his—a no-body murder.

Sean tried hard to suppress a smile. "And they still haven't found her?" he asked.

"Not a fucking toenail."

chapter

two

Sean pushed open the door to the jailhouse and began the long walk down the corridor to the lockup. He had made hundreds of trips to this dungeon, but he knew he'd never get used to it. The cold, inhuman touch of the place always chilled him. He guessed it was the metal—the metal doors with metal window frames and metal mesh running through the glass. The iron bars and the stainless steel commodes. Not the slightest touch of warmth anywhere.

Sean banged on the metal door of reception and saw Gloria Rodriguez's face peer through the mesh window at him. Rodriguez was short and over-padded, and she had those big Latin eyes that she guarded with a sullen expression. She could never smile or relax or show any emotion, or the men would bury her in a flurry of daily bullshit. Why they had her working here, Sean could never figure.

"Good afternoon, Gloria," he said as he shuffled past her. His briefcase had come unbuckled, and he was trying to wrestle with it while he looked for some paperwork.

"Good afternoon, Mr. Barrett. How are you?" She kept her voice flat, but her eyes were soft.

"Fine. How's Rosario?" Gloria had a little boy from when she was married.

"Honor roll this semester." Her eyes warmed a few more degrees. "Go ahead and put your things on the desk," she said and stepped away from the bullpen door so Sean could set down his bundle.

Patterson, the other jailor on duty, a beefy, beer-bloated deputy with rheumy eyes, swung his feet around off a metal chair in the closet-sized office. "Counselor," he shouted, nodding hello to Sean. "Say, who you got in the Packer game?"

"Frisco minus three," Sean said without looking up from his papers. "Ah, that reminds me," he said and fished in his pocket and pulled out a ten-dollar bill along with a green betting card and placed them on the counter next to the jailor.

Patterson was a near-celebrity during football season because he handled the Pick Six cards for a local bookie. If a guy picked six winners, he won a thousand bucks on a ten-dollar bet. Even the judges would swing by the lockup on Friday afternoons to drop off their picks and the ten bucks.

Patterson swung the key chain loose from his belt. "Okay, who's your fish today, Counselor?"

"We got every fish in the sea here in this aquarium," Patterson liked to joke. "We even got sharks. Of course, they're the ones that come in through the front doors with the briefcases."

Sean found the sheriff's report and read the full name of the man that Judge Macklin had asked him to interview. "Chad Lee Curtis," he said.

Patterson ran his hand down a wrinkled computer printout on a clipboard hung on the wall. "Oh, yeah, the piranha."

"Piranha?"

"Yeah, this is the no-body murder, right, Counselor? We figure he ate his victim, 'cause there's nothing left of her."

Patterson laughed and swung the door open. Sean cinched his briefcase tight, stuck the sheriff's report between his teeth, heaved his stuff up, and followed the jailor.

"Hey, you got a celebrity on your hands, Barrett. 'Rifleman' Chad Curtis," Patterson said, pointing at the report.

"Last time I read about him in the *Times*," Sean said, "he was burning up Triple A. What the hell happened?"

"Blew his arm out trying to throw a ball out of Yankee Stadium."

"Really!" Sean said, shaking his head.

"Yep. I heard it was a bet with a teammate. Probably both sucking up coke all day, for chrissake. 'Ah, hell, yes, I can throw it outa this fuckin' stadium!' " Patterson laughed at his own performance.

"Where'd you hear all this?" Sean asked skeptically. A jailor was worse than a bored housewife when it came to gossip.

"My kid caught him in high school. They still screw around together," Patterson said, then stopped a moment to reminisce, his hand resting on the bars of the lockup. "You know, I remember when my kid would come home after Curtis pitched. His hands looked like he tried to fix a car engine with the motor still running. All swollen and cut up. I clocked Curtis one time with a radar gun from a black-and-white. Ninety-eight just throwing on the sideline to my kid in practice. Ninety-eight!" Patterson whistled. "I figure he's the best athlete to ever come out of Orange County. All-CIF quarterback, led the league in scoring in basketball, and goes number three in the pro baseball draft. Three years later, Oakland brings him up at the end of the season to get a sniff of the Bigs, and the idiot tries to throw a fucking ball out of Yankee fucking Stadium."

"Thereby kissing off all chances for a twenty-five-million-dollar, no-cut, guaranteed contract," Sean said and whistled at the asinine way Curtis had blown his future.

"Tank three, Counselor," Patterson said and shut the door behind Sean with a loud bang.

Sean walked down to the far cubicle and sat down. It was about the size of a toilet stall at a gas station and just about as clean. There was a concrete-and-glass partition that divided the room in two. Sean had to hold an interview through the small wire-mesh window with fingerprints and spit and snot smeared so thick, he had to hunt for clean spots to see what his client looked like. The only difference between the two sides was the black marker graffiti covering the walls of the inmates' stall. Gang logos and swastikas peppered the wall along with encrypted messages like PUPPYDOG SUCKS CHIPS and BLOOD-TALK SACRIFICE!

Sean sat down and began reading Curtis's file again while he waited. He had already gone over it quickly, skimming the essentials of the prosecution's case so far. A few minutes went by before he heard the clank of the door, and he looked up to see Patterson leading Curtis in. He was a big, good-looking, light-haired kid with ice blue eyes. Six-three at least. But he'd filled out since high school, and he looked like he'd been spending afternoons in the weight room.

"Sit down," Patterson said, and Curtis dwarfed the stool like a parent sitting in his kid's desk on parent-teacher night.

"Hi, Chad," Sean said. "My name is Sean Barrett. I'm an attorney. Judge Macklin asked me to represent you. But I need to find out some things before I agree to take your case."

"I already have an attorney," Chad said warily.

"Yes, I know," Sean said. "Bill Pelzer has a conflict."

"What happened?" Curtis said with more than a trace of alarm. Sean knew that anything unexpected, no matter how trivial, can panic someone in lockup. And losing your attorney is not trivial.

"That's all I really know, Chad," he said and put the report he'd been scanning in his lap.

"I don't understand why I'm even still here," Chad said, raising his voice. "Mr. Pelzer told me I'd be out of here by now. After the preliminary hearing the judge was supposed to dismiss the case. That's what he told me." Curtis lifted off the stool a few inches, put his face closer to the glass, and raised his voice another notch. "They don't have her body. They don't even know if Robin is dead. Why am I still here?"

Ordinarily Sean would have held a client's hand a little, reassured him, but the clock read 5:11. At 5:30 they bused everybody back to the main lockup at County, and Curtis was catching that bus whether he wanted to or not. Sean picked up the "murder book," a compilation of the investigation on the case, and held it up in front of the window. "Look, Chad, there's over two inches of documents here, and all I've had time to do is get the basics of your case. So I'll make you a deal." He put the book down and lowered his tone. "First, let me ask you some questions and then, if we have any time left, I'll try to answer *your* questions."

Curtis lowered himself back onto his stool and nodded. "Okay."

Chad's quick compliance would have surprised Sean if he hadn't known the type. Chad was probably used to taking orders from coaches. Oh, he liked to bitch and whine, but he was relieved when someone else took the responsibility for his life.

"All right," Sean said, "the woman you allegedly murdered, Robin Penrose, what was your relationship to her?"

"Robin was my girlfriend in high school," Chad said.

Sean turned the report over and started taking notes on the back as Chad talked. "Tell me a little about her, Chad."

"I was in love with her," he said as if that covered everything.

"You *were* in love with her. Does that mean you're certain she's dead?"

"She has to be dead," he said and started to raise his voice again. "She loved me too. She would never let me stay in here if she were alive."

"All right," Sean said, raising his palms to Chad, "calm down. Tell me about her."

"Well, she's very pretty," Chad began. "She's an actress. She did a couple of those movie of the week deals and had a few speaking parts on some sitcoms like *Seinfeld*."

Sean nodded his head. "Go on."

"We were the big couple in high school. I was the quarterback. She was the head cheerleader. After school she went to Hollywood to pursue acting, and I got signed to play pro ball—"

"You mean professional baseball?" Sean asked. The last thing he wanted was to let Chad think he was a fan of his. This kid needed help, not hero worship. The D.A. wasn't going to offer him a no-cut contract.

"Yeah, baseball," Chad said. "I got some scholarship offers for football too. But all the smart people said my future was in baseball. A lot they knew." Chad leaned back and gave a short laugh. Sean could see that even in this dungeon, the kid had an easy smile. That was a plus. A jury would want to like Chad Curtis.

"And what about Robin?" Sean asked. "What happened to her in Hollywood?"

"Well, it was rough for her there, really. She fell in with a bad crowd. You know, drugs and stuff. That's about all I know. When she came back to Newport she was pretty messed up, and an old friend gave her a job." Chad put his head down and fought back some tears. "She was really doing good," he went on, "making good money and going back to school."

"All right," Sean said, "I'd like to go back to the last time you saw her alive."

Curtis shrugged. "Well, I dropped her off at her apartment on a Friday night a few weeks ago, and that's the last time I saw her."

"Do you know if anybody else has seen her since that night?"

"No. I mean, nobody's said anything yet."

"All right," Sean said and jotted something on the report. "Now, you were at the preliminary hearing. Tell me what happened."

"Well, a couple of kids said they saw me arguing with Robin at the beach and that I beat her up. They said they thought she was dead when I carried her to her car. But she wasn't, Mr. Barrett. She was just drunk."

"All right, Chad," Sean said softly. "Who else testified?"

"A guy named Frank Johnson. He said I asked him if he'd help me get rid of Robin's car. That's about it."

"Okay," Sean said. "Now, what about this fight at the beach?" He knew the statements of the two kids had prompted the police to charge Curtis with murder in the first place.

"It wasn't any big deal. She was drunk, so she was talking crazy and stuff," Chad said. "I might have slapped her once or twice to calm her down, but that was it. She was fine when I took her home."

Sean studied Chad for a moment. What he said conflicted badly with the kids' statements. They said that it looked to them as though he beat her to death.

"What were you arguing about?" Sean asked.

"Just things. You know."

"No, I don't know," Sean said, getting rough again. "Tell me exactly what was said and what happened."

"It was just an argument," Chad said quickly. "Nothing specific. I don't remember exactly what we said."

Sean looked down at the sheriff's report. He was fingering through the pages, looking for something that might help. "What about this guy you ditched the car with?" he said and looked down again to get the name right. "Frank Johnson?"

"I didn't give him the car. He's a damn liar. He's always in trouble. He's probably just lying to help himself out with the cops," Chad said. Then he added, "Can they keep me here like this, Mr. Barrett? Without her body?"

Sean put everything down and leaned forward to give Curtis a good look at him through the murky glass. "You know, Chad, I don't think you grasp just how serious this is. It appears they have quite a lot of circumstantial evidence built up against you. Some very damaging stuff."

"I don't know about that," Chad said. "Those kids at the beach couldn't have seen much because I didn't kill her. She was just passed out drunk. That's all. And Frank Johnson," he said and laughed. "Frank Johnson is a weasel. He was a weasel back when we played together, and he's a weasel now. He'd do anything for a buck so he can put some more stuff up his nose."

Sean studied Chad. He knew the kid was in for a shock. "That might all be true. But the way things are right now, your chances of convincing a jury aren't very good."

Chad's shoulders dropped. "But I didn't do it."

Sean paused for a second. An attorney was called a counselor because that was a large part of his job—to explain the law to his client, to counsel him on his rights and options, and just exactly where he stood with the law. Sean's counseling of Chad was about to begin.

"It doesn't really matter that much whether you did it or not. It's whether or not the evidence against you is strong enough to convince a jury," Sean said. "Sure, it's true that they don't have a body. But they don't have to produce a body. Without it, of course, it will be more difficult to prove she's dead. That's why a district attorney will rarely file a case like this, because once they decide to prosecute, that's it. They've got to get a conviction or the defendant goes free forever. So the odds are with you in this kind of case. Except the D.A. knows all this too, and he hardly ever brings a defendant to trial unless he's sure the circumstantial evidence is a dead-solid lock to bury you. And apparently he does. Because the D.A.'s office is going ahead with this prosecution all the way to trial."

Chad's eyes dropped and then his chin lowered until it rested against his chest. The next time he saw a lawyer, he had been expecting to walk out of jail with him.

"Mr. Barrett, I would never hurt Robin," Chad said without looking up. "I love her. You can ask anybody who knew us. Ask Carrie Robinson. She is her best friend."

"Carrie Robinson the attorney?" Sean asked. Although he'd met her a few times at parties and around the offices of their respective firms, he knew Carrie Robinson mostly by reputation. A full partner in her father's firm, she'd earned her position. She had represented several large companies in deals involving Sean's firm, and she'd handled the gorillas from his office like they were chimps. She was worth a bundle by now. And to complete the package, she had a face men would empty their money markets for. But she also had a reputation around the courthouse for being the kind of rich snob from the snooty end of Newport that Sean preferred to avoid.

"Carrie will tell you I couldn't have killed her. She knows how much I loved Robin."

"I believe you, Chad," Sean said. "Unfortunately, love is one of the first things a prosecutor will point at to prove guilt. Love often turns out to be the sole motive in the most brutal of murders."

When Chad finally raised his head, there was terror in his eyes. Sean saw it, but he still had work to do before five-thirty.

"I notice in Pelzer's file that he received several phone calls from an anonymous caller who spoke with a Caribbean accent and that the caller told him he knew where Pelzer could find Robin," Sean said. "Did he ever mention these calls to you?"

"No."

"Do you have any idea what those calls might have been about?"

"No. I don't know anything about it." Chad shifted in his seat until he was sitting almost sideways to Sean. His arms were folded on his chest.

Sean studied Chad for a moment. For a young man who had never spent a day in jail, he didn't seem to be trying very hard to help his attorney free him.

"You know, Chad," Sean said softly, "a good defense attorney's strongest asset is that he can read people. Read witnesses and clients and even other lawyers. A person's reaction to a question many times tells me more than what is actually said. Now, throughout this interview I've had the feeling that you were telling me the truth. Maybe it had a coat of wax on it here and there, but basically the truth. Until I mentioned this Caribbean caller."

He let Chad fidget a little more in his chair. "You want to tell me again what you know about this guy?" Sean finally asked.

"Look," Chad said, "I swear I don't know anything."

Sean hesitated again, watching him. With most clients it was best to let them know when he thought they weren't telling the truth, then drop it. After that he let the prospect of a long stretch in jail work on their memories.

"You really think they're going to go ahead with the trial?" Chad asked. "Pelzer thought that if they didn't find her body, they'd just drop the charges."

"I'm sorry, Chad. They're definitely proceeding with your case. They're going to set the trial date tomorrow."

"But I didn't kill her. I had no reason to harm her. It had to be—" Chad suddenly stopped and looked away from Sean.

"Had to be who?" Sean probed. "Do you know someone else who had a reason to kill her? If you do, you better let me know now."

Chad shook his head, still not looking at Sean.

"You're lying, son," Sean said. "I think you know she's dead, and you have a pretty good idea who did it."

Suddenly Chad cried, "I don't know who killed her."

"So you do know that she's dead, then?"

"I didn't say that."

"Come on. I know bullshit when I hear it."

Chad didn't answer, staring at the wall.

"Look at me, Chad," Sean yelled. "Look at me!"

The young man slowly raised his eyes.

"Chad, I don't think it would be wise for me to take on a case as complex as this one if I think my client is lying to me."

Sean stood up as if to leave.

"Mr. Barrett, I'm sorry," Chad pleaded. "Things just aren't working out like I thought. What I meant was she really had a lot of problems when she was in Hollywood. She was into a lot of drugs and knew some bad people. I think maybe she owed some of them money. I just don't know."

Now he was getting somewhere. "Do you have any names?" Sean asked.

"No, I'm sorry. I was off playing ball the whole time Robin was hanging around that place."

Patterson came into Chad's tank then and motioned to Sean. "Sorry, Sean," Patterson said. "We're lining 'em up for busing now."

Chad got up to follow Patterson and then he turned back to Sean, "Are you going to help me?"

"I can't answer that now," Sean said and watched Chad disappear through the door. The truth was, Sean already knew he wanted to take the case. Chad Curtis didn't know it yet, but he'd finally gotten himself into the World Series. Only it was the World Series of legal cases. What Sean couldn't figure was why the kid was being evasive. It was obvious to Sean that he knew more than he was saying. But why? What could be worth rotting in this cesspool—risking a murder conviction—to hide?

chapter

three

Sean pulled open the door of his beloved old 1977 Mercedes 450 SL convertible. The tired white paint was as gray as old dishwater and the seats were broken down, off-kilter, and sometimes slid forward on their tracks when Sean hit the brake hard. He had recently replaced the tattered old ragtop, but the top's frame was hopelessly bent, so it didn't fit snugly. If it rained, Sean had to plug the gaps with rags. In a good storm the floorboard was awash with murky water.

Sean took off his jacket and vest and threw them in the backseat. Sitting in the driver's seat with his feet still resting on the pavement, he pulled off his loafers and his socks, then reached behind the seat and got his yellow beach flaps.

He hated shoes. He'd lived at the beach ever since he was eight years old, when his father moved the family to Newport. As a kid he'd gone entire summers without ever putting on shoes. Even now he couldn't wait to get them off.

Sean pulled out of the parking lot and headed for the beach. He had lived in Newport for twenty-five years before L.A. had finally worked its way down there, crawled all over it like skin cancer. A flock of birds that inhabited the sanctuary of the back bay had finally been chased away by the houses now crowding the overlooking bluffs and the speedboats that butchered the silence and the R.V. park that paved the land right up to where the shorebirds made their nests. As kids, the back bay was Newport to Sean and his pals. Sean would borrow a dinghy in the morning and paddle across Newport Harbor through the inlet into the back bay—the little metal boat pushing through an acre of ducks that had grudgingly cleared a path for Sean, then closed behind, bobbing in his inconsiderable wake. That was all gone now, of course.

Newport Beach had been swallowed alive sometime in the last twenty years, and hardly anyone had taken notice. It was crowded with the worst L.A. had to offer—people looking for an address that meant something on the envelopes of their business Christmas cards.

The real beach folks, the surfers and the boat people—the people who didn't just live by the ocean so they could own a "view"— were forced to keep moving south away from the encroachment of "Greater Los Angeles." That left only Laguna Beach, San Juan Capistrano, and San Clemente. Laguna was owned and operated and ruined by "creative types," and Nixon had turned San Clemente into a right-wing mecca for TV evangelists. That left Capistrano. The only thing in Capistrano were the swallows and another endangered species—the last of the Southern California beach people.

Sean turned off the San Diego Freeway at the Camino Capistrano off-ramp and headed west toward the beach. The sun had been down for an hour, and he could see the light of an autumn half-moon dancing on the Pacific. He wound down off the bluff to Pacific Coast Highway and drove south a couple of miles before making a right across the railroad tracks.

Sean's place was the next-to-last house on the beach before Doheny State Park, which meant the public parking was within fifty feet of his patio. It got rowdy during the summer with the kids drinking and blasting rap, but of course there were always the bikinis to ease the annoyance. Most of the sunburn and beachball crowd just in from Omaha and Boise stayed down on the north end of the mile-long parking lot and beach area. The shore break was gentle there and a lifeguard tower lent peace of mind to the mothers. On his end of the beach was the hot surfing spot.

Sean turned his car into the Doheny parking lot and pulled right up to the edge of the sand. He got out, hopped the retaining wall, and walked along the beach and into the side door of his house—a sun-bleached wood bungalow with louvered windows and a shake roof. A utility room opened onto the back patio, where he kept his wet suit. He yanked his tie off, stripped off his clothes, and pulled on his wet suit without bothering about trunks. His board was leaning against the wall in front of the house. Throwing it on the sand in front of where his SL was parked, he hopped back up onto the pavement and snapped on the headlights of his car. When he flipped the brights on, the beams lit the waves enough so he could see the silhouette of the swells building up outside.

Sean threw his board into the surf and dived in after it. The cold of the winter water shocked him, but he knew his body would warm the water in the wet suit. In five minutes he'd be comfortable.

Since law school he'd taken up night surfing. It was the only time he had. And surfing was the one thing he found that could really relax him: out in the dark water, the waves lifting the board up, then speeding past, crashing ten yards on.

Tonight the waves were decent-sized, and the swells lifted him high above the sea and then dropped him into the pitch dark troughs behind them. When the waves rolled on, he could once again see the shore, the camp fires burning on Doheny Beach, and the cars going by on PCH.

Waiting for the waves rolling out of the vast Pacific was when he did a lot of his thinking, when he could best unravel those tough knots of a case.

A no-body case. Sean couldn't believe his luck. He hadn't heard of anyone being prosecuted for murder without direct evidence of death since law school.

The Scott case had been the first one in California history. In 1956 L. Ewing Scott had been accused of murdering his wife for her money. The only direct evidence of the wife's death was her eyeglasses that were found near the defendant's incinerator. Mrs. Evelyn Scott, the missing woman, had carried on close relationships with many longtime friends. When she disappeared, all visits and corre-spondence with those friends suddenly stopped without a word from Mrs. Scott. In addition, she was loaded with money and yet she never withdrew any of it from any of her accounts after her disappearance. So, if she was alive, how did she support herself? everyone asked. But what really sunk Scott, Sean knew, was the way he acted after his wife vanished. He immediately began to spend his wife's money, forge checks and safety deposit access slips, and started dating other women, whom he lavished with the jewelry and furs of poor Evelyn Scott, as if he was certain he'd never be seeing her again.

The circumstantial case against Scott seemed very convincing indeed. Yet how could a jury ever be convinced that someone was dead without a coroner or someone else testifying that a death had actually taken place? Didn't the absence of a body automatically cre-ate a reasonable doubt? All the same, the jury found Scott guilty in a matter of hours. The case was taught in every law school in the country to show that death can, indeed, be proved by circumstantial evidence. Rare as these cases were and as tough as it seemed for the prosecution to prove that a murder had even been committed, the defendants were almost always convicted.

Sean knew how difficult it was going to be to win this case. Chad Curtis had been arrested and charged with murder in the first degree, and the D.A. seemed confident that the circumstantial evidence against Curtis was strong.

Of course, all this conjecture was moot unless Sean could con-vince Jonathan Spann, the managing partner of his firm, to let him take the case. And what if Spann turned him down? Would Sean be willing to jeopardize his secure position at Spann, McGraw and New-some to go jousting with this legal windmill? The first two years out of law school Sean had hung out his shingle and nearly starved. Then, four years ago, Spann had hired him to handle the criminal problems of the firm's wealthy clients so that they wouldn't be lost to another firm. With Spann, McGraw, Sean had built his reputation and his bank account, but he had not been entirely content. As a criminal attorney in a corporate law firm, Sean knew that to become a senior partner he would have to forgo his criminal practice and become expert in business and corporate law. The thought appalled him. Maybe it *was* time for a change. Wouldn't it be nice to pick and choose the cases he took, rather than having Spann do it for him?

As Sean mulled over Chad Curtis's case, he spotted a set of big waves forming outside, beyond the range of his headlights but silhouetted by the moon, the high, rolling shadow of their crests rising slowly toward him.

Suddenly it got very dark. Someone had turned off his headlights. He could feel the waves somewhere out there rising behind him.

"Hey, asshole! What the hell you doing out there freezing your butt off?" someone shouted from the shore.

The lights snapped back on.

MacDuff.

Jesus! He was supposed to meet with MacDuff at seven-thirty. He'd forgotten all about it. No telling how long he'd been out here rhapsodizing about this no-body case.

Sean looked over his shoulder and saw a good one coming, gave a couple of quick paddles, and felt its smooth acceleration as he stood up. He rode the wave all the way into shore, picked the board up in a foot of water, and trotted over to MacDuff.

Craig MacDuff was a private investigator Sean had used before, an ex-detective with the Sheriff's Department for the County of Los Angeles. Sean knew if he took Chad's case he would need an investigator, and Mac was the best available. So after he'd interviewed Curtis, he'd given Mac a call from the jailhouse.

"Hey, Mac. How's it going?" he said and shook the investigator's hand. "Look, do me a favor. While I get showered, put my car in my garage. The keys are in it. And you better move yours too."

"Ah, I'll just leave it there," Mac said casually.

"You better not," Sean said. "It's one-hour parking here, and what we have to talk over could take awhile."

"Yeah? I don't see any signs," Mac said, looking around.

Sean dropped his board on the sand and stepped onto the asphalt and pointed at the metal poles that were planted up and down the parking area. "See those poles? They're supposed to have signs on them. But this is Beaver Beach and every time they put up a sign 'Beaver Beach—Violation!', some kid's got the damn thing in his bedroom in an hour."

Mac laughed. "Yeah, I know, but those meter bitches don't come around after dark."

"They do here," Sean said. "You know what a problem parking is at the beach. They're tough as hell. Even this time at night somebody comes every hour and chalks tires. If they come around the next time and see a chalk mark on your tire, it'll cost you twenty-five bucks."

"I get it. They don't care if you bang your honey on the beach. But you better get it done in an hour. Is that it?"

"That's it."

Sean laughed and trudged through the sand to the side of his cottage and leaned the board against the wall. Then he turned on the outside shower and peeled the rubber skin from his body. When he finally walked in the sliding door of the cottage, the phone was ringing.

"Sean, this is Carrie Robinson."

"Hello, Carrie. How are you?" he said, surprised to be hearing from her. They had met once or twice, but they'd never said anything more than "pleased to meet you."

"I'm sorry to bother you, but I understand you're going to represent Chad Curtis," she said abruptly.

"Who told you that?"

"I heard it from someone at the courthouse."

"Well, the truth is, I really haven't decided yet."

"Good, so then you're not going to take the case?"

Sean frowned at the phone. Carrie Robinson had a reputation as a tough, aggressive attorney, but so did he. "Like I said, I don't know yet."

"Well, I don't know if you're aware of this, but Robin Penrose worked for me," she said. "Actually, Robin was my best friend since high school."

"Yes. Chad told me."

"Then wouldn't it be difficult for you to represent Chad knowing how close she was to my family?"

"You mean my relationship to your father?" he said, a little baffled. Carter Robinson had been a partner of Spann's before Sean joined the firm. Sean's dealings with the man had always been strictly social. "Frankly, I don't see how that affects my decision. You know I like your father a lot, but I only see Carter a few times a year. There's certainly no grounds for conflict, if that's what you mean."

There was silence for a moment. When she finally spoke, all the warmth had vanished from her voice. "I don't want to get nasty, Sean. But I don't think Jonathan Spann is going to see it that way."

"Look, Carrie," Sean said, trying to contain his anger, "I know how upset you must be. But you're an attorney, and you know that Chad is entitled to legal counsel, the same as anyone else."

"But why does it have to be you?"

"Because Judge Macklin thought I was the best man for the job."

"Maybe, but when I get done talking to your boss, I don't think he's going to agree with the judge," she said and hung up.

Sean put the phone down slowly. The problem was, she was probably right. Spann wasn't likely to want Sean to take Chad's case but not for the same reasons as Carrie Robinson. Court appointments like the Curtis case paid less than half of Sean's normal billing rate, and the firm's bottom line was Spann's obsession.

Mac was rummaging around in the kitchen cabinets when Sean got off the phone. MacDuff was a bear of a man, a rusty-skinned redhead with a meandering handlebar mustache that hung below his chin. He was about six-four and closing in on three hundred, but he wasn't the body builder type. He was built more like a haystack. When he was with the Sheriff's Department, he had kept in pretty good shape playing for the department rugby team. But since getting booted off the force, he'd added twenty or thirty pounds and softened up. Hunting for Sean's booze, Mac looked like a grizzly ransacking a campsite for food.

"You got anything besides this fucking light beer?" he growled at Sean.

"Hey, you're in a lovely mood," Sean growled back. "Try looking above the refrigerator."

Mac yanked open the cabinet door, and with one hand he grabbed a couple of bottles of liquor. It didn't seem to matter what he fished out of there as long as it was alcohol.

"Want a drink?"

"Sure. Which bottle is yours?" Sean joked.

"Both of 'em!" Mac said in a pissed-off way that made Sean regard him more closely. Mac was the kind of guy who rode out a storm like a seabird—floating through whatever came. Except Sean knew there was one storm that sank big Mac every time—Hurricane Trudi.

"All right, spit it out," Sean said. "What's the problem? Trudi making life miserable again?"

"Ah, that fucking bitch!" Mac said, slapping shut the cabinet door.

Trudi was Mac's ex-wife—a woman he had had no business marrying in the first place. She was a Vegas glamour girl with breast enhancements and a shopping obsession. Every two or three days she'd come home with a carload of purchases, all on Mac's credit cards. It took about six months before Mac found himself staring bankruptcy in its hideous face. It was either get rid of Trudi or bring in more dough. The department's semi-annual raises weren't going to cut it. And no way Mac was going to get rid of his "Truds." A man like Mac dreams his whole life of coming home to a pillow full of blond curls and breasts like a Playmate's. So instead of getting rid of her, he tried a little "creative financing." Every time he busted a dealer, a little of the evidence went into his pocket. "You ax down a door and these assholes have twenty grand in hundreds lying next to their stereo," Mac told Sean one day after he'd been kicked off the force. "So only five grand ends up in 'evidence.' Big fucking deal!"

When the district attorney got a whiff of Mac's harmless little scheme, he unloaded on Mac and his pals like a dump truck of judicial boulders. Luckily, it was an election year and the D.A. wasn't looking for a public scandal to fuel his opponent's campaign. He gave Mac the option of resigning quietly or doing fifteen years at Soledad. Mac wisely decided to become a civilian. When he did, though, Trudi decided to resign too—from their marriage.

Mac grabbed a couple of cubes and slammed the refrigerator door. "Sean, the bitch got everything. The car, the house, the TV, the stereo. I got my clothes and a good-bye fuck. And it wasn't a very good fuck either." Mac dumped most of the bottle into a tumbler with the ice and drank half of it down. "On top of that, I can't get an assignment to save my ass. Nobody's getting divorced anymore, for chrissake. It's too expensive in this recession. And the D.A.'s office has me blacklisted, so I can't get any court appointments." Mac finished off the drink, cubes and all.

"You just got one."

"Huh? No way. They won't touch me."

"I'm telling the judge you're my investigator on this one or I don't take the case."

"You're shittin' me!" Mac hollered.

"Scout's honor," Sean said, holding up three fingers.

"What kind of case?"

"Murder, first degree."

"Yeah?" Mac said. "Who did who?"

"Ever heard of Chad Curtis?"

"Who hasn't?" Mac said. "It's in the paper every day. Killed his girlfriend. Only they haven't found her body. That's *your* case?"

"Yeah."

"That's an appointment, isn't it? Appointments don't pay diddly," Mac said, waving his hand at Sean. "The partners in your firm won't go for that. Especially that cheap bastard Spann."

"I don't know yet," Sean said.

"Shit, I know," Mac said and gulped down the rest of the drink. "I appreciate you thinking of me, buddy, but next time hire me for a case you're actually going to be able to take, will you?"

He got up and headed for the door. "Look, I'm going over to Tortilla Flats to watch the game. They got buck well drinks and free taquitos tonight. Wanna come?"

Sean had a weakness for Mexican food, but he was going to have to face Spann first thing the next morning and he had to find a way to persuade him that a low-paying, tough-to-win case that was going to take up all his time was a smart move for Spann, McGraw and Newsome.

"I'd better not, Mac. I've got a little homework."

"No shit, Counselor," he said and slammed the door behind him so hard that the house shook.

chapter

four

Early the next morning, Sean stood in his unlit office and looked down at the fading lights of Newport Harbor—the ferry boat dock strung with blue and white Christmas lights, the old cannery building now a restaurant with a red Christmas star bolted to its roof, a cardboard Santa leaning tiredly against it. The horizon was taking on an orange hue—probably a storm down below Baja somewhere, Sean thought. The waves would be big in a couple of days.

"If I can just convince Spann," he said to himself. Like many trial attorneys, he was in the habit of rehearsing his openings and closings out loud, often pacing before a mirror to see how it would look and sound to a jury.

Sean saw Spann's big silver Mercedes pull into the eight-story parking garage across the street. A pinstriped sleeve reached out of the driver's window and stuck a plastic card into a slot, the guardrail raised, and the Mercedes disappeared into the darkness of the concrete structure. A few minutes later, Sean saw Spann, a tall, slim man with slicked-back gray hair, carrying his wine-colored leather briefcase. His stride was long and upright as if it were already mid-morning. Sean didn't bother to look down at his watch. He knew it was exactly six forty-five.

Spann had been a highly respected criminal attorney in his early days, but he had eventually opted for a corporate partnership when he realized that only an elite few attorneys—the glamour names writing books who were more celebrities than lawyers—made a killing in criminal law.

Most people who committed crimes, Spann had told Sean, couldn't afford an attorney and usually settled for public defenders. And those who could afford a lawyer didn't always pay. They weren't exactly the cream of society, and if they lied, extorted, cheated, burgled, and murdered to get their way in everyday life, they couldn't be expected to suddenly change when it came time to pay their attorney. Part of being a good criminal attorney, Spann told Sean on a weekly basis, was making sure you get paid up front.

Spann's daily rounds brought him by Sean's office at exactly ten forty-five every morning when Sean wasn't in court. Before he spoke to Spann today, however, Sean wanted to discuss the Curtis case with Scott Powers. Scott had been hired by Spann seven months before, on Sean's strong recommendation, to help Sean and some of the other attorneys with their backed-up caseloads. He was a good criminal lawyer and an old friend. Sean had known him since their days together playing on the Newport Harbor High baseball team.

"Got your message, Sean. How'd that Berger confession go?" Scott asked as he walked into Sean's office. He was about the same age as Sean, but his thinning hair and pale complexion made him look older.

"The judge threw it out," Sean said. "You should have seen Gamboa's face when I brought the girlfriend to the stand. It was sweet."

"Great! Gamboa needs his ass trimmed on a regular basis," Scott said. "So how's the case going otherwise?"

"Well, that's what I wanted to talk to you about," Sean said as he walked over and sat in a chair by the wall. "I think it's going to be your baby now. I'm going to have to hand off most of my caseload for a while."

Sean knew he would have to have additional help in order for Spann to accept his plan. Scott was the logical choice. He could handle his current cases as well as Sean could. There was nothing on his docket at the moment that wasn't routine. And if he did encounter trouble, Sean would be right down the hall to bail him out.

But there were a few problems. In the first place, Scott's hiring the previous spring had nearly been a disaster. About a month after he joined the firm, he had been the only witness to a murder inside a gay bar. Scott, who knew it was useless to try to concoct a lie, admitted on camera he was gay. It was on Channels 2, 4, 5, and 7 at five o'clock and eleven. Spann stormed out of his office just as Scott arrived the next day and intercepted him. Spann pushed him in and closed the door behind him, and the whole office could hear the execution for the next fifteen minutes.

"I don't give a goddamn who you screw," they heard Spann yell, "but you start fucking with the reputation of this firm, and that is my business. You know, I've already had six calls this morning from long-time clients asking me what's become of Spann, McGraw."

Then Spann fired him. Sean, who was in court that morning, didn't witness Scott's dismissal. When he heard about it, he marched down to Spann's office and demanded that Scott be reinstated.

Spann flatly refused, and Sean was just about to say he could fire him too when he looked out the one-way glass of Spann's wraparound view and saw two dozen gays chanting and waving placards on the sidewalk in front of Spann, McGraw.

"Mr. Spann," Sean said, pointing out the window over Spann's shoulder. "You better have a look at what's out there."

Spann turned and Sean thought he heard his boss gasp. One look at the growing mob, at the sound trucks of Orange County's Own— KOST 91.5 AM pulling up, and Spann knew he had a public relations disaster on his hands that could demolish the firm's P&L.

It took him only a moment to gather his wits. He took off his jacket, rolled up his sleeves, and pushed through the front door to confront the homosexuals with his most concerned look. In ten minutes he'd convinced them that Scott's so-called firing was just another media screw-up.

That had been six months ago, and Scott was still with the firm.

Scott settled into the chair next to Sean. "What's the deal? Why do you have to lighten your caseload? You sick or something?"

"No, I'm not sick," Sean said and kicked his shoes off. "I've got another case now that's going to take up most of my time."

"For how long?" Scott asked warily.

"Several months at least. But it could be for as long as a year." Sean knew this would, of course, be a major obstacle. It meant he couldn't simply use delays to juggle his caseload. He was going to have to inform some very wealthy and influential people that he was no longer going to be handling their cases.

"You're kidding!" Scott said and pushed his blond hair back off his face. "What kind of case?"

"You're familiar with Chad Curtis?"

"Sure," Scott said and stopped again. He put his finger to his lips. "But that's a court appointment, isn't it?" He paused again to work out the next step in the puzzle. "Spann let you take an appointment?" He sounded as if someone had told him the sun wasn't coming up tomorrow.

"Spann doesn't know yet."

"He doesn't know yet!"

"I'm going to tell him as soon as he gets in," Sean said quickly.

Scott started laughing. "Whoa, señor," he said. "Hey, if I'd known we were going to be sharing our fantasies this morning, I would have worn my garter belt. No way Spann goes for that."

"If he doesn't," Sean said, "I'm prepared to walk."

His face was placid, but a wave of nausea rippled through his stomach as he said it. Until that moment even he hadn't known how far he was prepared to go for this case.

Scott saw something in Sean's eyes that frightened him. "You're serious, aren't you?"

"Yes."

"This case means that much to you that you'd give up a possible partnership?"

"Yes." He felt himself sinking deeper and deeper into a committed stance from which there was no return.

"What the hell for?"

"Scott," Sean said and put his hand on his friend's shoulder. "It's a no-body case. They come around about as often as a solar eclipse."

"Jesus Christ, I know that. But, Sean, you better think this over a little. There will be other cases you can hit a home run with, you know."

Sean looked at his friend and smiled. "Ah, who knows?" he said, slapping his knees with mock finality. "Maybe Spann will surprise us both and let me take the case and I won't have to worry about opening my own practice."

"Right," Scott said. "And I hear they're opening a ski lift in Death Valley this summer."

They were both chuckling when someone behind them said, "I understand you wanted to see me."

Scott and Sean turned to see Spann standing at the door dressed in a slim-cut Italian blue suit. With his silver and black hair combed straight back, with the manicured nails and the five-karat ruby pinkie, he looked like a model in a *GQ* ad.

"Mr. Spann! Good morning," Sean said, a little startled. He had been rehearsing all morning how he was going to approach Spann about the case, and his boss had caught him off guard.

"Well, I've got work to do," Scott said and gave Sean a raised eyebrow as he walked out.

Spann put his hand out and stopped Scott as he went past.

"I want to talk to you about that Gemco matter as soon as you're finished with the research," Spann said in a starched tone.

"I'm ready any time, Mr. Spann," Scott said and pushed quickly by.

Sean could almost hear him sigh out in the hallway. Spann managed to intimidate just about everyone. He was the only one in the firm who could fire you without a question.

"I understand you interviewed a man named Chad Curtis," Spann said, turning back to Sean, who had quickly hidden his stockinged feet beneath the chair and sat upright.

"Sounds like a very interesting case," Spann said while he watched Sean struggling to get his feet back into his loafers. "Have they found the body yet?"

"No. Not yet," Sean said. He could tell Spann already knew all about the case, including Pelzer's conflict and Judge Macklin's request that he take the case.

"A no-body murder," Spann said. "You just don't see that kind of case very often, do you?" His tone was suddenly so friendly that Sean felt uneasy. Spann wasn't a bad guy outside the office. In fact, after he had half a belly of scotch in him, he could get downright human. "In fact," Spann went on, "I've only heard of one other case the whole time I was with the district attorney's office."

"A no-body murder?" Suddenly he'd forgotten just about everything he was going to say to Spann.

"Sure. Didn't I ever tell you about that case?"

"No. What happened?" Sean said.

"Well," Spann said and perched on the side of the desk, one foot on the floor, "when the judge asked the defense attorney to call his last witness, he stood up, turned dramatically to the back of the courtroom"—Spann stood and faced the back of the office—"raised his voice much louder than normal, and called the victim to the stand."

"The victim?" Sean asked.

Spann smiled. "Yes," he said. "There was total silence in the courtroom when he called out the victim's name. 'Robert Sloan! Bailiff, call Robert Sloan to the stand.' Everybody, including the D.A., turned quickly and looked toward the back of the courtroom. The whole court was waiting for the murder victim to walk through those swinging doors into the court and exonerate the accused."

Spann paused, still facing the back, and looked over his shoulder at Sean. "Two minutes went by and nobody came through the door. They finally realized he wasn't going to appear when the defense attorney sat down. He'd made his point. If everyone expected the murder victim to appear at the mere mention of his name, then they must have a reasonable doubt in their minds whether he was dead." Spann spun around and slapped his palm on the desk. "It was brilliant. The attorney looked slowly around at each juror and even at the D.A. Then he turned to the judge and said, 'The defense rests.'" Spann had both hands spread out on the top of the desk, looking down at Sean. "The D.A. knew he was sunk. The jury deliberated and returned a verdict in less than a day." Spann hesitated a moment. Then sprung the punch line. "The verdict was 'Guilty'!"

"Guilty?" Sean said and laughed. The mood was barroom, two buddies exchanging war stories.

"Nobody could believe it, especially the poor defense attorney,"

Spann said. "He went up to the foreman of the jury in the hallway afterward and asked, 'How could you return a guilty verdict? You must have had a reasonable doubt because when I called out the victim's name, every single jury member turned and looked for him to come walking into the courtroom.'

" 'You're right,' the juror said. 'We did have a reasonable doubt at the time whether he was dead or not.'

" 'So what happened?' the attorney wanted to know.

" 'Well, when you called out his name, everybody in that courtroom turned around. Everyone except your client, that is. He was the only one in the courtroom who knew for sure that the victim wasn't going to be walking through the door.' "

Spann was pointing at the door. His smile gave Sean the feeling that his boss might actually go for the Curtis case.

"Who asked you to interview Curtis?" Spann asked gruffly, his smile suddenly gone. He had turned from a puppy to a growling guard dog in the time it took to blow out a candle.

"Judge Macklin called me to his chambers," he said. "The P.D. declared a conflict and Macklin asked me to replace him. So I interviewed Curtis."

"Well, that's fine," Spann said. His face was expressionless and his eyes steady. "You don't want to upset Judge Macklin. He could hurt you on another case if you aggravate him. You did him the courtesy of talking to the accused, and now all you have to do is come up with some legitimate excuse why you have to decline."

Sean sat there for a moment looking at Spann with grudging admiration. He'd gone from telling an amusing little story to ordering Sean to drop the most intriguing case of his life.

"I haven't decided whether to take the case or not," he said finally, looking Spann straight in the eye.

"I don't think your decision is that difficult, really," Spann said, turning away and staring out the window. "There is no possibility you can take that case. You're so busy now, you can't handle the cases you have."

"Yes, I know," Sean said. He was prepared to answer whatever Spann threw at him. "I was thinking that we could use Scott to help me for the next few months. At least until the trial is over."

"Let me remind you of what I told you the day you were hired.

We work as a team here. A team! Not individuals trying to further their own careers at the expense of the firm. Everybody works for the common good of the firm." Spann leaned over and tapped his finger on Sean's desk. "We hired you to take care of the criminal difficulties of our clients. These are very wealthy, high-paying, prominent people for the most part, and when they get in a spot of trouble, they expect you to be there to bail them out. They're not going to put up with some pinch hitter."

Sean held his temper but not without clenching his teeth. He could feel the heat in his chest radiating up into his collar. "Think what a case like this could mean to the firm's reputation," he said in a reasonable tone.

"Only if you win."

Sean finally understood Spann's real problem with this case. It was too risky. Forget that the publicity from a case like this could triple business in six months, or give the firm a prestige it couldn't buy. No. If he lost, it could hurt the bottom line. That was the corporate mind. Stay mediocre, stay solvent.

"You know, there's another point that needs to be made about that story I just told you," Spann went on. "The defense attorney who lost suffered considerable damage to his reputation. Now, call Judge Macklin," he said, putting his hand on the phone for emphasis, "and tell him you have checked your calendar and you can't fit this case in."

"I can't do that," Sean said quickly. His lack of hesitation surprised even him.

"Son, this is not a negotiable matter," Spann said. "You'll never defend this case while you're working at this firm."

The crucial moment had come more quickly than Sean had expected. All right, he thought, do I or don't I commit professional suicide?

"This isn't some messy little divorce," he said to Spann, starting out slowly. "It's the ultimate case. A no-body murder." Sean took a step toward Spann. "When I was in law school, I dreamed about getting a no-body case. And I'm not going to give it up."

He had gone too far already. Sean knew he was probably no longer a member of Spann, McGraw. Even worse, Spann had the power and influence to blackball Sean right out of Southern California and they both knew it. But Sean realized in that moment that he didn't care about the job, about the security, about the money, about the prestige. He wanted that damned case.

"You're jeopardizing what you have been working for the last several years," Spann said. "You walk out that door and it's like jumping off a cliff. And the only parachute you've got is this firm." He was pointing at the floor as if Sean's career were down there, obliterated by his own stupidity.

Then Spann upped the ante.

"You're this far from a partnership, son," he said, keeping his hands in his pockets, uncommitted. "And you're throwing it away for a case that will turn into a run-of-the-mill murder two as soon as some jogger stumbles on her body. That could be tomorrow morning, you realize. And you would have blown it all for some two-bit murder case that you'll probably end up plea-bargaining down to manslaughter."

Sean didn't say anything. Spann had the instincts of the craftiest criminal attorneys. He had been the best around at one time. Too bad, Sean thought, that he'd given it all up for the paperwork of corporate law just because he wanted his bottom line to bulge.

Sean stood up even-shouldered to Spann, an equal for the first time. The power Spann had over him was gone with his job. He could already feel the knot in his stomach loosening. Jonathan Spann and Sean Barrett were different kinds of men, and Sean finally understood that.

"I'm going to have to take that chance, Jonathan," he said calmly and walked out.

chapter

five

Sean pushed past the knot of smokers standing outside the entrance to the County Courthouse. Inside, the place looked like most government buildings, like a dog that nobody cared about. Dust and hair balls skittered around in the corners of the hall. A crippled chair, its black plastic seat split down the seam, sat alone in a corner. There were no plants or flowers anywhere, no colors except dingy beige and simulated walnut. Like a bus station, everybody was just passing through.

Sean weaved through a hallway filled with people nobody cared about either. Young women, their hair fried blond, with pretty faces and fist-sized bruises on their arms, slumped in chairs while their school-aged kids in mismatched clothes ran in and out of doors. Two or three grammar school dropouts in untied high tops were hunched over a form trying to read it. Greasy-haired men wearing jackboots and baseball caps with truck logos wiped their drug-ravaged noses.

Sean took the stairs up to the Superior Court on the second

floor. Carrie Robinson was waiting for him at the landing. She was nearly as tall as Sean, and her long black hair fell past her shoulders. She wore a navy blue suit with a red scarf tied loosely around her neck. Sean had forgotten how striking she was.

"Did you talk to Jonathan?" she asked without preamble.

Sean frowned. "Yes."

"Good. I want to thank the two of you for considering my feelings. I just didn't want either you or Jonathan to do anything to help that killer."

"I'm accepting the appointment," he said flatly.

The surprise was evident on her face. "But Jonathan told me he wouldn't let you—"

"I'm no longer employed by Spann, McGraw and Newsome," Sean cut in.

"He fired you?"

"Well, if he did, it was after I walked out," Sean said. "Now, if you'll excuse me."

He stepped past her, but she grabbed his arm as he went by. When he turned toward her, he had an annoyed look.

"You would have liked Robin," she said.

"I'm sure I would have."

"Tell me, Mr. Barrett. Does Chad know how much Robin's family and friends are suffering because we can't give her a decent burial?"

He looked her over for a moment, from the expensive shoes to the two-hundred-dollar haircut. "Chad was wrong about you."

"What does that mean?"

"He was certain you'd help him. He told me you were the one person who knew that he loved Ms. Penrose."

"It wasn't love. It was obsession," she said. "Ever since Chad came back to Newport, he followed her around like a damned bloodhound. She couldn't shake him." She still had her hand on his sleeve and she drew him nearer. "You know, she had just gotten herself through a rough period, and she had a bright future. She was the best assistant I ever had, and she was going back to school. . . ." She broke off. Sean turned to go, but she tugged his arm. "How can you represent him?" she asked. "He snuffed out a beautiful and gentle young life."

"Look, Ms. Robinson, I've heard what you have to say," Sean said coolly. "I'm Chad's attorney." He pulled free of her and walked away.

Sean saw the crowd of media surrounding Courtroom E as soon as he turned the corner. He could see that most of the newspapers on the West Coast had a reporter here with a steno pad stuffed in a rear pocket and a patter as tough as a career criminal's. " 'Course he did her. That's not the question. It's whether they can prove it."

This was Sean's first appearance for Curtis, so the media ignored him as he made his way toward the courtroom. By tomorrow the whole mob would break toward him as soon as they spotted him, shouting and pushing, the kliegs snapping on, the videos rolling.

Behind the herd of reporters Sean spotted Tom Gamboa. When the detective saw him, he stepped out of the crowd gathered at the courtroom door and stomped toward Sean. "Good morning, Counselor," he said. Coming from Gamboa, the word *counselor* sounded like an insult.

"What's all the excitement?" Sean deadpanned. He was wearing his best suit—a dark blue three-piece—and he'd put a new buff on his loafers with a dishtowel as he was going out the door. He also had on an impressive gold watch, one of those Singapore Rolexes that go for twenty-five bucks on every street corner in Little Saigon near Dodger Stadium.

"They're waiting to see who Macklin pulled out of the hat to save Curtis," Gamboa said and jabbed his thumb over his shoulder at the crowd. "Wait'll they hear it's you."

"It should be a lot of fun," Sean said, "especially with you being the investigating officer."

Gamboa motioned down the hallway with his head. "Mind if we have a little talk, Barrett?" He grabbed Sean by the sleeve before he could answer and led him around a corner out of earshot of the media.

"What is it, Sergeant?" Sean asked, though he was pretty sure he knew what Gamboa was up to. The prosecutor wanted to make Sean an offer, and Gamboa was his messenger boy.

"We both know your client is guilty and I can prove it with or without a body. Except now we've got the body." Gamboa's voice had an almost pleasant lilt to it. It got that way sometimes when he'd trapped a criminal, or a criminal lawyer, which was the same thing to him.

"Really?" Sean said, trying not to look concerned. "You found her body? I didn't hear anything about that."

"Well, we don't exactly have her yet," Gamboa said quickly. He knew he had to be careful with Barrett. "But we know where to find her."

Sean grinned at Gamboa and took a step closer. "Before you can present it as evidence, Sergeant, you actually have to have the body and somebody has to ID it."

Gamboa grinned right back. "Look, tell that client of yours we know she's buried on a hillside near Victorville. And if I were you, I'd tell him now, Counselor," he said. Then he got to what the prosecutor had sent him there to do. "The D.A. will agree to offer him second-degree right now. Once we find the body, it's going to be first-degree or nothing."

Sean nodded at Gamboa and said, "Sure, I'll tell him."

"This is a one-time offer, Barrett," Gamboa said and spat into the sand-filled ashtray next to Sean. "Good for today only."

Sean was tired of hearing the ultimatum "good for today only" that prosecutors were so fond of delivering. It sounded like they were selling used cars. Sure, a lot of the people a defense attorney represents deserve the harshest treatment the law can deliver. But did the system and everybody in it have to lower themselves to the same level as the criminals?

"If the legal system were run the way you wanted it, Gamboa, we wouldn't need courtrooms. We'd just scare a confession out of everyone and then hang them."

"Don't sound too bad to me."

"Except you'd be coercing confessions out of innocent people too."

"Innocent people don't drive around in the victim's car the next day, Barrett," Gamboa said, his nose right up next to Sean's. His voice had a hissing edge. "So don't give me any of your bullshit. Assholes like Curtis deserve to be gassed, but the old ladies sitting on the Supreme Court won't let us do it anymore without special circs."

Shaking his head, Sean stepped around Gamboa without answering and started walking toward the courtroom again. The bailiff spotted him and motioned him to hurry inside. Sean figured that Judge Macklin probably wanted to meet with opposing counsels.

As he neared the courtroom door, one of the reporters shouted from the crowd, "Mr. Barrett! Is it true you're representing Chad Curtis now?"

Suddenly the mob of reporters and their cameras closed in on him. He had to trot the last couple of steps to avoid being cut off.

"I'll talk to you later," Sean yelled back over his shoulder as the bailiff slammed the door behind him.

The prosecutor, Sherman Lowenstein, was already waiting at the counsel table. Lowenstein was in his fifties and a little heavier than Sean remembered, but he still had that gleaming smile from all those capped teeth and the power suits and the garish ties that were his trademark. Today it was a red number about a foot wide with French sex terms scribbled all over it.

"Mr. Barrett?" Lowenstein said and held out his hand.

"Yes," Sean said, shaking. "Mr. Lowenstein, how are you? I'm going to be representing Mr. Curtis."

"Yes, I've heard. Should be an interesting case."

"Yes, it should be." Sean laid his briefcase down on the counsel table. "So they sent over one of their heavy hitters, huh?" he said, acknowledging Lowenstein's high-profile reputation. He was the perfect prosecutor—clever as a hungry weasel with a deft touch for the politics of the job. "The point man in the war on crime," as the mayor was fond of calling him at the endless dinners, fund-raisers, and political meetings where Lowenstein was always being photographed.

"Well," Lowenstein said, "as you probably know, it can be very tricky if you don't know what you're doing." He gave Sean a long, sympathetic look as though he were the heavyweight champ and Sean some club fighter they'd set him up with for an easy payday. Then he added, "But to be perfectly honest, I just needed a change of scenery."

The first of many lies, half-truths, exaggerations, cons, trickery, and misstatements yet to come, Sean thought. Lowenstein had had a long, media-glorified run as chief deputy D.A. He'd tried the Midnight Strangler case, as well as the Children of Perdition, a satanic clan who had been murdering celebrities in alphabetical order. They were up to *C* when a SWAT team surrounded them as they were parked outside Johnny Carson's Malibu beach house. Lowenstein was the kind of D.A. who measured his success by how much air time he logged.

The bailiff approached and said, "Gentlemen, Judge Macklin would like to see you in chambers."

Judge Steven Macklin was sitting back in his chair with his feet propped on his desk and a cigarette stuck to his bottom lip, talking on the phone. By law, he could not light up in the courtroom, but a perpetual cloud of carcinogens hung in his private chambers. Sean took a deep breath as he entered. It might be the last pure air he breathed for a while, he thought, what with the smoke and Lowenstein's well-known penchant for bullshit.

Macklin motioned them to take a seat with his cigarette. A long ash fell as he pointed, and it splashed over his pants. Macklin fit perfectly into the unkempt atmosphere of the County Courthouse. His suits always looked like he'd spent the night on a park bench, and he rarely wore a jacket that matched his pants. His hair looked like he cut it himself—a dried-out straw manger of a haircut with a part that meandered from front to back like a drunk walking the line.

Macklin threw the receiver in its cradle, got up, and walked over to the chamber's rest room. With the door still wide open, he unzipped his trousers and began to relieve himself. "I knew you couldn't turn this case down, Barrett," he said over his shoulder.

Sean was used to Macklin, so he just kept right on with the conversation. "I didn't know my stupidity showed that much," he laughed.

"Hell, what are you talking about? This case will make you as famous as Lowenstein," he said.

Sean looked over at Lowenstein and grinned. The D.A.'s mouth was wide open in disbelief. Sean knew that look. At dinner tonight, Lowenstein would tell his wife, "This nutcase judge is taking a leak in front of us as we discuss the case."

"How did Spann take it?" Macklin wanted to know.

"Oh, just fabulous," Sean said. "Thanks to you, I'm now a former member of Spann, McGraw."

Macklin did a little dance, zipped up his pants, and came back into the chambers. He didn't bother to stop at the sink on his way out but marched right up to Lowenstein and stuck his hand out. "Been quite a while. How've you been?"

Sean could see Lowenstein trying to decide whether to shake. Finally he joined hands with the judge. A good trial lawyer will do anything to win a case.

"Fine. Thank you, Judge," he said and pointed at Gamboa, who had come in so quietly, Sean didn't even know he was there. "I guess you know the sergeant."

Without looking at Gamboa, Macklin said, "Yeah. Why's *he* here? I said I wanted to talk to the attorneys."

Macklin went over to an opened Diet Coke and shook it. There were cans of half-drunk soda all over his chambers—on the bookshelves, on the planters, and two or three on his desk. He went around shaking them until he found one with something in it and took a long swig.

While Macklin was hunting for something to drink, Lowenstein pleaded. "Your Honor, this is a very complicated case which I have only recently joined. We have gathered a lot of information, and yet it seems like we have just started. Mr. Gamboa is one of two investigating officers. He knows all the particulars of the case. Whenever possible I would like to request that he be with me during any discussions in chambers or at side bench."

Macklin walked back to his desk and lit another cigarette. "That's a little unusual. What do you think, Barrett?"

Sean figured this was all a prelude to something else Lowenstein was after. Conceding this point to get at it wasn't going to cost him a thing. "I don't have any objections *at this time*," he said, leaving the door open for a later objection.

"All right," Macklin said and shook another can of Diet Coke and took a drink. "But make sure you do all the talking, Mr. Lowenstein."

"Fine, thank you, Your Honor. Now I have one more suggestion," he said. "I know Mr. Barrett and I still have a lot of investigating ahead of us. So I would like to suggest that we put the trial date off for, say, three to four months to give us all time to prepare."

Sean eyed Lowenstein sourly. He had never known a D.A. to

give a damn about the defense's case. Lowenstein was trying to get more time for two very important reasons. First of all, the longer the delay, the more time the prosecution would have to find her body, and, second, if they couldn't find her body, the longer she would be missing and the more the jury would be inclined to assume she was dead.

"Your Honor," Sean said, "I certainly appreciate Mr. Lowenstein's sense of fair play and concern for the defense, but as the court and the prosecution are aware, my client has the right to have his trial commence within sixty days. He will not waive that right. I suggest January third."

Lowenstein looked at Sean a long time before turning back to Macklin. When he did, the TV smile was gone. "The third will do," Lowenstein said flatly.

"Anything else before we arraign?" Macklin said.

"Yes, Your Honor," Sean said. "So far I have a murder book over two inches thick. I need two things if I'm going to fulfill my responsibilities in this case."

"Yeah, what is it?" Macklin said, a little annoyed. Like all big-city judges he had a court calendar overstuffed with cases. His first impulse during any proceeding was to keep things moving.

"First, I'd like an order for the district attorney to turn over to me his daily investigation reports within twenty-four hours."

Macklin looked over at Lowenstein. "Sound reasonable, Counsel?"

Although Lowenstein would have liked to hold back his information for as long as possible, he knew there was no point resisting. Macklin was only asking out of courtesy. If the prosecutor didn't volunteer the reports, Macklin would force him to comply.

"That seems fair," he said with a sweep of his arm as if he'd given something away in a gesture of fair play. "The reports will be available by three every weekday."

"That it?" Macklin asked Sean.

"I need an investigator, Your Honor," Sean said. "The district attorney has two full-time detectives on this case and the use of the entire Sheriff's Department. If I'm going to adequately prepare, I'll need a full-time, court-appointed investigator." Sean emphasized the phrase *court-appointed*. It meant he expected the court to pay for him.

Since Macklin had handpicked him for this case, Sean figured he'd be inclined to be more generous than usual.

"Of course you can have an investigator," Macklin said graciously. This case could freeze his calendar for months, backlogging the whole system. He couldn't afford for this case to drag on for months and then fall through some trapdoor in the law because the defense attorney didn't know his stuff. That would mean a mistrial and six more months. That's why he'd appointed Barrett in the first place. If he wanted an investigator, sure, he'd pay for it gladly.

"Have anybody in mind?" Macklin asked.

"Craig MacDuff."

Before the judge could say anything, Gamboa exploded. "You're not actually going to let that lowlife work this case, are you?"

"This is none of your business, Gamboa!" Sean said, wanting to get the ground rules settled early. He didn't mind Gamboa hanging around, but he wanted him to keep quiet.

"That's enough!" Macklin said. "Sergeant Gamboa, you are here strictly as a courtesy. You better behave like a little schoolgirl, or I'll have the bailiff throw you out on your ass!"

He turned to Lowenstein. "Counselor, this is not really a matter that concerns the prosecution anyway. So if you'll wait in the courtroom, Mr. Barrett and I will iron this out."

After Lowenstein shut the door behind him, Macklin turned on Sean. "Jesus Christ!" he shouted. "MacDuff? Didn't he get booted off the force for tapping drug money?"

"Yes. But no charges were ever filed," Sean said. "MacDuff resigned and the matter was dropped. The guy had a ton of personal problems at the time, Your Honor, and the department accepted his resignation without sanctions."

"Don't bullshit me, Barrett," Macklin said and struck a thick wooden match that held a flame an inch high. "If he hadn't resigned, he'd be doing time." He puffed a new cigarette to life, then threw the still flaming match in a silver dish on his desk.

"All I know is I've used him before," Sean said, "and, quite frankly, he's the best investigator around who's willing to work for what the county will pay. If you expect me to give Curtis a good defense, I need a good investigator."

Macklin took a long drag on his new cigarette. "All right," he said, "but if we have any problems with him, he's gone. No questions asked. Agreed?"

"Agreed."

"Now let's get this arraignment over with. Tell the bailiff to bring Curtis out."

chapter

six

Sean dropped his coat across the cell bench, its wood pocked by black pustules of cigarette burns and carved with initials. There was a stainless steel toilet in the corner, and the place stank like a gymnasium crapper—urine and b.o. colliding. Somehow it seemed poetic to Sean because this was where his clients often did most of their bullshitting.

He sat next to Chad and laid his briefcase carefully down beside him. Chad asked him casually, "Now what?"

He had been arraigned earlier, and they were in the lockup directly behind the courtroom, a cell within a cell where Sean could visit with his client without looking through two inches of snot-smeared glass. He could pat Chad on the shoulder, get his face up next to him, or yell if he had to. Sean was the kind of attorney who needed to get close to his client, touch him, smell him, look in his eyes, read the fear jitterbugging in his pupils. Sean wanted to smell Chad out like a bloodhound when he first told his story. He wanted to press him for details because the hard grit of detail usually sandpapered away a varnished story.

That's all he wanted today—Chad's story. See how he looked telling it, see how it floated logically. If one little fluttering leaf of an objection knocked it out of the sky, Sean couldn't sell it to a jury. "The plane don't fly right," a jury foreman once told him, "I ain't gettin' on it."

Sean pulled a yellow pad out of his briefcase and unscrewed his fountain pen and set them both down on the bench. Before he started digging for Chad's story he had a duty to perform.

"Chad," he started out formally, "an attorney is obligated to present to his client all offers he receives from the prosecution."

Chad's eyes lifted from the floor and focused on Sean. "They made an offer?"

Sean didn't like to present plea bargains, but he knew they were as necessary as rain to the arid process of the law. They resolved cases in minutes that might take months to grind through the court. It was, however, the one real incursion into the defense's strategy that the prosecution could make. An offer could panic a defendant and his lawyer just when they were gaining confidence in their defense. That's why Sean liked to present a prosecutor's offer in formal law book terms, so the client knew a foreign third party was in the room with them.

"Yes, the prosecution made an offer," Sean said without expression. "Sergeant Gamboa has informed me that the D.A. is prepared to lower the charge to murder in the second degree. But you must accept today."

Chad was leaning casually forward, his elbows on his knees, like it was early in a game. "Why today?" he asked.

"Sergeant Gamboa left for Victorville immediately after the arraignment to look for Robin's body. He had a tip she was buried out by the new mall. If you accept the plea before he returns, they've promised to drop the murder-one charge."

"What does that mean?"

Sean uncrossed his legs and leaned forward until he was shoulder to shoulder with Chad. He was Chad's counselor again. "It means instead of life imprisonment if you're convicted of murder one, you could spend as little as seven and a half years in prison."

If Chad was guilty and her body was buried in the desert, Sean knew the offer would be tempting. Most men who knew they were guilty would take it.

"Seven and a half years!" Chad cried and stood up. The roar of his voice in the concrete echo chamber made the bars sing. "They're goddamn kidding, aren't they? There's no way I'm going to prison. Tell them to shove it up their asses."

"Chad, Sergeant Gamboa is pretty certain that he knows where the body is. The mall is just a couple of miles from where Frank Johnson lives and in the same area where they located Robin's car. Supposedly they've found parts of her already. Now, what are the chances that it could be Robin?"

"All everyone does is talk about her body like she's a piece of meat. But I loved her. I don't know if she's buried out in the desert, but if she is and I get out of this, someone's going to pay! If I have to spend my entire life looking for them, I'll find out who killed her!"

"All right, Chad," Sean said quietly. "It's just an offer. This early in the game an offer might indicate that they think their case is shaky and they want a disposition as quickly as they can get it."

Sean knew it might mean that or a dozen other things, including that Lowenstein knew that trying to get a murder-one conviction was a dicey matter. There was a huge burden of proof on the prosecutor's shoulders when he went for the big score. To get a conviction he had to prove malice and premeditation. Sean could figure what was going through Lowenstein's head. Why take it in front of a jury and risk losing the case altogether because he got greedy, when Chad, feeling the pressure of prison, of relatives, of the media, might accept the deal?

Chad turned and leaned his shoulder against the bars. "Mr. Barrett," he said calmly, "I'm not going to accept any offers. If I have to, I'm going to go to trial."

Sean looked at Chad for several long moments. He could smell microwaved pizza drifting down the hall from the guards' bullpen and heard Seelicke's unmistakable hee-hawing laughter.

"Okay. Fine," Sean said. "Let's get to work, then. I want you to tell me everything you know about the case."

Chad sat down next to his attorney.

"Now first," Sean said, "let me get something straight. Did you date Robin while you were playing pro ball?"

"Oh, no!" Chad said emphatically, giving his head a short shake. "I hadn't seen her in four or five years until we ran into each other a few months ago in Balboa."

"Then you began dating again?"

"Not actually dating. We saw each other a lot, but it wasn't like before. It was more like old friends."

Sean saw something surface for a moment on Chad's face, then disappear, so he dug for it quickly while he could still get at it. "Wait a minute, Chad, I thought you told me yesterday you were in love with each other. Now you're telling me you were just old friends. Which is it?"

"I've been telling you all along I loved Robin."

"Yes, but how did she feel about you?"

"The same way," Chad said quickly.

"Did she tell you that she loved you?"

"Well, not in so many words," he said. "But I know she loved me. She just needed a little time, a little space . . ."

"Did you give her that space?" Sean pressed.

"Of course."

"That's not what Carrie Robinson said."

"What do you mean?"

"She said you were suffocating Robin. So much so that Robin didn't want to see you anymore."

"I can't believe Carrie would say that. We've always been good friends."

"Well, she did," Sean said. "So, is she right? Is that what happened, Chad? Robin wanted to break it off, see other guys. Is that what the fight was about at the beach?"

"No."

"Maybe things got a little out of hand that night. Maybe you hit her a little harder than you meant."

"That's not what happened," Chad cried. He had risen to his feet, standing above Sean, his eyes wild and out of control. "Yeah, I did slap her. I never said I didn't. But she was drunk. I had to."

"And you knocked her out."

"No, she passed out. I told you that."

Sean looked at the kid standing above him. "All right," he said, patting his client's arm. "All right. I believe you." Chad sat down again. "Now tell me, what was the fight about?"

"She was afraid someone from Hollywood was out to get her."

"Did she say who?"

"No." He shook his head.

"Did she say what it was about?"

"Money. She owed someone money."

"What else did she say?"

"Not much. Like I said, she was really drunk. She wasn't making much sense."

"So the argument had nothing to do with her wanting to break off your relationship?"

"No, nothing at all."

"But you did want the relationship to be more like it was before? Isn't that right?"

Suddenly Chad had a sad, beaten look. "I asked her to marry me that first day we met again." He frowned and raised his eyebrows to Sean as if to say, "Pretty dumb, huh?"

"Jesus!" Sean said. "You didn't tell that to Gamboa, did you?" He could imagine what Lowenstein would do with a statement like that.

"No. He never asked me."

He never asked me? Sean thought. Is this one of those clients who couldn't keep his mouth shut? If Lowenstein got the least indication that Chad liked to talk, he'd plant an informant in here as soon as he could bribe one.

"Chad," Sean said, "I want you to listen to me very carefully now. From this moment on, I want you to discuss this case only with me. Do not talk to the prosecutor or Gamboa"—he waved the arrest report in front of Chad—"or any law enforcement officer, and that includes the jailor, even if he seems like some nice guy just shooting the crap with you. If they ask about your case, don't say a word. And especially," Sean said and grabbed Chad by the arm, "don't ever talk to another inmate about your case. This place is crawling with guys who'll do anything to make a deal with the prosecutor. And they know the easiest way out of here is to turn snitch." Sean released his hand slowly. "Do you understand me clearly on this?"

"Yes, I understand," Chad said, nodding.

"Good," Sean said. "Now, what did Robin say when you proposed to her?"

"She laughed," Chad said, and by the way he stared through the bars at the blank wall ahead, Sean could see Chad was reliving that moment.

On an impulse, Sean asked a question that as a personal rule he never asked a client. But this was a case in which he would have to break a lot of his own rules.

"Did you kill her?"

Chad looked at Sean as if he'd suddenly started speaking in Swahili. Sean put a hand on his shoulder.

"Son," he said, although he was only six years older, "I need to know what happened that night. I know you loved Robin. I know you wouldn't have done anything to intentionally harm her. If she's dead, I'm sure it was an accident, which means you either didn't commit a crime or whatever crime you did commit wouldn't amount to murder."

Chad just shook his head. "I didn't kill her," he said, looking directly into Sean's eyes.

Sean had seen clients lie to him every day for years, and he was willing to bet that Chad Curtis wasn't lying. Maybe they got into an argument after she'd laughed at his marriage proposal, and he'd slapped the girl to shut her up. Only that big paw of his snapped her neck, and suddenly this big kid who'd never had to grow up had a grown-up problem on his hands—a dead girl. So instead of facing it, he had ditched her somewhere. No way Chad thought he'd murdered her, though. Yeah, she was dead, but it was an accident.

"I believe you, Chad," Sean said finally. Then he got up and began pacing the small cell. "One thing that bothers me, though," he said and paused until Chad looked up at him. "It's the car. How did this Johnson character get hold of Robin's car?"

"I have no idea," Chad said, shaking his head.

"You have no idea?" Sean repeated.

"No."

"You're driving her car the night she disappears, and a former teammate of yours ends up with it the next day," Sean said. "And you don't know how he got it?" He touched a finger to his forehead in puzzlement. "That's the part I can't buy, and if I can't buy it, believe me, a jury won't either. It's too much of a coincidence."

He walked over to Chad and rested his foot on the bench next to him. "How did Johnson get the car, Chad?"

"I don't know!" he said a little louder. That little whine was back in his voice.

"Aw, bullshit!" Sean shouted. "I'm your goddamn attorney. How do you expect me to defend you when all you give me is a bunch of bullshit? A jury's going to laugh in my face if I tell them an old buddy of yours just happened to end up with the dead girl's car. It was all just a big fat fucking coincidence. 'Ladies and gentlemen of the jury, just ignore Johnson's testimony that my client asked him to ditch the car the day after the girl disappeared.' Is that what you expect me to tell them?"

Sean picked up his briefcase and yelled out to the bailiff, "See-licke, get me the hell out of here!"

"Mr. Barrett," Chad pleaded. He was standing at Sean's back. "Johnson's lying. I know him. He probably got busted for something and he's making a deal with the cops."

Seelicke came to the barred door of the outer cell and pulled out a big brass key and unlocked it. When he unlocked the inner cell, Sean stepped out and Seelicke slammed the door behind him. He'd escort Sean out of lockup first, then come back for Chad.

Sean turned around to his client. "I want you to think about this very hard, Chad," he said coldly. "This isn't a high school baseball game. Your life is at stake here." Then he turned back and nodded at Seelicke, who unlocked the outer cell. Sean walked out without looking back at his client.

When they got near the bullpen, Seelicke said, "Academy award back in there, Counselor."

Sean sniffed a sarcastic laugh. That was just the first of many little explosions he knew would be necessary to excavate Chad's story. The mystery of this case was bound to have many layers. He hadn't expected to dredge the bottom of Chad's story at this interview. All he wanted was that first clue, that hint, that piece that didn't wash. Maybe the big nugget hadn't come falling out of the pan this time around, but Chad's thoughts would bang around on the walls of that stinking cell awhile and the next time Sean saw him he'd be a little less tough. He didn't know when, but he knew that one day he'd walk into that cell and Chad would beg to tell the real story.

One thing was certain, he knew Chad was hiding something. Sean may not have liked Carrie Robinson, but her assertions about Chad and Robin's lopsided relationship rang true. Besides that, Frank Johnson couldn't have just coincidentally ended up with Robin's car the day after her disappearance. Something was wrong. Since Sean wasn't going to get any help from Carrie, the next step was to see what Carrie's father and Robin's boss—Carter Robinson—knew about the girl. Then he had to hope like hell that Gamboa didn't find her body out in that desert.

chapter

seven

The brilliant desert sunlight refracted off the mud-splattered windows of the idling Bronco. The feeble wipers had plowed a half-moon of visibility on the windshield that Emory Knox struggled to see through. He reached over and slipped a pen out of Gamboa's shirt pocket.

"Okay, so we're in beautiful downtown Victorville now. Where to?" he said to Gamboa while he jotted what he'd spent for gas on a blue "trip" card.

Knox was a young black cop who had graduated from Michigan with a degree in criminology. This was his fourth year on the force and he'd already made detective. In five more years, at the rate he was going, he'd probably be running for sheriff and Gamboa would be reporting to him. He was just about everything Gamboa mistrusted—a good-looking, well-spoken, educated minority. But despite all his prejudices, Gamboa liked Knox. He was smart, dedicated, and he handled a gun under fire with an unshakable precision.

"Victorville P.D. said two kids on bikes found a dog chewing on an arm over behind the mall somewhere," Gamboa said.

Knox grimaced when he pictured some mongrel tearing flesh from a dead girl's body. Even after four years of almost daily gore he still felt uncomfortable in its presence. He still didn't understand how Gamboa could sit in Denny's hungrily wolfing free jelly donuts and coffee and stare at photos of blood-covered women, or men with bullet wounds big as stepped-on tomatoes exploding out their torsos.

Gamboa looked down again at the Thompson where his finger was pinned to the page that showed Victorville and the surrounding area. "Take 395 to Navajo," he said.

Knox turned off Palmdale Boulevard onto Highway 395 and drove a few miles before Gamboa held up his hand.

"Somewhere along here," Gamboa said, "there's supposed to be a sign with 'Gomez' written on it."

"We turn there?"

"Nah, keep going to the first yucca, then turn."

"Oh," Knox said. He didn't know a yucca from a dune buggy.

"Slow down," Gamboa said. "This is it."

"What do you mean? This is it?" Knox said, leaning over toward Gamboa, trying to see what his partner saw. All around him was desert—waxy scrubs a couple of feet tall, dangerous-looking patches of cactus here and there, and sand, endless sand. He'd grown up in Detroit. He was used to being surrounded by a reassuring cocoon of human doings—buildings, street signs, people.

"Just turn the fucking car off the road, college boy," Gamboa said. "There's only three or four dozen things in the Mojave that can kill you."

"I hate these fucking out-of-county searches" was all Knox mumbled as he pulled off the pavement.

They bumped along in the Bronco, the four-wheel drive spinning in the air as it took the bumps. It wasn't a road. Some desert rat had just made a path by driving his car down there often enough to flatten the sand and kill off the brush. Desert rats were a breed found in these desolate spots. They'd get ahold of an old trailer, park it out in the middle of the desert, and that was home. They usually had four or five dogs too, wild as they were.

"What kind of maniac lives out here?" Knox asked.

"The kind that doesn't have a lot of use for his fellow man," Gamboa answered, his head hanging out the window, looking for washouts, potholes, boulders—anything that could turn the Bronco's axle into junkyard parts.

After about a hundred yards, the path widened into a cleared area. Two San Bernardino County deputy sheriffs were standing in front of a trailer with a man wearing ratty overalls who stank so bad Gamboa could smell him from the Bronco. He had a bottle of Thunderbird he was pulling on as he talked to the deputies.

"Tom Gamboa. This is my partner, Emory Knox," Gamboa said. He didn't wait to hear their names. "What do you have?"

"Not much," one of the deputies said. He was a potbellied Mexican whose *barriga* hung over his belt. "This guy's dog dragged a female arm out of the desert."

"You locate the rest of the body?"

"Nah," the Mexican said and pointed around at the desert. "Lot of real estate out there."

"How about the owner?" Gamboa asked. "He know anything about it?"

The Mexican shook his head. "Dog's smarter than he is."

"Great. What's his name?" Gamboa asked.

"Darryl Higgins."

"All right," Gamboa said and waved his hand in dismissal. "We can take it from here."

The Mexican looked at his partner, a wiry, red-faced alcoholic, and winked. The commander had said to "escort" an Orange County detective on a search of the Simon's Gulch area. A search like that would ordinarily eat up the rest of the afternoon, which meant they could take a three-hour lunch, down a few beers, and nobody would ever know.

"It's all yours, Sergeant," the Mexican said. "Have fun." The two smiling deputies climbed back in their cruiser and bumped back down the trail, leaving a high cloud of dust rising behind them.

"About the dog," Gamboa said. "We understand it was chewing on a human arm when the deputies showed up." He pointed to a bag that the deputies had handed Knox.

"All's I know is the dog likes to wander out that way. There's some abandoned wrecks—"

"Wrecks?" Gamboa asked.

"Yeah, you know, cars. Old cars. There's rats all over out there," he said, pointing off into the brush.

"Rats?" Knox asked.

"Oh, yeah. Big as cats. That's probably why the dogs like to chase 'em."

"Okay. Where'd you say the wrecks were?" Gamboa asked.

"Right through that little clump of joshua. Out to the clearing." The man got up real close to Gamboa and pointed at a spot that looked like every other place around there. His breath hung on Gamboa like a rotten fog. The cop held his breath until he was ten feet from the man, then exhaled.

"We'll check it out," he said and nodded at Knox. "Got the shovels?"

"Yeah." Knox handed one to his partner.

Gamboa rested it on his shoulder and took off into the brush. Knox followed him, his eyes inspecting the ground, holding the shovel in front of him like a spear.

They plowed through the desert, stumbling over wind-sculpted mounds of sand and pushing aside the greasewood. After a few hundred yards they saw a car marooned in the sand. A few yards beyond it, three or four more wrecks leaned together like derelicts. They marched over the next hillock of sand, and suddenly they were in a graveyard of stripped heaps.

The dog had followed them out there and immediately started sniffing around one of the cars. Gamboa and Knox dug there awhile. When the dog wandered off, Gamboa and Knox followed it. It went into a washout and started pawing around near a boulder. Knox and Gamboa shoved him away and started digging there.

This went on for several hours. Finally the two detectives gave up and trudged back to Darryl's trailer. And there was the dog sitting in the shade of the butane tank, chewing on another piece of the dead girl.

"Jesus!" Gamboa cursed and stepped forward and slapped the flesh away from the growling dog.

"Oh, there y'are," Darryl said, coming out of the trailer. "The dog come back again, and this time I got a look at what direction he come from." He stood up close to Gamboa again, and Gamboa held his breath. "See that hill there?"

He pointed and the detectives marched off toward a bump on the horizon.

The sun was almost completely down. The clouds hanging above the mountains were on fire. Gamboa knew they had to hurry. As soon as the sun fell behind Mt. Baldy, it would be black in a matter of minutes. That's the way it was in the desert: the sun went down and a few minutes later it was dark as a bank vault.

Knox slipped once in the loose dirt and went down on his hands and knees.

"Come on, college boy," Gamboa said. "We had our break already."

When they got to the top of the hill, Knox turned around.

"Look, you can see the guy's trailer from here," he said, shading his eyes from the low-angling sun. "This has to be the place."

Knox started poking around with the shovel. Then he stepped over a boulder, and his boot kicked back some dirt revealing something blue. "Look," Knox said, "some kind of dress or something. This might be her."

Gamboa stooped and started digging with his hands, brushing aside the dirt that covered a large swatch of blue cloth. Then he felt the leathery flesh. A handful of hair came next. He pulled slowly, and a woman's face came up out of the earth and stared empty-eyed at him.

"Female," Gamboa declared triumphantly.

"Yeah," Knox said like he was out of breath.

"Look, the right arm is gone. This has got to be the body that damn dog was chewing on."

Gamboa inspected the corpse for signs. "Dead about the right amount of time. Right age, right color, right area. This has got to be her." He stood up and took a deep breath. With the shallow grave uncovered, the sour smell of decaying flesh made the air rank.

"Look at her, Sarge," Knox said. He was standing over Gamboa, who was holding a clump of her hair. The last sliver of the sun winked above a hillside. "Look what he did to her."

"Yeah," Gamboa said absently.

"What would her father think?"

"The father's dead," Gamboa said. That was one of the first things her friends all told him about the dead girl.

"She was a beautiful girl," Knox said. He'd seen publicity photos of her in a bikini. "Now she's just a piece of rotten meat some garbage hound's after." He was leaning on the shovel, holding it in both hands, his chin resting on the handle top.

"It's not good to do a lot of that kind of thinking, Emory," Gamboa said without looking up. He was still uncovering parts of the girl. "Go get the camera."

Knox ran down the hill to the Bronco, taking deep breaths along the way. It was going to take quite a few Wild Turkeys tonight to wash away the putrid taste. He reached in the car window and pulled a Polaroid off the front seat and trudged back up the hill. When he got to the grave, he handed Gamboa the camera. Gamboa set the flash and took several shots of the grave as they found it. Then they pulled back the cloth that had been used to wrap the body before the killer had buried her.

Gamboa took a few more shots of the dead woman.

"Her hair looks brown," Knox said. "Robin Penrose's was blond, wasn't it?"

"Buried out here, the hair can turn," Gamboa answered matter-of-factly, still snapping. "It's her, all right. I'll bet my ass on it."

He took another shot and mumbled to himself. "Yeah, this is her," he said and thought about the look he was going to see on Barrett's puss when they identified her and he knew his client was staring down the barrel of a murder-one conviction.

chapter

eight

Sean was in his kitchen wrestling with a mattress when the phone rang. He had it partway into the utility room just off the tiny kitchen. It was folded like a wallet through the doorway, poised to snap if he let go. Sean tried to hold it against the wall with his foot while he reached for the phone.

"Yeah," he said.

"Sean? This is Jonathan Spann."

Sean straightened up a little out of habit, his foot still pinning the mattress.

"Sean, I want to apologize for the other day."

"Forget it," Sean said. "We both overreacted."

Even though it was a weekday, he was dressed in baggy Hawaiian swim trunks and a Hard Rock T-shirt. Beyond the counter was the chaos of his front room. He was in the middle of turning his two-bedroom beach cottage into a law office. Sean had cleared out one of the bedrooms and brought in two metal desks, a computer, and two phones.

"I'm sorry I missed you when you were here reviewing your cases with Scott," Spann said. "I appreciate your help. It was very professional of you after our little blow-out. But, of course, I'd expect nothing less of you."

Sean had returned the day after he was fired and gone over his caseload with Scott, explaining the peculiarities of each case and what was due to happen next. He'd done it for Scott, not Spann.

"Part of the job" was all he said.

"Do you have a few minutes?" Spann asked pleasantly. His overly polite manner surprised Sean.

"Of course."

There was a pause on the other end. Sean heard Spann clear his throat a little. "What I said about becoming a partner still goes, you know. Why don't you reconsider? You can have that office with the bay window you always wanted."

Sean's foot slipped when Spann said "partner," and the bed snapped flat. It slapped an unopened beer bottle off the sink. It landed in a corner and fizzed angrily. Sean eyed the phone suspiciously. What was Spann up to? He had never mentioned a partnership except in the vaguest terms—the kind of back-slapping rubbish that corporate types give out instead of raises. No matter what Spann was saying now, Sean knew that corner office with the bay window was still several years of groveling away.

"I think we both know I wasn't really right for the firm," Sean said finally. "It was a good time for me to go out on my own."

"Are you sure I can't talk you out of it? Take your time. You don't have to decide now." He sounded like a game-show host tempting a contestant.

"No, thanks," Sean said. "I've made up my mind. This is the right thing for me." He kept his eye on the fizzing beer bottle, ready to duck if it blew.

"I still think you're wrong," Spann said. "But that doesn't mean we can't be friends." He was so pleasant he was almost singing.

"Absolutely," Sean said.

"Another thing. You're all alone now. So when you run into a

problem with the case and you need someone to talk it over with
. . . well, I just want to let you know you can call me anytime."

That was the one benefit of belonging to the firm that Sean
would miss: his discussions with the firm's other attorneys, especially
Spann, about puzzling points of the law.

"I appreciate that," Sean said. "You know I've always valued your
opinion. And you're right, I'm going to need some advice on this
case. I hope you don't mind if I take you up on the offer, considering
this was the case that got me canned."

They laughed together.

"Nonsense," Spann said. "I look forward to seeing how you handle the case. To tell you the truth, I wish the firm could have afforded
to take it. But I'm sorry to say it was just too risky."

Sean had had a couple of days to cool down, and he could see
Spann's point. "Yeah, this kind of case is probably better as a one-
man show anyway."

They hung up after a few obligatory pleasantries. Spann wasn't
a bad guy, Sean thought, as long as the bottom line didn't interfere.

Sean was just putting the receiver down when Mac banged twice
and shouldered his way through the front door. He looked as though
he'd walked through a sprinkler. His red kinky hair, which usually
puffed up on his head, was flat and stringy. His shirt had dark patches
of sweat under his arms, circling his collar and down the front on his
chest.

"Hey, you're late," Sean said.

"Of course I'm fucking late," Mac said. He was puffing like an
old dog after a chase. "I had to park in Dana fucking Point, for God's
sakes, and walk all the way up that damn hill."

"I told you, just use the visitors' parking out back."

"Yeah, that's fine, except there's never any empty spaces in visitor parking," Mac growled. "You got fifty houses along the beach
here and six goddamn parking places for visitors!" He threw his jacket
down and looked around the place as if he hadn't been there a couple
of dozen times before. Sean's cottage looked like a typical Southern
California beach place. A rope rug covered the entire floor. Every six
months he rolled it up and swept half of Capistrano Beach back out
the door. In one corner was an orange naugahyde sleeper couch that
pulled out into a queen-sized bed. There were three more single beds
pushed up against the walls around the living room with oversize

pillows thrown on them to lean against. Next to one of the couch beds was a tiki-torch lamp with a few light fixtures running up its length. To complete the decor, scattered all around the room was beach detritus—two or three Frisbees, pieces of driftwood, a clam-shell ashtray, lava rocks, a belly board, fishnet curtains with plastic starfish hanging on them, and mildewed rattan chairs.

Mac slowly turned and gazed almost stupefied at Sean in his beach house attire—the loud trunks, the faded T-shirt, the old flaps.

"Jee-sus, Barrett," he said, "you had to be a surfer boy lawyer and have your damn office at the beach. It's a pain in the ass trying to find a parking place around here, you know that? Get an office in a business park like every other fucking attorney, would ya?"

Sean went back into the kitchen and gave the mattress a shove. It folded reluctantly and he pushed it into the utility room, slamming the door shut quickly before it changed its mind. Then he ducked his head into the refrigerator and pulled out a Tall Boy and tossed it to Mac.

"Here, drink this and cool off. We have a lot of work to do."

Grabbing the quart-sized can of beer like a lifeline, Mac plopped down on the divan, even though it blocked the doorway. It groaned under his weight. Sean threw a legal pad at Mac. "Take some notes. I've got some assignments for you," he said. "First, interview Robin's family. Particularly, find out from her mother if Robin ever got out of control as a kid. Did she run away? Anything like that. Also, find out who her friends were and have a talk with them. She and Curtis were hanging out before she disappeared, and it may help us to know how they got along. But forget Carrie Robinson. I've already talked to her."

Mac put his head back and drained his beer can, then got up and headed for the kitchen to get another beer.

"Also," Sean went on, "Chad said some of her friends in Hol-lywood were after her for drug money she owed them. I couldn't get any names out of him, but maybe you can find out from her mother who she worked for and start from there. I like the drug angle. Drugs make people do irrational things—like taking off without letting any-body know about it. If a jury thinks she's unpredictable and might just show up any day now, they're going to find it hard to send Chad to prison."

Mac just nodded as he sat back down with his beer.

"And we've got to rip Frank Johnson apart too," Sean went on. He had his bare feet up under him on the chair, sitting on his heels. "Remember, he's the one who claims he ditched Robin's car for Chad."

"Right," Mac nodded.

"He's done time before. See if he got arrested after Robin disappeared. If he did, he may be trying to cut a deal with the cops. I've got a feeling Gamboa may be incubating a few ideas in his desperate little mind."

"That's always possible. But he did have Robin's car," Mac said and took a long pull on his beer. "How did he get it unless Curtis gave it to him?"

"Quit thinking like a cop, would you, Mac?" Sean said. He had the legal pad in one hand, and he was pointing at Mac with the other. "Our job is not to answer questions, it's to raise them. See if the guy had a reason to lie. That's our starting point."

Sean ripped off the top sheet of the legal pad and handed it to Mac, who scanned it.

"Yeah, this should get us somewhere," Mac said. He had his big, meaty arms draped over the back of the couch.

"You know, Mac, something bothers me about this case."

"Yeah, what's that?"

"Well, in the police report Robin's best friend, Carrie Robinson, said that Robin, on the night she disappeared, was at a meeting with her at the Robinson law offices until nearly seven. Robin hadn't had a drink all day, supposedly. But an hour or so later she's out of her mind staggering on the beach. No reason for the kids to lie. Why did she get so wasted so quickly? She had to have gone at that booze with a vengeance. I want to know what really happened at that meeting."

"Okay. Who else was at the meeting?"

"Carrie Robinson's father, Carter, and another guy named John Krueger, president of an outfit called Laramie Homes. I'll go talk to Carter. I know him pretty well," Sean said. "He's an old partner of Spann's. Meanwhile, you see what Krueger has to say."

"All right," Mac said, sitting up. "You think this Robinson broad lied about something?"

"No. She had no reason to lie," Sean said, looking out the window. He could see that the wind was too high for good surf—white bursts of foam blew across the tops of the waves. "But this Krueger and Carrie's father were the last ones to see the girl alive. They might remember something."

"Check."

"Of course, this may all be a waste of time."

"Why's that?"

"Gamboa found a body buried in the desert," Sean said. He could imagine Gamboa's grin as he told the D.A. what he'd found. "The coroner said the girl is the right age and description. All they need is the dental records to positively identify her."

"So big deal," Mac said. "They find a hundred bodies a year buried out there. The Mojave is busier than Forest fucking Lawn, for chrissake."

Sean turned from the waves and looked over at Mac. The kitchen light behind him lit his red hair like a halo.

"Frank Johnson, the guy that ended up with her car, lives about a mile from where they dug her up," Sean said. It wasn't good news.

"Oops."

"Yeah, oops," Sean repeated. In a case built on circumstantial evidence, a piece that connected that strongly to his client could be the lynchpin of the D.A.'s argument. "Anyway," Sean said, "that stuff should keep you busy for a couple of days at least."

"Yeah, if I don't sleep or eat," Mac groused. "Speaking of eating. I need some expense money, partner. There's no way I can wait until the end of the trial to be reimbursed. Can you help me out?"

"Sure."

"And I need a little right now. Can you front me a few bucks?"

"How much do you need?"

"Two grand should cover it."

Sean stared at Mac and shook his head. Mac got a sheepish look on his face and shrugged his shoulders. "Hey, I have some old bills I gotta cover."

"I'll see what I can dig up," Sean said and stepped over the divan that was blocking the hallway. When he came back with Mac's check, the phone was ringing.

"That's probably Scott," he said. "He was supposed to call about meeting with Berger." He leapt back over the couch and trotted to the bar.

"Sean Barrett. Can I help you?"

"Now dat would depend, mon," the caller said and laughed. "Are you da gentle-mon rep-re-senting Meesta Curtis?" His voice was very low with a rusty undertone and a heavy accent.

Oh, crap, Sean thought. It's starting already. Whenever he got a high-profile case, anything that made TV, he'd get these calls. He could smell them out before they got finished saying hello.

The rhythmic accent of the caller caught his attention, though. Sean didn't understand him clearly the first time, so he asked the caller to repeat himself. He didn't.

Instead he asked, "How are things looking for our boy Chad?"

Sean was trying to place the accent, eliminating possibilities as he spoke. Something with a British influence but not from England.

"I'm afraid I can't discuss that unless you identify yourself," Sean said. "Who's speaking?" He was going to give this guy about thirty more seconds.

"Cut da shit, mon," the caller hissed. Sean held the receiver back away from his ear and looked at it with a frown. "I can help dee boy," the man said.

I doubt it, Sean thought. Then he placed the accent—Jamaican. This must have been the Caribbean caller who'd been pestering Pelzer.

"She's alive, you know," the man said. This time there was no laughter.

"What?" Sean said, standing straight.

"Alive and well, Meesta Barrett. Living free like a little bird. Ha, ha, ha!" He laughed loudly again, and then his low voice got very soft. "I know where you can find our little Robin."

"Where would that be?"

"She's a real Hollywood girl, our Robin. She dancin', dancin' all dee night. Ah, you know, mon, she have dat kinda body a lotta men goan kill for. So what you think, huh? You better be lookin' in Hollywood."

Sean hated riddles. "Where in Hollywood?"

"Sunset Boulevard. Dat's dee place, Meesta Barrett." And he hung up.

Sean stood with the phone in his hand for a moment or two. His first thought was that Chad had had some friend call. But what was he going to gain by the ruse? Or maybe it was the cops. A little dirty tricks maybe, to keep Sean busy chasing phantoms. Only about five percent of him believed that this guy could help him.

"A weirdo?" Mac asked.

"I don't know," Sean said and put the phone down. "He had an accent."

"Another goddamn wetback," Mac said, slamming his beer on the table.

"No, this guy's Jamaican, I think. Sounded like that guy on TV. You know, the big black, bald guy from the Caribbean that sold the soft drink."

Mac looked Sean over like he'd gone screwy. "You mean the Uncola Man?"

"That's it! The Uncola Man."

Mac spread his wings and put a hand on either armrest and pulled himself up, groaning. "That's our big fucking lead? The Uncola Man! I don't believe it."

"I've got a feeling this guy's not all b.s., Mac," Sean said. He respected Mac's instincts, but he hadn't heard the Jamaican talk. Maybe it was the accent that had him fooled, or the cocky vibrato of his laugh. But whatever it was, there was still that five percent of Sean that wanted to find out what this Jamaican knew. "Let's see what he's up to."

"Forget what he's up to," Mac said and swatted his hand at Sean's idea like it was a pestering fly. "He's a crackpot."

"Probably. But hear me out on this one," Sean said. "Mac, tell me, what makes it so difficult for the prosecution to get a conviction in a case like this?"

"There ain't no body."

"Exactly," Sean said with a poke of his finger. "So let them spend their time trying to find it. That's their job. Ours is to convince a jury she's not dead. Every person we can drag into court who'll say they've seen her alive since her disappearance will help us create doubt in the jurors' minds. Doubt, Mac. That's the name of the game for us. If we have to chase some weirdo's leads to find someone who'll tell us they saw her, then that's exactly what we're going to do." Sean walked over to Mac and handed him a manila envelope. "Here are some photos of the girl."

"Oh, shit!" Mac snorted. "You start out an investigation desperate, you end up desperate."

Sean ignored him. "Her mother lives in the San Fernando Valley. On your way to interview her, stop off in Hollywood and see if anybody's seen her."

Mac just shook his head as he made his way into the kitchen and got another beer from the refrigerator. "That about it?" he asked and headed for the door.

"That's good enough for now. I still have some loose ends to tie up at Spann, McGraw."

Mac gave him a quizzical look. "I thought you were outa there."

"I've still got to introduce Teddy Berger to his new attorney," he explained. "Then I'll go talk to Carter Robinson. He lives out on Lido Isle."

"Great," Mac said. "I get to hobnob with the perverts over in Hollywood, and you get to go slumming in Lido."

"You were a deputy sheriff for how many years? And you still think there's justice in life?" Sean laughed and closed the door.

This Jamaican was probably a nut, Sean was almost sure of that. But there was something that made him uncertain. And if he could nurture that uncertainty into a full-blown doubt, he could feed it to a jury and let them try to chew it apart. If they couldn't, they'd have to acquit his client. That was the law.

chapter

nine

When Sean drove up to the Orange County Jail, Scott was waiting out front. Still fairly new, the wholly unremarkable, windowless six-story cement block actually brightened the surrounding neighborhood. Santa Ana was occupied primarily by foreigners, mostly illegal aliens from Mexico and Central America. Driving in from the beach, Sean could see packs of them in their white shirts, black pants, and dress shoes with busted seams leaning around on the busier intersections, waiting for some non-union contractor to pick them up for a day labor job. They were living two or three families to an apartment, and the neighborhood reflected the per capita income. The chipped paint, the cardboarded windows, the bashed junkers in the street, the graffiti their sons left everywhere they went, all added to the blight.

Sean turned into the parking structure next to the jail and left the top down on his SL. If they wanted the car or anything in it, they would just rip the top up getting to it. After Sean lost three rag tops, he had to get rid of the high-tech sounds in the dash. The thirty-nine-dollar AM/FM he had now wasn't worth stealing.

"Let me brief you a bit on this case," he said to Scott as they walked up the steps to the building. He held the door open and Scott walked in ahead of him.

"First of all," he started, "Berger hasn't been completely candid. He says he knows nothing about the killing, but I'm pretty sure he does. Even without the confession, I think the odds are pretty good he'll get convicted unless he starts really opening up to you. Our first job is to make him understand that."

They took the stairs to the left, and Sean kept talking as they climbed, Scott one step above him. "It's pretty obvious he wasn't the one who pulled the trigger, but we have to find out what he was doing there. Berger went to work after hours that night. He was up to no good, all right, but I'm pretty sure someone else sent him."

Scott opened the door to Visitors' Reception and let Sean walk in ahead of him. Sean told the jailor at check-in whom he was there to see, then he and Scott took a seat.

"Maybe someone else is calling the shots?" Scott said, rocking his folding chair to test its stability. He didn't like the way it wobbled, so he got up and moved to the chair on the other side of Sean.

"Oh, I'm sure of it," Sean said. "Remember, he told Gamboa there were two others with him at the time. And the idiot's protecting them."

"Berger," a female jailor called out in a bored tone. Sean and Scott walked over to the door marked RESTRICTED ADMITTANCE. The jailor let herself through a locked door behind the check-in desk, and a moment later she opened the door from the inside. "Right this way, gentlemen," she said with mock cordiality.

"Thanks, McKinnon," Sean nodded.

After they were through the door, she swung around and unlocked another door that opened into a large room with a horseshoe-shaped counter in the middle. Inmates filed in from lockup and sat on the inside of the horseshoe and the visitors on the outside. A wire-mesh glass partition separated them. But it only extended up from the counter about three feet to enable paperwork, photos, and letters to be passed back and forth.

Berger was already sitting at the far end of the counter waiting when McKinnon let them in. From across the huge, yellow-hued room, Sean could see Berger hyperventilating. One hand was massaging the back of his neck, and his other hand was busy with an unlit cigarette. It struck Sean how different his two clients were taking their predicament. Berger was nervous as a weasel while Chad seemed almost unconcerned by the seriousness of the charges he was facing.

"How's it going?" Sean asked him.

"Jesus! How's it going? He wants to know how it's going?" he said to Scott. "The linebacker in the cell next to me proposed last night. Get me fucking out of here before I have this nigger's baby, for chrissake!"

"Okay, calm down, Ted," Sean said, patting the air with his palms to settle things. "We've got a lot to discuss today."

Berger looked at Scott as if he'd just seen him and pointed. "Who's this?" he asked Sean.

"This is Scott Powers, Ted. He's going to be taking over the main responsibilities for your case."

"Main responsibilities? What does that mean?"

"It means he's your attorney."

Berger's head jerked as though a little explosion had gone off in his brain. "I don't get it!" he said. "You got the confession thrown out. Things were looking good, weren't they?"

"That helped a lot, sure," Sean said. "But the prosecution still has a lot of evidence against you."

"In California," Scott explained, "under the felony murder rule, you can be held just as responsible as the one who did the actual shooting. Even if you had nothing to do with pulling the trigger. As long as the shooting took place during the commission of a felony, such as burglary, they can get you for murder."

"Murder? Jesus!" Berger mumbled. The cadence of his breathing was increasing. The air came snorting out his nose. His eyes took on a wired, unfocused glaze.

"Teddy, calm down," Sean said. "Just start breathing normally if you can."

He looked more carefully at Berger. Then he stood up quickly. "Oh, Christ! The guy's going out!" And he reached over the partition to grab Berger's shoulders.

"Jailor!" Sean yelled, but just then Berger's eyes rolled up and he went over onto the floor.

One of the jailors came strolling over. "Jeez, Barrett, you play it rough," he joked, looking down at Berger sprawled on the floor.

"Right," Sean said. "Get him a wet paper towel, would you? His nerves gave out on him. He'll be okay."

"The D.A. file special circs on this guy or something?" the jailor said.

"Just get the towel, Dooley, would you?" Sean said.

By the time Dooley was back, fifteen minutes later, with the dripping towel, Berger had lifted himself back onto his seat.

"You all right?" Sean asked.

"Yeah. Yeah, sure," Berger said. He was oddly serene, sitting with his hands folded in his lap, nodding at his attorneys. "Mr. Barrett," he said calmly, "I want you to represent me. I need you. No offense." He looked at Scott apologetically, then back at Sean. "But I don't know anything about this man. You can't leave me now with someone I don't know."

"Ted, you hired the firm of Spann, McGraw and Newsome, and the case was assigned to me. But I no longer work for Spann, McGraw."

Berger's eyes were dilated like a freshly fixed addict. Sean was watching him closely.

"Scott has just as much experience as I do in these kinds of cases. The firm would never assign you an attorney they didn't have complete confidence in," Sean insisted. Then he paused for a second to make sure Berger was listening. "Of course, neither one of us can really help you unless you decide to open up," he said.

He watched Berger's eyes bounce around the room, from Sean to Scott to the clock to his hands to Sean.

"What do you mean?" Berger said. "I told you everything."

"Look, Ted, it's time for you to tell the truth," Sean said. He was sitting back with his elbow cocked on the seat back, twiddling a pen nonchalantly in his fingers. "I know these two bozos put you up to it and one of them shot the guard. And I'm sure they probably threatened you. But what about it?" He gave a so-what wave of the pen. "What can they do to you that could hurt you more than what you'll get if you're convicted?"

"Hey," Berger shot back, "they can kill me!"

"They can kill you in here too just as easily," Scott said. Berger looked over at him like Scott had the gun.

"And," Sean said and Berger looked back, "if they'd kill you out there for talking"—he pointed through the solid wall out to the street—"they'd certainly kill you in here to make you *stay* quiet."

Berger looked puzzled. "Why would they do that?"

"Look, they know what it's like in jail," Sean said. "They know you'll have all kinds of time to think, and they know that any time you figure you've had enough, you can just cut a deal with the D.A. to testify against them."

"They're more afraid of you *in* jail than out," Scott added.

Berger's mind was being batted around like a squash ball. Then his eyes zeroed in on the trap he was in.

Berger slowly shook his head. "You're right, Mr. Barrett. I'm not going to eat this damn murder charge. Why should I, right?" Berger was talking himself into it. "Fuck those guys! What can they do? I sit in here and rot, and then someday one of their buddies shoves a shiv up my ass? What for, huh?"

Sean and Scott slowly shook their heads to ease him on.

"I was standing right next to the guard," he started. "But I wasn't the one who shot him."

It went pretty much the way Sean had figured it. Berger had been conned into helping a couple of career criminals pull off a burglary. He owed money to one of them, Eddie Romero, a medium-time meth dealer. He was into him for eight thousand dollars. If Berger got them some information on Medtech, the company he worked for, Romero would call it even. Teddy figured all he had to do was steal a few papers and he'd save himself from a couple of broken legs, because he didn't have the money to pay Romero and he didn't know where he was going to get it.

"What kind of information did he want you to get?" Sean asked.

"Whatever I could find on a large pharmaceuticals company called Kaufmann Industries," Berger said.

"Industrial espionage?" Scott suggested out of the corner of his mouth to Sean.

"Maybe something to do with product development," Sean said. "Medtech and Kaufmann are both high-tech companies. They have to stay on the cutting edge. They make their profits by staying a step ahead of their competitors."

"Sure," Scott said. He was busy jotting notes.

Sean tapped Scott's notepad with his finger. "Talk to the president of Medtech. His name is Schwitters. See if he's got any idea what they might have been after."

Scott nodded and Sean turned back to Berger. "Then what happened?"

"I got nervous," Berger said. "So I tried to back out."

So Romero just pushed a little harder. Enter the big bad wolf. Romero told him his boss, the biggest, baddest black son of a bitch in the galaxy, was going to eat them both alive if Ted didn't cooperate. And he threw in that this black guy "has a reputation for torture-killing anyone who crosses him." When Berger said it, he had the wide-eyed look of total belief that a kid has when he's told the Easter bunny is coming to town.

"Did Romero mention the guy's name?" Scott asked. Sean sat back now that he knew Berger was going to unload and let Scott establish a rapport. Berger probably needed a mother as much as a lawyer.

Berger looked at Scott as though he'd suddenly gone senile. "You kidding?" he said. "Not only wouldn't he say, I didn't want to know. Give him what he wants and get off the hook. That's all I was thinking about."

He nosed around at work, Berger said, and found out that the Kaufmann files were locked in the president's office.

"It didn't take much to get in there. You know what kind of locks they've got on those old file cabinets. I tugged extra hard and it opened. Then I just flipped through and found the Kaufmann file," Berger said, flipping his fingers through the imagined files in front of him.

Then he got to the shooting of the security guard. He'd gone downstairs and met the old guy at the door. When Berger signed out, he accidentally left his coat on the stool next to the guard's desk. The old retiree noticed it when Berger was already halfway to his car and started running after him, shouting Teddy's name.

When Berger saw the guard chasing after him, he took off. "Jesus, I had a briefcase full of stolen documents, so I started running," Berger said like he was adding two plus two. There could be no other possible solution. "That's when I heard the shots. Real quick. Pop! Pop! Pop! and I looked back and saw Joe fall to the ground. He was holding my coat." Berger stopped again and looked down. "God damn. He was a nice old guy. Just wanted to give me my coat."

Sean felt for Berger. Unlike a lot of his clients, Berger was actually sorry about something besides the fact that he'd gotten caught. The guard was a decent guy, and Berger had seen his blood running down the driveway of Medtech. A lot of that was Berger's fault and he knew it.

Berger turned after the guard went down, he said, and saw a big black man across the street with a gun.

"Eddie started screaming at me, 'Get in the car! Get in the car!' " Berger said. "He finally wrestled me into the car. And we got the hell out of there."

Sean studied Berger as he sat in the chair. He knew this was where the story was going to collapse for a jury. This mysterious black man. Who was he? Did he even exist? And why had he shot Joe? Had he only been following Berger's orders? There were still a lot of questions. But Scott would have to find the answers on his own. Sean had done his job. Scott could take the case from here.

"And you have no clue who the shooter was?" Scott asked.

"All I know is an hour later he showed up at Eddie's sister's, where we were hiding out," Berger said. "Eddie went outside to his car to talk to him and then came back in to get the Kaufmann files. Then he went back out and handed him the stuff."

"You never got a close look at him?" Sean asked.

"All I know is he's black. And big! Way over six feet. Two-fifty, two-sixty easy. And he's got that long, braided hair. You know, like the reggaes wear it."

"Yeah, I know," Scott said and showed Sean with a spin of his fingers the curling dreadlocks of a Rastafarian. "Now, how about his car? Did you see that?"

"All I know is it was red."

"Was it a big car, a small car, a sports car?"

"Yeah, it could have been. Yeah, a red sports car."

"Did you catch any part of the license?" Scott asked.

"Jesus," Berger said. "This guy just shot down a security guard without sneezing. I was in no mood to check out his plates."

"Okay," Scott said.

"You said you were at Eddie's sister's that night," Sean said. "Where does she live?" One good whiff of a trail and Sean knew Scott could track the shooter back to his hole.

"It's in east L.A. somewhere. Near Boyle Heights is all I remember. Those barrios all look the same," Berger said and gave his head a disgusted shake. "I know her name is Morales. Rita or Renee. One of those spic names."

"All right, Teddy," Sean said. "That was great. I think we've got enough to help you out now." He started packing his briefcase to go, shoving papers back inside. Scott was doing the same.

"Now, before we go, do you need anything?" Scott asked.

"I need you to get me out of here before something happens," Berger said. "Eddie kept telling me over and over this guy was bad news, and if either one of us opened our mouths about what really happened, we wouldn't live ten minutes." A heavy sweat had broken out on his forehead, and he was wiping it back up into his hair. "And I'll tell you, I believe it. I've already had two guys walk past me while I've been in here and tell me to keep my mouth shut. I'm fucking petrified."

"Don't worry," Scott said. He was standing now with his hand extended over the glass, shaking Teddy's hand. "If we can get Romero to verify a few things, we'll have you out very soon."

"How you gonna do that?"

Scott leaned in closer and whispered as if disclosing inside stuff. "It's a lovely little thing called immunity. Romero tells us the name of the killer and you both go free."

Sean and Scott got up, gave Berger a few more assurances, and walked to the exit. The jailor pulled back the heavy door, and as they walked out, Sean looked back and saw Berger still standing at the glass partition staring at them, hyperventilating like a heart patient. But this time Sean thought he'd make it.

chapter

ten

Sean slowly inched the SL along Pacific Coast Highway. The traffic slowed just as he came into Laguna and didn't get any better all the way to Newport. It was always a battle crossing into the crowded Balboa Peninsula, where six lanes of highway funneled onto the narrow two-lane bridge across the waterway. But this was the worst night of the year for traffic—the night of the annual Christmas Boat Parade. All the yachties dressed up their boats with Christmas lights and decorations and motored around the bay, stopping at every other slip to share Christmas cheer with a neighbor. Other yachties sailed in from Huntington, Morro, Tiburon, and San Diego and putted around in their garishly decorated boats.

Sean usually stayed away from Newport on Boat Parade night, but when he'd called Carter Robinson to set up an appointment, Carter had told him he was "slammed" the next two weeks and out of town the week after that. "Why don't you come by before the parade Saturday night and we'll talk a little over a drink?" Sean had reluctantly accepted.

Sean had grown up in Newport, so he knew the back way into the Bay. He took Jamboree Boulevard across the Balboa Bridge to Balboa Island, then down Agate to the auto ferry. He pulled onto the paved dock at sunset, just as they were about to chain the ramp closed and slipped into the last remaining space on the ferry. The ride took eight minutes and let him out on the southern end of the peninsula. Lido Isle, where Carter Robinson lived, lay at the far northern end.

When Sean passed 15th Street, he slowed and took a peek at the old beach house he had grown up in. It was a block up from the ocean and only measured about a thousand square feet, but it was worth close to a million now. Of course, when he was growing up, it had been a blue-collar neighborhood and the place went for $14,000. All the wealthy people lived on Lido Isle or in BayShores, where John Wayne and Bogie and the oil and manufacturing magnates from the Midwest had their summer homes. The Bal Peninsula was Newport's ghetto. The families that lived there were the working-class folks of Newport. They crewed the fishing boats, tended bar, ran the restaurants, or repaired the Cadillacs for the wealthy Newporters who treated them like an extension of their house staff.

The Newport Beach of his youth, however, now existed only in the photos that hung on the walls of old-timer hangouts like Snug Harbor. When the real estate market tripled overnight back in the mid-seventies, a lot of the local people had sold and moved away, and nobody knew anybody anymore. "Nouveau Newport," as the old-timers liked to call it now, was crowded with five-thousand-square-foot beach cottages, plastic surgeons, and fur salons.

Carter's house was a gray New England clapboard with no front yard, no side yard, and no backyard but Balboa Bay. It was one of the old "Lido Mansions," built back in the twenties by some Oklahoma oil man who wintered in Newport. Carter had bought it in the sixties when it was worth $100,000. Twenty years later it listed at over three million.

The sign on Carter's front door read: "Merry Christmas. Go right on through to the slip." Sean opened the door and made his way through an antique-stuffed front room that opened out onto the deck. Through the sliding glass door, he could see Carter's Baby Elliot: a fifty-eight-foot beauty with bleached teak decks and blue rigging. On the jackstaff, the blue and orange burgee of the Newport

Harbor Yacht Club flapped above the moniker *Poco Bueno*, stenciled in gold on its gleaming white hull. Sean had crewed on a boat just like it while he was working his way through law school at the University of San Diego. He still sometimes thought of those days as the happiest he'd ever had—sailing through the Panama Canal one summer, the smooth run of the Elliot beneath him.

Sean spotted Carter lugging a case of scotch to the boat. Carter had left Spann's firm before Sean joined, but the two still knew each other from social events—office Christmas parties, professional seminars, and other functions. Although Carter was only five years younger than Jonathan Spann, he looked half his age. He kept his hair blond at the same place he got his mani and pedi, and he kept his stomach flat at the Newport Athletic Club, where he had a daily squash game and steam.

"Sean, how are you?" he hollered and put down the case.

"Good, how are you?" Sean said and shook Carter's hand.

"Can't complain and nobody would listen if I did." He laughed and slapped Sean's shoulder. Although he wasn't a big man, he had a big laugh, the kind acquired as a fraternity brother. By the way he was swaying with that case, Sean could see he'd already put a serious dent in a bottle of something ninety proof. But, like a lot of lawyers Sean knew, Carter was positive he held his liquor with the same sure-footed swagger that he held court.

"Where've you been? The party's cooking, sport. We're just about ready to shove off."

Sean knew that Carter would want to sail his two-million-dollar ego trip around Newport Harbor tonight. Sean had hoped to catch him before he shoved off.

"Can't make it," Sean said.

"What?" he said and spread his hands out as if offended.

Sean unlatched the little white picket swinging gate of the dock and held it open so Carter could get through. "The Chad Curtis case has me hopping," he said.

"Jesus, I hate criminal attorneys," Carter laughed. "They're all so damn serious. You should be a corporate attorney. They pay us obscene amounts for pushing paper."

"That's why I'm a criminal attorney," Sean said and pushed his hair back off his face. "I hate paperwork."

Carter shrugged. "So how's Jonathan?" he asked as they walked on the dock. Sean could see the dark blue water through the white slats.

"He's fine, still coming in at six forty-five and leaving at dark."

"Some things never change, huh? Except that Curtis case fooled me." He put the box on the swim step and turned and faced Sean. "Boy, I never thought he'd let you take a court-appointed case. Not that tight-assed bastard."

"He didn't let me take it," Sean interrupted.

Carter looked puzzled. "I thought you told me that was your case."

"I'm not working for Spann, McGraw anymore."

"Oh, I see," Carter said. "Well, hell, Spann, McGraw's no place for a criminal attorney anyway." Then he took Sean's arm and turned serious, the alcohol whipping his mood around like a tailless kite.

"I'm sorry," he said solemnly. "I gotta tell you this. I hope your client spends his golden years at San Quentin. Robin was a nice girl."

Sean was amazed at how even an experienced lawyer like Carter could jump so whimsically to a verdict of murder one from the tidbits he'd gathered from the media and the gossip around the office.

"I'm sure Robin was a wonderful person," Sean said. "I'd like to talk to you about her when you get a chance tonight."

"I'd be happy to help you out any way I can, but, to tell you the truth, I'd just be a waste of your time. I didn't really know Robin that well, you know. Except I saw her around the office, of course. I mean, she used to drop by now and then when she and Carrie were in school, but I haven't seen her that much since."

Sean might have found this hard to believe if he hadn't seen the partners at Spann, McGraw treat the secretaries and clerks and even some of the associates like office furniture.

"She was Carrie's secretary. She's the one to talk to," Carter continued.

"I already talked to her."

"And?"

"She wasn't very cooperative."

"Try her again. Now that she's over the shock of the murder, she'll probably agree to talk to you."

"Yeah, maybe so," Sean said, but he knew it was a waste of time.

He had been an attorney for only a short time when he realized that one of the axioms of criminal law is that clients and witnesses change their minds. Sometimes they change their minds because of sheer confusion—the bullets boring through flesh at supersonic speed, the sirens cymbaling against their eardrums, the cuffs and the coke and a jail term longer than they've been alive. Sometimes they change their minds when they see the iron-barred jaws of a conviction gaping before them. But he was willing to bet just about anything that Carrie Robinson wasn't going to change her mind. One of the first things Sean had put down on the "knowns" side of his case-strategy checklist was that the only talking he'd be doing with her was when she took the stand as a prosecution witness.

Carter picked up the booze again. "Ah, enough about business. It's party time!" The big fraternity laugh was back.

He stepped onto the swim step of the yacht and through the transom. Sean followed him onto the aft deck, where a table of food and liquor was set out on top of the bait tank. The boat was packed with guests. It was only six and the party was already revved up. The Beach Boys were blaring and a boatload of people were dancing and drinking and yee-hawing to "Little St. Nick." Sean looked down at what he was wearing—cords and an orchid print aloha shirt. Half the men there were in tuxes, the women in designer cocktail dresses. He looked like one of the crew.

He followed Carter to the packed salon and stopped by the door. Then the crowd parted a little, and he saw Carrie Robinson in a red cocktail dress that fit her tight on top and showed off all but six inches of her beautiful legs. She put her champagne glass on the piano and embraced a man who had just come in, kissed his cheek, and then rubbed her lipstick off him with her thumb.

Sean turned and walked to the deck rail. There were several boats out on the bay already cruising slowly by, everybody on board yelling Christmas greetings and sexual innuendoes to people on the other boats. He was tossing back the last of his scotch when the yacht suddenly pulled away from the dock. Sean laughed to himself. He'd come here to interview a witness for his big case, and before he knew it, he was joining the annual Christmas Boat Parade. Just Sean Barrett and the rest of the stinking rich.

Sean turned around and leaned cross-legged with his back

against the rail, and for the next hour he watched people who could barely walk jump-stepping from boat to boat in search of a better party or a better drink or a better-looking woman to share it with.

Christmas he could take or leave. His mother had walked out on a bitter cold Christmas Eve the year he turned eight, and he had never seen her again. That pretty much shot Christmas for good.

Sean would remember that night forever. It was one of those snapshots that he carried around in his head. They had been living in North Carolina then—his father and mother and his sister and brother and himself—when a hurricane hit Cape Fear. His father came skidding into the gravel driveway in their old Buick as the black clouds were gathering over the Atlantic, turning the day so dark the streetlights went on at noon.

"Come on!" he said to Sean. "Gather up your sister now. Let's get out to the shelter." He herded them by the shoulders through the door of the kitchen porch out to the bomb shelter he'd built the summer before during the commie A-bomb hysteria.

"Is Mom coming?" Sean asked. He hadn't seen her in two days, and no one had told him where she was. But she'd gone away before for a day or two on a "vacation," she called it. It was his six-year-old sister who finally let him know she was gone for good when she took his hand softly in hers and held it. Then he put together what his father had said about the golf course and the fights his parents had when his mother would come back from her vacations and his father slammed through the screen door late at night, wildly drunk, screaming about her "and that golf bum."

They went down into that bomb shelter, and the next morning, after the wind screamed for hours and the trapdoor banged all night like a gorilla was out there trying to get in, they crawled out, his father pushing a fallen tree off the trapdoor, and everything that Sean possessed, everything he loved—his home, his bike, his bat, and his books were gone. And so was his mother. That's when his father decided to pack up the family and move to California, as far away from his wife as possible.

Nothing was really certain for Sean after that except what he could do himself. That meant school. He was salutatorian in high school. Got a full ride to UCLA. Then he won the prestigious Samuel Harnett Wilkes grant to USD law school and graduated number one in his class. Six years later he had become a highly respected defense attorney on his way up. "A shooting star" was how the *Orange County Register* had described him.

"Sean, how are you?" a voice behind him said.

He turned and there was Carrie Robinson. He figured she wasn't going to pass up an opportunity to take another shot at him. He was about to say something, but she spoke before he could answer.

"Sean, I want to apologize for the way I acted at the courthouse," she said. "It wasn't very professional of me. As a lawyer, I should have known you had a job to do." She held her hands open in front of her. "Now I'd like to help Chad if I could."

The first time they'd met, she had bit off the conversation with a snap he could almost hear, and now she wanted to help. "That's all right," Sean finally managed to get out. "You were upset."

"When I got over being angry, I realized that Chad was my friend too and I was convicting him without even hearing his side," she said. "What is it you'd like to know?"

Later, when he looked back on this moment, he realized he should have known something wasn't right. She had made a complete turnaround overnight. Maybe it was her luminous green eyes or her voice or the way she rested her hand on his sleeve, or maybe it was his eagerness to get a handle on this case, but he never really questioned her motives when she looked in his eyes and said she wanted to help him.

"Well, I'll tell you. What I'd really like to know more about," he said, "is what happened to Robin when she was in Hollywood."

"Of course," Carrie said and leaned against the rail next to Sean. "Actually, she did very well for a while. Landed a few TV commercials and some bits in a couple of movie of the weeks. She was even a Laker girl for two years. Danced with Paula Abdul before she got famous." Carrie laughed softly to herself. "She used to joke that it didn't do her much good except she got to meet Jack Nicholson—and that didn't do her any good at all."

Sean smiled. "But what happened?" he said, dropping the grin.

"She met a creep named Gregory Pope."

"Who is he?"

"Some big-shot wheeler-dealer Hollywood agent," she said.

Every word had a contemptuous punch to it. "I blame him for everything."

Sean could feel an opening and he pushed to get through. "What do you mean, everything?" he asked.

"Everything," she said. "Drugs, parties . . . everything." She stood back from the rail and turned to face Sean. "Robin was a gorgeous girl with a ton of talent in a town filled with rats," she said and looked out at the harbor.

Sean could see that Robin's disappearance had been roiling around in her mind for days, and she was striking for the cause of it.

"Creeps like Gregory Pope know just how to exploit a girl like Robin. They go to school to learn how." She paused again and her eyes narrowed. "I'd like to get my hands on Mr. Pope," she said and strangled the air in front of her. "Robin was an innocent young girl when she left, and when she got back she'd changed."

"How do you mean?"

"She was harder. I guess that's the word," Carrie said, looking at Sean for confirmation. But he gave her nothing. He wanted her to ramble, let everything come out—the guesses, the suspicions, anything that he might be able to turn into reasonable doubt.

"Everything about her was tougher," she said. "Her looks, the way she walked, her language. Even her eyes. She looked like she'd lost her youth at twenty-two. Do you know what I mean?"

He raised an eyebrow and nodded to keep her going.

"But she was never hard with me, though. When we were together, we were still just two kids. If she ever really needed something, she'd always come to me." She looked down, cataloging memories.

"Like for a job?"

"Yes, she asked me for a job," she said. "It was kind of sad, really. She always used to say, 'I'll kill myself before I'll be a desk slave for some old fart.' " Carrie's cheeks rose as if she were about to smile, but she didn't. "She started out as a gofer at the office and, despite herself, I think she really began to love the law. She started taking some pre-law classes at night. Then, lately, she got very interested in the stock market, and she always had a book or two with her about stocks and bonds. Robin was a very smart girl, and it was great to see her enthusiastic about something again."

Sean turned and they stood together silently for a while and watched the parade of boats and the stream of party goers on shore.

"It would help if you told me about the last time you saw Robin," he said finally.

She was silent for a while longer, then she straightened up and turned to him. "It was late," she said. "We had a meeting—my father, myself, Robin, and a client."

"Would that have been John Krueger from Laramie Homes?" Sean asked.

Carrie's eyes narrowed. "That's right. It was in the police report, wasn't it?" she said, and a faint smile lifted her lips. Their eyes held on one another for several seconds. It was more than two attorneys sparring.

"Robin was at the meeting to take notes," she said without releasing his eyes. "We finished a little after seven, and I sent Robin home a few minutes before we broke up. That's the last time I saw her."

"Anything unusual happen at that meeting?"

"No, not really."

"Was she drinking?"

"No," Carrie said. "In fact, Krueger and my father and I had a drink and she didn't."

Then how, Sean thought, did she get black-out drunk in an hour or so? That meant something happened after the meeting. "Was she fooling around with any drugs that you know of?"

"Absolutely not!" she said. "Pope had her strung out on coke pretty bad when she came back to Newport. She weighed about a hundred pounds, and she was going nowhere a hundred miles an hour. She shook it all by herself, though. No clinics. No trips to Betty Ford. She just said I've got to get through this. And she did. I was damned proud of her." Carrie slapped her palms down on the rail. "That's another reason I've been so angry. She was doing so well with her life and then—"

A tall dark-haired man stuck his head out of the salon and interrupted her. "Carrie, come on, we need you to play the piano," he said, waving for her to come in.

"Oh, all right," she said and shrugged at Sean. "Duty calls."

"I understand," he said.

"Can we talk later?" she asked.

"Of course," he said and watched her leave. A broad smile grew slowly across his face. If Carrie Robinson was coming over to their side, she could do a lot to save Chad. A respected attorney who was a longtime friend of both the alleged victim and the accused could counteract a lot of media gossip, innuendo, and rumor for a jury.

He got himself a drink and found a rail in the stern and watched the parade. It was a beautiful night. The wind had blown the last couple of days, so the smog was pushed out to sea and the stars were bright. Carter's boat, in parade, motored down the length of Lido into the Rhine Channel and made a lazy turn past the old tuna factory and the Lido Shipyards, where Sean's father had worked for years wiring boats.

"Come on, Dad! You can't steer this thing!" a woman yelled and pulled Sean out of his thoughts.

The yacht was sliding dangerously close to the old docks by the cannery. Sean could see the swollen pilings encrusted with barnacles and the black, oily rot of timber only a few feet from the stern.

"Hell, I can't," a man shouted.

Sean stepped back, looked up, and saw a man and woman struggling in the shadow of the pilothouse.

"Will somebody help me out here?" she cried, her voice breaking into a desperate pitch.

Sean ran aft down the gunnel decks and up the stairs to the fly bridge. When he pulled himself over the top deck, he saw Carrie trying to restrain her father.

"Now let me at least steer," she said.

Carter Robinson was completely drunk. Sean knew that trying to talk sense to him now would be impossible.

"Bullshit, I'm piloting my own goddamn boat," Carter growled and pushed her aside.

Sean looked aft and saw that the *Poco Bueno* was now only a few feet from the boat slips, where a row of the gold-platers were moored. He liked Carter enough not to want him to have to wake up in the morning and face arrest for sinking a one-hundred-foot yacht while drunk.

Carter had his back to Sean as he wrestled with Carrie for the wheel. "Carter," Sean said and slapped him on the shoulder. When Carter turned, Sean snapped an uppercut into his chin. Carter's legs gave way, his shoulders followed, and he went down in a heap at his daughter's feet.

Sean pushed past Carrie quickly and took the wheel. Carter's boat was no more than a foot from a yacht Sean knew was probably worth six or seven million. He calculated at a glance that if he accelerated away from the slips too quickly, he'd risk center-punching one of the boats in the parade. Instead he centered Carter's twin-screw by using the dual throttles to spin the boat on its axis away from the moorings. When he saw an opening, he eased the boat back into the procession.

Carrie was trying to pull Carter up to the padded bench along the far wall of the pilot house when Sean took his other arm.

"Sorry," he said as he grunted to lift Carter. "He was just about to sink several million dollars' worth of boat."

She looked at her sodden father. His tongue was hanging out the corner of his mouth, a line of drool on his upper lip. "It couldn't be helped," she said. She propped his head on a life jacket. Then she turned to Sean, who was at the wheel again.

"Can you drive this thing awhile?" Carrie asked. "I'm going to get someone to help me bring him downstairs."

"No problem. I'll take her," Sean said, delighted at the chance to pilot a buffed-out Elliot. It had been a long time since he'd piloted a boat in the harbor. He'd spent a lot of his youth there hosing down decks, painting masts, scraping hulls and decks—whatever odd jobs his father set him up with. That was another mental snapshot—the rotting fish guts in the water, the *buddha-buddha-buddha* of the diesel engines, the slap of water on the docks. By the time Sean was thirteen he was piloting boats around the dock area—down to Lido Shipyard or Harry's Dock, the scroungy hull-scrapping outfit near the cannery, or to the valet dock of the Stuffed Shirt, where the owner had gone for dinner. When he was sixteen he captained the ferry in summer, and on school weekends he crewed on some of the most famous sport fishers around—*The Dorado*, *The Joker*, and *The Wahoo*—the thirty- to forty-foot high-speed fish killers of that era.

A few minutes later Carrie came back with two good-sized men, and they carried Carter off the bridge, slobbering and moaning as they lugged him down the stairs. Carrie stayed in the pilothouse with Sean.

"Do you really think she might be alive?" she finally asked, with a lift of hope in her voice.

Sean looked over at her. "I see as much evidence that she's alive as I do that she's dead," he said. "Don't you?"

"I was too close to Robin to think clearly," she said. "I'm just going on prayer now."

Carter's boat was under power, and yet Sean had the feeling it was sailing. The *Poco Bueno* was a lovely boat to handle. The wheel spinning with an eager-to-please precision, the bow cutting the water like a silk zipper, the engine whining for more leash. It sliced through the harbor past the Yacht Club, past China Cove, and around Balboa Island to the Yacht Basin at the entrance to the Back Bay.

The idea was to round the buoy and slide back around into the harbor and stay in the parade. But when Sean got to the buoy, he pulled the yacht around and took the long, slow run into the dark of the Back Bay. As he approached the bridge where Highway 1 crossed over the water, Sean lowered the hydraulic tower so that the mast of the big boat cleared the overpass. He could hear the *thrump-thrump* of the cars on the bridge above him as he passed under. The cliffs of the Back Bay rose straight above the water on both sides of the *Poco Bueno*. The multicolored holiday lights of the expensive homes planted on the edge of the cliffs twinkled. He leaned back in the chair and tilted his face to the evening stars.

"When did Robin and you first meet?" he asked out of politeness.

"Oh, gosh, way back in junior high. About a hundred years ago." She smiled and Sean smiled back. "She was the girl all the boys were after. But who could blame them? She had the most beautiful crystal blue eyes and a long blond mane. Of course, I was insanely jealous." Her hands were dancing on the dash as she talked. "In spite of how much I hated her, we hit it off immediately. You couldn't dislike Robin even if you tried. She was so full of beans."

"You two must have been quite a team," Sean said. He could imagine these two beauties, one blond, one brunette, cruising Bal in daddy's Jag, heading for two very different futures.

"Oh, we were! We got into more trouble together!" she laughed.

"You also knew Chad in school, right?" he asked, looking up.

"Who didn't?" she said. "Chad and Robin were *the* couple in high school. She was homecoming queen and he was the quarterback of the football team."

"Sounds like a made-for-TV script," Sean said dryly. He'd never seen one of those perfect couples yet that any decent D.A. couldn't find, scattered among the snapshot good looks, some unflattering detail.

"Doesn't it?" she said and rolled her eyes. "I think that's what makes it so sad if he did . . . if she *is* dead." She corrected herself.

"So what happened to the fairy tale?" Sean said.

"Like just about everybody else who swears they'll never forget each other, they went their separate ways," Carrie said. "He went off to play baseball and she moved to Hollywood to pursue acting. Everybody knew Chad was a star, but Robin was talented too," she went on. "She used to do impersonations, and she was an absolute genius with makeup and disguises. In high school we'd all sit around at lunch, and she'd imitate anybody you could name. Barbra Streisand, Bette Midler, Nancy Reagan." She shook her head and smiled, remembering. "She did a fabulous Nancy Reagan."

Sean circled the Back Bay once, then instead of turning into the long parade of boats motoring into the harbor, he banked Carter's yacht around again. No one seemed to mind. The party was reaching a crescendo below, the music louder than ever, except the tempo had slowed. Natalie Cole was singing her father's tunes again, and the roar of party talk and the tinkling of glasses had settled. From the bridge Sean could see a couple leaning against the aft rail, her arms around his neck holding a full champagne glass. The man kissed the woman, leaning her back a little as he bent for her lips, yet she never spilled a drop. Another couple was hidden in the dark under a cover in a deck lounger. Their champagne glasses were on the deck next to them, and the man had settled half on top with one of her legs wrapped around his waist, her foot resting on his buttocks. Her other foot, adorned with a silver-sequined high-heeled sandal, pointed straight to the heavens above them.

"It was stupid of me to listen to the bilge the media was pumping out about Chad," she said. "Now that I'm not angry, I realize I don't really believe Chad did it."

"You don't?" Sean said, a little stunned. Feeling compassion for a friend who was in trouble was one thing. But thinking him innocent? Even Sean hadn't come to that yet.

"No," she said. "Maybe he caused her death, maybe he didn't. But whatever happened, I can't believe he murdered her. And I'd like to find out what did happen. I don't think we've got the whole story."

She was beginning to read his mind.

"You know," she said at last, "I really liked Chad. He was the center of the whole class in our school. He loved to go to Del Mar to surf. He had a beautiful old woodie and we'd pile about ten of us in there and drive down for the day. Those were great times." She was smiling again. She reached over and put her hand on his. "By the way, thanks for helping me out with Carter tonight."

"Sure," he said and looked at her. He noticed for the first time that her eyes weren't really green. They were an ocean blue with spokes of yellow in them. His mother had had eyes like that. They changed color according to the light she was in. Sometimes they were blue, sometimes green, sometimes the color was impossible to name.

"You had your hands full," he said. "Sorry I had to pop him."

"Yes," she said. "And I've been such a bitch." She raised her eyebrows, easing the apology with a laugh.

Sean laughed and squeezed her hand. All right, he thought, so she was gorgeous and stinking rich. "Hey, forget it, okay?" he said. "Let's start over."

"All right," she said and smiled.

"Besides, I had a great time skippering the *Poco Bueno*."

"Really?" she said with a doubtful look.

"Absolutely," he said. "A Baby Elliot is one of the finest boats ever built in that class."

She smiled. "Well, I've got to get downstairs again before we pull in so I can get Daddy taken care of," she said and touched his arm again. Then she leaned over and kissed his cheek. "Merry Christmas, Sean."

"Merry Christmas," he said. "Can we talk again?"

"Of course," she said. "Why don't you call me next week and we'll have dinner? I'll help in any way I can."

"All right, I will," he said and watched her disappear down the steps. It sounded to him like they'd just made a date.

chapter

eleven

"Well, what happened?" Lowenstein asked when Gamboa and Knox walked in. "Was it her?"

The local district attorney's library had been converted into a command post for the Curtis case, and Lowenstein was sitting behind a requisitioned gunmetal desk. Behind him were photographs of Robin Penrose—a publicity shot of her in a frolicky pose, her fingers fluffing her hair out; a full-length rear shot in a thong that showed the breathtaking stretch of her dancer's legs; and one at a party, her hand draped across Carter Robinson's shoulder.

"Nada. Zip!" Gamboa answered and cleared a place for himself on top of another metal desk by dropping a pile of police reports on a chair. "Same age, same body type, same everything. But it wasn't her. The damn dental records didn't match."

"There are bodies buried all over that stinking desert," the D.A. said.

Knox spoke up. "Frankenstein said, and I quote, 'If all the bodies that were buried in the Mojave were to rise to the surface, you could walk all the way from San Bernardino to Vegas without ever touching sand.' " He was referring to the chief deputy coroner, a four-eyed creepy lizard with patches of psoriasis up and down his arms and neck. "A lovely little man," he added, shaking his head.

Gamboa yanked a couple of notes off the corkboard leaning against the wall that served as a message center. He waved the notes in front of Lowenstein's nose. "Look at this crap! There must be over twenty leads here. Not a one of them worth a shit. This one says she was seen in Granada Hills yesterday," he said and began throwing the notes in front of the D.A. one by one as he read them off. He and Knox had spent the past four days poking into every possible shallow gravesite they knew of, without luck. "This woman spotted her in Phoenix. This one says he dumped her in a cesspool out in San Bernardino."

"A cesspool?" Lowenstein said, scrunching his face up and leaning his head away from the imagined stench.

"Oh, yeah, that's a favorite," Knox said, stepping away from the doorjamb. "You dump a body in there, who's gonna bother looking?"

"Here's one from a psychic," Gamboa went on, still dealing the notes to Lowenstein. "Says she had a vision the girl was dumped in the ocean. We've got fifteen more of these crackpot leads, and they're spread all over the fucking state. And there's only two of us. If you've got any genius ideas, I'd like to know what the hell they are."

"How about the psychic?" Lowenstein asked.

"No goddamn psychics!"

"Now, wait a minute," Lowenstein interrupted. "I've used them before and sometimes they turn out to be helpful. We can't afford to ignore any leads since you two superstars haven't come up with diddly squat."

"Jesus!" Gamboa sighed. These goddamn Hollywood lawyers with the fag boots and bun-huggers, he thought to himself. "I'll make love to a transvestite before I let some weirdo tell me they got a vision about my goddamn case."

"Yeah, well, I hear Frederick's is having a half-off sale, Sergeant," Lowenstein said with a sweet lilt. "You two better get your ass in gear. I have to give Barrett daily updates on our leads, and I want you to stay two steps ahead of their investigator."

Knox could see Gamboa was steamed at the D.A.'s crack. He knew enough about his partner to know that it wouldn't take too much for Gamboa to climb over that desk and strangle Lowenstein by his hand-made tie. Not that he'd mind seeing the pompous ass with his eyes bulging out of his skull.

Knox slapped Gamboa on the shoulder. "Come on, Sarge. If we're going diving in any cesspools, we've got to rent some scuba gear."

The cesspool in question was out in San Bernardino, a glorified lettuce field on the outskirts of Riverside. The local farmers had put up a traffic light and called it a town. Gamboa and Knox drove around for an hour trying to find the place, an old vineyard no one had lived on for years. The cesspool was out behind what was left of the barn. When they drove up, the sanitation man had already arrived with his pump truck. On the side it read: "Tommy Tucker Sanitation—We'll take crap from anyone."

Tommy was built like an East African famine victim. His shirt hung from his shoulders and never touched another part of his body. His pants did the same thing. After the belt, they fell straight to his shoes. He had an old cigarette burning in his mouth, and one side of his face was sunken in, with a long, raised scar running from his ear to his Adam's apple, the unmistakable sign that he'd had a tumor the size of a grapefruit removed.

"Howdy, you Sergeant Gamboa?" Tucker said to Knox.

"Nah, I'm Knox," he said and shook hands. "That's Gamboa." And he pointed over his shoulder at his partner.

"Pleased to meet ya," Tucker said. Gamboa looked him over while they shook hands. Tommy had on a pair of overalls stained top to bottom with God only knew.

"Where's the cesspool?" Gamboa grunted.

"It's a septic tank."

"Whatever."

"Big difference," Tommy said. "See, a cesspool runs on a whole different sci-en-tific principle."

"Is that right?" Knox said, encouraging Tucker. He knew Gamboa didn't want to hear any of it.

"See, with your cesspool you got a chemical reaction that produces certain lethal gases. That's why they've been outlawed for twenty years. You still see 'em, 'course, but the state of the art is your septic."

"Great," Gamboa said. He was looking around for the hole in the ground. "But all we want to know is, is there a body in there?"

"Can't tell from here," Tucker said. "We'll have to open her up."

"No shit, Sherlock," Gamboa said. "Let's get to it." And Tucker led them to a patch of weeds near his truck. Gamboa was surveying the area with a hand shading his eyes like an Indian scout. "Where the hell is it?"

"You're standing on it," Tucker said. "I'll need some help here. If you'll lend a hand." He was motioning at Knox. "This is one of the early models of septic. Looks to be an Owens 55 or 75. Not worth a shit. Grab that piece a plywood there, would ya?" he said, pointing at a scrap over by Knox. "See, no cap to it. And the innards usually last less than ten years. That means as soon as the jacket goes, what's left in there seeps out into your water table." He had his arms fully extended at his sides, and he was wiggling his fingers to demonstrate what the refuse was up to while the unsuspecting owner slept peacefully in his house.

"I seen these Owens ruin more wells than all the insecticides in the world," Tommy said. "Now, on three, let's pull her loose. One . . . two . . . three." The plywood came up easily, and Knox dropped it off to one side and walked off a few steps and took a deep breath. Tommy walked right up to the edge of the tank, knelt down, and stuck his head in the hole. There was a visible greenish fog of stench hovering around his ears.

"Yep, it's an Owens, all right," he said. "Only it's a 40. Those are rare as hell." Gamboa could tell Tommy was impressed, like a wine taster just before he spits the medal winner into a spittoon. "They only sold a couple thousand before they took 'em off the market. Biggest pile of shit they ever made. You flush down your morning crap and that night you'd be washin' your dishes in it."

Tommy pulled his head back out, chuckling to himself. Knox still had his head between his legs trying to recuperate.

"Damn, that *is* ripe, Tommy," Knox gasped. His lungs were desperately searching for clean air.

"Aren't they supposed to drain those things before they abandon them?" Gamboa asked. He was standing next to Tucker, looking down into the bowels of the tank. It had taken him five or six years before he got over the knockout punch of a decaying body. After that he could stand the smell of anything. Except my ex-wives' perfume, was his barroom joke.

"S'pose to do a lot of things," Tommy said. Then he walked over to the truck and unrolled a three-inch hose. He tried to hand the hose to Gamboa, but he wouldn't take it.

"I think I'll just watch, thanks."

"Well, somebody's got to help me," Tucker said, holding the hose out. "I need one of you to unclog the line when the bigger pieces come through and get hung up. I can do it myself, but it'll take five or six hours that way. Couple hours if you lend a hand."

"Hey, Knox," Gamboa shouted at his partner, who still had his hands on his knees trying to get the burn out of his nose. "You're up."

Knox held up his hand to Gamboa. "Aw, partner, I hate to do this. But remember on that Tyler deal?" he said pathetically. "I got your ass off the hook on that surveillance fuckup. You said you owed me one. I'm calling in my marker now, Sarge."

Gamboa cussed while he put on the yellow rubber gloves Tucker handed him.

"We got another cesspool and two pigpens to check out yet," Gamboa said. "My marker's been called. Next time you're up."

"Yeah, well, hopefully she's in this one and we can skip the rest of them and get back to a nice clean gang murder. At least they have the decency to leave the victim in the middle of the street where they shot him."

Tommy went to the side of the pump truck and attached the other end of the hose. Then he went over to the septic and knelt down.

"Wait'll I tell you," he said, "then flip that switch next to where the hose is attached." And the man stuck the hose and half his body down into the bowels of the tank.

Tucker pumped for twenty minutes, then, finally, yelled to Gamboa. "It's clogged!"

Gamboa lifted the hose, and he could see some type of clothing blocking the end of the hose. He pulled the material away and threw it on the ground.

"What is it?" Knox asked.

"It looks like a pair of women's panties!" Gamboa said. "Jesus! This may be it!"

Then he called down into the hole to Tucker, who had climbed in. "Can you pump any faster? We just found her panties."

Tucker pulled himself part of the way out of the tank and rested his elbows on the rim.

"Can't do it, Sergeant. The whole jacket is shot to hell. I pump any faster, we'll clog the hose up in two shakes. I told you, these damn Owens 40's ain't worth a shit."

Behind Gamboa, Knox was rolling over on his side, laughing. You go to the University of Michigan for four years, he thought, spend weeks at the murder investigation seminars they got—ballistics, forensics, witness management, the works. And what was homicide all about? Fighting over who's gotta hold the hose while some Okie pumps out a hole full of shit.

chapter

twelve

Rita Morales, Eddie Romero's halfsister, lived with a black man in a kind of demilitarized zone of L.A. where the barrio coexisted alongside the black ghetto. There were no Latino *garachos* gangs who hung their banners, the spray-paint script that proclaimed their *zonas*, as a dog pisses to mark its territory, because they would be instantly challenged by blood gangs that ran the 'hoods directly across the Harbor Freeway. If a person didn't wander outside that four-block neutral zone of shops and homes that ran alongside the freeway, he was almost safe. A tortilla shop was flanked by a soul food joint, and the record store stocked R&B and salsa, sure signs of an uneasy peace. It was almost safe—if someone was brown or black. But for a white lawyer like Scott Powers, staking out a house waiting for a homeboy to sneak back home, it wasn't safe at all.

Scott pulled a Raiders cap down low on his forehead. He'd borrowed a black and silver Kings jacket and had the collar pulled up so just a hint of his pale skin showed as he slumped in the front of his rented Buick. He'd had the good sense to leave his white BMW back in Orange County and rent an old Riviera from the local Rent-A-Heap. The crappier and dirtier the better, he'd told the rental agent.

Scott scrunched down in his seat so that only the black cap showed over the top of the driver's door. This was the third day he'd squeezed the time to stake out the Morales house. But it had been nearly a week since he'd been able to get over there. He knew this hit-and-miss approach wasn't likely to catch Eddie, so he'd made up his mind that this was going to be the last day he wasted.

Berger had given Scott a detailed description of Eddie, including the tattoo of vipers and women and daggers in a satanic ménage à trois that ran the entire length of his upper left arm. On the back of his right shoulder was a dripping heart lanced through with a jagged knife. Except for a blue knit *cholo's* cap, he dressed in black, favoring tight leather pants and long-sleeve silk shirts.

Dusk was settling in around the neighborhood when a lowered Chevrolet Impala pulled up in front of the Morales house. A short, thin *pachuco* crawled out from behind the wheel and stroked up the walkway to the front door.

As soon as Scott spotted him, he knew it had to be Eddie. He threw off the Raiders cap and the Kings jacket. When he emerged from the car he looked like an attorney again—the wide tie, white shirt, gray gaberdines, and blue blazer. Eddie looked back, saw Scott coming, and ran for the door.

"Hold it, Eddie!" Scott said, breaking for the house before Eddie could get inside. "I'm not a cop! I'm not a cop! I'm Teddy Berger's attorney. He needs your help."

As soon as Eddie heard Berger's name, he wheeled around, his hand still on the doorknob, and instantly changed his demeanor from the hunted to the hunter.

"What's that *chingadera* want?" he yelled.

When Scott kept coming, Eddie stepped behind the door, back on the defensive. "Let's see some fuckin' ID if you ain't a cop," he said. "If you're a cop you gotta tell me now or any judge'll throw it out. I know my rights," he said, spewing out some of the misinformation that passes for legal advice on the streets—until they get arrested and their P.D. tells them it doesn't mean a thing.

Scott didn't want to spook Eddie, so he stopped two or three feet from the steps and pulled out a business card from his briefcase. When he offered it to Romero, the Mexican snatched it from his hand.

"Hey, do I look like some kind of *cabazon*? I know a card don't pass for no fucking ID," he said and threw it down in the dirt.

Scott bent down and picked it up. He didn't want to leave a trail that one of Romero's friends or enemies could follow. "They don't give attorneys ID's, Eddie. That's only the police," he said. "If I showed you an ID, I'd be a cop, now wouldn't I?"

Eddie thought it over. "How do I know you're Berger's lawyer?"

"Well, let's see," Scott said, thinking. "I think I have some paperwork that will prove I'm his attorney."

He fished some papers out of his briefcase and held them up for Romero to see. "See there, where it says '*Theodore John Berger* v. *State of California*.' And right above that, 'Attorney Scott L. Powers.' That means I represent him."

Romero's eyes roved the page. He didn't see what Scott was getting at because he'd dropped out in the eighth grade, and most of his first seven years in school had been a naively ambitious waste of taxpayer money. He finally shook his head. "I guess it's okay," he said. He stepped out from behind the screen door. "Now, what the fuck do you want?"

"Can I come in?" Scott said, motioning toward the door with his head.

"No, you can't come the fuck in!"

"I will be a lot less . . . conspicuous inside."

Romero looked Scott over a long moment and, finally, swung the door open.

"Thanks," Scott said and slipped by him into the kitchen.

Neither Scott nor Romero had noticed the two black men sitting in a furniture van down the street. One of them got out of the passenger's seat. He was a massively wide Rastafarian with dreadlocks. Another Rasta, this one enormously tall, got out of the driver's side. They crossed the street and edged up near the side of the Morales house, next to the kitchen window.

Romero sat at a table covered with drug paraphernalia—a metal pipe clotted with gooey black resin, and razor blades and dishes and cups with dark, grainy residues left on them. Scott stood on the other side of the room and leaned against the refrigerator. The temperamental old thing rumbled loudly when he touched it, so he stood clear.

"Now, first of all, Eddie—mind if I call you Eddie?"

"It's better than motherfucker."

Eddie sat back. A gold chain hung down his chest between his unbuttoned silk shirt.

"Yeah, well, first of all, I'm not here to get you in trouble. Although Ted has told me everything."

"What's everything?" Eddie asked.

Scott stared at him a moment. When he had been a P.D. in San Diego, before Sean had thrown him a lifeline and pulled him into the firm, he had dealt with Romero's type every day. They all thought in their druggy haze that they could bluff their way through any jam. The quicker they understood how deep they were buried in their own shit, the quicker the facade dropped.

"Everything, Eddie, is how you asked him to break into the Medtech offices and steal any information he could get on Kaufmann Industries," Scott said.

Romero didn't react. His hands didn't fidget and his eyes stayed fixed on Scott. "That's it?" he finally said.

"No," Scott answered and added some more weight. "I know you were there when the guard was shot."

"That's bullshit!" Romero cut him off.

"*And,*" Scott went on, "I know you know the guy that pulled the trigger."

That did it. "Okay, motherfucker!" he exploded. "Get the fuck out of here!"

Scott didn't move. He had been expecting a violent bluff from Romero when he mentioned the killer. He outweighed the drug-emaciated Mexican by nearly fifty pounds. All he had to do was keep him clear of weapons, and they could continue their little chat.

"I said get the fuck out of here!" Romero screamed and grabbed a butter knife off the sink. When he realized what he had, he put it down and looked around frantically for something that would do some good. He reached for one of the drawers, and Scott stepped across and slammed it shut with his foot.

"Calm down, Eddie," he said. "If I leave now, I'll call the cops in. Five minutes from now you'll be sitting in the back of a squad car answering a lot of tough questions."

Romero looked over at the door, then into the other room. Dark half moons were growing beneath his arms, and drops of sweat ran down his brow. He started to say something, but all that came out was a whimper.

"You said you weren't here to get me in trouble," he finally managed to get out. "The first thing you do is say you're gonna call the damn cops. Jesus!"

"Look," Scott said, "you've got to see it from my point of view. I have a client who's sitting in jail ready to go down for a murder he didn't commit. And you know who did it. What do you expect me to do?"

Eddie didn't answer. He went over to the kitchen door and pushed aside the curtain on the upper glassed portion. "You can't prove a goddamn thing or you wouldn't be here," he said with his back still to Scott.

"You might be right, Eddie," Scott said. "But you've got to start thinking clearly if you're gonna save your own ass. If I know what went down that night, how long before the cops get onto it? Tomorrow night it'll be the Orange County sheriffs knocking on your door. Wise up, Eddie."

Romero didn't answer.

"What do you think's going to happen when my client gets up on the stand and testifies to everything he knows and I subpoena you into court?"

"Then I'm a dead man," he said.

"Not if you cooperate," Scott said.

Eddie dropped the door curtain and turned around to Scott. "You don't know your ass. You know that?" he said. He walked over and put his fists on the table and leaned close to Scott. His gums and lips had a chapped, shredded look. "As soon as I open my mouth, I'm a fucking corpse."

"Don't worry, Eddie," Scott said. "The police will protect you."

Romero barked a quick, short burst of laughter. "They can get you anywhere, asshole," he said. "They got Hoffa. They got Kennedy. They got Jesus fucking Christ, man! They can sure as hell get Eddie Romero."

Scott knew that the Mexican, despite his protestations, was going to give it up. He wouldn't have let him in the door if he wasn't going to tell. Romero had been hiding out for weeks, sneaking around, looking for a way out of this death trap. He just wanted a little reassuring before he changed sides in the deal.

"Tell me who killed the guard," Scott said evenly. "Who is he?"

"God damn it!" Romero said and looked around nervously. "Shut the fuck up! Don't fucking do this. He sniffs any part of this . . ." Romero didn't finish. He turned as if he was going to bust out the kitchen door and run for it. Then he turned and slapped the wall with his palm. "I don't want to talk to you. Leave me alone."

"You don't have a choice, Eddie. You know that. If you cooperate now, tell them everything you know about this guy, I can guarantee you'll walk out of this without doing hard time. Maybe a little county time. Maybe not even that." Scott knew he couldn't really promise a thing. Only a D.A. could do that. But why spare a little exaggeration when Romero was ready to roll over?

Romero looked at him suspiciously. "Shit!" he mumbled.

"I know you and Ted didn't kill the security guard," Scott went on, pressing Romero's crumbling will. "You drove there with Berger in his car, and the shooter pulled up later and parked on the other block. That's the way it happened, wasn't it?"

Romero shrugged. He was listening closely to his alibi taking shape.

"He had the gun," Scott said, feeding Eddie his way out. "He pulled the trigger. You had nothing to do with it. But unless you cut a deal with the D.A., you'll go to the gas chamber. In case you don't know the law, if someone dies during the commission of a felony, they can be charged with murder one, special circ."

Romero looked up.

"You know what that means, Eddie?"

Romero shook his head.

"It means the death penalty," Scott said and let the phrase roar around a few moments in Eddie's brain. "The only way out of this mess is to tell the police the whole story and let the guilty party take the heat. He's the one who should be in custody. Not you or Berger."

Romero was standing with his back to Scott now, leaning over the sink. Scott thought he was going to throw up. The Mexican turned around and put his dark hands over his colorless face.

"Who's the shooter?" Scott asked. "Just tell me who he is, and Teddy and you both walk. All just a bad dream."

"He's the baddest motherfucker you'll ever meet," Romero moaned. "You want somebody dead, he can do it. And he's fuckin' immune from the cops, man. He's been vaccinated or something."

Scott smiled to himself. The first thing these small-time gangsters did was build a myth around themselves. If the homeboys could see their heroes in an interview room sobbing their eyes out to their public defender, that myth would disappear overnight.

"What's his name?" Scott pressed.

"Shiiiiiit!" Eddie said, shaking his head. He walked to the cupboard and pulled down a bottle of a clear liquid in a recycled whiskey bottle. Scott figured it was home-brew tequila. Eddie took a long, urgent pull on the bottle. Then another. His eyes watered immediately.

Scott knew Eddie was breaking. He walked over to him and put his hand on his shoulder. Romero started sobbing like an old Mexican woman at a funeral.

"There's only one thing to do," Scott said. "Go to the cops now. If you hand them the killer, they'll probably let you walk."

"Do I got a choice?"

"None that I can see," Scott said. "As soon as Berger testifies, you're out in the cold—with the cops and this black guy both looking for you. And no place to hide."

"Motherfucker!" was all Romero said.

"Come on," Scott said, motioning toward the door. "I'll buy you a drink before we go to the police."

That was the moment when the kitchen doorknob exploded. It bounced across the floor and hit Scott in the shin. The door slammed open, and an enormous black man with shoulders as wide as the frame stepped through. He held a long blade that extended to the floor. It took Scott a moment before he realized it was a machete. But this was an aficionado's machete. The wooden handle, long enough to accommodate both hands, was leather like an expensive tennis racket's. The blade started near the man's pocket—a three-inch-wide cut of metal that grew to five toward the floor. It shone like chrome and the edge was milled lovingly. The man had used the machete to hack the doorknob off.

Another huge black man stepped in after him. This one was

thinner than the first, and tall as a professional basketball player, so he had to duck to get through the door. He had a gun with a silencer. He took one enormous step and was next to Scott in the doorway that led to the living room. He put the long snout of the silencer in Scott's ribs.

"Well, well, well," the man with the machete laughed, swinging the door shut. It was a friendly chuckle, as though they'd just arrived at a party. Both men were dressed for a formal do, in expensive tailor-made suits. They both had a matted mop of dreadlocks and dark sunglasses, even though the sun had set a half hour before.

"Ha! Ha! Ha! Now, where dee hell you goan, Eddie, with Mr. Ham-berger's attorney?"

Scott was pretty sure this was the guy that had shot the security guard at Medtech. Apparently, they'd been staking out Eddie too.

Romero immediately started pleading with him. He had both hands locked on the chair back, and his face was bloodless.

"Look, Shabba! I wasn't going to say shit to this asshole," he cried. He dismissed Scott with a sideways wave of his hand. "He's just a faggot wants a blowjob. I didn't tell him shit!"

The big man showed a face-wide grin. He was very black, and his teeth, the two front ones edged in gold, punctuated the twilight in the kitchen.

"Hey, don't get excited, Eddie," he said. "We're tight, mon. I don't fuck with my friends. It's dese nosy white boys dat piss me off." And he pointed at Scott with the tip of the machete.

Scott noticed then that both men were wearing leather gloves. And that's when he knew for sure that this was a hit. Nothing else. They were just maneuvering closer, checking the other rooms for witnesses. The last thing they wanted was a lot of noise, screaming, running, a mistake.

Romero took a deep breath and relaxed when the big man told him it was Scott he was after. Then Scott saw a blur and Eddie Romero's hands were separated from his wrists. They were still gripping the chair back, but the two handless arms were at his side and blood was pumping out of them with the rhythm of his heart—hard spurts of blood coming from the arteries that suicides always go for. Eddie began to scream. Then the big man whipped his blade again, and Eddie never got the scream all the way out. His head flew across the room as if a baseball bat had caught it flush. It was a brutal hacking sound, like an uprooting. Scott could hear tendons and arteries ripping and pulling apart. Pieces of Eddie's neck splattered against the refrigerator next to Scott. Then Eddie's body collapsed, his shoulders thudding against the cabinets below the sink, blood gushing out of the hole in his trunk where his head used to be.

In that frozen moment, as the tall one with the silencer jerked back away from the splattering blood, Scott chopped his arm down on the gun and it bounced across the floor.

The massive black man took a quick step across the kitchen and swung the machete as Scott ducked and spun away into the living room. He could feel the whoosh of air across his cheek. The big man tried to get past the table that separated him from Scott, while the tall one went for his gun. Scott was through the living room into the back of the house before they were out of the kitchen.

He could see blood soaking his pants. As he hurdled through a bedroom and slammed the door behind him, he could hear them banging their way through the living room. Two giants who barely fit through a door bulling through a small, unfamiliar room. His hand hurt. The hand, he thought. He dived out the bedroom window, and he landed on something hard and went over on his face. His left hand was burning, like acid was leaking from his sleeve down on his fingers. He reached down with his right hand to inspect it, and it was wet and small and fleshy. He felt around. The pain was rising up his arm. Something was wrong. His hand wasn't all there. A finger was missing, two fingers maybe. And the wetness felt as thick as paint.

He hopped up onto a wooden fence and caught the splintered top with his right hand and tried to pull himself over, but he couldn't. He could feel his senses going, his vision narrowing, a humming in his head. His life was draining from the hole in his hand. The machete. The big one Eddie had called Shabba had hacked off his fingers on the doorjamb with the machete.

Scott turned as they came through the back door—the tall one first with the gun, a monolith of black granite in his gloved hand—then Shabba with the machete dripping red.

Scott put his butchered hand on top of the fence and screamed as he went over. He found himself in an alleyway of cinder-block walls and garage doors. He took off running, his mutilated hand held against his hip. With his other hand he was trying to pull his tie off as he ran. He had to get the bleeding hand tied off or he would die. One of the black men scaled the fence, dropping to the pavement fifty yards behind him. Scott slowed, fumbling to knot the tie around his arm. It wasn't working. There was nothing to grab onto. No way to make a knot with one hand.

Something *thwapped* against a garage door across from him. Looking back, he saw that the tall one had stopped and held the long-nosed gun at eye level. Scott shouldered through a gate and started running through a backyard. He took another fence and he was in the front yard now and out onto another street of old houses.

He couldn't hear the tall one anymore. He ran down to the next house and hid in some hedges next to it. A dog was barking several houses down in the other direction. He was hoping it would draw them away from him.

He slumped down against the stucco wall of the house, his feet the only things showing under the hedge. He wrapped the tie around his arm and, with the thumb and remaining finger of his left hand, held it while he knotted it with his teeth and the right hand. He screamed but only his breath came out.

Then he remembered: his car was parked in front of Romero's. If he was going to survive, he had to get to his car. It wouldn't do any good to try to get a neighbor to help. No one was going to help him around here. Gang members shot each other up every night of the week in this neighborhood, and all they did was lock up a little tighter and keep low. What were they going to do? Walk out on their porch in the middle of a firefight and try to save one asshole from killing another asshole?

He figured he was on the street behind Romero's place—if, that is, he hadn't gotten hopelessly confused during the chase. That meant he needed to make his way down the block, then cross the street, and he'd be directly across from his car. He'd parked it almost on the corner, so he'd be only about fifty feet from it. Getting across the street, though, would be a problem. If they spotted him before he could get the car started, he'd be dead.

His hand was burning, but the blood had stopped gushing. He had a little more time before he had to get to a hospital.

Scott crawled beneath the hedge to the corner of the house. The street was empty, but he could hear heavy-footed clomping down the block, and the dog was barking more furiously. The first wave of nausea poured over him as he ran past another house and he stopped to rest. He was very weak from all the blood he'd lost. He prayed his adrenaline would keep him going awhile longer. He got up again and ran past the next house and the next and came to a walkway between houses. He cut through it and he was in the back alley again. At the far end of the alley he saw the tall one, his right hand dangling heavily at his side.

There was a breeze scattering scraps of newspaper in the alley. An old junker was parked there, and Scott crouched behind it. He looked down the alley through the windows of the car. The tall one had ducked back into Eddie's yard, and Shabba was nowhere in sight. Scott crossed quickly to the other side of the alley and stood up against the cinder-block wall. The cold of the stone on his back re-suscitated him. He could feel something besides the numbing fire in his hand. The muscles of his left arm had gone dead, and it felt like a piece of concrete was hanging from his shoulder—cold and hard and unresponsive. He edged down to the end of the wall and there it was—the old Rent-A-Heap slumped against the curb. All he had to do was get lucky. Make it across the street and to the car without them spotting him. He had to get to the hospital quickly, though. His legs were twitching and wobbly, and nausea was pushing against his throat. He stepped around the fence.

Shabba was right in front of him with the machete in both hands. He grinned as he drove the long, cold blade up into Scott's stomach. All the way up, three feet of blade cutting the life from him. Scott felt the fire in his hand spreading, rampaging up through his belly and his chest, and sweeping into his brain, a red, violent storm of fire that flashed like Hiroshima.

Shabba pulled the long blade out and stepped back as Scott buckled to the ground, vomiting his life away on the cold, merciless pavement.

chapter

thirteen

MacDuff drove up Gower in his Honda with a beer wedged between his legs. Checking the rearview for cops, he drained the can and stuffed it into a paper sack behind the seat. When he got to Hollywood Boulevard, he made a right.

He'd spent all day cruising up and down Sunset and Highland and Vine and Western, slowing down when he saw a girl who might be Robin Penrose. All morning and all afternoon and part of the evening trolling this worn-out legend.

Hollywood was a beat-up old piece of L.A. now. There weren't any Lana Turners waiting to be discovered at Schwab's. The only girls waiting to be discovered weren't looking for any six-figure, long-term contracts. A half hour for twenty bucks at the Stardust off Sunset would do.

The studios that had made the area famous had all gone Chapter 11 or moved over the hill to the Valley, where land was cheap. All they had left behind were grimy coffee shops with cracked linoleum, secondhand clothes bins, liquor stores that sold twist-top wine and the Daily Racing Form, and a scattering of rock clubs like Whiskey's and The Roxie.

On the streets, besides the hookers, were would-be rock stars with iridescent pants, out-of-towners with zooms, and people of every ethnic origin except American. All the shops were run by Asians. Underneath a sign proclaiming Huan's Fatburger was a scrawl of hieroglyphics. What it said only a Taiwanese would know for sure. The liquor stores were run by Arabs, though, and that's where Mac concentrated his search.

He had spent hours going into one liquor store after another, showing Robin's picture without luck. It was time to go home. Mac couldn't figure out why Sean would want him to spend all this time looking for her alive anyway. Everybody knew she was dead. Why not spend his time on more constructive pursuits?

He spotted Hussein's Little Cairo Superette, made a U across six lanes of traffic, and parked on the street in front of the place. He was through searching for the day. He just wanted to pick up some refreshments for the long drive back to Capistrano.

He grabbed a sixer of Meisterbrau and laid it on the counter and then out of habit flipped the picture of Robin at the Arab behind the cash register.

"Ever see this girl, amigo?"

The man nodded no without looking at the photo until Mac revealed the numbered corner of a fifty he had folded behind the photo. The man's eyes pinned the bill like a cat spotting a robin.

"Tell me where I can find this girl, and the fifty is yours," Mac whispered.

"Sure thing, dude," the Arab said, still looking at the fifty. A lot of these new arrivals liked to use all the latest expressions. The problem was the words were slightly altered to fit the cadence of their native language, so they came out like Mexican food cooked by a Greek.

"You Hussein?" Mac asked.

"You got that one right."

"Well, Hussein, can you help me?" He was wagging the photo and the fifty in front of him.

"Sure. This chick big-time fox. Only this not good picture of her. Different hair. And dress," he said, wagging his finger in the negative, "not the same."

"Forget the dress and the hair. These bitches have ten wigs apiece now."

"There's a ticket. But same fox, for sure. Slam dunk, baby!"

"Yeah?"

"Yeah, you bet your bookies! See the necklace?" Hussein motioned Mac closer and pointed at the heart-shaped locket around Robin's neck. "Different hair. Different clothes. Same necklace."

"When was the last time you saw her?"

"Hard to say, for exactly," the Arab said, bobbing his head uncertainly. Mac knew it was crap. This guy knew exactly when he'd seen her. He was holding back his big cards was all.

"Well, was she with anyone?"

The Arab offered a wide-eyed look as if Mac had asked him if he knew which way was east. "What you think? Hey, she's hooker," he said.

"A hooker?" Mac asked incredulously. "Around here?" It wasn't that he was surprised by the news. He'd spent too much time in Vegas to be surprised by much of anything these bimbos would do. He'd had every kind of bitch from a cheerleader to a minister's wife trying to woof his tool for a buck. But he pictured Robin for the grand-a-night dinner, dance, and jerk-off call girl. If Mac flashed so much as a twenty at a hooker around here, he'd be looking for change.

"Yeah. You know, hooker." The Arab put his hands together and pumped his pelvis a few times and grinned.

"Yeah, I know," Mac said and flipped Hussein ten dollars.

"Hey, you say fifty bucks!" the Arab screamed. He was waving the ten around like it was on fire.

"That's right. If you see her, let me know and you get the fifty."

Hussein nearly vaulted the counter getting to Mac. It was time to play that big card he figured he was holding. He only came to Mac's shoulder, but when he grabbed the big ex-cop by the sleeve, he nearly picked him up, dragging him out the door. When he got to the corner, he pointed down the street to a woman leaning in the window of a car.

"Are you sure?" Mac asked, squinting down the street. "It's got to be the right one or you don't get zilch, Abdulla."

"From my mouth to God's ears, praise Allah," he said and raised his eyes heavenward. Mac didn't know what the hell he was talking about.

Mac trotted across the street. When the man in the car saw him coming, he took off with a squeal of tires, leaving the girl talking to a bunch of air. When she spotted Mac, she turned and started walking in the other direction as fast as her spiked heels and tight skirt would take her. She knew a cop when she saw one.

"Robin," Mac yelled and began to trot, his belly leading the way.

When she heard him call out, she hiked her skirt to her ass and started running, a wink of hot pink panties flashing with every stride.

"Ah, shit," Mac groaned. "I'm too old for this." After a couple of blocks he caught her by her tank top and spun her around. He stood for a minute trying to catch his breath.

"Robin?" Mac asked. He was looking her up and down, checking the hair, the eyes, the height. They didn't add up. This girl was blond but the nose was all wrong. She was tall like Robin, but when he looked down he saw she was wearing four-inch spikes.

"What?" she said. Mac could see close up that her nostrils were raw from cocaine.

"You're not Robin, are you?" he said.

"No, and I ain't Julia Roberts either."

Mac still held her shoulders. She tried to slap his hand away when she realized he wasn't a cop.

"You wearing a locket?"

"What of it?"

Mac didn't want to stand around on Hollywood Boulevard and argue with some hooker. He reached inside her top and pulled out the chain that was around her neck. He had the picture of Robin out, checking the locket around her neck with the one on the girl. He could see right away it was much smaller than Robin's and shaped differently.

"Sorry, wrong bimbo," Mac said. He took aim and dropped the locket back between her pushed-up tits and started to walk away. But she didn't appreciate some guy running off her date, chasing her down, asking a lot of dumb questions, and then reaching inside her blouse. Especially for free. Before Mac got two strides away, she jumped on his back and started kicking and screaming.

"What the fuck do you think you're doing, you fuckin' weirdo . . . ?" She stomped her heel on his toe, and he swung his big arm around and caught her shoulder. She went sprawling, her blond wig hanging down her back, attached to her brown hair by a lone bobby pin.

Then Hussein ran up and started yelling, "Where's my fifty bucks, you sonafabeech! Where's my fifty bucks!"

Mac reached in his pocket and took two twenties and a ten and threw them up in the air. "Fight over it!" he snarled. And the Arab and the girl were all over each other in the street, kicking and slapping and scratching each other trying to get the bills. Mac trotted over to his Honda, crawled in, and drove off.

Nothing but a great big waste of time, he thought. Robin might have been selling her bush, but he could tell by looking at her she wouldn't be doing it around Hollywood. This was strictly the needle crowd. Why Barrett had listened to that dipshit Jamaican he couldn't figure. It was Barrett's nickel, though. If he wanted to waste his court-appointed hours chasing these bullshit leads, okay by Mac. As long as the checks didn't bounce, he'd be glad to do it.

chapter

fourteen

Sean still ate breakfast at the Back Harbor once every month or so. They put out big portions of bacon and eggs, and many of the old harbor rats from his father's era still came in to eat before work. It was the same bunch that had been there the night his father had his heart attack. Only now some other red-faced old working slob had his father's stool, the one with the best view of the TV.

"Hey, Sean, what's the word?" Blaine said from behind the bar. He'd owned the place for forty years and was also one of the Back Harbor's best customers. He had the rotting body to prove it—the nose corroded like a leper's, his pupils swimming in skim milk, the rims swollen with blood, his bowels hit and miss.

"Not a thing," Sean said.

"Scotch?" he asked and started to reach down for a bottle in the well.

"Draft'll do, Blaine," he said.

It wasn't yet noon and they were all lined up: Gerty, George,

Crane, Weidemeyer. Nothing changed. The place still had the same wormwood walls and fish nets hanging from the ceiling and old pictures of the Newport Harbor during World War II, when these same guys were building PT boats instead of outfitting one-hundred-foot sport fishers.

"George, Gerty, how's it going?" Sean waved. They waved back.

"Hey, Sean! Hey, Sean!" the two old guys said one on top of the other.

"Read where you're defending Chad Curtis," Gerty said. He was a tubby, gray-faced ex-Marine who dug in his nose with his thumb.

"Yeah."

"Jesus, what a fast ball!" he said. They all shook their heads in agreement. Then went back to their drinks and a hockey game on the flickering TV mounted on the wall.

That's about the way it always went. Except sometimes they'd start in about his father, whose prowess as a boatman and a drinker, the two skills they admired most, had grown with the years.

"Your old man could wire a boat faster'n a whore can get you to come," Weidemeyer used to say reverentially. He had been his father's second for eleven years. "He was a class-A screw-up," he said, meaning it as a compliment, "but the guy had a sweetheart pair of hands. He could get inside a gnat's asshole and build a whole instrument panel."

His father had always got the three kids home by seven, in bed by nine or ten, most of the time with their homework done. He had only started staying all hours after Loretta was in high school. By that time Sean was a junior, busy with school sports and surfing, and his older brother, Petey, was going to Colorado State.

His father's first heart attack came while Sean was in his first year of law school in San Diego. Two days after that he had a stroke that left him speechless and paralyzed on one side. He still went to the Back Harbor to drink every day, though, sitting in a booth, no longer able to balance on the wobbling bar stools next to his friends.

Then came another heart attack seven months later and a quick funeral. His sister and brother flew in from Idaho and Texas, where they had gone to live, his brother transferred by his computer company to San Antonio, his sister to marry a pilot based in Boise. The house on 15th quickly sold and the monies were divided. And, like that, Sean was alone, a first-year law student struggling over contracts and torts.

Sean was nursing a draft Bergie, the only beer poured at this establishment since it had opened, when Blaine came over to him. "Sean, phone for you, buddy."

"Thanks."

Sean walked to the end of the U-shaped bar. He hadn't told anyone he was here except Mac. "That you, Mac?" he said. The receiver was greasy, so he switched it to the other hand and wiped the other one on his pants.

"You remember me, Meesta Barrett?" It was the Uncola Man.

"Sure, I remember," said Sean, surprised. The only way the Jamaican could have known he was in the Back Harbor was to have followed him. "But I forgot your name, sorry."

"Ohhh, ha, ha, ha!" he laughed heartily. "Don't try to trick your friend. Or maybe you regret it. Know what I mean?"

"Save your dime," Sean said. "Your hotshot leads suck. My investigator spent all day in Hollywood and got zilch."

"Ohhh, my gawd, mon," the Jamaican laughed derisively. "Dat ding-a-ling don't know his booty from a lava rock. Ohhh, the mon don't understand what kine girl our Robin is. She be a crystal goblet, and he lookin' for a old beer bottle rollin' 'round dee gutta. Liquor stores! Shit!" He said it like a Prohibitionist. "Now, what kine girl you goan find outside liquor stores and dose topless joints? Huh, mon? You tell me dis now. What's he goan find dere? Dis girl is a jewel, a sparkly diamond. You send dat big ol' corn boy to find her. Dat boy can't see pass dee broom under his nose."

Sean was taken aback for a moment. No crackpot would ever know these kinds of details about a case or the ongoing investigation. This Jamaican, or somebody he knew, had to have followed Mac. "Look, mon," Sean said with a bite, "Robin Penrose could be next in line for the throne. But the fact is, we still haven't found her in Hollywood or anywhere else," he said. "Who the hell are you? I've got a client to defend. I can't be screwing around chasing your bullshit leads."

The Jamaican said something, but just then Gretsky slapped one in. There was a boozy roar from the patrons, and Sean couldn't hear what he said.

"What was that?" he said loudly over the commotion.

"I'm dee only one can save Chad," the Jamaican said. There was no accompanying laugh. "Why don't you go dis time yourself, mon? Let dat dumb ol' corn boy play with dee ragheads in Hollywood. You goan see for yourself our little bird's alive."

"All right," Sean shouted into the receiver. "You keep telling me you're Chad's friend. So far you haven't been much help. Where can we meet?"

"Ohh, no, no, no! No meeting. But I tell you where to find our little bird."

"Quit screwing with me," Sean cried again, only just then a commercial came on and the place was quiet as a tomb, so he heard his own shouted "asshole!" starch the place. He turned away from the bar, where Gerty and a couple of the others were looking at him.

"Tell me what you know," he said into the cupped receiver.

"Bakersfield. Red Lion Inn. She just waitin' for you in dee bar. Been dere couple days now. Maybe she gettin' bored. Better hurry, Meesta Barrett."

Sean put the phone down when he heard the click on the other end and slid it back across the bar to Blaine. The Jamaican was right. Even Chad wasn't as eager to help him. He couldn't just throw these leads away because the guy was taunting him. The Uncola Man knew something. Maybe Robin wasn't alive. But if he could keep supplying girls who looked like her and Sean could find credible witnesses who'd testify they'd seen Robin, then the Jamaican and the dead-end searches he was sending Sean on would be worth it.

"Girlfriend giving you the raw one, Sean?" Weidemeyer asked after Sean hung up.

"Yeah, Weed, you know how it is," Sean said, even though he was pretty certain that Weidemeyer, a lifelong bachelor, didn't know a thing.

Sean picked his beer off the bar and went to sit in the back booth. Mac was supposed to meet him here at twelve. It was already twelve-thirty. He spread Gamboa's reports out on the chipped formica top and began reading.

"What did you find out?" Sean snapped when Mac lumbered in an hour later.

"Well, Merry Christmas and Happy fucking New Year to you

too! Ain't you even gonna say hello, give me a big wet kiss?" He had a couple of shreds of notepaper rolled in one hand that passed for case notes.

"Don't tell me you couldn't find anywhere to park."

Sean was a little more upset than he should have been. He had known the way Mac was when he hired him. Mac would do a hell of an investigation, but he'd do it on his version of time.

"I was waiting at the Harbor View for a half hour before I realized you'd said *Back* Harbor," Mac explained, wrestling his way into the booth. He took the table and shoved it against Sean so he was wedged against the seat, then he slid in and pulled it back so Sean could breathe again. "Christ! Where'd you find this dump? Strictly the d.t.'s crowd," he said, looking around at the bar's patrons.

"We used to eat in the back when I was a kid," Sean said, pointing at a four-table anteroom off the kitchen that passed for a dining room. "Now, what did you find out?"

"Well, I talked to Robin's mother," Mac said, unrolling the sheets of notepaper. There were a few three- or four-word phrases, names, and telephone numbers but mostly a lot of doodles, underlines, and stick figures. "Nice lady. Kahunas out to here." Mac leered, holding his hands cupped a foot in front of his chest. "Loved her daughter. Liked Chad too. Until now, that is." Mac reached over and finished Sean's half-full beer.

"She's like everyone else," Sean said, shaking his head. "As soon as they arrest someone, they figure he's guilty."

"You got that right. As soon as she found out I was there to help out Curtis, she wouldn't say shit," Mac said. "Except I did manage to get one interesting piece of information before she got lockjaw. Remember that locket around Robin's neck in all her photos?"

"Yeah?"

"The old lady said her father gave it to her on his deathbed, and Robin never took it off. Took showers in the damn thing." Sean thought about his old briefcase. He could understand the sentiment. "The old lady told me Robin said it had some kind of magic power in it. Jesus! It had magic in it, all right. Probably kept her coke stash there."

"Anything else?" Sean asked.

"Yeah," Mac said and screwed his face up in a question. "I'm not sure exactly what to make of it. But remember that guy from Laramie Homes you wanted me to talk to?"

"Krueger?"

"Right," Mac said and looked at his notes, turned the page, then turned it over and gave up. "Well, anyway, it seems the SEC red-flagged the buying and selling of large blocks of Laramie Homes stock. The purchases all took place a few days before an announcement of a huge land-development deal in Apple Valley. Two thousand homes, a shopping mall, the works."

"Was there something illegal going on?"

"They don't know yet. But some old lady bought up a bundle of Laramie stock, the price doubles in three days, and she unloads and walks away with a million plus profit. Not bad for a few days' work." Mac blew a long, slow whistle like an incoming mortar shell.

"Does Krueger think there's going to be indictments or anything like that?"

"Nah. He was just pissed at the SEC was all. Claims they got Ivan Boesky fever these days. Every time somebody makes a profit they go ballistic. They were climbing all over Krueger's tree."

"That's what his meeting with Carter was about?" Sean asked.

"Yeah. He wanted Carter Robinson to get them off his back," Mac said. "Krueger was claiming he didn't know shit about it."

"All right. So what's it got to do with our case?"

"Nothing really," Mac said. "I was just saying that's what came up at the meeting."

"Man, I'm lost," Sean said.

"Well, hang on, I'm getting to the interesting part," Mac said. Blaine came over and put two more beers on the table. Mac leaned his head back and drained one of them in a couple of swallows. "Robin got up in the middle of this meeting and ran out. Krueger said one minute she's taking notes, the next she's out the door with Carter Robinson in pursuit. Then Carrie Robinson takes off after them. Meanwhile this guy Krueger's in there whanking his dick, trying to figure out if his deodorant maybe quit on him or something."

"What time was this?" Sean asked. He was rolling his empty beer glass between his hands like a piece of molding clay. This didn't jibe exactly with what Carrie had told him—that she had sent Robin home early because Robin wasn't feeling well.

"Krueger figured seven, seven-thirty. Anyway, ten minutes later, Robinson and his daughter come strolling back in. But no Robin. A couple hours later, Miss Penrose gets herself permanently lost. Sounds like she was back on the vitamin C."

"Could be. That about it?"

"Yeah," Mac said and reached for Sean's beer.

"Okay, good, Mac," Sean said. "Now, there's just one more thing on the agenda."

"Yeah?"

"The Uncola Man called."

"Oh, shit." Mac's big paw came down on the table, and the salt and pepper jumped. "What's that asshole want?"

"He wants you to go to Bakersfield."

"Ah, crap! This is dogshit, Sean!" Mac said. His hands were swatting the air. "The guy's a fuckin' fruitcake and you got me chasing his cream dreams."

"It can't be helped, Mac. You know what these circumstantial cases are like. You've got to stack up the witnesses like cordwood. We need as many as we can get," Sean said. He knew Lowenstein would be calling in Robin's friends, family, people she worked and played with, all to testify that they hadn't seen or heard from Robin since her disappearance. Circumstantial cases often hung on who had the biggest stack.

"But Bakersfield! Why not Hawaii or something? I could interview a few hula girls and chug-a-lug those fruity-tootie drinks all the gay boys suck up. How about it? Ask the Uncola Man if he's seen her in Lahaina."

"Sorry, Mac." Sean laughed and reached into his pocket and pulled out some gas money. "The I-5 awaits you. You don't want to disappoint all those horny women in that godforsaken wasteland just waiting for a real man like you to show up."

Mac grunted out a laugh. Then he brightened. "Yeah," he said, "but remember, you wanted me to follow up on Gamboa's witness list."

There was an ever growing list of people who had called the sheriff's office saying that they had seen Robin Penrose. Gamboa ignored them, of course. He was interested only in witnesses who had seen her dead. This was standard procedure with the police. They ignored all evidence that could prove a defendant's innocence, but they doggedly tracked down anything that looked bad for him. They were trained to find people guilty, not innocent. But since Macklin had ordered a copy of all prosecution investigations be handed over to Sean, unless Lowenstein wanted a mistrial, Gamboa had to furnish the list.

"Oh, Christ! I thought you were on that already," Sean said.

"I am. But the damn thing's growing like a tumor."

Sean sat back in his seat and sighed. He didn't have time to take any trips to Bakersfield or Lahaina or anywhere else. The trial was starting in a few days, and he needed to prepare Chad's defense. But the Jamaican knew something. Maybe it would turn out to be something he could use, maybe it wouldn't. But he had to find out.

"All right," Sean finally said. "You're off the hook. It looks like I'll have to go to Bakersfield myself. That's what the Jamaican wanted anyway."

Mac smiled broadly. "Well, have a jolly fuckin' time with the rattlesnakes," he said and sloshed down the rest of Sean's brew.

Sean wanted to get to Bakersfield while the Jamaican's lead was still fresh. The sooner he arrived, the more likely he would find witnesses who thought they had seen Robin. He reached Gorman in an hour and a half. Then he fought his way through the Grapevine, the twisting interstate that threads death-defyingly through the mountains, until he wound down into the dust-blown, fog-plagued San Joaquin Valley. If Sean hadn't known better, he might have thought he'd been dropped into the Texas panhandle, the flat, windy parts that people drive through with the windows rolled up tightly to keep out the dust, constantly spinning the radio searching for anything to break the monotony of the interminable miles of cotton and oil derricks nodding in fields of weeds.

Thirty minutes later he was sitting in the bar at the Red Lion Inn. The place was filled with dark mahogany, red velour, and businessmen in Tony Lamas. The bartender was a between-gigs country and western singer named Randy Lubbock. He was a thin ropey-armed man with an eye patch that he lifted to read the scribble of the cocktail waitresses. After they visited a spell, Sean showed Randy the photo of Robin. "Yeah, I've seen this gal before," he said.

"When?" Sean asked.

"Last night." Randy turned to his right and pointed at a table in a dark corner and said, "She sat right over there. Drank white wine the whole night."

"Was she alone?" Sean asked. There was always a possibility she'd run off with some guy.

Randy gave him a cautious look. "She your girlfriend or wife or something?" He sang about this kind of deal every night, and he wanted no part of it. The worst kind of trouble a man can get is from a mistreated hound dog or a husband that just can't forget.

"No, she's not my girlfriend," Sean said. "You sure it was this girl?" and tapped the picture. "You said she was sitting way over there."

"Yeah, but when she first came in, she stood right there where you are and ordered a drink."

A young couple came into the bar and sat at the far end. Randy went to see what they were drinking. When he returned with Sean's drink, Sean put a twenty on the bar and said, "It's yours."

"Hey, thanks. You want to know anything else?"

"Well, you can tell me if you'd seen her before."

"No," he said, "and, believe me, I'd remember. Bakersfield ain't exactly Malibu Beach."

"No, I guess not," Sean said. It wasn't even Santa Ana. "Do you know if she's still around?"

"That I don't know," Randy said. "She left around one last night. So it's possible she stayed in the hotel. You might try the front desk. . . ." He paused for a second, twisting his neck to see past Sean. "Hey, wait a minute. Ain't that her out front?" he said, pointing out through the lobby.

The doors that separated the bar from the lobby were smoked glass, so Sean couldn't see much. Running into the lobby, he saw, parked in the front of the hotel, a red Corvette, its rag top up. There was a tall blonde just getting in it. Her hair was cut like a stewardess's, parted in the middle and flipped under on the ends an inch or two below her chin. If it was Robin, she'd cut her hair, or she was wearing a wig. The rest of her was the expensive hard sell of a starlet or an escort-service whore—long legs in sheer black stockings beneath a rivetingly short yellow leather skirt with matching yellow spikes and bag. It was a hey-look-me-over getup, not something a girl on the lam would pick out.

She backed into the passenger seat rear end first and then swung her legs into the car and the valet shut the door. There was someone big behind the wheel. The valet still had the handle of the car door in his hand when the 'Vette reared up and took off.

Sean dashed through the lobby, stumbling over the oddly placed furniture. A circular couch made him veer left, and an unkempt ficus blocked him again. Every picture he'd seen of Robin resembled some part of the girl—the bold chin, the pinched waist, and the surgically inflated breasts. He hurdled the chair at the concierge's desk, and when he looked up, the red Corvette was gone.

He got through the front entrance after waiting a half stride for the electronic doors to whoosh sluggishly open, and by that time the tail of the car was winking left at the light at the hotel entrance.

He could see a big black man at the wheel as he ran through the vast lot. There was a convention of Basques in town, and he had had to park on the last row next to the street. When he got to his car, he could see the 'Vette turn up the street heading for the freeway.

A thickening fog was descending, and the car disappeared into the mist as it approached the on-ramp. He couldn't tell which way they'd turned. North—San Francisco. Or south—Los Angeles. He plopped into the seat and turned the key, and the old Mercedes ground over. It had 261,841 miles on the odometer, but Sean personally knew that the guy who had sold it to him had run it with a bum speedometer for over a year. So it was entirely likely that "Sir Lawrence," the name he'd dubbed it because of the chrome monogram SL on the trunk, had over 300,000 miles on its old bones. Its galloping stallion days were definitely over.

The SL ground on, but its engine hadn't sparked to the idea yet. "Come on, Larry, baby. You can do it," Sean coaxed, patting the dash gently. It caught once and coughed, and on the next crank it sputtered to life. Sean pumped it to a full rev. "That-a-boy!"

Shoving it into reverse, he swung back out and sped down the lane of the parking lot. He tapped his brake quickly for each speed bump, timed one wrong, and his head nearly punctured the rag top. As he sped through the reddish-hued yellow light, the SL belched, then started to accelerate in fits and starts.

When he got to the on-ramp, he pulled onto the overpass. Getting out, he looked north, where the fog was building fast. He couldn't see a hundred yards. If the 'Vette had gone that way it was already swallowed. He ran across the road. A mile or so up, just fading into a drift of low clouds, was the red Corvette.

Sean ran back to the SL, rammed it into drive, and U-turned onto the ramp going south. "Okay, Larry. Do your stuff!" he said.

The SL climbed quickly to eighty going down the long incline to the highway. And kept accelerating faithfully to eighty-five, ninety, and then began to vibrate, then shake, then shudder violently when it got close to ninety-five. Sean stepped down harder on the pedal, even though it was already flush to the floorboard. The SL groaned past ninety-five, rattling like a dying man. Then near one hundred it suddenly stopped shaking and began tracking smoothly again.

The Corvette had climbed the rise in front of him. He could see the hulking back of the driver and the blonde beside him. But between the crest Sean was on and the crest the 'Vette had climbed was a deep valley. The Mercedes accelerated to nearly a hundred ten as it fell down the face of the grade. As the SL began the climb up the far slope, though, it slowed to seventy-five almost immediately, then sixty-five, then sixty. As it came to the crest, he spotted the 'Vette far ahead.

The 'Vette wasn't speeding, so the SL began to make up ground again—seventy, eighty, then shimmying again past the mid-nineties. It kept plugging, trying to get past one hundred, but it couldn't. On the flat it held at ninety-nine.

"Come on, Larry, come on," Sean cajoled. The old car sputtered and dropped to ninety-seven. Then he lost his patience. "Come on, you old goat! Do something good for once!" and he slammed his fist against the dash. "Show me some guts, you piece of shit!"

The old car responded by dropping down to ninety. But it was gaining on the 'Vette. Sean wedged by a huddle of semis, and there it was two hundred yards ahead, cutting through the gray, horizonless acreage of fallow cotton fields, where tumbleweeds bounced as agilely as gymnasts across the highway, striking cars as if radar-guided.

The 'Vette swerved to avoid a monstrous tumbleweed. It exploded on its hood and was crushed underneath, splintering finally to nothing, the last few fingers raking across Sean's windshield as he drew closer.

Sean slowed as he finally pulled even with the passenger's window, but the woman had the back of her head to him, talking to the driver. All Sean could see was one meaty black hand on the steering wheel. The blonde's hands gesticulated in the air in front of her, and by the way her head jerked forward, Sean could tell she was screaming at the guy. Then she turned her head, and Sean was suddenly looking into the face he had stared at for hours every day for the past six weeks. A close-up of that beautiful face—the long drop of her thin nose, the stunningly immense blue eyes, the thick, cascading hair—was pinned to the wall in his living room. He knew Robin Penrose.

She slowly raised her eyes to him, but she was looking at something beyond him. Then she turned to the driver and started screaming again.

"Goddamn it! That's her!" Sean said to himself. The 'Vette had drifted a few feet ahead, and Sean accelerated and caught up and got another good look at her. Robin Penrose was being driven around Bakersfield by a huge black man in a red Corvette.

"The driver of the white Mercedes, pull over now!"

Sean jerked the steering wheel when the loudspeaker blared and looked in the rearview mirror. There was a CHP cruiser standing on his ass with its headlights flashing and a red spot pulsing.

"Shit!"

Sean accelerated to catch the 'Vette again, and the CHP blasted his riot siren, the ululating scream of the damned. Then he gave another amplified order.

"This is the Highway Patrol. Pull your vehicle to the side of the road now!"

Sean let off the pedal and slowly pulled to the side of the highway onto the banked shoulder. He watched the red blur of the 'Vette disappearing into the haze of the San Joaquin.

Sean reached in his pocket for his bar association ID and handed that and his driver's license to the cop. The officer, wearing aviator reflector sunglasses, had his book out flipping for a new citation. He took the driver's license from Sean and handed back the bar card without looking at it.

"Officer," Sean pleaded, "I'm an attorney pursuing a possible suspect in a murder case."

"You should leave that up to qualified law enforcement officers," the cop said without looking up from his pad. He was checking off this box and that.

"Have you heard of Chad Curtis?" Sean tried.

The officer shook his head no and kept writing.

"He's on trial for murder, and the girl he allegedly murdered is a passenger in that red Corvette," Sean said, pointing down the empty highway.

"Fine," the cop said, handing the pad to Sean to sign. "Did you get a license number?"

"A license number?" Oh shit! Sean thought. I didn't get the license. The first thing any decent investigator would do is write down the license of a car he was pursuing.

"No, I forgot to get the license," Sean said. Then he looked at the citation. "Ninety-nine in a sixty-five? This is going to cost me a fortune. Jesus, give me a break here."

"I gave you a break," the officer said. "If I cite you for doing a hundred, I'd have to cuff you and bring you in for reckless driving. If you go up before Judge Singletary, you're looking at mandatory jail time, Counselor."

Sean signed the ticket, and the patrolman tore the citation out of the book and handed it back. "Next time, Counselor, leave the high-speed pursuits to someone who knows what he's doing," he said, and his boots crunched on the gravel shoulder as he walked back to his cruiser.

"Yeah, thanks a lot," Sean said under his breath and sat there for a second, looking up the highway where the 'Vette had disappeared. There was no use trying to catch it now.

Robin Penrose was alive. He'd seen her. At least he'd seen someone who looked so much like her he'd swear to it in a court of law. And that, short of actually dragging her into court, was as good as he could expect. The bartender at the Red Lion would probably swear to it in court too. And maybe one or two others she'd sat next to last night. People wouldn't forget a woman who looked like Robin.

Sean took the first off-ramp and got onto the highway back to Bakersfield. He was about to gather the first material witnesses in his attempt to save Chad Curtis's life.

chapter

fifteen

On his way back to Capistrano from Bakersfield, where he managed to get a signed statement from the bartender, Sean exited the freeway near UCLA and turned down Wilshire heading toward Gregory Pope's office. It was a warm day and he had the top down, but that didn't turn out to be such a good idea. The weatherman had called for "Unhealthful" smog levels that day, Sean remembered as he sat in exhaust-belching traffic at light after light down the Miracle Mile.

Pope's office was in a new high-rise near the Beverly Wilshire in the hundred-dollar-a-foot district. The building had elevators that whirred like computers as they rose, with a leather bench and Berber carpeting that covered the walls. It whooshed past all thirty-eight floors in a few seconds. Sean got out and found 3810 and pushed through the door.

It was a large office where a decorator had run amok. A black enamel table shaped like a pear dominated the center of the room.

Most of the avant-garde chairs and sofas spread around the place took some figuring to sit in. The walls were high-gloss black and covered with photos of celebrities framed in polished ivory, all being hugged by the same short, dumpy man with a full head of straight black hair.

Behind the reception desk, a ton of green-speckled granite with no drawers and no counter space, was a girl who looked so much like Robin Penrose that Sean stopped in the doorway. When she looked up at him and smiled, he could see it wasn't her. This girl was barely twenty, but her blond hair was poofed up in a sophisticated cut that made her look older at first glance. When she opened her mouth, Sean wasn't surprised that she had a southern accent. North Dallas was his guess. Another Highland Park, SMU, beauty pageant clone on the loose. God help us all, he thought.

"May I help you, sir?" she said with a big, perky pageant smile, bright as patent leather and about as genuine.

"Sean Barrett to see Mr. Pope." And he laid a card in front of her.

"Oh, yes, Mr. Barrett. If you'd please have a seat," she said as she pointed toward a sort of asexual love seat in the corner of the room. "Mr. Pope will be with you as soon as he can. He just took a call from Kevin Costner this very moment."

Just as Sean sank into the couch, the girl said, "Mr. Barrett?" and he pulled himself from the sofa's clutches.

"Mr. Pope will see you now," she said and opened one of two large doors.

Pope was just hanging up the phone when Sean walked in. He was a little heavier and dumpier than in the gallery out front. His hair was still dark and full, but it was fashionably longer and knotted into a tiny flap of a ponytail. He was wearing a cream-colored linen suit with a red paisley ascot, a pinky ring on each pinky, and the gummy smile of the Cheshire cat.

"Mr. Barrett," Pope said. As he stepped enthusiastically forward to shake, Sean saw his two-toned brown shoes fit for a buck and wing.

"Thanks for squeezing me in on such short notice," Sean said.

"No problem. But I have to be out of here in ten minutes." Pope bent his wrist to show Sean his watch. Clustered diamonds marked the hour. Sean knew it was the stones, not the time, he was meant to note. "I just this second got off the phone with Sharon Stone.

Damn! She's so hot I had to wear asbestos gloves to hold the phone. Know what I mean?"

Sean had to smile. He had the Hollywood connections of a wino, and Pope was into overdrive with him.

Sean sat on a big leather couch and fished his notebook out of a manila envelope. His briefcase had disemboweled itself that morning. "Now," he said, "I know you're a busy man, so why don't we get right to Robin?"

"Oh God, of course," Pope said and sat on his desk. It was a big dark teak monstrosity crowded with a dozen frames of more celebrities schmoozing with Pope. "That was terrible about Robin. But, frankly, it doesn't surprise me. She was on a collision course with disaster." He looked at Sean expectantly. "How did you like it?"

"Like what?" Sean asked, a little confused, looking up from his notepad.

"The line," Pope said. "A collision course with disaster. Good stuff, huh? I'm doing a screenplay with Monty Dennis. He wrote *Dangerous Weapon II* and *III*."

"Oh, yeah. Good line," Sean nodded. It occurred to him why movies were so hopelessly banal: blunt minds like Pope were at their creative core. "Now, about Robin," he said. "From what I gather, Robin was a nice girl who got in over her head in Hollywood. And as her agent, you were in a position to see it all."

"Oh, Robin was a nice girl, all right. When it suited her." Pope sat next to Sean on the couch. He looked at his watch for the third time since Sean had arrived. "We don't have a lot of time, so let's cut to the chase, shall we?" Pope was a compendium of the latest bad movie dialogue.

"Okay," Sean said.

"I do a little teaching at the Hollywood Actors' Workshop. It's a private school for young actors. Up-and-comers. Keifer Sutherland came out of there. River Phoenix. Phoebe Cates. A lot of the brat packers." He was ticking them off his fingers. "Anyway, Robin at the time was working makeup at Universal and taking these acting classes at night. She was very serious. She wanted to be famous. But that ain't news here, right?" He pointed out his picture window that overlooked Los Angeles. "You know, she had incredible potential. I dated Madonna when she first came up. You look at the two of them together, you gotta pick Robin for the superstar."

"What happened?" Sean asked.

"What happened is she wanted it now. She wasn't going to wait around, schmooze it up, pay the heavy dues like all the other schmucks and schmuckettes. She looked around and decided the express route to stardom was through the bedroom. You know the line. It's not who you know, it's who you blow in this town. That's where I came in. Big-time agent-producer." Pope rolled his eyes to let Sean know his lofty stature hadn't gone to his head. "A few trips under the sheets and she figures I'll make her the next Demi Moore."

Sean knew Robin wasn't the first homecoming queen ever to try to sleep her way to the top. The image of the wide-eyed girl come to the big city was quickly disintegrating, however.

"And you couldn't deliver, is that it?" Sean needled Pope and got the reaction he was after.

"It's not that I couldn't," Pope quickly corrected him. He was up on the edge of the couch, ready to sell, but then suddenly something in him deflated. He gave a derisive grunt. "Get this. I thought the girl really liked me," he said almost touchingly and shrugged. "When Robin wanted to treat you right . . ." His voice trailed off. "She was pure genius in the bedroom. An artiste." He touched his gathered fingertips to his lips and smacked.

For the first time that day, Sean sensed that what was coming out of Pope's mouth wasn't bullshit.

"Anyway," the agent went on, "it didn't last more than a couple months. One evening after she was passed over for a speaking part on a *Cheers* episode, she came unstitched. Started throwing vases around. The whole Bette Davis scene. Said I'd never get her anywhere in this town. Then she grabbed her things and walked out with me standing in the middle of the room holding my dick wondering what happened." Throughout this little speech Pope had been doing choreography, unstitching his shirt front with a double-fisted yank, throwing imaginary vases, grabbing his crotch.

Sean thought the agent was about to cry. But Pope must have had another movie in mind because instead he raised his voice. "She was wrong, you know," he said. "I could have done big things for her if she'd been patient." He dropped his head and then he slowly raised it until his eyes met Sean's. They were having a moment.

"You know this town, it's a user's town," Pope said. "I know the rules. You don't open your veins when you jump in a shark tank. So like a putz I slit 'em wide open for Robin Penrose. Christ, I'm supposed to be a tough guy. Tear your balls off first chance I get." He was dangling a pair of torn-off testicles in the air. "I guess we're all saps inside, huh? It just takes the right bitch to suck us dry."

"That a line?" Sean asked.

"Hell, no. That's straight from the heart," Pope said, poking a finger into the right side of his chest. Sean would have bet Pope didn't know where his heart was.

"I swear I thought she loved me, you know. She was sooooo *good* at it. In bed, out of bed, Robin made you think you were the only man who ever made her come. Know what I mean? The only one."

Sean nodded, thankful Pope hadn't choreographed that last bit. "I talked to several friends of Robin's, and they said she was caught up in drugs at the time," he said. "Do you think that was part of her problem too?"

"No, the drugs came later," Pope said. "After she left me, she started sleeping with every jerkoff in town who promised her stardom. That's what gets them every time, isn't it? The bitch-goddess fame is what Henry Miller called it. It's just like the damn movies. *All About Eve.* You ever catch that flick?"

It was the quintessential Hollywood bitch-eat-bitch story that nobody in Hollywood seemed to have learned anything from.

"Sure," Sean said. "The one where Bette Davis gets what's coming to her."

"Exactimento!" Pope said, shaking his head. "As smart as Robin was, she was blinded by her own greed. They weren't going to do a damn thing for her. Sure, she got some bit parts but—ah, hell."

Pope's intercom buzzed, and he pushed a button on a black box on his desk. "Yeah, Sherry?"

"Meryl Streep is on the line, Mr. Pope."

"Tell her five minutes."

Sean looked at his watch. He'd been with Pope exactly ten minutes. He could guess what had happened. Pope had told Miss Dallas out front to give this schmuck ten minutes and buzz. Sean figured he'd better get to the rest of what he'd come for before Elvis tried to get through.

"What about the drugs?" Sean asked.

"The drugs were just a by-product of the life. The whole world she got involved in is drowning in drugs. She got hooked because that was what everyone else did. You ever do coke?" Pope asked.

"A little may have wafted by my nose in college."

Pope sniffed a little laugh. "Anyway, it just got out of control with her. She was sleeping with anyone. Not to become a star anymore but just because. You get strung out, after a while you don't know what the hell you're chasing. You just know you've got to have it. Believe me, I know. I had to do a month at Betty Ford one time. That's where I met Liz," he said and pointed back over his head at a photo of Elizabeth Taylor prominently hung on the wall behind his desk. It was the kind of publicity shot any fan could send away for. Scrawled across half the photo was a long, schmaltzy inscription Sean guessed was in Pope's hand.

"I tried to help her. I really did," he said, sad-eyed. "Gave her the use of a friend's apartment while he was in Spain doing a movie. No strings. No sex. Just because I liked her." He said it like he was Mother Teresa doling out love in a children's cancer ward. "She fucked that up too. Sold the guy's fuckin' big-screen Sony and moved out. It was sad to watch. The corruption of a beautiful young girl," he said as if he were reading a film synopsis in *TV Guide*. "She was doing night work before it was over."

"Night work?" Sean asked, surprised. "You mean prostitution?"

"We don't call it that here."

"What do you call it?"

"Customer relations," Pope said. "Couple grand a night dating money guys some producer's trying to hustle."

Whatever euphemism it went by, it was the first dark pocket of reasonable doubt that Sean could try to mine. If Robin Penrose was a high-priced call girl, she might have known a hundred men who would want her quiet.

"Was she killed because of drugs?" Pope asked.

"That's one of the things I'm trying to find out."

"I heard some ball player killed her." Pope brushed both hands through his hair and fell back in his seat in the same motion. "Athletes and drugs. That's a tired script."

"That's for sure," Sean said and kept pushing. "Tell me, when was the last time you heard from Robin?"

"It had to be at least three or four months ago. Not long before she died. She came by the house to see me. Same old Robin. She wanted to see me, all right, but only because she wanted something."

"What was that?" Sean asked.

"Money," Pope said. "I should have known she was up to something because before I knew what hit me we were in bed. That's how Robin always got what she wanted. Her negotiating table was a Posturpedic. She wanted to borrow some money. Big surprise, huh?"

"Did you give it to her?"

"Believe it or not, I finally came to my senses and turned her down. As soon as she could see I wasn't her all-day sucker anymore, she hauled ass. I haven't seen her since."

Pope made a show of looking at his watch again. Sean was through with him, though, so he beat him to the good-byes. "Well, I guess that's all I need," he said. Pope started to get up, but Sean put his hand out. "Hey, don't get up, Gregory. I can find my way out. Besides," he said, pointing at the phone, "you've got Meryl on hold."

"Hey, that's right!" Pope said and stood up anyway. He shook Sean's hand and held it. "Look," he said, pulling Sean closer and lowering his voice as if they were poolside at the Beverly Wilshire. "If this case looks like it could be a movie—you know, beautiful chick comes to Hollyweird, gets blown away kind of hook. Let me know. I can get you something in the mid-six figures. Slam dunk!"

chapter

sixteen

Sean had tried to arrange a meeting with Carrie. He wanted to clarify what she'd told him about Robin. But one thing or another got in the way. When she was free, he was in court. When he was free, she was tied up with clients or out of town for the day. After a week of phone tag, she suggested that they have dinner the following evening.

The law offices of Robinson, Racine and Robinson were situated on the tenth floor of a high-rise down the street from Fashion Island, the mammoth shopping complex in Newport Beach. Carter was just coming out the door of the office as Sean walked up. It was the kind of warm December day that hits Los Angeles before the January rains. But Carter was dressed for a ski weekend—a cable-knit sweater, dark blue cords, and boots out of an L.L. Bean catalogue.

"Sean, how are you?" Carter said. "Thanks for saving my tail on the boat the other night. Boy, you've got a hell of a right hook," he laughed. "My jaw still hurts."

"Sorry about that, Carter."

"Don't be. I should never have been in that condition," he said. "So what brings you here?"

"I'm going to talk to your daughter about the Curtis case," he said as he held the door open for Carter. Sean had left the cumbersome load of his crumbling briefcase in his car. Instead he had a notepad and a small manila envelope of papers. "I was also hoping I might have a word or two with you, if you've got a second."

"Ah, geez! Actually, I don't." He raised his wrist nearly to his nose and made a show of looking at his watch. "I've really got to hustle now but, look, talk to Carrie and if you still think we need to meet, give me a call, Friday." He was already walking backward down the hall, his finger pointing at Sean. "Deal?" he said and pulled his trigger finger.

In Sean's mind, that was what had gone wrong with California. It had degenerated from people who shook hands to seal a deal with a neighbor they'd known since grammar school to a smart-ass twitch of the finger that shot nothing but noncommittal blanks.

Sean nodded with a frown. He knew a brush-off when he saw it. Carter probably didn't want to get roped into testifying because he knew a witness might have to hang around the courthouse for ten days waiting to testify for ten minutes. That could seriously decrease billing hours. If Carter could keep putting Sean off, though, the trial would be underway and Sean might not have time to bother with him.

"I need to talk to you sometime soon, Carter," Sean called after him. "I want to know what Robin was doing the night she vanished."

"No problem," Carter said as his head disappeared into the elevator.

"Yeah, no problem," Sean repeated to the empty hallway.

He checked in with the receptionist and took a seat to wait. There was a feel to the place he wasn't expecting. The French provincial was there, and all the law books were lined against the walls to inspire confidence. But the faxes, copiers, and computers were lost among flowers and plants and art nouveau lamps and mirrors. On the walls were prints by modern masters and oils someone had bought at a Laguna art boutique. Sean spotted a woman's influence. The more you saw of them in law, the less you saw the clubby leather and mahogany, the pipe-smoke meetings, the monochromatic gaberdine and subdued ties.

After a few minutes Carrie opened the inner door of reception. She was dressed in a royal blue suede suit that fit her like silk. The skirt was cut just above her knee, and she had on a cream blouse with a high collar.

"I'm starving," she said. "How about you?"

"Famished. Mexican all right?" he asked.

"Perfect. As long as they've got Tres Equis."

They drove to a little café called El Tecuan off the Ortega Highway, a place filled with khaki pants and straw Stetsons. They were the only gringos there. They talked nonstop about everything except the law all the way through the green corn tamales and the carne asada and stacks of handmade tortillas, finishing a six-pack of XXX between them.

After the meal, the conversation drifted toward the courtroom and Chad's case. Sean deliberately did not tell her that he thought he'd spotted Robin in Bakersfield. All he'd really seen was a woman's face for a few seconds in a speeding car. That moment in Bakersfield when he'd glimpsed her face, he would have wagered anything that Robin Penrose was alive. But as each day passed, his certainty weakened into a reasonable doubt. As Chad's attorney, that was all he needed from the sighting. Carrie, however, wanted her friend to be alive.

He finally got around to asking her about what Krueger had said about Robin running out of the meeting the night she disappeared.

"Robin was upset all day," Carrie said with a nonchalance that perturbed him.

"Well, why didn't you mention that?" Sean asked. She was an attorney, she should have known he'd want to know about it. "You had to think that it would be important considering she disappeared two hours later."

She reached over and took his hand across the table. "Sean," she said, "she was having a bad period. That's all it was. You're not going to solve this case because Krueger doesn't know a bout with PMS when he sees it."

"That was it? Her period?" he said. Like most men, the mysteries of the female hormonal riot that wreaked havoc once a month bewildered him.

"She was a raving bitch all day long. Up and down. Crying and laughing. The whole schizophrenic ride," Carrie said, her hand undulating on an invisible roller coaster. "Did your investigator ask Krueger if anything happened or was said that would have upset her?"

"Yes," Sean admitted.

"And?" She was still holding his hand.

He shook his head. "It was a mystery to him."

"Tell him not to feel too bad. Women don't have a clue either. It just happens to us. We didn't invent it." Laughing, she leaned back and took her hand away. "She'd been a pain in the ass all day. When she disrupted the meeting, I told her to go home."

They talked further about the case, and he filled her in on how it looked from the defense side. He enjoyed chatting with an attorney who understood what he was talking about.

Once they were back on the Ortega, winding through the dark of the coast hills toward San Juan, they fell silent. Pavarotti sang softly an old Neapolitan love song. The air was heavy with the sea. In the darkness Sean could see only glimpses of Carrie as they passed under streetlights. The wisps of hair about her neck, the plump of her lips, the elegantly long fingers resting in her lap.

Finally she said, "I've been watching you for years now."

He looked toward her, but her face was veiled by the shadows. "What do you mean?"

"I've gone to at least three of your trials to watch you work."

"What in heaven's name for?" he laughed.

"My father told me to. He said if I wanted to see how a good young attorney handled himself in court, go watch Sean Barrett," she said and leaned forward so her face was lit again. "He was right."

Sean flushed at her flattery. It was one thing to have some balding attorney slap him on the back and tell him what a great job he'd done. But quite another to hear it from a gorgeous woman.

"That's awfully nice of you to say, Carrie. Thank you."

"Oh, Spann and my father used to talk about you all the time," Carrie went on. "Spann told him he knew he'd never be able to keep you." She patted his knee with just her fingertips and laughed.

"You're kidding," he said.

"No, they knew you'd go out on your own sooner or later. And it would probably be sooner. You were too good to stay at a corporate firm."

"They told you that?" he asked, starting to feel almost weightless.

"Oh, sure," she said. "Daddy can't keep anything from me. I've got his number but good. Spann and Daddy were laughing over drinks because Jonathan thought he'd carried off quite a coup keeping you a year or two longer than he'd hoped."

"So the big scene that Spann and I had in my office . . . ?"

"Choreographed for years."

"I'll be damned." He shook his head. Spann had worked him like a marionette.

He turned onto Camino Capistrano and headed toward the cliffs above Capistrano Beach. When they got to Palisades Road, he pulled up at Pines Park, a grassy knoll atop the bluffs that overlooked the entire area.

"Come on. I want to show you my part of town," he said.

They walked across the grass to a concrete bench that overlooked the cliff. There was a redwood split-rail barrier in front, and Sean stepped over it and held Carrie's hand while she did the same, pulling her skirt up to the top of her thighs without a thought and hopping over. He saw then that she had left her shoes in the car.

She saw his look. "I hate shoes," she said.

He moved carefully to the very edge in the dark before stepping down to a pad of dirt below and then down again to a flat pedestal. They were completely hidden from anyone in the park above them —like two seabirds perched on the cliffs. Where they stood, the bluffs jutted out enough so they had a sweeping view of the coast. To the north was the Dana Point jetty knifing out into the Pacific like the nose of a landed swordfish. To the south stretched Capistrano Beach and San Clemente, still sleepy beach towns. Only the old San Clemente pier was alight. It still attracted baby-faced Marine recruits from Camp Pendleton who shuffled around the old wooden structure, hoping some bikinied high school girl would forgive their shaved heads and talk to them.

"I wanted to show you this," Sean said, his hand sweeping across the horizon. "That's my place right below us," he added, pointing across the highway at his cottage.

"You live on the beach?"

"Old surfers can't be more than a hundred feet from the water or they wash up on the pavement." He was pointing down at the sea where a line of surf broke white in the moonlight.

"You're a surfer?" she asked.

"I used to live on a board. Now I live in court, of course." He snapped the line off like a stand-up comic, and she laughed. "But I still get out maybe once a week at night."

"What do you mean, at night?"

"When I get home in the evenings, I try to get in the water."

She stepped back and looked at him, a warning smile edging up one side of her lips. "Nobody surfs at night."

"Sure they do. It's not dangerous. In fact, it's much safer than swimming at night," he said. "You've done that, haven't you?"

"Sure. In college we drank a lot of beer and went skinny-dipping. Who hasn't?"

"Tonight is a perfect night, in fact," he said, getting an idea. "Look at the swells. Five or six feet. Perfect shape, not too fast, not too slow. Full moon. We wouldn't even need lights."

A speeding car filled with teenagers honked by on the highway below.

"What do you mean, 'we'?" she said.

"Why not? You've surfed, haven't you?"

"Are you kidding? In high school Robin and I spent our lives on the beach. We surfed all day long. But never at night."

"Well, now's the perfect time to try it."

He grabbed her hand and guided her back up the cliff, took ahold of the fence railing, and stepped across. She followed right behind, her skirt hitched up.

"This is crazy!" she kept saying, but he knew she was going to do it. That was the first thing he ever really knew about Carrie. She could be seduced by adventure, by something dangerous.

She protested the whole time—about ruining her hair, putting on the wet suit, about the first sting of the icy water, about paddling into the blackness. But all the while she had a look not of anxiety but of exhilaration. She rode the waves like a kid, paddling to beat Sean out to the next wave.

"That was a hell of a ride," he said, pulling the board around after one of them. They were sitting on their boards face to face on the ocean.

"Wasn't it?" she said. "This is fantastic! You feel so lost out here."

"Everything's back on shore," Sean said and pointed over his back.

"Let's try a couple more before we freeze to death," she said and took off again.

They rode for a half hour, until it got too cold. Then they surfed in to shore and laid the boards against Sean's patio before going inside to take a warm shower.

Carrie showered first and then came into the living room tucked in a beach towel. Taking his turn, Sean stripped off the black rubber suit and laid it on the floor next to hers and got into the shower. The hot water had just taken the last chill out of his body when the shower door opened and Carrie stood there naked with the same look of adventure as when they had stood on the cliffs together, one misstep from falling.

She stepped into his arms, and they kissed for a long time as the warm water ran over them. He bent down and kissed her breasts until the nipples were firm on his tongue. Then he moved his hand down her belly and between her legs. When he touched her, he could feel her suddenly let go. Her head rested against his chest, and her hands slid down his arms and held him around his waist. Then she edged her legs apart enough for him to feel how wet she was inside.

She raised her face to his with her eyes still closed and found his lips. She groaned while they kissed.

"Oh, Sean," she whispered and lifted one leg and put it around his hip. Reaching up to his shoulders, she lifted herself up onto him. Then, with one hand still around his shoulders, she reached down and took ahold of him. When she eased back down, he slipped inside her for the first time.

They were asleep in each other's arms when the phone rang. Sean looked over at the red numbers of the digital clock across the room. It read 4:38. A phone call at this hour was either a wrong number or life and death.

He left Carrie in bed asleep and stumbled out to the living room to answer the phone.

"Yeah?" he whispered.

"Sean? This is Jonathan Spann."

"Jonathan," Sean said. "What's the problem?"

"It's about Scott. Did you know he's been missing the last few days?"

A pump of adrenaline revved his heart, and his brain started clearing. "I didn't know," he said.

"Yes. Well, nobody could find him. We didn't know what to think with his life-style and all."

Sean was suddenly scared. Spann was trying to tell him something had happened to Scott, and he didn't know how. "What is it, Jonathan?" he asked.

"He's dead."

"What?" Sean said. "Are you sure?"

"He was murdered," Spann said. "The police found Scott and a, well, a friend of his, in Laguna. They say it has the signs of a gay bashing."

"A gay bashing?"

"Yes," Spann said softly. "Apparently, the bastards did a real job on him. They made a pretty big mess."

"What kind of mess?" Sean asked.

"Well, they were both mutilated pretty badly."

"Jesus!" Sean muttered and sat on the back of the divan. The digital clock flipped over the next number.

"The police said the other victim they found with him was some kind of male hustler. He'd been booked a dozen times in Hollywood Division for solicitation, public lewdness, indecent exposure—you name it. It looks like Scott got involved with the wrong guy at the wrong time."

Sean had heard only about half of what Spann said. He rested the receiver on his arm while he gathered himself.

"Sean?" Spann said when he heard nothing on the other end. "Sean? Are you okay?"

Sean slowly lifted the receiver to his ear. "Yeah, I'm fine."

"I'm sorry, Sean," Spann said. "I know you and Scott were good friends."

Sean could hear Spann clear his throat, and for some reason that sound calmed him. The falling sensation in his stomach abruptly turned to anger. "Yeah," he said, not really talking to Spann. "He was a good guy." A gust rattled the sliding glass door. A storm had arrived in the middle of the night.

"Where was he murdered? A hotel?" Sean asked.

"Well, actually, they don't know yet. Their bodies were found in a truck parked behind an apartment complex in the hills behind Laguna. They were killed somewhere else. No clue where, apparently."

"Really?" Sean said. "That's unusual, don't you think?"

"Why?"

"Because gay bashing is usually a spur-of-the-moment thing. A gang might beat someone senseless, but they don't usually put them in the back of a truck and drive around with them. They leave them where they killed them."

"Not if it was on their doorstep and most certainly not in this case," Spann said sharply. He didn't like speculation.

The light in the kitchen flickered a moment, then came back to full.

"Maybe not," Sean said. "But how about the rest of it? That doesn't fit a gay bashing either."

"Look," Spann said, running out of patience, "Scott was a homosexual. He apparently liked to go down to Laguna Beach and pick up young boys of ethnic origins and—"

"Who in the hell told you that?" Sean interrupted. He could hear Spann take a deep breath on the other end.

"The police," Spann said.

The light in the kitchen wavered and the digital clock snapped off, then on, then off again, and the place went completely dark.

"Have they identified the other victim yet?"

"Some Hispanic," Spann answered flatly.

"Did you get the name?"

"No, I didn't."

"Why not?" Sean said, irritated.

Spann didn't answer right away. "Because, Sean," he said, trying to restrain his anger, "I'm not the investigating officer. I'm the head of a law firm that's now about to be buried under an avalanche of very adverse publicity. I don't give a shit who Scott Powers was sucking off while he was murdered. I'm concerned with the clients the firm is surely going to lose when the details of this damned thing show up on the front page of every goddamn paper in Southern California!"

Sean shook his head in disgust. The bottom line again. "You
don't mind if I find out who he was, do you?"

"Since you're no longer with the firm, it's not my concern how
you waste your time."

"Right," Sean said.

Carrie came up behind him and held him with her face resting
against his back.

"Look, Sean," Spann said after they'd both calmed a little, "the
reason I called was because Gamboa asked me to identify Scott's
body. Both his parents are dead and he had no brother or sister. So
they asked me." He hesitated. "The problem is, I have to be at the
airport at six-thirty to catch a morning plane to Dallas. Since you
were his good friend, I thought perhaps . . ."

"Yes, of course, Jonathan," Sean said. "I've got a meeting in
Macklin's chambers first thing in the morning. I'll drive to the
morgue right after that. Will that be okay?"

"Of course," Spann said.

"Is he at the M.E. in Santa Ana?" Sean asked, referring to the
county medical examiner's office.

"Yes. Thanks, Sean," Spann said and hung up softly.

Sean put the receiver down and turned and held Carrie. Another
gust of wind buffetted the window. It wasn't yet dawn and already
the gulls were out there crying.

chapter

seventeen

The meeting that morning in Macklin's chambers had been called by the judge to try one last time to settle. The Curtis case was one of twelve on the docket that was ready to start trial. Only one of those cases would begin that day, and if this case could not be settled with a plea bargain, it would have to take priority over the others.

Macklin did his damnedest to get the case settled, coaxing and threatening in equal proportions. Finally, Lowenstein gave in minimally and reinstated his original offer of murder two, which Sean told him wasn't going to get the job done.

"Too bad," Lowenstein snapped like a man who knew he had a conviction sewed up. Sean had to take the offer to his client anyway because he was obligated to do so by law. Chad turned it down again, as Sean had told them he would.

When Sean left Chad in lockup, he walked down to the parking lot and drove the few blocks to the county medical examiner, where Knox was supposed to meet him at ten o'clock to identify Scott's body.

"Emory, how are you?" Sean said as the detective walked toward him.

"Good, man. How about you?"

Knox and Sean had been on the same softball team one summer. The young cop turned out to be a good third sacker and a decent guy. Knox knew what side of the law he was on, but he didn't take it personally like Gamboa.

Sean looked around at the cold concrete graveyard. "It's been better."

"Yeah," Knox said. "I guess so."

Sean was wearing only his white shirt and dark gaberdines, having stripped off the tie, coat, and vest in the car. "What happened, Emory?" he asked.

Knox walked him over to the elevator and punched the down button. The M.E.'s office, the fax machines, and the secretaries were on the second floor, but the real business of the medical examiner went on downstairs. The lab was one floor down and the morgue, where Scott's body was waiting to be identified, was one floor below that.

"We found his body in the back of a furniture van up the block from a gay bathhouse."

"I thought they did away with bathhouses," Sean said.

"There's a few left. They're always tucked away somewhere quiet, though. That's where this one is. Back behind the Pottery Shack."

"I know the area," Sean said.

When the elevator door opened, the chill air swept over them. It reminded Sean of a walk-in meat locker. He let the thought pass.

"Spann said it was a mess," Sean said.

"Yeah, I meant to tell you. I want you to prepare yourself. It's pretty rough stuff."

A sign across from the elevator read MORGUE with an arrow pointing right.

"Like what?" Sean asked.

Knox hesitated. "Well, both victims had their heads pretty much hacked completely off," he said awkwardly. "Powers was eviscerated as well, and both victims suffered mutilation of the genitals."

Sean took Knox's elbow and pulled him to a stop. "Let me have the whole thing, Emory."

Knox took a breath. "Their genitals were cut off and stuffed in the other one's mouth."

Sean nodded. "Is that why you think it's a gay bashing?"

"It's got most of the signs of one," Knox said and began using his fingers to keep count. "It happened close to a known homosexual hangout. One of the victims had a record of homosexual prostitution. And the part with the genitals is an old way of telling everyone that these guys were no-good fags."

Sean understood how the police could see it that way. He didn't believe it, though. "What was the other victim's name?" he asked the detective.

"We're not releasing that at present, Sean."

"Emory," he said softly. "Look, Scott was investigating the Berger murder case at the time. I don't think this was a gay bashing, and I don't think you really do either. They don't usually do this kind of damage. They chopped their heads off, for chrissake! That's not an M.O. for any gay bashing I've ever heard of. And neither is the transportation. They usually leave them for dead where they beat them."

Knox didn't answer. It was tough to get a cop to say where the toilet was, much less give details of a murder investigation. They turned a corner and walked into the room. One entire wall was chrome, lined with four-by-four doors with horizontal latches.

Sean grabbed Knox by the elbow again and pulled him around. "I want the assholes that did this worse than you do," he said. "And I don't mind revealing a few confidentialities to help you get them."

Knox appraised him a moment, then flipped his file open. "Guillermo Jesus Estaban Romero," he read.

"Jesus Christ, I was right," Sean said. "That's Eddie Romero! This wasn't a gay bashing," he said. "Romero was supposedly with Berger the night of the shooting. He put Berger up to it. The shooter was a big black man."

"A big black man? Can't you give me a better description than that?" Knox asked.

"No," Sean said. "But I know who can." He was thinking about Berger. If the little weasel knew anything, Sean was going to get it out of him. "Just give me a day or two."

Knox nodded and stepped into the room. Sean had never been in a morgue before. Oddly enough, a defense lawyer may deal with a murder a month, and yet Sean had never before had to view a body. He'd seen hundreds of photos of dead people in every position, condition, and state of decay. And he'd seen dozens of autopsy reports. But he'd never had to come down into this chilly place with its flat green walls and its chrome glaring back at him.

Knox handed an orange carbon to a thin bespectacled man in a green smock sitting at a table writing on a clipboard. He took the paperwork and began walking the length of the room without saying, "Follow me," or anything else.

"Number eight-two-seven-one-seven," he said, reading the paper. "White male about thirty-two, five-eleven, one sixty-eight?" He stood with his hand on a latch. When Knox nodded, he pulled the drawer and it slid effortlessly open.

There was a dark green, almost black, vinyl body bag on the table. The technician reached down and took a zipper at the head of the bag and pulled it as far as the knees. Then he pulled it apart so Sean could get a good look.

Scott's head was tilted back away from his body. It had been severed almost completely. His stomach and chest were cut open, and most of what was inside lay open to plain view—gray, blood-caked piles of viscera. A dark patch of blood was cut below his belly, and an opaque plastic bag filled with bloody flesh had been tossed between his legs.

Sean was strangely unaffected by the slaughterhouse look of Scott's body. Or the bittersweet stench of his corpse that to Knox was like being forced to gag down glasses of curdled milk. The only thing Sean felt, staring down at his old friend, was anger. How long did it take for you to die? he thought. Did they make you suffer? Did that black son of a bitch try to make you beg for your life?

Knox looked over at Sean. One of the refrigeration units shut down and the place fell silent. The technician stood with his hand on the chrome table ready to shut it, while Sean stared at Scott's body.

"Motherfucker!" he finally whispered with an intensity that left Knox chilled.

From the morgue, Sean drove directly to the county jail. Berger was going to tell him who the shooter was and where he could get ahold of him, or he was going to drop the greasy son of a bitch off the first convenient judicial cliff.

He still had some old paperwork on Berger's case from when he represented him, and he flashed it at the guard, who nodded at Sean without really looking at it.

When Berger came out, he gave a surprised look when he saw who had come. "Where's Scott?" he asked.

Sean ignored his question. He leaned in close to the glass. He was seething and Berger could see it.

"I want you to tell me who this black asshole was who killed the guard."

Berger looked around him nervously. "I told you."

"You told me a bunch of shit," Sean said a little louder.

Berger's hands began to shake.

"Tell me who killed him. And don't pull any fainting jags on me either, or I'll jump over this partition and slap your stupid face until you come around."

"You can't talk to me that way. You're not even my lawyer," Berger said. "Scott's my lawyer."

"Scott is dead!" Sean shouted and stood up. One of the guards looked over, saw it was Barrett, and relaxed again.

"What do you mean?" Terror was spreading in Berger's eyes.

"Romero too!" Sean said. "Mutilated! Their heads were cut off, and their dicks were shoved down their throats!" Sean was standing, leaning over the glass, in reach of Berger. "So you better cough him up or he's going to get you next."

"He knows I won't say anything," Berger said.

"What the hell are you talking about?" Sean yelled. "I told you he had to be the one who killed Scott and Romero."

"He's still got no reason to think I'd snitch on him."

"Don't be stupid. He already knows you talked. How else would Scott have known about Romero unless you told him?" Sean said, shaking his head. "Now tell me his name and where I can find him."

"Why, so the cops can put him in the cell next to me?" Berger said. "No thanks."

"Don't worry, Ted," Sean said firmly, looking directly into Berger's eyes. "I won't let anything happen to you while you're in here."

"Yeah. And just how the hell are you going to do that from out there?" Berger said, pointing out at the street. "All I know is, if I tell you, I'm dead. If I don't, maybe he'll leave me alone."

Sean leaned forward. "Look, Ted, I'll make you a deal. I promise you I won't tell the cops a thing unless you say it's all right."

Berger slowly nodded his head no, but Sean could tell he was ready to crack.

"All right, Ted," Sean said as he stared at Berger, whose hands were now trembling, "I'll tell you what. How about if I agree to represent you again?"

"Can you do that?"

"I don't see why not. I just won't be able to spend a lot of time with you until the Curtis case is over."

Berger hesitated. "I'm still afraid he'll find out if I tell you."

"How? If I'm your attorney, anything you tell me is confidential. There's no way I would ever repeat privileged information. I'd lose my license. So have we got a deal?"

Berger shook his head reluctantly. "His name is Shabba. Shabba St. James. That's all I know."

"Where do I find him?"

"God, I can't tell you that. He'll kill me!" Berger moaned.

"You're dead if you don't tell me. You want a chance? This is it. He killed the guard. He killed Romero. He killed Scott. There's only one witness left," Sean said and pointed down at Berger.

Berger shook his head. "If Eddie wanted to get ahold of him, he'd go down to the Huntington Beach Fun Zone. That's where he hangs out," he said. "That's his office."

It took Sean forty-five minutes from the time he left Berger to get to Huntington Beach. The Fun Zone was an amusement park that spread over a huge acreage along the beach. There was an arcade of video and pinball games in a place as big as a warehouse. There was also a ten-story roller coaster and rides called "Colossus" and "The Viper." In the center of it all was a midway of fast-food booths mixed in with an assortment of sucker games—overinflated basketballs shot through undersized hoops, optical illusions that looked like an easy score if you wanted to win two dying goldfish, lead bottles that a cannon couldn't topple.

The Fun Zone was filled with a lot of kids who had nothing

better to do. Sean had heard about a few drug raids that had gone down there in the past few years, and like a lot of other places, gang colors had begun to stain the area. There had been a couple of shootings, although nobody had died yet, and the locals had begun to call the place the "Gun Zone."

Sean was so upset by the way Scott had died that he made a mess of trying to find Shabba. He couldn't tell Gamboa what he'd pulled out of Berger because he was a client now. Instead, he started asking around the Fun Zone if anybody knew "a friend of his named Shabba."

"If he's a friend of yours," one belligerent black kid in two-hundred-dollar high tops spat at him, "how come you don't know where to find him, cop?"

No one knew nothin'. No Shabba. No big black brother who might be dealing meth. They just knew they weren't going to talk to no white motherfucker who looked like a cop. Sean stayed until the place closed at midnight, and all he came home with was a bad sunburn and a gut ache from the Fun Zone "fire dogs."

chapter

eighteen

When jury selection began in the case of the *State of California* v. *Chad Curtis,* Sherman Lowenstein was at his flamboyant best. He wore a gray suit and tie with a crimson shirt and socks and oxblood Italian boots. He'd had his hair lightened for the trial, and a red hankie flashed from his jacket pocket. The only thing missing, Sean thought, was the studio rouge.

Lowenstein had spent the weeks leading up to voir dire turning the upcoming trial into a media event. He was a favorite of the press and TV crews because he was the embodiment of what the public expected in a prosecuting attorney. He was a tall, kinky-haired, flamboyant crusader for the public safety. He'd stop at nothing, he was always saying, to put "the bad guys" behind bars, to protect the good citizens from the slime that threatened to overrun them at any moment. On TV talk shows audiences often gave him standing ovations when he was through, with hosts like Arsenio winking and applauding right along with them.

The Curtis case was just the D.A.'s latest high-profile publicity vehicle. Lowenstein was portraying Chad through the media as a callous but clever killer who had disposed of his victim's body knowing that the absence of such would be an enormous burden of proof for the prosecution were he ever arrested. But, of course, this ploy would not stop Lowenstein from bringing this heinous criminal to justice. He would need all the genius he could muster to beat this clever killer, but, luckily for the law-abiding citizens of this great state, Lowenstein had genius to spare. By the time the trial of Chad Curtis opened, anyone in Southern California who owned a television knew that Lowenstein was the star of this particular show.

Lowenstein's first ploy was to drag out the jury selection as long as possible. He began by requesting that the jury be questioned one at a time in chambers. Sean knew what he was up to. The longer they took to select the jury, the more likely it became that Robin was dead. He started to object as soon as Lowenstein proposed the idea, but Macklin was a step ahead of him. He not only denied Lowenstein's request, but he had the jury come in eighteen at a time. To speed the process up even more, the judge did not allow either attorney to ask individual jurors any questions. Instead, all the questions were asked by Macklin himself. To Lowenstein's chagrin, by noon on the fourth day of voir dire, a jury of seven women and five men, including two blacks, three Hispanics, a plumber, a retired schoolteacher, a Little League coach, a Safeway assistant manager, two divorcees, and a female weightlifter, were sworn in.

Macklin walked into the court still buttoning his robe. He had his favorite old desert boots on, and in the hall behind him he'd left a bank of smoke. He looked around at his courtroom as he sat down. The audience had been growing throughout voir dire. That morning every seat had been taken. But now the media, who knew when the real action started, had descended. Most of them came in immediately after Macklin had called for recess and placed official-looking placards on the front-row seats like COURT ARTIST or L.A. TIMES OFFICIAL MEDIA meant to shoo off the uninitiated. By one-thirty, two hundred fifty spectators were standing against the walls and in the aisles, stuffed into an eighty-seat courtroom. Another five hundred that the bailiffs held back were outside in the hall.

"Although we're probably breaking every fire code in existence,"

Macklin said, "as long as you behave yourselves, I'm going to let all of you spectators remain for the opening statements. I know that's always a big crowd pleaser," he said and smiled. Then the smile dropped. "But let me warn you, if there is any disturbance at all, I mean *anything*, I'll have the bailiffs clear the court.

"Now," he said, looking down at the D.A., "are you ready for your opening statement, Mr. Lowenstein?"

"Yes, Your Honor. Thank you," he said.

Sean watched Lowenstein as he took his time getting to his feet. He knew how to milk a dramatic pause as well as any actor. He rearranged a few things on the table in front of him, leaned over to a clerk and whispered something, then pushed his chair back with a screech across the wood floor and stood up. As he walked the twenty feet from the prosecution table to the jury box, his face showed the momentous burden he had of putting another of society's enemies behind bars. His eyebrows were bunched tightly, and his lips were working together like a woman applying her lipstick.

"Your Honor," Lowenstein started and tipped his head to Macklin, "Counsel, ladies and gentlemen of the jury, I will make my opening statement a short one." His voice was very low, so the audience had to strain to hear him. "I wish I could say short and *sweet*, but I can't. Because there is nothing sweet about this case. This is a bitter case. Very bitter." Lowenstein stopped as if it were too much for him to go on.

"Why is it bitter?" he asked and walked over to Chad. Leveling his finger just inches away from his face, he suddenly began to yell. "Because this *man* brutally killed a beautiful, sweet, young, innocent girl named Robin Penrose."

Chad flinched as the D.A. roared in his face. Sean moved his hand under the table and patted Chad on the knee.

Lowenstein walked quickly back to the jury.

"Ladies and gentlemen, you will learn that the prosecution will not be able to present any direct evidence of this beautiful girl's death because this . . . *man*," he said, again pointing over at Chad, "Chad Lee Curtis, has made that impossible. Don't let that nice new suit and the All-American face fool you. Behind that facade lurks a monster. He killed that innocent young girl, and he is such a monster, so devoid of any human feelings, that he hid her body so no one can find it. Not even her mother! Who knows where that poor girl is lying right now? Where did he hide her? In a garbage can? In the woods so wild animals could tear apart her innocent flesh? Or maybe he just dumped her in the ocean. Who knows what lengths this monster would go to in order to cover his hideous crime?"

Sean took scrupulous notes as he listened to the D.A. He had helped bury Scott the previous morning, and his present work kept him from dwelling on his friend's brutal murder.

Lowenstein moved back to the lectern and spent the next hour summarizing the evidence the prosecution intended to produce. Contrary to his promise to be brief, it turned out to be an unusually long opening, but that was part of his strategy too. He wanted to prepare the jury right from the start for the long parade of witnesses to come. The evidence was going to be a slow drip, not a rushing waterfall, and Lowenstein wanted them to know it. After his summary he came over to the jury box again and put both hands on the rail.

"At times this case may become boring to you," he said. "But let me assure you, every piece of evidence that I present is necessary. Because this man has forced me to spend weeks and months simply proving that this young girl is, in fact, dead.

"Again, ladies and gentlemen," Lowenstein went on, "this man not only murdered Robin Penrose, but he cold-heartedly hid her body because he thought he couldn't be convicted without it. As you will find out, and as the court will continue to inform you, that is not the law. After you hear all the evidence you will reach only one reasonable conclusion, and that is, Robin Penrose is dead and this man"—he pointed over his shoulder at Chad without turning his head—"Chad Lee Curtis, is her murderer."

Pausing in front of the jury, he swung around dramatically and gave a small bow to Macklin, as if he were in an English court. "Thank you, Your Honor. Nothing further."

"Well, thank you, Mr. Lowenstein," Macklin said, raising his eyebrows at the histrionics. He'd heard all about Lowenstein's showboating in court, and he was ready for it. "No need to bow. I haven't been coronated yet."

The newsboys chuckled loudly in the back, and Macklin acknowledged them with a wry smile.

"Mr. Barrett," the judge said, turning to the defense table, "are you going to make an opening statement?"

Sean normally did not like to give one, and this trial was no exception. In an opening statement an attorney introduces to the jury his client, and the evidence he intends to present. But the problem was, in this case Sean would never know from minute to minute what would happen next. Would they find Robin's body after he'd spent weeks trying to convince the jury she was probably walking around no more dead than they were? If they found her body, would it be a mutilated mess, belying all his efforts to show his client incapable of any violence? Or maybe he'd get lucky and Robin Penrose would walk through the door and the case would be won. Anything could happen in a no-body case. Sean knew, however, that he had to risk giving an opening statement even if it meant making the jury prom- ises he might have to break later. As Lowenstein had warned, the prosecution's case would likely last for months. Witness upon witness would be called, all saying they hadn't seen or heard from Robin Penrose. Those were the only voices the jury would hear day after day, week after week. No one could resist that kind of psychological barrage. The chances were very high that the jury would already have made up their minds that Robin was dead before Sean had a chance to convince them otherwise.

He knew he had to give an opening statement so the jury would have a mental hold on the defense's case while Lowenstein tried to drown them in a deluge of prosecution witnesses.

Sean stood and looked around at Macklin, leaning back in his swivel chair, at Lowenstein, his ferret eyes working the room, at the crowd reshuffling before he began. Then he saw Carrie for the first time. She was in a back seat, second from the corner, wearing an apricot suit with her hair in a French braid. When he'd left her at six-thirty that morning, she had still been in bed, the sheets half cov- ering her back, her head resting on her arm.

Sean turned to the jury and took his time walking over to them. In court he liked to take it slowly, as if he were on a warm beach and the sand felt good between his toes.

The jury was the kind a pollster would choose for a cross-section opinion. He had spotted two hardheaded men who'd worked thirty- five, forty years: they'd seen what the world gave a man for free. Sean knew he wouldn't convince them with fancy clothes or eloquence. He'd look them in the eye, they'd read him like the morning paper, and he'd start from there. That was fine with Sean. If he could win those two, he figured he'd win them all. Sean was convinced that's where most attorneys fresh out of law school blew it. They acted as if they were addressing fellow grads, instead of people who understood only the laws of common sense.

Sean had one hand in his pocket, and as he began, he gestured with his right. Nothing dramatic, just an underline, a little point, a pause.

"Your Honor, Mr. Prosecutor, and ladies and gentlemen," he began, "you have all just heard Mr. Lowenstein say that he will be unable to produce any direct evidence of Robin Penrose's death. That he will convince you she is dead through circumstantial evidence. He also told you that circumstantial evidence is as good as direct evidence and should be so regarded by you. Mr. Lowenstein has stated the law correctly. You can base your verdict entirely upon circumstantial evidence.

"But he is wrong," he said and held his hands palms out to halt everything, "when he tells you that circumstantial evidence is just as good as direct evidence." Sean took another step toward the jury. "Mr. Lowenstein will try to bury you in an avalanche of circumstantial evidence to make his case seem substantial. Don't let him fool you. Circumstantial evidence, by its very nature, is open to doubt. It's *not* just as good as direct evidence, no matter what Mr. Lowenstein has told you. If the district attorney had the smallest shred of direct evidence, believe me, he wouldn't bother for a moment with circumstantial evidence. Why? Because circumstantial evidence, no matter how much the prosecution digs up, is open to more than one interpretation.

"Now, just ask yourselves one question. Why is the prosecution being forced to prove its case only through circumstantial evidence?" Sean waited a moment. "If you think about it, the answer is obvious. Because Robin Penrose is not dead. Therefore, it's impossible for the prosecution to produce any direct evidence of death because, ladies and gentlemen, there is none." Sean walked to the far end of the jury box and turned so that he was facing the judge.

"Now," he said, "I'd like to talk about another area in which Mr. Lowenstein may have misled you—the missing girl, Robin Penrose herself," Sean said, scanning the double row of faces turned toward him. "The prosecutor has just characterized Robin as a sweet, beautiful, innocent young girl. He's certainly right about the young and beautiful part. Robin Penrose is very, very beautiful. But as to the rest of Mr. Lowenstein's description of the missing woman as sweet and innocent, well," he said and cocked his head doubtfully to the side, "that is not entirely accurate. Please," he said, coming closer, "let me emphasize this point. The question of Robin Penrose's character is at the heart of this case."

Sean stepped back from the jury again. "I'm not going to try to convince you that Robin Penrose is a bad person. I'm not here to ruin a young girl's reputation. But I will produce evidence that Robin Penrose is really no different than many aspiring young actresses her age in Southern California, trying to make it in a highly competitive business that has an often unsavory reputation. She isn't sweet and innocent. Just like nearly every other struggling actress in Hollywood, she did whatever she had to do to get a break."

Sean was hoping that would score with this jury, who'd probably seen enough Hollywood Babylon movies to graphically fill in the details he was inferring.

"No, I do not agree with the prosecutor's characterization of Robin Penrose as a sweet and innocent young girl, and by the time the trial is over, neither will you."

Sean walked back to the lectern next to the counsel table to give the jury a chance to catch its breath.

"Now, I'd like to bring up a sore point for me. Mr. Lowenstein," he said in a derisive tone, "has just stood before you and called my client a monster. He said, without a scrap of proof, that my client hid the body of the alleged victim so the prosecutor would be forced to prove his case through circumstantial evidence. Forget the fact that he wants you to believe that my client knows all the sophisticated legal ins and outs of a no-body case. That my client killed her in a jealous rage and then had the presence of mind and the legal sophistication to hide her body. We'll let that pass for now, ladies and gentlemen." Sean raised his eyebrows at the absurdity, then he became angry. "I'll tell you what I won't let pass, though. I'm issuing a challenge right now to Mr. Lowenstein—to you, sir," he said, advancing on the prosecutor, pointing his finger and shouting the way he'd shouted at Chad, "to prove that allegation. Not only can't you prove that Robin Penrose is dead, but you can't even offer any plausible explanation why my client would have killed her." Sean remained in front of Lowenstein. "You keep telling us what you are going to do, now let me tell this jury what you are not going to do. You, sir, are not going to be able to call anyone to the witness stand who will say they saw Robin dead. You, sir, will not bring forward anyone who will say they saw Chad Curtis kill her. Or to tell this jury why Chad Curtis would have even wanted to kill her. Why is that? Because, Mr. Prosecutor, Robin Penrose is not dead."

Sean slowly approached the jury again, leaving Lowenstein steaming in his fifteen-hundred-dollar suit.

"Now, keep in mind the prosecutor's strategy. He warned you he will be using hundreds of Robin's friends and relatives to testify that they have had no contact with Robin since she was last seen with my client. He also said he would call hundreds of witnesses from a variety of government agencies to testify that they also have had no contact with a Robin Penrose," Sean said. "Why is he going to do this? To try to convince you that because those people haven't seen Robin since her disappearance, she must be dead. That's nonsense!" he said and dismissed the notion with a wave toward the D.A. "I have talked to nearly half a dozen people who will testify before you that they have both seen and talked to Robin Penrose since her so-called disappearance. These are credible witnesses, and they will testify that Robin is alive, hiding for her own reasons. Maybe she'd just had enough. Maybe she wanted to start fresh somewhere else. You see it in the papers every day. A guy runs away from his family, and ten years later, he runs a red light in some small town in Texas, and they discover he was alive all that time."

Sean looked several of the jurors in the eye. "Are you going to send a decent kid," he said and pointed at Chad, "to prison for life because the D.A. wants a big win?"

Sean took another stroll to the lectern and checked some notes. Then he turned to the jury again. He could tell by the way they were watching him that for the moment he had them on his side.

"I know you all want to see justice done in this court. So I want to ask a favor of you," he said softly. "Please maintain an open mind throughout this long trial. The first couple of months you will be hearing nothing but the prosecution's case day after day. You wouldn't be human if you didn't at least start to form an opinion before the defense has a chance to present its case, especially with a skilled attorney such as Mr. Lowenstein bombarding you day after day with his side of the story. I'm asking you not to let him fool you. Fight against forming any hasty opinions. I urge you, in the name of justice. If you can keep an open mind until the defense is concluded, I promise you will find my client, Chad Curtis, 'not guilty.' "

chapter

nineteen

When Sean walked into his cottage after court, the phone was ringing.

"Meesta Barrett!" the Jamaican shouted into Sean's ear. "Dee sun is shinin' and dee girl is still a-runnin'. Whatchu think? She goan stay in one place dee rest of her life so dis in-ves-ti-ga-tor, he can trip over her? Huh? Now whatchu think?"

"We haven't found her yet, cowboy," Sean said. He didn't want to pump him too high about the help he'd given. If a crackpot like this thought he was really needed, who knew what he'd ask for?

"Maybe not. Maybe not. But I know more dan you do. Is dis not so?"

Sean had to laugh. He was probably right. "All right. So tell me what else you know."

"Oh, I know our little bird Robin, she fly north dis time to dee Golden Gate."

"Now she's in San Francisco?"

"Ah, ha, ha, ha. Baghdad by dee bay."

Sean was beginning to really hate that laugh. "That's a pretty big city," he said. "Can you narrow it down some?"

"Fisherman's Wharf. She like to eat with dee Yankee Clipper."

"All right, maybe we'll give it a try," Sean said. Then he took a stab at a hunch he had. "Oh, by the way, I loved your red 'Vette."

For the first time there was silence on the other end. Sean knew he was right about the Jamaican being in Bakersfield. It was Sean who laughed this time. "I know what you look like now. I saw you driving that girl around," he needled.

There was still nothing from the Jamaican for a few seconds. Then he said in a low, cold tone, "Then you already seen too much." And there was no laughter before the phone went dead.

The Jamaican squeezed out of the telephone booth and adjusted his wraparound reflectors. His dreadlocks bounced heavily on his shoulders as he hummed an old reggae tune.

When he got to the pickup, he pulled a pistol from his pocket. Leaning through the passenger window, he handed the gun to the driver, whose head pushed against the ceiling.

"Keep dis warm for me, Hoops. I goan take care of our Mr. Ham-berger."

The driver nodded behind reflectors, and his mouth slowly slid open, revealing two gold canines. "Just another white boy needs a shave," he said, grinning.

Shabba walked up the street to where his Corvette was parked, went around the back of the car, and stopped for a moment to buff a smudge off the hood with the tail of his shirt. He stood back a moment to see if he'd gotten the blemish, then walked to the driver's door and swung it open. He turned his backside to the car and backed into the opening, plopping down into the low-slung bucket, his massive rear end filling the entire dimensions of the seat. Then he maneuvered one leg in the door, then the other. The top of his dreadlocks mashed against the ceiling of the sports car.

He stuck the key in the ignition, and the big cat of an engine roared. Shabba pumped the accelerator, and it growled on command. He let the Corvette idle, occasionally making it roar to keep it ready to pounce. He was only a few blocks from the Civic Center, so he knew a squad car would happen by sooner or later.

Several minutes went by before a black-and-white pulled up to the intersection in front of him. Shabba rammed the gear shift into first and stood on the accelerator. The car squealed from the curb and shot ahead. Shabba shoved it into second, and he was doing sixty when he hit the intersection. He pulled the wheel hard to the left and the back tires of the 'Vette slid, the car making a dizzy spin in the middle of the intersection. Cars slammed on their brakes to avoid the fiberglass dervish whirling in front of them. It kept spinning until it came to rest against the curb.

Shabba crawled out of his car and stood towering over it. Grinning, he stood with his feet spread and his hands on his hips staring at the squad car.

The driver, Gino DeLong, a ten-year veteran, grumbled, "Oh, crap," when he saw Shabba standing in the middle of the street grinning. "I smell another Rodney King here," he groaned at Cece Marin, his female partner. "Get on the fucking box and tell them to send a bunch of backup."

DeLong got out of the car. The tall, wiry Italian had his stick ready, dangling in his right hand at the side of his leg. "We had a little bit to drink, huh?" the cop said to Shabba from across the intersection.

Shabba looked at the cop with the grin still in place. "Fuck you!" he said.

DeLong sighed.

His partner was out of the squad car by now, approaching the suspect on his left. DeLong glanced over at her and motioned with his hand to slow her down. A few minutes and backup would be swarming all over this asshole. They could stun-gun him, and nobody would have to risk so much as a broken fingernail.

Shabba knew all this too, and he wasn't waiting around for a street full of uniforms to spoil his show. As soon as the cop looked over to see what his partner was up to, Shabba took an enormous step forward. When DeLong looked back, a big mass of black muscle was all over him.

Shabba pinned the cop's right arm so he couldn't use the club. Taking the cop down to the ground, he rolled the smaller man on top of him and began squeezing the breath out of him. The female cop moved around the two bodies rolling on the ground, but all that was exposed was her partner's limbs. DeLong tried to yell instructions to her, but couldn't catch his breath. All he could do was grunt and struggle.

When the other squad cars came sirening into the intersection, Shabba put his hands around the cop's waist so they were easily accessible for cuffing.

Three of the bigger cops pulled DeLong out of Shabba's grasp and yanked the big Jamaican to his feet. When DeLong finally managed to catch his breath, he rammed his stick into Shabba's crotch. The Jamaican collapsed, and the two cops on either side holding him by the elbows went down with him.

"DeLong, you fuckin' turkey," one of the cops yelled from the ground. "This asshole weighs five hundred pounds, for fuck's sake."

"Well, goddamn it, this queer bait was trying to cornhole me," DeLong moaned. He was wagging the stick, looking to get in another shot.

Two more patrolmen came over and helped pull Shabba up again. Then all four of them threw him in the back of DeLong's squad car.

"Goddammit, don't put that motherfucker in my car," DeLong yelled. "He smells like chicken manure, for chrissake. It'll take a month to get the goddamn smell outa the car."

The problem was the other cops knew that too.

"It's your collar, DeLong. You gotta furnish the transportation."

"Shit!"

Shabba slumped in the back of the car. His nuts would probably swell up like a couple of coconuts, but the arrest had gone much easier than he thought it would. His lawyer would have him out on bail as soon as his work was done, and he'd plea it down to almost nothing. But first he was going to pay a visit to Mr. Theodore Berger in county lockup. And that would be the end of that problem.

Carrie came by Sean's place late that evening around ten, just as he was going over some final notes. They were in the early stages of a strong sexual affair, and it had been three days since they were together. So when she knocked once and came in, he took her in his arms and kissed her. A minute later they were shuffling into his bedroom, their lips still locked together, giggling as they tumbled into bed.

In spite of how happy he was around Carrie, in the back of his mind somewhere lurked a nagging question. He just couldn't figure what Carrie Robinson saw in him. She could have anyone. He was too lost in the swirl of this case and their sexual energy, however, to really stop and look hard at their relationship. When he felt uneasy, he simply told himself that any man was bound to feel insecure around a woman as beautiful and intelligent and talented as Carrie.

When she awoke, he wasn't there. Then she noticed the light in the living room. When she went in there, Sean was frowning over a book, his head in his hands.

"What's the matter?"

"Oh, hi. This case is driving me crazy. I'm flying around solo here with nothing to guide me. I have almost no precedent to go on. The entire body of trial law concerning murder is based on a case in which they know a murder has been committed."

On several occasions he had taken Spann up on his offer to help Sean with the case. And Spann with his experience had helped a great deal. But Carrie was there for him every day. She would come by at night now as often as possible and she and Sean would talk about the case before and after and while they were making love. They'd get up in the morning and have breakfast together and discuss the case some more. He'd call her at her office when she had a moment and she'd hold his hand while he walked with her through some briar-patch of the law. She had a brilliant, creative mind, always on the lookout for that sliver of judicial light that would help lead Sean out of this cavernous case. She steadied any doubts he had and helped him focus on the real issues and problems of the case. And day by day he came to depend on her more and more.

Carrie sat down next to him on the couch, and he put his hand in her lap. She cleared her mind and began digging with him. "What are you hung up on?"

"Ah, I'm trying to decide whether to put Chad on the stand." His hand was idly caressing her.

"If you don't, how's the jury going to know what happened?" she asked. "They're going to want to hear it from your client."

"It's a gamble anytime you put your client on the stand, you know that. Who knows what a prosecutor like Lowenstein would do to a kid like Chad?" He shook his head. "It's so risky."

"But if it's looking bad, then you're going to have to put Chad up there," she said, pulling his hand down from under her camisole so she could think better. "Besides, I think a jury usually likes to see the defendant up there so they can see his face when he says he's innocent."

"No," he finally said. "If Chad has to take the stand, then we're in big trouble. And the D.A. knows that. As soon as I call Chad, Lowenstein will move in for the kill."

"Yes," Carrie said. "I think you may be right."

"Plus, at any moment," he went on, "they could come up with her body. Every time I hear that damn phone ring, I think it's Gamboa telling me they've found her."

"And if they find her with a bullet hole in her?" she asked.

"Then that could give the jury enough to convict him of murder."

"So unless he's got a very good story how it happened accidentally, they've got him for murder two, at least."

"At least," Sean said. "Of course, it wouldn't be much of a stretch for the prosecution to argue that he brought the gun along to kill her. And that's premeditation."

"And that's murder one."

"Yes," Sean said.

"Well, the way I see it, whether or not the witnesses will hold up on the stand is always a major problem for any lawyer. Do your homework, trust your legal instincts, and then go get 'em. That's what Dad always told me."

"Yeah, and a little luck wouldn't hurt either."

Sean gazed at her a long time, and then he bent over and kissed her. He knew he was going to wake up soon and be back at Spann, McGraw working on a divorce case. Not here, not now, falling in love with Carrie and fighting the legal battle of his life.

"How do you know so much about criminal law?" he asked.

"Remember I was raised on criminal law. My father and Mr. Spann were the best criminal law team in the county when I was growing up. Dad had me working on cases when I was still in high school. You know how some fathers train their daughters to be world-class tennis players. Well, my father brought me up to be a world-class attorney. He started me out with Sherlock Holmes and Erle

Stanley Gardner—all the mystery classics. Got me hooked on solving cases. Then, in high school, he'd have me in the library looking up precedents. I used to tell my friends I couldn't go out because I was in the midst of a big case." Carrie laughed. "Can you believe it? I was wrapped up in a case back in high school."

She ducked down to meet his lips, and this time when she kissed him there was a sexual note attached he had no trouble reading. But he was curious about something.

"So why did Carter and Spann switch over to corporate law if they loved criminal law so much?"

"Money. Plain and simple. The more they got into that life-style with the homes in Lido and the fancy cars and the yachts, the more they phased out their criminal practice. The money was so clean and fast. Corporate pockets are so deep! What do they care if you bill five hundred hours? As long as they come out on top, your measly $250,000 in fees doesn't mean a thing. Especially if you just helped them close a deal worth a hundred million. Four or five of those a year, an attorney's making seven figures and never misses a tee time."

"Strictly money, huh?"

"It's not exactly that simple, Sean. Everything just builds until there's no way you can turn back."

Sean could see she was upset. Whenever the subject wandered onto her father, she always seemed to get defensive.

"I'm sorry. I didn't mean to sound like I was judging your father."

"Oh, I know. You're in love with criminal law. I can't blame you. So am I. But when Daddy went into corporate, I followed right along."

There was regret in her voice as she said it. She had a gift for criminal law, the same kind of innate understanding of what counted most in a courtroom that Sean had.

"Well, when you decide you want to be pure and poor again, let me know," Sean said. "I know an up-and-coming one-man firm that could use a partner."

"Is that a proposition?"

"Absolutely."

"Well, it's about time," she laughed, and they reached for each other.

chapter

twenty

Teddy Berger crouched every night on his lumpy cotton mattress and stared out the bars of the cell, his eyelids pinned open. Noises spooked him, especially the soft ones that had the sound of a carefully placed foot. He felt comfortable only with a wall at his back. Whenever he was forced out of his cell, he approached a corner cautiously, slowing to take it wide, his head craning to see around the corner before his belly met an upthrust knife.

He slept in a crouch on the bed, as far from the bars as possible. If he stretched out, someone could grab his foot, pull him forward, and sink a jagged blade into his belly. That's how he heard Buzzard got it. Then there was the beaner that they'd shoved bars of soap down until he suffocated. These were the stories that terrorized him most. Teddy sat on his bed every night and went over and over in his mind the horror the other inmates fed him every day.

The day after he had heard that Scott and Eddie had been murdered, some choke told him how they got it. Slit right up the belly, their heads hacked off. This Mexican had been out in the recreation yard with him smoking a Delicado, and the foul Mexican crap weed was making Teddy's head spin. The choke leaned in close and said, "Oh, man! Eddie's sister told Rodriguez that the walls in the kitchen was all red, man. Blood all over the place—the stove, the refrigerator," he said and puffed his Delicado. "Like somebody took a bucket of blood and threw it against the wall."

Berger sank onto the concrete bench and leaned against the wall, staring. Everybody in the joint knew that crazy fucking Jamaican had whacked them. That was the funny part. The cops had been trying to find the Medtech killer for weeks, and everybody inside already knew who he was.

Since Sean had told him about Romero's and Scott's murders, Teddy was becoming more and more paranoid by the day. He rarely ate and even when he did, he had a difficult time keeping any of it down. He was dropping weight like a flatbed truck on a bumpy road.

Other than meals, the only time he was forced to mingle with the other inmates was the mandatory exercise period just after lunch. He'd gotten out of it the first day or two after he'd heard about Eddie and Scott by claiming he was too sick. They let him stay mostly because of his terror-induced diarrhea. But when the guard told him that if he was too sick to exercise, he'd have to go to the infirmary, he got well in a hurry. Teddy figured he'd take his chances in the yard, where at least he'd be on his feet when they tried to butcher him.

The exercise yard was on top of the building. A ten-foot chain-link fence with rolled razor wire strung along the top enclosed the area. The fence was strictly for effect, however. It was a straight hundred-and-twenty foot drop to the asphalt below down sheer, windowless, ledgeless, featureless concrete.

For winter, it was a hot day and the sun bore in on the skin. Shabba stood in a far corner, in shadow. He had a six-inch jigsaw blade filed down to razor sharpness taped to the inside of his pants hip. Berger hadn't showed up the first two days after Shabba had gotten himself arrested. The Jamaican had found out he was faking the flu and staying in his cell. But he knew sooner or later Mr. Ham-Berger would have to come out and play.

Berger came into the yard last and as close to the trailing guard as he could possibly get. When he came through the chain-link inner gate, he moved up against the nearest wall, and with his back firmly against the concrete, he moved down to an unoccupied bench ten feet away. A group of blacks were pumping iron in the far corner, and another group was shooting around on the basketball court. The Chicanos in bandanas and knit caps took up a section of the yard in a corner farthest from the entrance—a foot-high concrete slab originally meant as a boxing ring. The guards called the corner "Burrito Heights."

Berger cautiously scanned the yard. If anyone approached the bench, he would immediately get up and stand as far away as he could without getting closer to anyone else. He hadn't had a very good look at Shabba the night he blew the guard away. All he remembered was he was big. But then half the blacks in this place were big. Besides, it didn't have to be Shabba himself who got to him. It could be anyone, anytime. But especially now out in this yard with three hundred other prisoners and only two unarmed guards. If a fight broke out, they could slice and dice him into stew meat in a matter of seconds, and the guards wouldn't even know it until he was gone.

Berger stood against the wall, his eyes never stopping, checking his watch every minute or two to see how much longer he'd have to stand there naked. Every day his goal was to stay alive, and every night he had the same nightmares of Shabba sneaking into his cell with that machete. Every night was worse than the last. He couldn't sleep, he couldn't eat, he couldn't do anything but think. His mind, sick with terror, had taken him over. He crapped soup. His head spun dizzily from no sleep and nothing to eat. He shivered during the day when it was hot, and he sweated at night. He knew he was cracking up, but what was he supposed to do—relax?

Shabba slid his hand down his pants and ripped the tape off his leg. Pulling the blade out, he held it against his side under his arm. He moved over by the trash cans about twenty feet to the left of Berger. When the bell rang signaling the end of exercise, he waited until Berger was circling near the back of the pack, then he moved quickly. Berger sensed something behind him and began to push forward, but Shabba caught him by the neck with a monstrous hand before he could safely wedge himself into the crowd.

Shabba clamped Berger's windpipe and choked off his scream.

He was an efficient killing machine, clinical as a surgeon when he had to be. But he liked it too. Killing had the sudden rush of the best drug—making someone beg, the terror electrifying the eyes, the frantic looking around, then the realization that they were going to feel that blade. That's why he liked the machete, it exaggerated the terror—the whimpers of regret as their life played back all the way to that last cry for Mama and the pain that scores the mind. You could ride C-biscuit all night—the cocaine like a stallion, the heroin making the ride golden—and it wouldn't touch the feeling in his hands as the first shiver of death ran through them.

Shabba forced the blade into Berger's back. Once through the outer muscle it began a long, easy slide up through his kidneys. He kept pushing until the tip of the blade poked out his belly just below the ribs. His left hand still clamped on the jugular, Shabba cranked the blade around like an organ grinder so it sliced repeatedly through Berger's internal organs. The heart kept pumping, though, so when Shabba let go, Berger fell to his knees and blood began pumping in spurts out the hole in his stomach. Then his face banged against the asphalt. He was choking and wheezing like a horse with waterlogged lungs. Then blood came spurting out of his agonized mouth, the red stream starting to spread, the daylight flickering in his eyes like those spring mornings in Albuquerque before his mother had been killed and he would ride his trike past the picket fence, the light strobing. And there would be his mother smiling. "Mama!" he moaned, seeing her, the blood pooling beneath him, warm as her breath on his face.

Shabba was through the gate and down the long, windowless corridor to lockup, sitting in his cell, before a guard spotted Berger lying facedown on the pavement, already dead.

chapter

twenty-one

The Uncola Man had said Robin would be at the Yankee Clipper restaurant, so the first thing Mac did when he got off the plane in San Francisco was find a phone booth. He tried four of them before he found a phone book that didn't have all the local hotel and restaurant listings ripped out. He looked under "Restaurant" in the Yellow Pages, but he found nothing for the Yankee Clipper. He tried the Clipper. Nothing. Then he looked in the white pages. Nothing. So he plunked a quarter in a pay phone and called information. The operator couldn't find a number for the damned place either.

When Mac told some honey he was trying to impress that he was a P.I., they got the idea he was like Magnum. Oh, maybe they didn't expect to see the red Ferrari, and he sure as hell didn't look like Selleck. But he said P.I. and automatically they had this vision of a sleuth—a cross between Sherlock Holmes and Columbo. A guy who could put two and two together and come up with four to the power of ten. A couple of obscure clues and he could tell you who killed

JFK. Of course, Mac never tried to clear up these little misconceptions the dollies harbored, not if it was good for a night in the sack. Why tell them it was just a bunch of boring hard work? Putting the leather to the pavement, that's what being a P.I. was all about. Toting around this picture of a dead girl, asking questions for hours. Nothing glamorous about it. No need to call 221B Baker Street. The only "superior intellect" he needed was figuring out who was bullshitting him. And all those decisions happened in the gut. Was the guy full of shit or wasn't he?

The most important ingredient to a good P.I. is luck. Mac would drag around all day, going from one dead end to another, looking for a lead, and nine times out of ten it was just dumb luck that led to his big break. Maybe he'd hit just the right bartender at the right time. Or some woman who wanted a little revenge on the dirty rat. Or a fag maître d' who took a liking and kept his mascaraed eyes open for him.

Mac was a drunk and a gambler and he couldn't pick an honest woman out of a convent, but he was a dogged investigator. He rented a car at SFO and drove up into The City past Golden Gate Park to Lombard, down through the Mission District, and finally to the Embarcadero on the bay, then west toward Pier 9 to the street mall the tourists all called Fisherman's Wharf, where the Jamaican had told Sean to look for the girl.

Mac wandered in and out of the restaurants that crowded the area—chowder houses, pasta joints, and bistros, mostly. It was an hour or so before dinner, and the business crowd from the financial district that stormed the wharf during lunch had already gone back to their offices half loaded. It was still too early, though, for the tourist crowd that arrived by trolley car from the swanky Nob Hill hotels. That meant the owners and bartenders and hostesses and maître d's didn't mind Mac asking a few questions.

"The Yankee Clipper? Never heard of the place," an old Italian behind the bar at Luigi's Italiano told him. The other dozen wops he talked to had all said the same thing.

"This broad tells me meet her at the Yankee Clipper on the Wharf," Mac told the old guy. He was a potbellied little Italian named Guiseppe. Mac wouldn't have been surprised if his son was Pinocchio.

"Maybe she don't like you so much," he laughed.

"Yeah, probably not," and Mac laughed too. "Maybe it's all for the best, though. That husband of hers won an Olympic gold medal in trap shooting. He'd probably plug me as I was crawling out the window."

Guiseppe's eyes crinkled like Santa's. He'd taken an instant liking to Mac. Nothing was more romantic to an old Italian than risking getting your botchies blown off for a little piece of proscuitto.

The old man reached across the bar and clapped Mac on the shoulders. "Oh, paisan! Let me buy you another glass of whiskey." He poured a full glass for Mac and then said, "You know, there is only one Yankee Clipper in San Francisco."

"Yeah, where is it?" Mac asked. He could feel a break coming.

"The Yankee Clipper is not a place."

"No?"

"No," Guiseppe said. He shook his head as if Mac had just blasphemed. "The Yankee Clipper is the greatest baseball player of all. Joe DiMaggio."

"DiMaggio? He live here?" Mac said. "I thought he played for New York."

"Sure, he played for the Yankees, but Joe DiMaggio was born two blocks from here on Polk. Same as I was," he said and arched his back so his belly strained against his shirt. "I grew up playing ball with Joltin' Joe at Golden Gate Park right up until Joe and his brothers signed with the San Francisco Seals back in nineteen hundred and thirty."

"That right?"

This was where the real P.I. work came in, Mac thought. Listening to some old coot lie about how DiMag and him were like this as kids. If Mac encouraged the old fart, he'd rhapsodize for hours about how him and DiMag jerked off together.

"That's probably what your gal meant about the Yankee Clipper," the old man said.

"That right?" Mac said without listening. He was looking at his watch, just about to say, "Well, better be going," when Guiseppe delivered.

"The Yankee Clipper owns a restaurant on the Wharf."

"He does?" Mac said. Here it comes—the lucky break falling out of the sky.

"Sure. Two blocks down."

"What's the name of the place?"

"What you think? DiMaggio's, of course."

"Thanks, Pop. I owe you one," Mac said and got up and threw a wad on the bar.

"Geeve her one for me." Guiseppe clenched his right fist and slapped it into the palm of his left as Mac went out the door.

DiMaggio's was tucked away behind another, newer restaurant, and it took Mac twenty minutes to find the place, even though it was only three blocks away. The bartender and the waitress who had worked the previous night came on at six, so Mac sat at the bar drinking beer for an hour until they showed.

"How ya doing?" he asked the bartender as he was putting on his apron to start his shift.

"I can't help you," he said and turned his back to Mac and started arranging some bottles below the bar.

"Why not?" Mac said. Like a salesman, he was used to hearing the word no.

The bartender kept moving the bottles around on the shelves. When he was finished, he looked around at Mac. "Look, buddy, the last time I did something like that, the guy was a cop and he waited here for two days. The bum he wants finally shows up and he busts him right here." The bartender pointed at the bar stool next to Mac. "We were packed, for chrissake. It's happy hour. They jumped on the guy, rolled around on the floor, and knocked over stools and tables. Scared the hell out of the customers. The place emptied out in three minutes. I can't afford another scene like that." He stood up with a bottle of vodka in each hand. "Give me a break, okay?"

"Jim," Mac said, reading his name tag, "let me be honest with you. I'm not a cop. I'm a private investigator."

"Oh, yeah? Like Magnum?"

"Yeah, like Magnum," Mac said. "I'm working for the family of a girl whose father is dying of cancer. He lives in Southern California. She ran off when she was a teenager. Big misunderstanding. You know how it is." He was checking Jim's eyes to see how he was taking this fable. So far, so good. "Well, anyway, he's dying and he's leaving her a lot of money and he wants to see his only daughter before he goes. Last thing he heard, she was in the Bay Area. Can you help me here?"

"Well . . ." he said.

"Look, I'm not going to grab her or anything. I just want to let her know what the situation is. Her daddy loves her and he's dying and wants to make sure she's going to be all right when he goes. You understand," Mac said and laid one of his business cards on top of the bar.

"P.I., huh?" Jim said, picking it up. Sometimes the card impressed them. They could see themselves talking to Selleck, the Ferrari idling out front. "I'm not too good with faces, but let me take a look at the photo."

MacDuff opened the folder lying in front of him and pulled out several photos of Robin. The bartender looked at the pictures briefly and gave them back to Mac without saying anything. When a couple sat down at the end of the bar, he went over and got them a drink. Finally he came back to Mac's end of the bar and started washing glasses.

"What do you think, Jim? Can you help me?"

"What can I get you to drink?" he said.

"Nah, I'm okay," Mac said.

"Well, if you don't order anything, you can't leave a big tip, now can you?" Jim said.

Mac's eyes came level with the bartender's. The way he said it, Mac knew this guy had negotiated similar deals. He was playing Mac for a good payday. "Sure, give me another beer."

Jim placed the bottle in front of Mac, and Mac handed him a ten.

"I thought you said the girl's father had dough?"

Reaching into his pocket, Mac came out with a fifty and put it on the bar. "I'll be looking for change if this beer is flat," he said.

The bartender took the fifty and went to the cash register. Ringing up two dollars for the drink, he put the change in his pocket and came back.

"She was here the last two nights. Sat right where you're sitting. Drank wallbangers. I know 'cause I had to go in the back for the Galliano."

"You think she'll be back?" Mac asked.

"That depends on whether she's working."

"A hooker?" Mac asked, trying to sound surprised. From what

Sean had picked up from Pope, it sounded exactly like what Robin would be doing.

"What do you think?"

"It'll kill her father," Mac said, shaking his head sadly. "You sure about this?"

"Hey, I've been behind this oak for twenty-five years. I don't know a whore?" He had his shoulders hunched, his hands out Italian style.

"Did she leave with anyone, by any chance?"

"No way we put up with that crap in here. Probably came by for a rest. Besides, Sally was here," Jim said and pointed at a young macho sitting down the bar.

"Who's Sally?"

"Beat cop."

"Oh," Mac said and looked at Sally again. He was greasy as an olive factory and dressed like a wiseguy with a black shirt, black tie, and white loafers. Like a lot of cops, he was having trouble deciding which side he was on.

"He walks in, she walks out. That's how I knew for sure she's professional. Cops and hookers can smell each other from two blocks away." He put his elbows on the bar and leaned close to Mac so Sally couldn't hear. "I don't think she was working the streets anyway. She's not the type."

"I don't get it. I thought you said she *was* the type," Mac said.

"What I mean is this girl wasn't any street-corner hooker. She wouldn't come in just any bar and try to score. She was class, a real beauty. That type works only the top hotels," he said, shaking his head grandly at the inside stuff that he was passing off. Mac wasn't paying dime one for that. "I got a cousin works concierge at the Mark Hopkins," he went on. "He says it's like an amenity at those five-star joints. Tennis courts, fitness club, business center, and hookers. Those high-rolling executives pay three hundred a night, they expect fax machines, Nautilus equipment, and beautiful women along with their room service. Know what I mean?"

Mac nodded. "Got a guess on what hotel she might be working?" he said, getting to the question he wanted to ask.

"Hell, there's several of them. But I don't think you'll find her at any of them."

"Why not?" Mac asked.

"Because I think she was a circuit girl on her way out of town."

"Circuit girl? What the hell is a circuit girl?" Mac asked. He'd never heard the expression before. The bartender's face brightened and he started to back away. Sighing, Mac pulled out another fifty.

Jim picked the bill off the counter and palmed it. "The way my cousin tells it, they got a circuit," he said. "Week or two at one city, then off to the next. That keeps the heat down. By the time the cops get wise, they're gone."

"What cities are we talking about?" Mac asked as he reluctantly peeled off another fifty.

"The girls start off in San Diego, then go to Los Angeles, Bakersfield, San Francisco, then to Las Vegas." The bartender made a circle with his finger. "Then back to San Diego."

"Damn," Mac groaned to himself. That Uncola Man knew exactly what he was doing. He had Mac chasing this bitch all over hell. He had told Sean three times that it wouldn't surprise him if Gamboa himself was the Uncola Man, and Mac was chasing down these bullshit leads to keep him from doing some real investigation.

"What makes you think she was a circuit girl?"

"Just a hunch. She was on her way out of town."

"She didn't say where she was going?"

"Not exactly, but if she's on the circuit, her next stop would be Vegas. That would be my guess."

Mac shook his head and slid the bottle across the bar. "Thanks," he said. "Get me a double Wild Turkey this time, would ya?"

"On the house," Jim said and slapped a glass on the bar in front of Mac.

Mac tossed the drink down in one go. He was going to need a little painkiller if he was going to drive ten hours to Vegas. First he had to leave a message on Sean's recorder, though. Tell him he had a hot lead that Robin was in Vegas.

This wouldn't be so bad after all, he thought as he sipped a second whiskey. Vegas was his favorite place. He had about a grand left of the money Barrett had fronted him for expenses. He planned to do a little investigating and a lot of serious drinking and gambling. Make a vacation of it. Yeah, that's what he'd do. Maybe this Jamaican wasn't such a bad guy after all.

chapter

twenty-two

Knox pulled the Bronco in at the sheriff's substation, where Narco had its headquarters.

"Looks like there's something to what Barrett's been bugging us about," Gamboa said. "Berger's death confirms it for me. The Romero and Powers killings weren't any gay bashings. It all has to be connected somehow."

"Maybe, but I've got a feeling Berger was the last one who could help us," Knox said.

"What about the asshole who killed them?"

"Sure, if we can find him. The only lead we have is the names of a couple hundred inmates who were on the roof when Berger got it," Knox said as he motioned to the computer printout Gamboa was carrying. "It'll take us months to track them all down. Half of them are out on bail already."

"So what else we got?" Gamboa said.

Knox shrugged and got out of the car.

"Look at those dismissals, would you?" Gamboa said, pointing at Romero's rap sheet. "Ten, eleven, twelve, thirteen," he counted them off as they walked down the long hallway to the narcotics bureau. "Thirteen fucking dismissals."

"Looks like Romero was working with Narcotics, if you ask me," Knox said.

"No shit. Fourteen arrests and thirteen dismissals. That's got Narco's trademark all over it," Gamboa said and spat into a trash barrel as he went by. "Rutledge and his band of merry men. Jesus Christ! They dress like a bunch of gang-bangers and they smell worse. Take away their badges and they're as bad as half the pukes they arrest."

"Come on, Sarge. They're on our side," Knox reminded his partner. "They can't work the streets in three-piece suits."

Gamboa shook his head. "It's their priorities. They're all fucked up. They go undercover for a while, and pretty soon they don't know it's supposed to be an act."

The two of them pushed through a set of double doors marked NARCOTICS. They weaved their way through a long room of file cabinets and then into a larger room with several desks parked here and there.

In the far corner a group of men in civilian dress were gathered around a blackboard. A big, beefy man about Gamboa's age with dark olive skin and huge, hairy hands was banging on the blackboard with a piece of chalk. It looked like a football team going over plays, if Haight-Ashbury had a team.

"Rutledge is the worst of the bunch," Gamboa said to Knox, nodding toward the big man at the blackboard.

"I thought you liked Rutledge," Knox said.

"Like a case of herpes."

"Hey, gentlemen, look who's here," Rutledge said when he spotted Gamboa and Knox at the back of the room. "Well, if it isn't the 'Bash Brothers.' Violated anybody's civil rights lately, Gamboa?" Rutledge said.

"Still misplacing confiscated drug money, Rutledge?" Gamboa came back.

Sam Rutledge and Tom Gamboa had hated each other since the Academy. Not because they were so different but because they were so alike. Right out of the Academy, both of them would walk all over anyone to get a collar. Since they had become sergeants, the rivalry was even worse. Any chance to insult each other they took with pleasure. A couple of times it had actually come to blows.

"So what're you doing slumming in Narco?" Rutledge asked. It irked him that Gamboa's department got most of the flashy press. When Gamboa captured a murderer, he usually got his picture in the paper. Narcotics got some ink too, but it still didn't have the glamour of Homicide. It was a dirty business, and the sleazy clientele rubbed off on the department.

"I wanted to see what retirement's going to feel like," Gamboa jabbed.

"If you've come by to give us any tips, Gamboa, thanks anyway but we've already seen 'Singing in the Rain,'" Rutledge said.

The illegal questioning of Berger had obviously made it down to Narco already. Gamboa said, "Fuck you," through a clenched-toothed smile.

"And besides," Rutledge went on, "we don't need any contempt charges right now. We like to stay in business." That last crack drew a chuckle from his team. "You don't mind if we finish our briefing. We got a bust planned for tonight. I'd invite you along, but we're not planning on sending anyone to Emergency."

"What happened?" Gamboa shot back. "Your surveillance team find some eighty-year-old grandmother smoking weed to help her appetite?"

"Tell us all just one thing, would you?" Rutledge said. "How the hell can the district attorney prosecute someone for murder when his chief detective can't even find the fucking body?"

"Fuck you, Rutledge, you goddamn poor excuse for a hippie. Can't you guys at least look like cops?" Gamboa said as he walked by a young cop with a ponytail, talking with another cop wearing a fu manchu and jeans. "You guys not only look like shit, but you smell like it too."

"You should talk," Rutledge sneered. "I hear you do most of your investigating in cesspools these days."

Jesus! They'd heard about that episode down here too?

Gamboa walked up to Rutledge and stood eye to eye with him. They'd gone a round or two on more than one occasion. Knox, though, wanted to avoid any trouble. They needed Rutledge's help now, so Knox wedged himself between them.

"You know, Gamboa," Rutledge said, still looking over Knox's shoulder straight into Gamboa's eyes, "there would be nothing I would like better than to kick your ass again, but my crew and I have to be on the street in two hours."

"Look, Sergeant Rutledge, sorry about the interrupt," Knox said, trying as hard as he could to keep things calmed down. "We just came down to find out what you can tell us about a guy named Eddie Romero."

"I know he's dead," Rutledge said.

Gamboa showed Rutledge the rap sheet he'd been carrying. "Looks like he worked a few cases off for you guys," he said. "That right?"

"Yeah, we used him a few times. Followed regs on all of it," he said. Like all narcotics dicks, Rutledge was paranoid about scandal. Everybody knew there were drugs and money just lying around every time they made a bust. It was the easiest way to get corrupted in law enforcement.

"There a problem?" he said.

"Oh, no. Nothing like that," Knox said. "But this rap sheet shows he was arrested last month for possession of controlled subs. Was he working that case off?"

"He was, before someone got to him."

"Can we ask what he was doing for you?" Knox asked.

"Same thing they all do. Ratting out his connection. This time it was some brother by the name of Shabba St. James."

"Guess what, partner?" Gamboa said as he shoved a computer printout at Knox. "Shabba St. James was on the roof at County the night Berger got stuck."

"Jesus!" Knox said and slapped the sheet. "Let's go see what that asshole has to say."

"Too late, genius. His lawyer already bailed him out." Gamboa pointed at the notation next to the Jamaican's name. "Besides, I'm not in any rush to grab his ass anyway."

"Why not?"

"I want to check him out for a while. See who he's hanging around with. This guy's muscle. Let's see who does the thinking for him."

Knox nodded.

"Was Romero working a sting on this asshole for you?" Gamboa asked, turning to Rutledge.

"Nah. We wanted to set something up, but Romero refused. He was scared shitless of him."

"Maybe that's what this is all about," Knox said. "St. James suspected Romero was going to turn on him, so he kills him."

"Maybe," Rutledge said. "But he had no reason to believe Romero was working for us because Romero backed out. Besides, why kill the attorney too? That's just more trouble."

"Exactly," Gamboa said. "And why kill Berger? Nah, this thing's bigger than just some puke worried about one of his runners turning snitch." His voice trailed off. Then he looked at Knox. "Wait a second, college boy. Didn't Barrett tell you the shooter at Medtech was a big black man in cahoots with Romero?"

Knox nodded.

"Let's stake the son of a bitch out awhile. See what he's really up to."

With the mood a little more relaxed, Knox asked, "Sergeant, you think your boys can nose around for us a little and see what they say on the streets? Maybe help us locate St. James?"

Rutledge nodded. "I'll tell my boys to see what the street noise is. As far as St. James, he hangs out at the Fun Zone in Huntington Beach."

"I know the place," Knox said. "Thanks. Anything your boys can find out, we'd appreciate."

"Yeah," Gamboa said as they started out the door, "if they have any time between hits of coke."

"Anything for you, you know that, Gamboa," Rutledge shouted at Gamboa's back. "If I hear anything I'll be sure to call you at your office. Tucker Septic, isn't it?"

Knox could hear the room burst into loud har-har-hars. He grabbed Gamboa by the shoulder and pushed him through the door before Gamboa had a chance to say anything back.

chapter

twenty-three

After San Francisco, Mac's luck faded. He spent two days in Las Vegas, driving from casino to casino, chasing empty leads. He had been on the road nearly a week, and he was ready to go home. But first he wanted a good meal and a good night's sleep. And he didn't have much money for either.

He turned his rent-a-car into the Desert Sands casino. It was one of the old Vegas Strip hotels. The neon wasn't as bright, didn't dance with the same computerized brilliance of places like Circus Circus or the Flamingo. The cocktail waitresses weren't as young or enticing as they were at the Rio. The naugahyde was wearing thin. No high-rolling Arabs or celebrities hung around the baccarat table. No one played baccarat at the Desert Sands at all, in fact. Most of the floor of the casino had been given over to quarter slots with blue-rinse grandmothers pulling on their metal arms by the hour while their Winnebagos hogged four spots in the back parking lot.

Mac had met his ex-wife, Trudi, at Caesar's Palace. He had been sitting front row with a table of other cops, breaking every law they could, throwing money around like they were drug dealers. It was pure, unadulterated chemistry when their eyes met. After the last show he caught her coming out of the casino, and they went for drinks. Before the night was out, she was his prisoner, handcuffed to his bed, begging for mercy, which he gave her for a couple of hours before he finally fell asleep in her arms.

Those were the good days, the high-living days when he had Trudi and all that drug money. He'd drive out on 15 doing a hundred all the way, flashing his badge whenever a CHP pulled him over, then flat-out again until he could see the huge yellow glow in the desert and he'd get that feeling like he'd just snorted a mirror full. That's when life was good. He'd wheel into Vegas in his candy-colored Cadillac, a beautiful blond show girl waiting to go down on him all night. He always seemed to have a hot hand at the tables too. For three years he never felt his feet touch the pavement.

That all seemed like decades ago. Now his job was gone, the money gone, Trudi gone. He couldn't even afford the breakfast buffet at the Desert Sands anymore. The only thing good about the place was the crew boss, a guy named Pete Terwilliger. He was an ex-cop Mac had ridden with for a couple of years while he was with the Sheriff's Department. Terwilliger would usually comp him a meal or two and sometimes a room if it was slow.

When Mac walked in, Terwilliger was standing in the center of the blackjack tables, looking over the shoulder of one of his dealers. He had the dyed jet black pompadour and the mutton-chop sideburns like Elvis. He'd also put on thirty to forty pounds in the past few years like Elvis. And hadn't admitted it to himself yet either. He still wore his shirts cut as tight as he had on the force, so his ballooning belly threatened to rip the buttons off.

"Terwilliger," Mac said when he got up close.

"Hey, Mac, you old bastard," Terwilliger said, genuinely glad to see him. By now he could do without just about everyone. After twenty-two years on the force and a few years in Vegas, he figured everyone for an asshole just waiting for a decent opportunity to crap in his face. The only spark of any feeling he had left was for his old friends on the force like Mac.

"How's Trudi?" Terwilliger wanted to know and slapped Mac on the shoulder.

"I dumped the bloodsucking bitch," Mac said.

"So she finally took off, huh?"

Mac smiled at Terwilliger sheepishly. Might as well try to fool God as try to con Terwilliger.

"How much she get?"

"Everything."

"I coulda told you that the first night you two locked eyes. I knew she'd get those painted claws into you and you'd be history. You should have just signed over your house and car to her right then and there for two years' worth of blow jobs. Would have saved you a lot of time. That's all you ended up with anyway, right?"

Mac smiled, remembering.

"Jee-sus Kee-rist! Look at you! Busted down to nothing and you still get that look on your face when you think about her." Terwilliger shook his head. "So what the hell you doing here, old buddy?"

"Working."

"Working? You a salesman now or something?"

"P.I."

"Jumpin' dogshit! A P.I.? Why don't you just go rape your grandmother so you can sink all the way to the bottom?"

"What the hell else can I do?" Mac shrugged. "Become a junior executive?"

"Nah, I guess not. I'd give you a job here, but soon as they found out you got caught dirty, they'd throw us both out."

"Thanks anyway, Terwilliger. I'm all right."

"Sure ya are, Mac," Terwilliger said and put his arm on Mac's shoulder. "You eat yet? Of course not. Or you wouldn't have come by to see me, right?" He laughed. "Look, here's a meal ticket." He took a light green coupon out of his pocket and slipped it surreptitiously into Mac's pocket as if it were a packet of cocaine. "Go fill 'er up and I'll get you a room. How 'bout it? I know a couple of women worth knowing. I get off at nine or ten. We'll have a few drinks and trade 'em back and forth, if you still got the cojones for it. What do you say?"

"Hey, can't dance!" Mac said and headed for the buffet.

As soon as he grabbed the tray and started sliding it down the stainless steel tray rack, he began to get that old feeling back. Sure, the Desert Sands wasn't the Mirage with its caviar and Russian vodka, but who ate that crap anyway? The Sands had one of those great

Vegas buffets with food piled two feet high on a serviette a mile long. Every kind of salad he could think of—Waldorf and cole slaw and potato salad and Jell-O with the fruit and tiny marshmallows in it. Then came the soups—chile con carne and gumbo and french onion and three or four others. Then the casseroles and ragouts and three kinds of lasagna and carbonara this and that. Then the rice and potato dishes—mashed and baked and home-fried and ten other ways. Next were the meats. Piles of chicken wings and baby back ribs, Salisbury steak and pork chops and baby lobster tail and deep-fried shrimp.

Then came the dessert table, set off all by itself so he didn't have to get back in the main line again. Pies and cakes and tarts and ice creams and three flavors of Cool Whip—bowls and bowls of it. He could stay here all night and not try everything.

By the time Mac got to the end of the line, he had two plates piled in a pyramid with a bread basket clutched under his elbow. He took a seat where he could watch the blackjack tables and chowed down. No, it wasn't the Mirage, but it was still pretty darn close to paradise.

The bell captain dropped by Mac's table as he was digging into a pile of pastries. "Mr. Terwilliger asked me to give you your room key, sir. I hope you have a pleasant stay at the Desert Sands, Mr. MacDuff. Did you want your bags brought up?"

"Nah, that's fine."

"Yes, sir."

When he got through with dinner, he went out to his car and got his bag and took the elevator up to the top floor. When Mac opened the door of 830, the first thing he saw was a sweeping view of Vegas. The sun had just gone down, and the full lights of the town were starting to make their dazzling effect against the darkening sky. Mac stood at the door for a few seconds, stunned. It took him awhile to realize that this was a penthouse suite. When he'd swung the door open, he'd expected the dark, claustrophobic feeling of a tiny Vegas room meant only to sleep in.

But this room was enormous. It spread out in front of him for thirty feet and then dropped down a step and went on another thirty feet to plate glass windows that made up two entire walls of the room. There was a crystal and teakwood bar that ran the length of one window, stocked with rows and rows of liquor. For what this place cost a night, the management threw in the booze. Big, soft, over-stuffed couches were scattered around the room with glass tables and fancy vases and fake plants. Next to the bar was a slot machine.

Mac dropped his bag in the marble entryway and slowly walked toward the bay windows. Sliding open the glass door, he walked out onto the wraparound balcony. To his left the Strip and its famous hotels and casinos—the Flamingo, Bally's, Caesar's—spread out in front of him. Just across the street was the Mirage, its marble facade lit by a thousand spots, the long line of expensive cars serpentining to its covered entrance, while the valets ran around unloading and parking cars.

Mac went back inside and poured himself a Chivas and checked out the bedroom. In the master suite was an acre of bed covered with a crushed velvet crimson spread. Fantasy-breasted nudes lounged on the walls. The bathroom was bigger than his whole apartment in Capistrano, and everything, the walls, the floors, the ceiling, the clamshell-shaped sinks, the sunken Roman tub with the nymph fixtures, was jade-colored simulated marble. Even the toilet was jade with a green crushed velour seat cover and a green shag throw rug.

He put his scotch down on the marble sink, stripped off his clothes, stepped in the shower, and let the ten-gallon-a-minute flow work on his aching shoulders. As he stood there in the marble tub, he almost felt like Caesar again. That's what Trudi used to call him. She would climb into the shower with him. The water pouring over them made her breasts feel like satin against his chest. She'd reach out of the shower and take a big mouthful of champagne and kneel before him, and the cold, fizzing liquid in her mouth would set him straight again. He'd take her right there in the shower, her back pressed against the marble, her legs wrapped around his waist, drinking from the bottle of champagne while he drove into her, pouring it down his back and giggling, the endless flow of hot hotel water screaming from the shower head.

Terwilliger called at eight and said he'd be by at ten with a couple of girls. So Mac sat out on the balcony and drank half the bottle of scotch while he waited and dreamed of the old days.

It was nearly eleven before Terwilliger finally showed up with the girls. The one on his right arm was for him, he said, a black girl with very dark skin and a red wig. She looked exactly like an airport hooker Terwilliger used to bang for free when he worked LAX.

The girl on Terwilliger's left arm was for Mac, and he pushed her gently toward him.

"I thought you and Candy might get along," Terwilliger said and laughed. The girl was a dead ringer for Trudi, only she was younger and her hair was blonder and her chest was bigger. Mac got that old tingle in his stomach. As Candy slipped her hand around his waist, he knew he'd ascended into heaven again. And he never wanted to leave.

Terwilliger was in the penthouse living room when Mac woke up the next morning and stumbled out to the kitchen. The scotch was playing kettle drum in his skull. Candy was still sacked out in bed. Mac knew she'd be useless until two or three in the afternoon, and he had to get back to L.A.

"Mac," Terwilliger said. He was one of those people who was awake as soon as his eyes snapped open in the morning. Mac needed two or three cups of coffee or a stiff bloody mary before he was civilized enough for chatter.

"Are these the photos you were showing Candy last night?" Terwilliger asked, chipper as a born again. He was looking at the pictures of Robin and Chad from the stack of reports on the table.

"Yeah, the girl that disappeared may have been hooking, so I thought Candy might know her."

Mac poured a cup of coffee and plopped down on the couch next to him.

"Hey, I know this guy," Terwilliger cried.

Mac focused on the picture and realized he meant Chad.

"Jesus, Terwilliger! Hold on to your pecker, will ya? Of course you know this guy. He's been in every fucking paper from here to Las Cruces."

"No, not from the papers. This guy stayed at the hotel for a couple of weeks. That's why I remember him. Nobody stays at a Vegas strip hotel more than two or three days. You don't come out to this stinking desert for a fucking tan."

"Was he alone?" Mac asked, waking up quickly.

"No, he was with some woman."

Mac poked the picture of Robin with his finger. "That the woman?"

"Nah."

"I'll be damned! Curtis had another chick he was porkin'?" Mac said mostly to himself. His mind was spinning. If Curtis was two-timing Robin, this case was really a mess.

"Not unless he was a necrophiliac," Terwilliger said.

"What was that?"

"I said not unless he liked 'em dead. This woman was sixty-five, seventy."

"I don't get it."

"Hey, what's to get? A young guy comes down to a Vegas gambler's hotel for two weeks with his granny and he never gambles." Terwilliger laughed. "I think you got a client ain't coughin' up the whole truth and nothing but."

"No shit."

"I think I know who can help you, though," Terwilliger said. "One of our drivers named Felipe. Comes in about an hour from now. He spent most of his time while they were here chauffeuring them around. For a hundred a day these guys will take you up and down the strip. High rollers use 'em 'cause they think they know the best places to gamble."

After a gallon more of coffee, Mac went downstairs to talk to the driver. Felipe was a short Marielito Cuban with pants so tight his machismo was stuffed up into a tight wad halfway to his waist. He was polishing his metal-flake Continental when Mac walked up to him in front of the hotel.

"Felipe?"

The Cuban didn't say anything. He just looked Mac up and down, sized him up as a cop, and went back to polishing his car.

Mac knew there was only one way to open up a tough guy. He reached into his pocket and laid a fifty on the fender. Felipe kept shining and Mac put another fifty on top of the other bill. The driver picked them up and stuffed them in his pocket.

"What do you want to know?" he asked.

"This guy," Mac said, showing him the photo of Chad and Robin. "You recognize him?"

The Cuban looked at the photo a long time. When he spoke he was strictly business. "Early October. Here with his grandmother, I figure. Wasn't banging her, I know that. Either a straight business deal, no sex, or a relative. Probably both."

"Terwilliger said you drove them around town?"

"That's right. That's the interesting part! Want to hear it?"

Mac frowned and dug in his pocket again and pulled out two twenties.

"It's more interesting than that."

"It better be the fucking Encyclopedia Britannica," he said and fished out forty more.

"Usually I drop the customers off at a casino and either wait for them or pick them up at a designated time. Casino to casino, right?"

"Yeah," Mac said. "That ain't worth eighty."

The Cuban rolled his eyes. "But these two have me shuttle them from bank to bank."

"Banks? I don't get it."

"I don't know what they were doing exactly, but I can tell you, the old lady had a bundle of cash. I leaned over once and saw stacks of it in her bag."

"So they'd go in the bank together?"

"Only the old lady," Felipe said. "He'd wait in the car."

"What banks did you take them to?"

"That's another question," he said, grinning.

"Jesus, Felipe, you trying to take early retirement?"

"This is the information age, no? You wanna keep up with CNN, it's gonna cost you."

Mac pulled out another twenty.

"Bank of Laredo, Nevada National, and one other off the strip. I can't think of it right now. I'll get you the name later."

"Is that gonna cost me any more?"

Felipe gave him a hurt look. "Hey, I'm not greedy, man," he said in a bruised tone. "I'll throw it in for free."

chapter

twenty-four

Lowenstein had a simple strategy for the testimony portion of the trial. In order to prove to the jury that Robin was dead, he paraded before them forty-three friends, relatives, and business acquaintances who had had regular communication with Robin prior to her disappearance. All testified that they hadn't seen or heard from her since the kids had seen Chad slapping her on the beach.

By the time Lowenstein unearthed a cousin of Robin's who hadn't seen her in three years, Macklin stopped the procession.

"Mr. Lowenstein," he said at sidebar, "I think we've seen enough of Miss Penrose's family tree. Let's get on to your next party of guests."

"Yes, Your Honor," Lowenstein said and began calling the first of nineteen local California Highway Patrol officers, twelve Orange County sheriffs, and eight Newport Beach policemen who had all been on duty since Robin's disappearance. He asked them all the same series of questions, ending with "Have you had any contact with the missing girl or heard of anyone who had?" When they answered that they had not, as everyone in the courtroom knew they would, Lowenstein gave a satisfied "I see," and looked meaningfully at the jury. It was all stagey bunk, and Sean was hoping the jury could see that.

All the same, Sean faced an inescapable avalanche of amorphous, snowballing evidence that he couldn't escape. The girl was missing. No one had seen her since the night Chad Curtis had carried her off unconscious in a car he later ditched. Until Sean presented his defense, there was nothing he could refute, nothing he could conjure up that would spark a question in the minds of the jurors that collapsed the prosecutor's argument. All this tonnage, this weight of circumstantial evidence that the D.A. kept shoveling on witness by witness, hour by hour, day by day, was crushing the life out of his client.

When Lowenstein called a CHP officer from San Diego to the stand, Macklin halted the parade once again.

On the eighth full day of prosecution testimony Lowenstein finally called Tom Gamboa to the stand. He was wearing a dark brown tweed jacket with tan pants that didn't match. Gamboa had put on a few since he'd pulled the jacket off the rack at Sears eight years ago, and the shoulder seams were straining from the added bulk. The clerk swore him in, and he took his usual hunched posture in the witness box.

Gamboa testified for several hours about the Sheriff's Department's exhaustive state and nationwide search for Robin Penrose.

"Did you contact any city or county morgues to see whether a Robin Penrose or any Jane Doe matching the description of Robin Penrose had been admitted?" Lowenstein asked.

"Yes," Gamboa answered. "Our office contacted every coroner's office in the state of California and every state in the continental U.S. It took us over a week, and our finding was negative. None of those agencies had come in contact with a Robin Penrose or anyone matching her description."

"When you say anyone matching her description, what do you mean?" Lowenstein led him.

"Well, we gave every office a physical description of Miss Penrose. The description we gave was a female approximately twenty-seven years old, five feet eight, one hundred and twenty pounds, long blond hair, and a blood type of A positive. They did uncover several Jane Does who matched the general description, and we then had to forward them her dental records for a positive ID. Once the dental records were compared, it was ascertained that none of them were Miss Penrose."

Lowenstein approached the witness stand. "Sergeant, have you ascertained whether or not any person named Robin Penrose has been issued or renewed a driver's license since her disappearance?"

"Yes, we have. We contacted the Department of Motor Vehicles in every state to see if a driver's license had been issued to a Robin Penrose," Gamboa said.

He wasn't a bad actor really, Sean thought. He recited this re-hearsed testimony as though every question was a surprise.

"We also check almost daily the computer printout from the Department of Motor Vehicles for the state of California, which lists new or renewed driver's license applications."

"And what were your findings?"

"Negative," Gamboa said without a gesture. "A new or renewed driver's license has not been issued to a Robin Penrose in any of the fifty states since she disappeared."

Lowenstein raised his eyebrows as if it were news. "And you say you review the records almost daily?" he asked.

"Yes, in fact, I just obtained a new printout before I came to court this afternoon. I can show the court if you want," Gamboa said and reached into a file he had brought along.

"I think that would be very instructive for the jury."

On and on it went. Gamboa testified that he had spoken to a long list of Robin's closest friends and relatives and contacted every hospital in the state in an attempt to find her. It was a long, exhaustive attempt to prove to the jury that there wasn't a trace of Robin Penrose. By the time Lowenstein had finished questioning Gamboa, it was late afternoon.

When Lowenstein finally sat down, Macklin looked up at the clock. It was almost four. "Do you want to cross-examine, Counsel?" he said to Sean. "Or hold it for tomorrow?"

"Yes, Your Honor, I would," Sean said. "Since we've already gone over every minute of Sergeant Gamboa's life since the girl disappeared, there won't be much left to do."

Macklin smiled, showing most of his smoke-stained teeth. "Well, thank God for that," he said, and this time even a couple of the jury members laughed.

Sean slowly pulled himself out of his chair. There was nothing really concrete in all this testimony that he could chip away at in cross to raise a reasonable doubt in a juror's mind. How do you fight a witness that testifies to what he hasn't seen? But Sean thought he noticed a fundamental weakness in the way Lowenstein had asked his questions that opened the door for other questions.

"Now, Mr. Gamboa," Sean said as he approached the detective, "the essence of your testimony is that you contacted all these agencies to verify if any of them had contact with Robin Penrose and none of them had. Is that correct?"

"That's correct."

"You testified you contacted every morgue?" Sean asked and started picking up the pace of his questions. He didn't want Gamboa to do a lot of reflecting as he led him along.

"Yes."

"Every hospital?"

"Yes."

"Every jail?"

"Yes."

"The Department of Motor Vehicles?"

"Yes."

"And many other government agencies?"

"Yes."

Sean retrieved a stapled document from the table and walked back to Gamboa. "Now, I wonder if you'd tell us why you contacted all of these morgues," he said and fanned the stack of papers.

Gamboa stared at Sean a moment. He knew that tone Barrett got when he was heading toward an execution. "We wanted to know if any of them had received Robin Penrose or anyone who matched her description," Gamboa said.

"And none of them had?"

The detective hesitated again. It was the same instinct that made him pause before a door when he didn't know what was on the other side. "That's right."

"So when you contacted these morgues you were looking for a dead person?"

Gamboa's face took on an imperceptible smile. "That's all you find there."

Sean gave him back the little smile. "You certainly weren't contacting these morgues about Robin Penrose to see if she were alive, were you?" Sean said and looked over his shoulder at the jury. He could see they were curious too.

"No," the detective said.

"So the fact that you didn't find her at any of these morgues only proves she wasn't dead?"

"It proves she wasn't in a morgue."

Sean looked up at Macklin and gave a disgusted look.

"Come on, Sergeant," Macklin said. "You know the routine here. Keep the answers yes and no, unless you're asked for more."

"Thank you, Your Honor," Sean said and turned back to Gamboa. "So she could easily be alive and not at one of those morgues?"

Gamboa didn't answer, so Macklin nudged him. "Sergeant Gamboa?"

"Yeah, I guess so," he said irritably.

"And when you contacted the hospitals that you and Mr. Lowenstein so laboriously listed, you were trying to find out if Robin Penrose had been admitted either sick or injured. Is that right?"

"Yes," Gamboa said weakly. He didn't bother to fight it anymore. He could see Barrett was going to get his score. Lowenstein was signaling him with a razor to his throat that he was killing them. Seventy-five witnesses about to be shot to hell.

"So if Robin was not sick or injured, you wouldn't expect to find her there, would you?"

"No," Gamboa said, narrowing his eyes. His face was turning the purple hue that was Sean's favorite.

"And the fact that the Department of Motor Vehicles has not received any information concerning Robin Penrose in the last few months does not mean she isn't alive and well and driving in California or any other state in the union, does it?"

"It means the DMV has had no contact with her," Gamboa said.

"Well, if I told you I hadn't applied for a license or received a ticket in the last four months, would that surprise you?"

"I've been on the force twenty-six years, Counselor," Gamboa said. "Nothing surprises me."

"No, I guess not," Sean said. "But as a matter of fact, it's probably not unusual for someone to have no contact at all with the DMV for months."

"I wouldn't know." Gamboa wasn't going to give anything for free.

"Well, let's see what you do know, Sergeant Gamboa," Sean said loudly. He stood close to the witness and started a rapid-tempo battering of the cop's testimony. "The fact that she wasn't found at the morgue only means she wasn't found dead. Isn't that right?"

"I guess so," Gamboa admitted.

"And the fact you couldn't find her in a hospital does not mean she isn't alive."

"Yes."

"Or in a jail?"

"Yes."

"And the fact she has had no contact with DMV since she disappeared does not mean she is not alive, does it, Sergeant Gamboa?"

"No."

"Fine," Sean said and walked a step closer. "Now let me ask you one more question, Sergeant. Except in the line of duty, have you been admitted to a hospital, been incarcerated, or applied for a license or even been given a ticket in the last four months?"

Gamboa took a long time before he answered. The gallery was whispering. Macklin picked up his gavel and gave a stern look at the back of the room. The place quieted.

"Sergeant Gamboa?" the judge asked.

"No, I don't think I have."

"Thank you, Sergeant. I have nothing further," said Sean and turned his back to the witness and walked to the defense table.

Several reporters slipped out the door to get a head start on the phones.

"All right," Macklin said and looked up at the clock. It was 4:45. "Since no one around here gets time and a half, let's call it a day, shall we?" And he gaveled the court dismissed.

Sean stood up and blew a sigh of relief. The long parade of witnesses who had testified they hadn't seen or heard from Robin since that day at the beach was finally over. Next would come the eyewitnesses—the kids and the man who had ditched Robin's car among them. They were a different kind of problem—witnesses who were going to testify that they'd actually seen his client engaged in suspicious acts to which, frankly, he had no logical explanation. Sean could only try to find holes in the eyewitnesses' own logic and question their credibility.

Sean talked to the reporters in the hallway and let the photographers get their shots. Then he did a TV interview. He knew they had a job that fed their families, so he did his best to give them what they needed. He tried to talk with them a little every day to satisfy them, and the strategy was working. No one was calling him at home, stopping him in front of the jail, or dogging him around town.

Gamboa was at the end of the hall waiting for him when they finally let him go. "Barrett, I need to talk to you," he said. His voice had an almost polite ring that caught Sean off guard.

"Yeah, I wanted to talk to you too," he said. "What have you found out about Scott's murder?"

"About the same."

"What does that mean?" Sean said. It came out a little louder than he'd intended in the echoing hall. He looked around and lowered his voice. "I told Knox who killed him."

"You told him Powers was staking out Romero's," Gamboa said flatly.

"And that whoever killed the guard at Medtech probably killed Scott and Romero."

Gamboa frowned. "We don't know that for a fact."

"What the hell do you want?"

"I want to go into court with something besides my dick in my hand, so shysters like you don't blow me out of the water in prelim." Gamboa poked Sean's chest lightly with a finger. "First of all, hotshot, we need a suspect. A big black guy," he said, repeating the description Sean had given Knox, "narrows the suspects down to a half a million brothers."

"If you didn't spend all your time looking for bodies that don't exist, maybe you'd have some time to investigate who killed Scott," Sean shouted. The reporters at the end of the hall were staring now.

"I need to know more about what Berger told you," Gamboa said.

"That's confidential. You know that," Sean said. Because he had been furious that his friend was so savagely butchered, he'd probably told Knox a little more than he should have at the morgue that day. He was chest to chest with Gamboa now, a new briefcase that Carrie had given him hanging in his left hand, his right pointing in the detective's face. "Berger's my client again."

Gamboa's eyes narrowed. He realized Barrett hadn't heard yet about Berger getting it on the rooftop. After what Sean had just done to him in the courtroom, he was going to enjoy this. "Look, Barrett, you can forget about protecting Berger's rights now. He's a fucking corpse."

The air went out of Sean suddenly as if Gamboa had punched him in the gut. "What are you talking about?"

"I saw him on a slab at County Morgue."

"Jesus! What happened?" Sean asked.

"A blade in the back. Bled to death on the roof of the jail."

"You mean to tell me that the guy was murdered *in the jail* in front of, what, fifty guards? Jesus Christ!" Sean was shouting again. "Somebody pops one of his accomplices *and* his lawyer. Didn't it occur to you that maybe he might go after the only other witness?"

Gamboa stared at Sean, fuming.

"You're telling me that you've got no idea who did it?" Sean said.

"It's ongoing," Gamboa said, using the expression a cop employed to mean that's all he was going to say.

"Ongoing, my ass. This black s.o.b. is running around Orange County killing everybody in his way, and you're standing around with your finger up your butt."

Gamboa stuck his nose up next to Sean's and said in a low, mean growl, "We know his name is Shabba St. James."

"I can't believe it, Gamboa," Sean said sarcastically. "You actually have been doing something besides swimming in cesspools."

"Fuck you, you shyster asshole!" Gamboa cried.

"Now that you have his name, I wonder how much longer it's going to take you to pick him up."

Gamboa noticed the reporters were in full gallop now, heading toward them. The kliegs were on and the red indicators on the mini-cams were winking. Sean looked back over his shoulder at the stampede.

"I guess I have to do your goddamn job for you, Gamboa!" he said as he pushed through the glass door and trotted out to his car.

Gamboa stepped through the door after him and yelled, "Just stay out of it, Barrett!" But Sean didn't hear him.

He yanked open the door of the SL. It needed oiling and made a terrible creaking sound of rusted metal. He threw the briefcase down on the passenger seat, yanked his coat off so it came off inside out, and tossed it over the seat into the back. The tie was jammed in one of the coat pockets.

He was tired of waiting for Gamboa to arrest Scott's killer. And now Berger was dead. He turned onto the 405 and pushed the old car up to seventy-five. He had some Xeroxed descriptions of Shabba left from the last time he'd tried to find him and a stack of twenties in his briefcase that was supposed to be for Mac. He was going to spread some of that cash around and find the killer. Then he was going to call Gamboa and tell him to get his fat ass down there fast and arrest him.

He took the Magnolia off-ramp and drove west until he got to the beach. The sun had set and the garish lights of the Fun Zone blazed against the darkening sky. Already the Ferris wheel was spinning, lit up by long spokes of red and white neon, and he heard screams coming from the plummeting roller coaster.

He parked down the street from the place and grabbed the briefcase. He planned to charge in there, throw the twenties around, and flush the asshole out.

He started talking to anyone in gang colors, and if they gave any hint at all that they wanted to help, he peeled off a twenty. In a half hour he'd found out that Shabba hung around with a seven-foot Sudanese named Hoops. He could smell the break coming. That's what Mac always said. It was something like that whiff of gun metal an old cop'll smell right before a suspect pulls a pistol on him.

He scoured the park for another half hour before he felt a hand the size of a baseball glove on his shoulder. Sean turned and found himself looking at a man's belly. He leaned his head back and looked up another foot and a half until he was staring into the blackest face he'd ever seen.

"Shabba looking for you," Hoops said.

"Good, I'm looking for him," Sean shot back. A ripple of fear tickled his stomach, but he wasn't about to let on. He followed the tall one to the storage and maintenance areas at the back of the amusement park. The bright lights were behind them. In the shadows of the buildings it was black.

"Hey, mon," he heard someone say, and Hoops pushed him through an open gate and blocked it off behind him.

"Come right in, Mr. Barrett. Ha! Ha! Ha!" someone laughed in the dark. Sean knew that laugh. It was the Jamaican, the guy who had been phoning him. That's when he knew—somehow the Jamaican was involved in both cases.

"You're the asshole that's been calling about Robin Penrose," Sean said.

"Dat's right," the Jamaican said and stepped out of the shadows.

The first thing Sean noticed was how wide he was—shoulders the width of a team in a three-legged race. He had light green eyes that shone in the moonlight, and he was wearing a dark, expensive suit with an embroidered tie. The Jamaican stood with one hand behind his back, and when he brought the hand around, it was holding a machete.

Sean realized in that moment how Scott had died. He remembered the way his head and belly had looked. Not sliced but hacked open. The Jamaican saw Sean staring at the blade.

"You like my maw-che-tay! Back home we use it for everything. Open dee coconut, chop dee cane, clean dee teeth." He raised it effortlessly like a toothpick to his mouth and grinned. "Good for gettin' rid of pests too," he said. "Dee cock-a-roach, dee blackmouth snake. Those are dee nasty one, mon. Come crawlin' in dee night."

Sean took a step back, his eyes dancing, looking for a way out.

The Jamaican smiled. "Nosy white boys. Dat's dee other pest we don't like. Dey burn dee cane fields twice a year, and dey always find a couple bodies. Most of 'em nosy white boys," the Jamaican said and laughed. Then suddenly he whipped his arms around.

The machete swished through the air, the lights of the Ferris wheel reflecting against the blade. Lurching back, Sean instinctively held the briefcase up like a shield. The heavy blade chopped it in two. Twenties flew out of the rent halves, the green flutter of money catching the Jamaican's eye for an instant. Sean flung the two halves of the case into his face just as the Jamaican slashed again. The blade sliced into the post next to Sean's ear, a salvo of wood chips and sawdust spraying across his face.

Sean dived, rolled once, and was up on his feet running down a fenced alley behind the building. The chain-link fence was ten feet high with razor wire along the top. Hoops stayed behind at the corner of the building and watched the chase. Sean took his shoes off and put them on his hands. Holding them in front of him, he started shouting for help as the Jamaican kept coming at him. Shabba stopped and began to laugh, "Ha! Ha! Ha!" That same corrosive laugh Sean had heard so many times on the phone. Shabba held the machete pointing up at the night and put the finger of his other hand to his ear as if to say, "Listen!"

Sean stopped, and he heard the hundreds of screaming voices all around, pouring unheeded into the night. A volley of screams followed every drop of the roller coaster, every time somebody won a stuffed animal, just kids screaming bloody murder for the fun of it.

All Sean had now was the shoes, and he knew from what the machete had done to the briefcase that one swipe would cut through both hands effortlessly. Sean dropped the shoes. Now all that was left was begging.

Shabba advanced, and Sean backed against the corrugated metal building. The blade flashed and sliced across his belly, the shirt cut open, blood beginning to seep from the cut. He looked up at Shabba and saw his big smile spreading.

"Fuck you, you son of a bitch!" was the last thing Sean shouted before Hoops stepped around the corner and yelled, "Cops!" and took off running.

Shabba raised the machete high above Sean's head. Then there was an explosion of blood out of the Jamaican's chest, and he fell on top of Sean with a heavy thud, the machete clanging along the pavement beside Sean's head.

Seconds later Gamboa came running toward them, his .38 held at his side. He rolled the Jamaican off Sean. "There's an ambulance en route," Gamboa said. "You gonna make it?"

Sean got up to his knees and took his hand off his belly. "He just cut the skin a little," Sean said, then looked at Shabba. "Is he dead?"

"Nah, but he probably will be if they don't plug him up pretty soon."

"Try to keep him alive. I've got a lot of questions I want to ask him." Then he looked at Gamboa. "What the hell are you doing here?"

"I had Knox stake him out. He radioed me as soon as you showed up here and did everything but challenge the asshole to a duel."

"You mean you were here the whole time?" Sean said. His mouth was open, his eyes disbelieving.

"Just on the other side of the parking lot," Gamboa said, pointing over his shoulder with his thumb.

"And you let him do this?" Sean said and lifted his hand off his belly. "Why didn't you just arrest him?"

"All we had was a bunch of circumstantial evidence. Any shyster could have had him out in fifteen minutes. You should know that, Barrett."

"But he almost killed me!" Sean cried.

"Quit whining, Barrett. It's only a fucking scratch." Gamboa grinned. "But I do want to thank you because now we can charge him with your attempted murder. That'll keep him in custody until we can get enough to nail him for the other murders."

"Yeah, if he lives long enough."

Knox came trotting around the corner just then. "You all right?" he said.

Sean nodded.

"The ambulance just pulled up," Knox said, pointing over his shoulder.

"Did you get the other guy?" Gamboa asked.

"No, he's got this place wired for sound," Knox said. "Knows every way in and out. But we know where he eats, sleeps, and plays. We'll get him."

Sean pushed past Gamboa and Knox without saying anything.

"What's up his ass?" Knox asked as Sean stomped off. He noticed then that Barrett wasn't wearing any shoes.

"Ah, he's pissed because we let the Jamaican get a swing at him."

"Yeah, well, that's his own damn fault for sticking his nose in our business," Knox said.

"Yeah, but I'll say one thing about Barrett. He's got cojones the size of a cantaloupe," Gamboa said, laughing. "He knew the way Powers and Romero bought it, and he came wading in here with just his goddamn briefcase." He nodded over to where the two halves of the briefcase lay on the pavement next to some blood spatters.

"Yeah, he's got balls, all right," Knox said. "Or he's the dumbest son of a bitch I ever met."

"Probably both," Gamboa said and slapped his partner on the shoulder.

chapter

twenty-five

After the ambulance attendant bandaged him, Sean drove home. When he arrived, Mac and Carrie were already in his living room waiting for him.

"What happened to you?" she said when she saw his bloodied shirt and pants.

"Nothing much," he said and opened his shirt to show the bandage. "I ran into our Jamaican friend, and he tried to shave me with his machete."

"The Jamaican," Mac said. "He do that? Goddammit, Sean! I told you he wasn't right."

"He's the one who killed Scott and Romero and probably Berger."

"Berger get it too?" Mac asked.

Sean nodded.

"God, and you went after him?" Carrie said. She had her arm around his back. "That was foolish, Sean."

"How'd you know he was the Jamaican?" Mac asked.

"I didn't until he opened his mouth."

"Oh," Mac said and nodded over at Sean's belly. "How'd he do that?"

"Same way he got Scott," Sean said. "With a machete." He shook his head at his own stupidity. "Gamboa showed up just as he was going to finish the job."

Carrie sank onto the old divan, put her face in her hands, and began to cry. Mac looked over at her, a little surprised.

Sean held Carrie for a long time, and Mac wandered out onto the deck. When she finally pulled herself together, she kissed Sean and went into the kitchen.

Sean walked out to Mac and pulled the glass door shut behind him. A half-moon hung only a few fingers above the horizon.

"What did you find out in Vegas?" he asked.

Mac turned around. "Zero on the Penrose girl. But I think Chad was up to something," he said. Then he filled Sean in on what the people at the Desert Sands had told him about Chad and the old lady.

"He's sure it was Chad?" Sean asked.

"Hey, Terwilliger's not a window washer. He's an ex-cop," Mac said. "Trust me, it was Chad."

"When did he say he'd seen him?"

"Two or three weeks before Robin disappeared," Mac said. "I'm telling you, Sean, our choirboy was up to something and it wasn't legal. I can smell it. I think you need to talk to Curtis again and ask him what he was doing in Vegas with Grandma Moses driving from bank to bank with a handbag full of dough."

Sean looked out at the ocean. The waves were breaking roughly that evening. They rolled in out of the dark unseen, and suddenly there they were, like a fully developed idea, their heads reared back, ready to collapse onto the shore. Maybe Vegas was what Chad had been hiding the whole time.

"I've got an idea," Sean said.

"Good. 'Cause I don't know where to go from here. Unless you can get Curtis to start coughing up the truth."

Sean shook his head at the prospect. He'd been hammering away at Chad for over a month, and all he got was the same old story.

"Look," he said, "I had a client once who was arrested for embezzling eight million dollars from his firm and fleeing the country. He was in Chile for *fifteen years* before the insurance company tracked him down." He put his hand on Mac's sleeve. "You know how they found him?"

Mac belched a beery burp. "Sherlock Holmes came out of retirement?"

Sean ignored the crack. "They computer-aged a photo of him, passed it around, and somebody recognized him."

Mac shook his head. "You've lost me, Counselor."

"Take that picture of Robin down to one of your buddies at the Sheriff's Department and have him age it about thirty years," Sean said. "Can you do that?"

"Sure, I can get that done. But what are you telling me? You think that old lady was our girl?"

"Why not? It makes as much sense as anything else about this case," Sean said. "If Chad and Robin had some kind of scam going, then it all makes a lot more sense."

Mac turned around and rested his butt on the deck rail. "You're reaching on this one. You know that, Sean."

"Why?" Sean said, throwing his palms out. "Robin was an actress. Did impersonations. Was a makeup artist. She could pull that off easily. Besides, what else have we got? Take it down to the lab. Have them age the photo. Then get back to Vegas and see who recognizes it."

Sean could see a frown growing on Mac's face.

"Now, listen to me," Sean said. "First, go back to the Desert Sands and then to the banks that the shuttle driver took them to, and show the photo to anyone you can get to talk to you. Maybe now we can find out what they were up to."

"That all sounds great, Sean, *if*," Mac said, poking his palm with a finger, "*if* Robin turns out to be the old lady in disguise. And *if* the aged photo looks like the old lady the shuttle driver took to the bank. And *if* one of the bank employees recognizes the photo. Jee-sus, are we that desperate?"

Sean shrugged. "We can't take anything for granted. We need this as fast as you can do it, and we need to stay in constant touch just in case. We're coming down to the finish line here. So if I need to get ahold of you and I can't get you at the hotel, I'll leave a message on my answering machine. I want you to call every day and listen for messages. All right?"

"Yeah, no problem. I'll use the remote," Mac said. "But, look, I've been on the road a long time. I need a few more bucks."

"How much?" Sean asked, thinking about the two thousand he'd already lost when Shabba destroyed his new briefcase.

"Hell, I don't know," Mac said, fishing. "Three or four thousand should handle it."

"Come on, Mac! Three or four thousand? What the hell for?"

"I'm not saying I'll need it. But it usually takes a few bucks to get someone to open up to you, and half the time what they know isn't worth a shit. The problem is, the money's already in their pocket. And it would be nice, Barrett, if I could have a decent meal and a place to stay. That asking too much? I'll bring back what I don't use," Mac said, knowing he intended to spend every dime.

"Yeah, well, I know what you're like in Vegas," Sean said as he walked into his bedroom. He returned a moment later and handed Mac an envelope with three thousand dollars in twenties.

"That's all the cash I have left," Sean said. "It will have to do. Just make sure you give me back what you don't use. I don't know how I'm going to get Macklin to reimburse me for half of what I've given you already."

"Hey, no problem," Mac said. He counted the money quickly and put the envelope into his inside coat pocket.

"When can you leave?" Sean asked. They'd gone back into the living room, and Mac was finishing off another beer.

"Jesus, Barrett! I just got here. Gimme a break."

Sean shrugged. "Mac, you come up with information like this, what do you want me to do? Sit back and watch the tide come in?"

"Yeah, all right." Mac shook his head and picked his coat off the divan. "I'll go to my place and change, and I'll be back on the road in an hour. That soon enough for you?"

"Thanks, Mac," Sean said and patted his shoulder as he started out the door. "Call me as soon as you come up with anything else."

Mac turned around when he got to the step. "You gonna be safe here? You know that cane cutter is just somebody's muscle. The guy that's calling the shots is still out there." He raised his eyebrows to

Sean. "He had the Jamaican kill everybody involved with the guard's shooting, and now you got him hooked up with Robin's disappearance. Say," Mac said, his face brightening, "do you suppose that really could have been the Jamaican with her in Bakersfield?"

"I don't know. I wouldn't be surprised," Sean said. "We'll probably find that out when Gamboa questions him." He shook his head. "Of course, he might have killed her too."

Mac lowered his voice so Carrie couldn't hear. "Button it up, Barrett. Bullets can go through you too. You're only fucking Superman in the courtroom, you know."

"Yeah, I know," Sean laughed.

"At least keep her away from here," Mac said, nodding his head toward the kitchen. "I'd hate to see that pretty face of hers messed up."

Sean hadn't thought of that. Of course, when he lost his temper he usually forgot everything. Now that he was back here licking his wounds, he was shocked at his own stupidity. Trying to corner a killer like Shabba. What the hell had he thought was going to happen?

Mac turned and Sean shut the door behind him.

Carrie drew close to him and they held each other. "Promise me you won't do anything that stupid again," she said with her face against his chest.

"You mean like face down a machete with a briefcase?"

"That's exactly what I mean."

"You've got my solemn promise."

A few minutes later Mac barged back through the front door, walked up to Sean, and threw a yellow parking citation down in front of him. "God damn it, Barrett," he said. "You and your fucking surfer boy office is costing me a bundle. I'm going to have to use all the fucking money you gave me just to pay for all the damn parking tickets I get every time I come here."

"All right, all right!" Sean growled back. "I'll take care of it. Give me the damn thing."

"That's great," Mac said. "Why don't you take care of these too while you're at it? I think a couple might be in warrant status by now." And he dropped a stack of violations on Sean's desk and rushed out.

———

Sean lay awake in bed that night for some time, while Carrie dozed. A hurricane near the Hawaiian Islands had kicked up the ocean, and ten-foot waves boomed outside the cottage.

He was thirty-three years old. First had come college, then law school, then right into practice. He had never had time for a relationship like this one. He was just too busy. How could he average fourteen hours a day in his practice and have any time or anything left for a woman? Except, of course, for the most casual of romances. Marriage and kids were ridiculous to even consider now. Maybe in three, four, five years. That had been his plan anyway. Then Carrie had come along, and right away she had answered a lot of questions he didn't know existed.

They both woke just before dawn and decided to go for a walk on the beach. The tide had ebbed, and the sand was cold on their bare feet.

"I wish I knew what this Jamaican has to do with all this. You never heard Robin mention the guy?" Sean asked.

"Not even anybody resembling him. Maybe he's one of the crowd she hung around with in Hollywood."

"I guess that's a possibility. But why's the guy going around killing anyone who has anything to do with the Berger case?"

They strolled silently hand in hand down the beach toward the pier. "Do you really think that was Robin with him in Bakersfield?" she finally asked.

"Who else could it have been? He tells me where I can find her and, bingo, there she is."

"Or someone who looks enough like her to fool you," Carrie said. "Remember, you've never seen Robin in person. So all you can go by is her photos. You can't be certain that was her."

"I know."

They watched a gull come squawking down the beach and land on a huddle of rocks. She turned to him. "Another thing, why would Robin go along with it, and why would she let Chad stand trial for her murder? None of it sounds like Robin."

"Maybe not the Robin you knew as a kid, but it does sound like someone Gregory Pope told me about."

"You don't trust that creep, do you? It wouldn't surprise me if he has something to do with all this."

Sean shook his head. "I don't think so, Carrie. I mean, nothing would surprise me, but I think Pope honestly loved Robin in his own demented way."

She moved closer to him to protect her face from the wind, which was growing stronger by the minute. "So where does that leave us?" she asked.

"I don't know about us. But it leaves Robin in some very deep trouble. If she isn't dead already, she may be soon. Every person Shabba came in contact with has ended up on a slab."

Carrie shivered in the cold wind. "But what could they have in common? What's the link between Robin and Berger's death?"

"I don't know." He stopped walking and turned to her. She was beautiful in the half-light of dawn. "Maybe it wasn't Shabba and Robin I saw in Bakersfield. Maybe it was a lookalike."

"You don't believe that."

"No. But I hate to think of the alternative."

They walked for another hour. He'd never been so confused, so frustrated, so stumped by a case. He doubted everything and everyone, including his own abilities. He put his arm around Carrie and they strolled in step down the beach. They walked a long distance without talking. The clouds were black and the waves were gray and fast and windblown. The gulls were beginning to take cover.

Sean stopped and turned to Carrie, and she smiled. When he kissed her, the warmth of her face sheltered him from the bite of the wind. Despite all his doubts, he knew he only had to have his arms around her to feel at ease. Surrounded by a swirl of doubts and self-doubts, of uncertainties and suspicions, the one thing that he could be certain of was Carrie.

chapter

twenty-six

Lowenstein planned to finish with a one-two-three combination that would floor Sean's client. He was going to put the kids, Todd and Nicole, up on the stand to tell the jury how Chad had beaten Robin that night. Then he would bring up Frank Johnson, who said he had ditched Robin's car at Chad's request. If there was an attorney in America who could explain Johnson's testimony in Chad's favor, he'd like to meet him. Then Lowenstein planned to bring Robin's weeping mother on as the coup de grace, make sure the jury knew that Robin was somebody's daughter, that her mother wept for her nightly and cursed the day she'd ever heard the name Chad Curtis.

"Call Todd Grant to the stand," Lowenstein announced.

"Todd Grant," the bailiff called out.

"Here," the kid said as if at roll call and got up quickly from his seat next to his mother in the second row of the gallery. He was dressed much the way he had been the night Robin disappeared. Cords, loafers, no socks, and a Hang Ten inside-out shirt. He excused his way past the knees of the three men between him and the aisle. His whole body was shaking as he walked to the witness box.

Lowenstein was in a burgundy suit with another smutty two-hundred-dollar tie. This one had naked Grecian golden boys and girls running amok on its gray silk. He stayed at the lectern as he questioned Todd, taking a lot of time to have the boy describe with as much detail as he could the condition of the murder victim as she appeared to him from his perch at the beach.

"I thought she was dead," the kid finally told the court.

"Thank you. I have nothing further," Lowenstein said, and he left the boy in the stand watching his back until he sat down. Todd looked around the court, then back at the judge, waiting for some signal of what he was supposed to do next. When Sean stood up for his cross-exam, Todd's eyes immediately went to him. This compliant lost look worried Sean. Todd wasn't a smart-ass gang type. The jury knew that everything he'd described at the beach was told without lies. Sean could only hope to make the jury think, and maybe even the witness by the time he was through, that perhaps he hadn't seen what he thought he had. Sean knew he had to be careful, though. Todd was a decent kid. He dressed like their sons, talked like their sons, took a girl to the beach like their sons. If Sean attacked Todd too harshly, he would be harassing a defenseless young boy only there to do his civic duty.

The minute hand on the old school clock fell the final click straight down to 3:30 as Sean began cross-examining the kid.

"Mr. Grant. Or would you prefer I call you Todd?" Sean said as he approached the stand.

"Todd's fine," the kid said, too nervous not to smile at the idea of being called Mister.

"All right, Todd," Sean said in a friendly manner. "You said this girl looked dead to you."

"Yes."

"How old are you, son?"

"Almost seventeen. Sixteen really until next month."

"And you're in high school?"

"Yes."

"So you haven't made it to med school yet," Sean said, smiling. Todd just gave a little chuckle in reply.

Macklin leaned forward. "Son," he said, "you're going to have to answer the questions even if they seem funny to you."

Sean could tell by the way the judge addressed the kid that even he liked him.

"No," he said. "I'm just in high school. Sorry."

"That's all right, Todd," Sean said. "I was just wondering, if you haven't been to medical school, how did you know she was dead?" It was the first assault on the veracity of the kid's story, and the jury leaned in to hear more. So far Sean was doing well. But he had to be careful. If Todd broke down and started bawling on the stand, the cross-examination would be disastrous. The jury wouldn't hear a thing. All they'd see was their son up there being bullied by this big-shot attorney.

"Then why did you think she was dead?"

Todd began to stutter. "I-I don't know," he said. "She wasn't . . . you know. She wasn't moving."

"Well, she could have been asleep or passed out, couldn't she?"

"I guess so, yeah."

That's as far as Sean dared to take it without completely embarrassing Todd. He'd made the point that when it came to corpses, the kid didn't know what he was talking about. It was time to move on.

"Now, when you saw her walking before that," Sean said, starting off in another direction, "was there anything unusual about her walk?"

"She seemed okay, I guess."

"I see," Sean said. The kid had forgotten his written statement to the police that the girl appeared drunk to him. This happened sometimes. The witness was just so nervous, he'd forgotten. "Now, Todd, you understand that it's very important that you make sure of every detail of your testimony here today."

"Yes, sir," he said, shaking his head earnestly.

"I realize it's been a while since that night, so perhaps we can help you remember. Okay?"

"Sure," he said.

Sean went back to the defense table and picked up a transcript. When he came back, he placed it on the railing of the witness box. The kid wiped his sweaty hands on his pants before he picked it up.

"Now, Todd, please read to yourself page three, the second paragraph."

Todd looked down at the manuscript. Every so often he put his finger on the page, and his lips moved as his eyes shifted along the print. When he was through, he looked up. "I'm done," he said.

"Good," Sean said, taking the transcript back from Todd. "Now, does that refresh your memory about how the girl was walking that night?"

"Yes," Todd said, shaking his head. "I guess I said she was sort of stumbling a little."

Sean needed something more definite than that, and he led the boy there. "Have you ever seen any of your buddies walk that way?"

Todd's face brightened. They were finally talking about a subject he knew something about. "Oh, sure, when they've really got a buzz on."

"A buzz on?" Sean asked, looking at the jury with raised eyebrows as if they all didn't know exactly what Todd meant. One of the old hard-ass jurors gave off a sarcastic knowing grunt.

"Yeah, you know, if they're drunk or something."

"I see. Then would it be fair to say she appeared drunk to you?"

"Sure."

"Did you notice anything else that would lead you to believe she had a buzz on?" Sean asked.

"No, I didn't really see her that long."

"Well, you told us you saw Mr. Curtis carrying her."

"Yeah?" the kid said with a question mark.

"And was there anything about her condition at that time that may have led you to believe she was drunk?"

"No, that's when I thought she was dead," the boy said.

Sean cringed. The last thing he wanted was for the jury to hear the word *dead* in reference to Robin Penrose. He hurried on to the next question.

"You said you've seen people who were drunk. Is that right?"

"Sure, plenty of times."

"Have you ever seen anybody who was passed out?"

"Sure," Todd said, then he paused. Sean could see him figuring it all out. "Oh, I see what you mean. She was probably just passed out," he said and hesitated again. "That's what I told Nicole that night."

A door as wide as the Golden Gate had just opened for Sean, and he stepped through. "You told Nicole Hardaman, the girl who was with you that night at the beach," Sean said, looking at the jury, "that the girl was just passed out?"

"Yeah," Todd said, happy to please.

Sean saw Lowenstein drop his head in disgust. A lawyer could never tell about kids. They were as unpredictable as a wild animal show. Put them up on that stand and just when you figured they were going to jump through another hoop for you, they'd turn around and devour you in one mouthful.

Sean smiled over at the prosecution table, then turned back to Todd. "Now, you said you didn't observe them that long. Is that correct?"

"Only when they were under the tower, really."

"Was the lighting good?"

"Yeah. There's a light there."

Stepping away, Sean walked to the end of the jury box and rested against it nonchalantly. He was about to undress the boy, and he didn't want to seem to be attacking him. He was one of the jury now, searching for the truth.

"And you never told us what you were doing up on that tower with Nicole," he said softly. He was smiling and the kid was smiling back, like a couple of friends in the shower room talking about girls.

"Well, we were . . . you know, just talking and stuff."

"How long had you been . . . just talking?"

"About a half hour."

"Did you do anything else?"

"You mean . . ."

"Well, like kissing, for instance," Sean prompted him, his voice still as soft as a confessor's.

"Sure, we were kissing."

"Anything else?" Sean said, waving his hands out in a general way.

"You mean like was I feeling her up?" Todd offered.

The courtroom burst into laughter. Sean tried to keep a straight face, but he couldn't. The bailiff was leaning over a file cabinet, his belly heaving, the gun jostling in its holster.

Even Macklin was laughing as he gaveled the courtroom to order. "Oh, boy," the judge said and took a long drink of water until he could ease the smile off his face.

Sean looked at the kid. His face had gone from red to ashen and back to red. He was suffering the worst fate a teenager can endure —embarrassment. Sean walked up to the witness box with a serious, businesslike expression. He looked Todd in the eye until the boy calmed a little. Then he said, "Actually, Todd, I wanted to know if you were drinking."

The boy had his hand on his face, stroking a beard that wasn't there. "Yeah," he said, "we had some beer."

Sean hurried through the next few questions to keep Todd's mind off his embarrassment. "Then you were both drinking?"

"I guess."

"How much?"

"Three or four beers."

"Nicole had three or four also?"

"No. She had two, I think."

"Did you have a buzz on when you saw the two people under the tower?"

"Not really."

Sean stopped there and looked back at the jury, giving a doubtful shrug of his shoulders. He was letting them know that he was going to have to slap the kid some to get at the truth. "You had three or four beers and no buzz?"

"You know, maybe a little. No big deal, though. My dad lets me drink beer at home," the kid said, not knowing he'd just accused his father on public record of committing a crime. He was making excuses, trying to squirm his way out of punishment. That's exactly what Sean wanted. "I can handle it pretty good," Todd went on.

"Whose car did you take to the beach?"

"Mine."

"And who drove the car to the beach?"

"I did."

"And who drove the car home?"

The boy hesitated and looked away from Sean. He knew he was

trapped. His parents were sitting right in the gallery. And they were going to give it to him but good now. No car for a month.

"Answer the question, son," Macklin said. Even he felt sorry for the kid.

"Nicole," Todd said softly.

"Why?"

"I don't know." He was still squirming, still trying to stall the ax that was falling on his driving privileges.

"Did it have anything to do with the fact that you had too much to drink?" Sean asked.

Todd leaned forward, his hands flying around, his voice whiny. "It wasn't any big deal," he said. "I could drive okay. But she wouldn't get in unless I let her drive."

"Thank you," Sean said, "I have nothing further."

"Mr. Lowenstein? Redirect?"

Lowenstein didn't bother to get up. "I have nothing," he said disgustedly.

"You can go now, son," Macklin said.

Todd walked past the counsel tables and down the aisles as if condemned. His father followed him out of the courtroom with the dour look of an executioner.

As Sean sat down, Chad said, smiling, "That went good."

"Not bad," Sean said. "Except Lowenstein's going to call the girl up next, and the girl wasn't drunk."

"Oh," Chad said, and the smile was gone.

chapter

twenty-seven

Mac pushed through the door at the Southern Nevada National Bank just after nine the following morning. Since he was sure Robin hadn't used her real name, all he had to go on was the tip Felipe had given him and the aged photo of Robin.

The first person he approached was the guard, an old geezer about seventy standing to the right of the door in a faded blue off-the-rack uniform. A badge with the name Metro Security was sewn on his front pocket.

"Hey, Sheriff, I was wondering if I could ask you a few questions," Mac said with a smile.

"I'm not a sheriff," the old man said. He had a gray stubble under his chin that he'd missed when shaving. "I used to be a sheriff. But that was back in Tulsa. 'Course, now that was in the thirties before the Depression wiped out all them jobs."

"That so?" Mac tried to sound impressed.

"Oh, yeah," he went on, "they didn't have no money to pay

deputies. That's why Dillinger, Pretty Boy, and that bunch pretty much had their run of things." The old-timer folded his arms and his eyes glazed over as he reached back. "There wasn't a hundred lawmen between Topeka and Denver, I'll bet. I remember seein' Bonnie and Clyde. . . ." The guard droned on for another minute before Mac could get a word in. He didn't dare show the photo of Robin. By the time the guard got done telling Mac all he knew about photography, the bank would be closing.

"Can you tell me where to find new accounts?" Mac asked quickly when the old man took a breath.

"New accounts? Yeah, right over there," he said, pointing at a railed-off area.

The woman behind the desk was in her early fifties, but she was trying to pass herself off as thirty-five. It wasn't working.

"Howdy, ma'am," Mac started out. He pegged her for a woman who had grown up doing the two-step. He wished he'd worn his boots. "My name is Craig MacDuff."

"Nice to meet you, Mr. MacDuff. My name's Darlene," she said, looking over this big cowboy with the sexy handlebar.

"Oh, call me Mac, would ya?" he said, smiling.

"All right, Mac," she said and smiled back, showing off a lot of bridgework. "Do you want to open an account with Southern Nevada National Bank?" she said and let the heavy gold bracelet on her wrist clang against the desk.

"Darlene, I'll tell you what, I sure would 'preciate it if you'd allow me to ask you a couple questions." He was trying not to sound too much like Johnny Cash but still get the point across that he was just plain folks.

"About the bank?" she asked.

"Sort of. I have a photograph of someone I'm lookin' fer, and I'd like you to tell me if you know who she is."

The woman's expression soured. "You mean a customer of the bank?"

"Prob-ly," Mac said. He knew this is where he was going to really have to start to sell.

"Oh, I'm sorry, Mr. MacDuff," she said, shaking her head, "but I'm not allowed to give out that kind of information."

"Darlene," he said, looking deeply into her rheumy eyes, "I only want to know if this lady has conducted any business with your bank."

"That's exactly what I'm not allowed to divulge," she said. "Our clients deserve every confidentiality."

Mac had the aged photo of Robin out so she could see it in his hand. He wanted to know if she recognized the woman in the photo without asking her to ID it yet. When Mac saw her glance at the photo, he was sure she knew something. If the lady in the photo wasn't a customer, then Darlene wasn't breaking bank rules by telling him she hadn't seen her. But if she recognized the photo, she had to throw up the roadblock.

Mac put his big paws on her desk and gave her the hurt-doggy look. "Can't you make an exception?" he asked.

"I'm sorry."

Mac took a deep breath. He was going to have to do whatever it took to get this old saddlebag to open up. "Look, honey, can you keep a secret?" he asked, leaning over the desk.

She flushed a little at the nearness of the big galoot. "As well as anybody else, I guess," she said with a little schoolgirl giggle.

"Here, let me show you something," Mac said and reached inside his coat pocket. "I haven't been entirely up front with you, Darlene. I'm sorry," he said. "I'm Sergeant MacDuff with the L.A. County Sheriff's Department." He opened a black leather wallet and inside was a badge with LOS ANGELES COUNTY SHERIFF'S DEPARTMENT written across the top.

"I see," Darlene said, but Mac knew she didn't. That's the way he wanted it. He was making this up as he went along.

"Now, I'm not going to lie to you." He leaned over the desk, his face within inches of Darlene's, and began to whisper. "I'm supposed to be here on vacation. Sort of R and R, I guess you could call it. See, last month I had this heart attack. A pretty bad one. I'm not supposed to even *think* about working for at least two more months."

"Uh-huh," she nodded. She was trying to figure out what this gorgeous hunk was getting at. She looked deeper into his blue eyes.

"Well, to make a long story short, I work for Homicide and for months I've been looking for a suspect. She's really the one who caused my heart problem. I was working eighteen hours a day trying to find her."

"And you think she killed someone?" Darlene whispered and glanced around. The bank manager was looking her way.

"Not just someone," Mac said ominously. "Have you ever heard of the Crosby murders? It was all over the papers about six months ago."

"No, I don't think so," she said, shaking her head.

"You're lucky, then. I've been on the force for twenty-five years, and I've never had a more gruesome case. This sweet old lady killed her three grandchildren while she was baby-sitting them. Mutilated them and ground them into hamburger. She had a couple of big Dobies. . . ." Mac's voice trailed off.

"Oh, my God," was all Darlene could say as Mac slumped back in his chair.

"Yeah, I haven't slept since the day I walked into the kids' bedrooms. The blood . . . and . . . well, I been havin' these nightmares ever since."

He could tell by the look on her face she was hooked. Now to reel her in.

"I still don't know how you think I can help," she said.

"Well, I have reason to believe the grandmother's living in the Vegas area and that she may do business at your bank," Mac lied some more.

"Mac, I really want to help you, darlin'," she said and touched his hand. "But I could really get in trouble discussing our customers with anyone."

"Darlene, you've got to help me," Mac pleaded and took her hand. "Like I said, I'm leaving town tomorrow and there's no way I can get back out here. Can't you just look at this photo?" he said, sliding it across her desk. "For the kids?"

Darlene glanced at the photo again and began to inspect the face.

"She's been here before, hasn't she?" Mac asked, bending down to catch her eye.

"You're really going to have to talk to the manager," she said and slid the photo back toward Mac.

"Come on, Darlene. I need your help. She blew all three of them away with a shotgun and fed them . . ." Mac broke off again. He began to hyperventilate and rub his chest under his jacket.

"You all right, Mac?" Darlene asked.

"No, I'm not all right," he said. "I won't be all right until I get this monster. She needs to be brought to justice, and I know if I don't do it, no one will. I was the one who stood in those kids' bedrooms. . . ."

Darlene finally broke. "You're not the only one looking for her," she said.

"So you've seen her?"

"Several times."

"When?" Mac asked.

"Let's not discuss it here," Darlene said, looking around again. The manager was still staring. "I could lose my job." She leaned closer to him. "I'm off at four-thirty. Why don't you meet me at the Wild Horses? It's down two blocks on the left side."

"I know the place."

"I'll meet you there," she said and smiled into those great big blue eyes of his.

"Great," Mac said as he got up to leave.

"It'll only cost you a few drinks," she said and winked.

"You got it, honey! Maybe you can help me get rid of all my nightmares," he said and winked back.

Darlene was too old to blush, but a tingle rushed up her thighs and she knew just the cure for that. She wanted to find out what that big crazy mustache of his was going to feel like tickling every inch of her body.

chapter

twenty-eight

The next day Lowenstein called to the stand Frank Johnson, a tall, bulky black man about Chad's age. Johnson had a lopsided strut, one arm stroking broadly as he walked, the other held motionless against his side. He was wearing a cheap blue polyester suit with a conservative cut—the uniform of a scrubbed-up prosecution witness. The outfit was all wrong, though. The shirt was unbuttoned nearly to his navel, and he had thrown away the tie and replaced it with a large gold medallion that was furrowed among his chest hair. His hair was done up in cornrows, and there were lightning bolts cut in the sides. As soon as Sean saw him come through the back doors, he knew Mac was right. The D.A. had made a deal with Johnson. When he walked past, Sean noticed a small square tag still stapled to the tail of the coat.

"Excuse me, Your Honor," Sean said and followed Johnson up to the stand. "Mr. Johnson, you've got something stuck to the back of your coat."

Sean walked up quickly to the witness and yanked the tag off the coat. Dressing Johnson, an ex-con, to look like a churchgoing citizen had to be Lowenstein's idea. He'd probably pulled it off the rack last night and given it to Johnson to put on in lockup.

"Oh, it's a price tag," Sean said and held it up for everyone to see. "Let's see," he said, squinting at the tag. "J.C. Penney, $69.50. Say, that's a good deal."

"The sergeant bought it for me this morning," Johnson said, pointing in Gamboa's direction.

"Yeah, it's nice," Sean said, nodding.

"Your Honor," Lowenstein said as he slowly got to his feet, "do we have to put up with defense counsel's jibes?"

"Hey, the guy's a sharp dresser," Sean said and winked.

"You know better than that," Macklin scolded, but by his smirk Sean knew he'd enjoyed it too. A judge like Macklin saw an endless parade of these spruced-up hoodlums trying to testify their way to a reduced sentence.

Lowenstein began his examination of Johnson by reading each question from his legal pad and ticking them off one by one with his pen. After a series of questions establishing that Johnson and Chad had known each other playing professional baseball, Johnson testified that on Saturday morning, October 15, Chad had driven up to his house in a white 1987 Ford Mustang convertible. The two of them sat in his living room drinking beer and watched a football game until Chad brought up the subject of the Mustang.

"He asked me to get rid of it," Johnson said. Lowenstein had started him out slowly with the basic questions of name, address, do you know the defendant, and so on. By now Johnson was comfortable, and the career con bravura was beginning to animate every gesture.

"What exactly did he say?" asked Lowenstein.

"He said I need you to ditch this baby, brother," Johnson said and raised his chin at a cocky angle. "Lose it so nobody can ever find it."

Lowenstein did a little prancing now. Johnson was the centerpiece of his case. He was the witness who was going to put Chad Curtis away, and he'd dressed special for the occasion.

"Did you ask him why he wanted you to ditch a car?"

"I asked him if it was hot. That's the first thing you gotta know,"

Johnson said authoritatively. When it came to grand theft auto, he was an expert.

"What did he say?"

"He said it wasn't stolen. But the owner wouldn't be needing it anymore."

"I see," Lowenstein said and rubbed his chin. "Did he say anything else about the owner?"

"Just that she was in no position to complain." He smiled and gave the jury a knowing look.

Lowenstein looked at the jury too with a quizzical expression. What does this all mean? he seemed to be wondering.

"Did you ask him what he meant by that?"

"Why would I care? He was giving me the damn thing, and I could get a couple grand for parts alone. I ain't no damn fool," Johnson said.

"So what happened next?" Lowenstein asked.

"He threw the keys at me and said, 'Just make sure the car vanishes from the face of the earth.' "

Lowenstein narrowed his eyes and came in close to Johnson. "Were those his exact words?"

Johnson didn't hesitate. "Exact," he said and fired a finger at Lowenstein for emphasis.

"I see," the D.A. said, milking the scene for as long as he could. He stood with one hand on an elbow, one on his chin, contemplating what the witness had just said, as if he hadn't gone over every word of the testimony for days. "What happened next?" he finally asked.

"He left and walked down the road. He musta hitched outa there. That's the last time I seen him before today."

"Thank you, Mr. Johnson. Your witness," Lowenstein said to Sean.

Sean got up slowly from the defense table. Of all the prosecution witnesses, he feared Johnson the most. The one question Sean couldn't answer for the jury was not so much why Chad had been in possession of Robin's car the day after she disappeared. After all, they were good friends. But how had Johnson ended up with it? No matter what he did to discredit the witness, Sean could not explain how he got ahold of Robin's car unless Chad had given it to him. No matter how much the jurors distrusted Johnson, that was the question that would sit in their stomachs like a raw apple.

"Now, Mr. Johnson," Sean began, "how long have you known Chad Curtis?"

"Maybe five years," Johnson said, sitting with one elbow cocked on the chair back. Like most ex-cons, Johnson had a practiced nonchalance. His walk, his talk, the way he sat, said that he wasn't afraid of anything, least of all some cupcake attorney. Sean planned to find out how deep that cool ran.

"Where did you meet?"

"Like I said, we played ball together."

"Professional baseball?"

"Yeah, for Medford, Oregon. That's an Oakland single A club," Johnson said, offering more than had been asked. Sean was hoping he'd keep it up. There was no telling what might come rolling out of that cocky mouth.

"And how long did you and the defendant play together?"

"Part of one season. 'Bout three months maybe. Then he went on to double A in Texas."

"And what about your career?"

"Got cut that year and went back home."

Sean moved a little closer to the witness. "Now, were you and Mr. Curtis friends in Medford?"

"We had a beer or two."

"Alone. Just you and him?"

"No, with other guys on the team."

"Then he wasn't your best friend or anything like that?" Sean asked. He was next to the jury box now, a step closer to Johnson.

"No, we weren't best friends." Johnson still had his elbow over the chair back, fending off the questions with a wave of his other hand.

"Or even a good friend?"

"We were teammates."

"Teammates?"

"Yeah, teammates," Johnson said impatiently, swinging his arm off the back of the chair and sitting up straight.

"And when was the last time you saw each other before October 15?"

"When he was playing against the San Bernardino Spirits, he came by my place for some beers after a game once," Johnson said. "That's how he knew where I lived," he added, driving the nail in.

"So let me get this straight," Sean said, leaning right over the witness box rail. "You were teammates for three months over five years ago?"

"That's what I just told you," Johnson said in a bored tone. There was only so much stupidity a man could suffer.

"And you weren't good friends?"

"Nope."

"And since that time you saw him only once. Is that right?"

"That's right."

Sean leaned in close to the witness and raised his voice. "And you want us to believe he'd trust you with this car?"

"Doesn't matter what you believe," Johnson shot back. "That's the way it happened."

"Mr. Johnson, have you ever been convicted of grand theft auto?" Sean asked.

"Yeah, why do you think your boy come to me for help? He figured I knew how to get rid of a car."

Sean turned his back on the witness. "I see," he said, talking right to the jury. "And that's not all you've been convicted of, is it?"

Johnson looked around at Macklin.

"Answer the question," the judge said.

"Yeah, I've had another conviction."

"For selling drugs?" Sean said and locked eyes with one of the old hard-asses, who was shaking his head slowly at the slime that had crawled into the witness box.

"Yeah."

"Did you go to prison?"

"No, six months in County."

"But weren't you still on probation for auto theft at the time?" Sean said and swung back around to face the witness.

"Yeah," Johnson said, irritated.

"And you only got county time? You must have had a good attorney."

"Objection!" Lowenstein said, standing. "He's badgering the witness."

"Overruled," Macklin said and turned to Sean. "But get to the point."

Sean nodded and went right back at Johnson. "Mr. Johnson, did you ever testify as a witness in the case of *People* versus *George McLann?*"

"I think so, yeah."

"What was your testimony?"

"McLann told me he robbed two or three liquor stores."

"And that was after you were arrested on the drug charge?"

"Yeah," Johnson shrugged. "I guess so."

"And because you testified for the prosecution you received a suspended sentence," Sean said a little louder. "Isn't that right?"

"Yeah."

Sean was shaking his head as he turned to the jury again. "Were you arrested after the night Mr. Curtis supposedly told you to make that car vanish from the face of the earth?"

"Yeah," he said with a so-what shrug. The elbow was back up on the chair back.

"What was the charge?"

"Possession for sale," Johnson said, bored.

"And you were on probation at the time?"

"Yeah."

"Have you been sentenced on that case yet?"

"Not yet."

Sean paused for several long seconds, turned to face Johnson but not so completely that the jury couldn't see the disgust in his face. "And you're testifying here today for consideration on that charge, aren't you, Mr. Johnson?" Sean said. "You cut yourself another deal, didn't you?"

"They said they'd give me a break, sure."

"And who is they?" Sean said, narrowing his eyes.

"The D.A. and the cop," Johnson said, pointing at the prosecution table.

Sean followed the witness's finger over to Gamboa and Lowenstein. "That would be the district attorney, Mr. Lowenstein, and Sergeant Tom Gamboa?"

"Yeah."

"No further questions," he said.

Sean walked back to the defense counsel's table and threw his pad down with a satisfied grin. He patted Chad on the shoulder, as if to say he'd taken care of that problem. But he knew he'd done

nothing of the sort. How else could Johnson have come into possession of Robin's car unless Chad gave it to him? And if that was so,
what had happened to Robin Penrose? No matter how much the
jurors disliked Frank Johnson, once they were sequestered alone, the
twelve of them with the job to see justice done, that's all they would
ask themselves. No matter how sleazy the witness, no matter how
assured Sean appeared, Johnson's testimony confirmed Chad's guilt.
There was no doubt about that—reasonable or otherwise.

Macklin adjourned the court with a swing of his gavel, and the room
emptied quickly. Lowenstein nodded at Sean as he hurried by. Then
the D.A. caught Gamboa by the arm and pulled him aside into the
hallway.

"How are we progressing on our other informant?" he asked.

"Well, I've got a guy who was in the cell with Curtis for a week
or so earlier this month who will say Curtis told him the whole story.
How he killed her. How he dumped her body. Everything but where
the body is."

"That's good," he said, giving Gamboa an approving pat.

"It's not that good," the detective said. "I had a note from him
saying he needed to know more about the particulars of the case if
he's going to testify."

Lowenstein shrugged. "Have you used him before?" he asked,
ignoring the implications of what he had just been told.

"The department has," Gamboa replied. Then he looked at
Lowenstein menacingly. "Look, I don't like this. You know what he's
doing, don't you? He wants to get familiar with the case so he can
make it look like Curtis spilled his guts to him."

"Sergeant, I don't give a damn whether you like it or not," Lowenstein said, poking Gamboa's lapel. "Frank Johnson may have
helped us, but you never know what those fucking clowns on the jury
are thinking. I want to make sure that the only way Barrett can win
this damn thing is if he waltzes into the courtroom with Robin Penrose herself." The D.A. shook his fist. "This'll break Barrett's back."

"Hey, I ain't Mother fucking Teresa," Gamboa said, knocking
Lowenstein's hand away. "But this is pushing it."

"Don't get righteous on me now, Gamboa," he said. "Why do
you think I kept you on this case? You've got a reputation for doing

whatever it takes to get a conviction." He leaned into the cop's face. "So now I want you to do whatever it takes!"

Gamboa didn't say anything. He just stared back.

"So we showed him the police report first and told him what we needed," Lowenstein said. "We didn't instruct him to lie. Curtis is guilty, right?"

"I guess," Gamboa said, his face getting purple.

"That's all that matters. The rest of it is just details," Lowenstein said. "Now, what did you promise him?"

"No violation of probation on his old beef and straight probation on his pending drug case," Gamboa answered.

"Beautiful! Let's go with it," the D.A. said.

Lowenstein played with these cases like they were cards, Gamboa thought. Drop a few hands to win a big pot. That's the way the flashy bastard did things. He didn't care if this snitch went out and raped a few more old ladies as long as those headlines read "Lowenstein Wins No-Body Case!" Gamboa wanted to puke.

"Does Barrett know anything about him yet?" Lowenstein asked.

"Not yet."

"Perfect!" Lowenstein said. "I want to save this little surprise as long as possible. When Barrett finishes with his defense witnesses, I'll put the informant on in rebuttal. But we can't wait too much longer to inform him, or Macklin will flip. As soon as I tell you, give him the report."

Gamboa nodded.

"We got him now," Lowenstein said, clenching his fist. "When we hit him with the informant, he'll be pleading for mercy. He'll beg us to let Curtis have the murder-two plea. That's when I'll tell him his warranty is up."

"You mean the offer is off?" Gamboa asked.

"It's murder one or nothing," Lowenstein said, then added with a gay little laugh. "And I might even go for special circs. See if we can get him reservations for the gas chamber."

chapter

twenty-nine

Robin's mother, the last prosecution witness, was ready to testify, so Sean knew he didn't have much time. The prosecution was about to rest. He could prolong the trial a little by cross-examining her at length. Ordinarily, that was a poor strategy because of a jury's natural sympathy for a victim's mother. But he simply needed more time to develop Mac's information into something concrete enough to turn their case around. Unless Mac found out something important in Vegas, all Sean had were the people who thought they saw Robin in scattered locations around the state. How they were going to hold up under cross he couldn't guess. Lowenstein was known as a deadly cross-examiner, and inexperienced witnesses with nothing to gain could be easily led into contradictions and doubts.

But that was the nature of a no-body case. Sean had no sense of how well he was doing because he'd never defended a case like this —and nobody else had either. The only positive was that he was certain that Lowenstein was experiencing the same doubt. It was difficult for either attorney to know exactly where he stood in this case. All the same, Sean sensed, especially after Johnson's testimony, that he needed something more to win and he was praying that his investigator had an answer.

Mac didn't call until later that night, two days after he had left for Vegas again.

"Could anybody at the hotel ID the aged photo?" Sean asked.

"Nothing you could put up on a stand. Terwilliger and the shuttle driver, Felipe, both said the photo resembled the old lady. But they couldn't swear it was her."

"Shit!" Sean said and threw his pen down on the table. "Then we're sunk."

"Hold on there, pardner. We struck it rich at the bank. I went to Southern Nevada National, one of the places she had Felipe take her, and a woman in new accounts recognized her."

"No kidding," Sean said, sitting up.

"Yeah, I knew as soon as she saw the photo she'd seen the old lady before. But she didn't want to say anything 'cause she's afraid of losing her job. So I tell her I'm from out of town and show her my badge."

"What badge?"

"My old sheriff's ID."

Sean rolled his eyes. "Did it work?"

"She cut loose like a dog with diarrhea," Mac said. "Of course, I had to put a grand down with it," Mac lied, angling for more expense money. "She looks at the badge and puts the money in her purse and then tells me the whole damn thing."

"A thousand bucks?" Sean cried. "You gave her a thousand bucks? Damn, Mac, she better have admitted to killing Robin herself for that kind of money."

"Oh, it was worth it, all right. She told me the old lady opened a new account months ago. And then once a week like clockwork she deposits large sums—like fifty grand or more. This goes on for a few months until one day last October she comes in and gets a cashier's check for $500,000 made out to Hutchison and Sloan."

"Who's that? Attorneys?"

"Stockbrokers."

"Stockbrokers?"

"Yeah. Looks like she was playing the market," Mac said. "But hold on to your horse pistol. Three days after that, she cruises in with a check from Hutchison and Sloan for better than a million bucks and she deposits *that* in her account and tells the bank manager she would like to withdraw it all in two days. The bank president gets involved then, and he verifies the check. Sure enough, it's legit," Mac said. "The old lady comes back a couple days later and picks up her cash and drives away with our altar boy."

"The whole million in cash?"

"Yeah," Mac said. "And ten days later she vanishes into space."

"Jesus," Sean said softly. "What the hell is going on, Mac?"

"I don't know all the details yet, but something ain't kosher because the woman at the bank told me the Securities and Exchange Commission is involved now."

"The SEC? What's their angle?"

"Well, this sweet little old lady buys more than a million bucks worth of stock—the day before it doubles in value."

"Wait a minute!" Sean said. The figures were spiraling upward at a dizzying pace. "I thought you said she bought a half a million."

"She did. From her deposits at *that* bank. I found out she bought another half million from deposits at two other banks. That's what the merry-go-round with the shuttle driver was all about," Mac said. "A couple days later she sells it all for more than twice what she paid for it."

"And now the SEC suspects insider trading?"

"Sure does," Mac said. "The stock doubled because the company announced they had finalized negotiations on a major new contract. So the SEC is investigating."

"The old lady?" Sean asked. He was up out of his chair, pacing as he talked.

"Yep. And not only the SEC but the IRS. It seems Granny Goose closed her account and flew the coop and they can't find her. She used a bogus name. No such person exists. The SEC wants to investigate the transactions, and the IRS wants the taxes. The lady filled out all the right forms. She had the driver's license, Social Security card—the works. But it was doctored goods," Mac said.

"So this old lady who's shuttling all over Vegas with Chad Curtis makes a million plus profit in a few days," Sean said. "Now, what are the chances that our old lady is Robin Penrose?"

"Well," Mac said, "what do you think was the name of the company whose stock made her an instant millionaire?"

"I give."

"Laramie Homes."

"I'll be damned!" Sean said. The whole picture of what Robin was up to and what Chad was trying to hide was suddenly becoming clear. "Anything else?" he asked.

"That's all I could get at the banks. But my next stop is to talk to the broker where she bought the stock. If I can't catch him tomorrow or the next day, I may have to stay over until Monday."

"Good. I've got plenty to work on with this stuff. Try to dig up everything you can there. If we're going to cut Curtis free of this mess, we'll need a lot of evidence and witnesses," Sean said. "If I need you and I can't catch you at the hotel, I'll leave the instructions on my message phone, all right?"

"Got it."

"And Mac?"

"Yeah."

"Try to go easy with the money," Sean said, quickly figuring what he had left from a personal loan he'd taken out to float the expenses of this case until the court paid its costs. "You can't shell out a grand to everybody you interview."

"Hey, it was worth it, Sean. But you're right. I'm already almost out of money, and I still have a hell of a lot more witnesses to talk to."

"Where are you going now?" Sean asked.

"Well, if it's all right with you, mother superior, I'd like to get a little shut-eye. If I can find a place cheap enough, that is," Mac said and hung up.

He turned and put his arm around Candy, who was lying next to him in a suite at the Mirage. "You ready for one hell of a blowout, babe?"

"I heard you tell your boss you were almost out of money," Candy said. "Blowouts take the big bucks, honey."

"Well, look what I found, sweetcheeks." Pulling an envelope from the drawer of the nightstand, he took out a stack of the remaining twenties and fanned them in front of her brightening face. "I've been stashing some of his cash for my retirement fund."

Candy giggled and began to kiss her way down Mac's belly.

"Plenty of time for that later," Mac said, getting off the bed. "Right now we're going to hit the tables because, you see, my little darlin', I feel like one lucky son of a bitch. You and I are going to make this casino regret they ever saw us."

After talking to Mac, Sean hung up and walked out onto the deck. The puzzle for the first time was becoming intelligible. There were quite a few pieces that he couldn't snap into place yet, but he knew eventually that he would. Laramie Homes was the key. Robin had been last seen by Carrie and Carter at the meeting with John Krueger. With the information Mac had just given him, he knew Robin was the person the SEC was looking for. Laramie Homes was Carter's client, so either he and Robin were in on it together, or Robin stole the information and purchased the stocks by herself. But Sean was certain Robin couldn't have acted alone. Even if she was smart enough, she never could have come up with the money she needed to pull off the scam. Robin had to have had a partner, and Carter was the likely choice.

Sean walked down to the shore and waded into the water up to his knees. The energy of the surf always stimulated his thoughts. The undertow grabbing at his heels, the wavelets lapping against his knees, the swells moving across the ocean. He waded back out and began to walk down the shore.

He still didn't know whether Robin was dead or alive, of course. Or whether Chad had killed her. And there was one thing he couldn't get out of his mind. Shabba St. James had to be the Jamaican making the telephone calls, and he had to be the same person with Robin Penrose or her lookalike outside Bakersfield. If Shabba was the Jamaican caller, then the two cases had to be connected. But how? No one involved with the cases could help him now. Berger and Romero were dead, and Shabba was still in a coma. Sean knew that whenever Shabba was well enough, Gamboa would figure out a way to get him to talk. But for now it was up to Sean to unravel the mystery.

He walked on. Carrie would be waiting for him at her place. Ever since the run-in with Shabba, they had been spending a lot of time at her house. He would come by most nights after he was through with work, which usually meant he crawled into her bed sometime after midnight and they made love for a while before they fell asleep. He was thinking about their talk that morning. She had brought coffee and sat next to him on the bed and begun to talk about their upcoming trip to San Francisco. They were going to visit the wine country as soon as the trial . . .

Then it struck him. What if the burglary at Medtech had been to get information to be used the same way as for Laramie Homes —for insider trading. If he just knew more about the break-in at Medtech, it might help solve this mystery. He just needed one more piece to fit the two crimes together.

As Sean watched the blinking lights of a boat out in the darkness, he suddenly realized exactly where to find that missing piece.

He started running back to his cottage, his cold, wet pants legs flapping loudly as he ran. Pulling off the pants in the living room, he put on a pair of dark blue jogging sweats and some beat-up running shoes and ran out to his car. He checked his key ring to make sure he still had his old key from Spann, McGraw. During the hectic few weeks following his resignation from the firm, he had forgotten to return all his keys. He started up the SL and it belched, then coughed, and finally turned over.

He backed out of his carport and headed out the Doheny Park lot and onto PCH headed for Newport. He motored along the coast highway, past Dana Point and through Laguna. It was after one and the stoplights were all blinking yellow, so he had to slow a little going through town. He accelerated to sixty once he got out of Laguna and pulled up to Spann, McGraw fifteen minutes later.

The problem was, Spann had already turned Sean down once when he had asked to see the Berger file immediately after Scott's murder. It was privileged information and Sean was no longer Berger's attorney, Spann had politely explained. But now it was ironic, Sean thought, because he really was Berger's attorney. The problem was, Berger had been killed before Sean's representation of him had become official.

Technically, he was committing burglary. If Spann or the D.A. wanted to get tough, he could serve prison time for this little midnight excursion. It probably wouldn't get anywhere near that, though, he thought. Spann would be furious, threaten legal or even criminal action, but he'd probably back off eventually.

At this time of night it was so quiet Sean could hear the waves crashing on Balboa Beach two miles away. As he opened the SL door, it made a loud creak that sawed its way down the silent street.

He pushed through the heavy glass doors of the lobby. That was the one door he didn't have to worry about. Law office buildings are always left open because lawyers are notorious for their crazy hours, especially criminal attorneys. If his client is about to be sentenced to suck cyanide gas, an attorney tends to spend his sleepless nights going through law books or trying to sharpen his delivery.

Sean got off the elevator and fished out his key ring to unlock the front doors of Spann, McGraw. The janitor was just finishing up and nodded as he backed out the door with his pail and rags hanging from hands and belts and shoulders. Shit! Sean thought. If Spann ever found out, there was his witness.

Sean went to Scott's old office, the third down the hall, and tried the door. His key wouldn't get him in if it was locked. Luckily it was open. But when he turned the light on, he knew he was in the wrong office. That wasn't Scott's mahogany desk or leather chair. Sean looked back at the front of the door: Scott's nameplate now read JACOB DYSON. He turned around a photo on the desk: it was Dyson and his wife. Of course! Jacob Dyson had been hired to take over Scott's caseload. He'd worked at Carter's firm before he took a raise and joined Spann, McGraw.

If Sean was lucky, though, the Berger file would still be there. Dyson had the new file cabinets that look like dresser drawers and a new oak desk to match that had to have come from a discount joint like Office Mart. Sean pulled out a few drawers before he found the case files and flipped his way to B. Barnaby . . . Benson . . . Black. But no Berger. He fingered his way to P and looked up Powers. There it was, a whole section of Scott's old cases. Dyson was probably making his way through them one by one. Sean shuffled through the manila tabs once more. Banazek . . . Bender . . . Burnell. No Berger.

Damn! Where the hell was that file? He sat back on the desktop a moment.

Of course, Sean thought. Spann would have any frozen files kept in his office, safe from any leaks. Sean walked down the hall to Spann's office and tried the door, but it was locked. Spann locked his door even when he went down the hall to pee. Now Sean could either break down the door or go home. And he wasn't going home without Berger's file.

He went out to the front doors of the firm and cautiously looked down the hallway and checked the elevators. Both cars were parked at the lobby. He went quickly back to Spann's door again. He knew this was crazy. If he broke down Spann's door, he was almost certainly looking at a criminal charge. Spann would be furious. It would surely get around the law community as well. He couldn't break into Spann's office. Could he?

He stood there with his shoulder leaning against the door, weighing the pros and cons. If he won this case, his future was set. But if he went up on burglary charges, that could lead to prison and the end of his career.

Just as he'd decided to break down Spann's door, an easier way to get into Berger's files finally came to him. There was a computer in every office that came as part of the furniture. Dyson's computer was probably Scott's old machine. So it might still have Berger's file on its hard disk.

Sean ran down to Dyson's office and flipped the red switch on his computer. Scott had been a computer junkie. He'd gotten the firm to buy him a monster machine with a mammoth hard drive and the latest Intel chip to run it. And he always put his files in there, so he had a paper copy and a computer copy of everything he did. The screen fired up after the computer blinked and beeped itself to life.

GOOD MORNING, SCOTT. LET'S FREE THE INNOCENT

it said, followed by an alphabetical menu of programs.

Sean bet that, like most people, Dyson was leery of his computer. It had appeared in his life one day, and now he needed it to keep in step with everyone else. But he was afraid to do anything that might screw things up in the confounded machine, such as change the greeting from "Good Morning, Scott" to "Good Morning, Jacob."

Among the list of directories on the menu was one for CRIMINAL CASES. Sean punched it up, and when the program appeared on screen, he scanned down the list of cases. Bender . . . Burnell. But no Berger. The file had been erased.

But Sean had been half expecting that. He wasn't through yet. He knew enough about his old boss to know that Spann didn't know shit about computers either. Sean knew that all a computer did when someone erased a file was delete the first letter of the file name, not the whole file. If the Berger file wasn't already overwritten— and Sean was betting it wouldn't be because Dyson probably only used this monster when he absolutely had to—it meant the file was likely still there.

Sean went back to the computer menu and found the program that could recover an erased file. He'd seen Scott use it himself. After a few commands the computer whirred, and on the screen appeared a list of files that had been deleted. On January 18, the day after Scott's funeral, someone had erased the Berger file. There it was: "?ERGER."

"Do you know the first letter of the erased file?" the program asked. Sean typed B and a moment later Berger's file appeared on the screen. He scanned down to the notes on Medtech. Under "Schwitters, James: President, Medtech," Scott had entered a flurry of notes. Sean read down the screen, scrolling as he went. Then he saw what he was after.

"Schwitters stated that on February 15 a merger between Medtech and Kaufmann Pharmaceutical was to be announced. This would double, maybe triple current Medtech stock within a few days of the announcement."

Underneath that Scott had typed, "Schwitters believes the break-in involved *insider trading*."

"Yes!" Sean cried. "Thank you, old friend."

He made a printout of the entire Berger file. Then he shut off the computer and hurried out the glass doors. When he got to the elevator, he saw that someone was coming up, so he took the stairs just in case. He sneaked down all nine flights and hurried out to his car. He was too wired to go back home and sleep yet, so on the way back to Capistrano, he stopped in a twenty-four-hour Denny's on the coast highway for a cup of coffee.

He knew now that Shabba and Berger and Romero and Robin had all been involved in insider trading. But still, it made no sense. Berger could barely tie his shoes without help. Romero was a doper without a scrap of education or ambition. Shabba, even though he walked around in Wall Street threads, didn't figure to be a Dow-Jones terrorist. He was a killer, muscle, he took care of street business. And Robin? Maybe she knew a little about stocks and bonds, but she couldn't pull off a scam like this without a lot of help. No, somebody else had to be involved. Somebody with solid knowledge of stocks and bonds and access to privileged information or how and where and when to get it.

Sean read through the rest of the Berger file as he sipped coffee. Near the end Scott had listed the Medtech board of directors. Sean glanced quickly through the dozen or so names. Suddenly he stopped in the middle of a sip and stared for a long time at a name near the bottom: Carter Robinson.

chapter

thirty

After court the next day, Sean made his way across Balboa Bridge toward Lido Isle. At long last this case was beginning to make sense. He had talked to Chad the first thing in the morning, and Chad had denied everything, as usual. The next step was to confront Carter Robinson. He was well versed in stocks and bonds, was on the board of Medtech, and he had been at the Laramie Homes meeting with Krueger. But why had Robin run out of that meeting? Maybe she had overheard something from Krueger that scared her, or maybe something she wasn't supposed to hear. Then she had been murdered. Or she'd run off before she could be murdered.

Once Sean suspected the crime that connected both cases was insider trading, a suspicion confirmed by Scott's computer file, it was easy to see that Carter was the common link. Still, Sean owed it to him and, most of all, to Carrie to see if her father could explain whether these incriminating pieces were just coincidence. It was the murders Sean was having a tough time with. He simply couldn't believe that Carter was involved in the killing of three, maybe four people. But then in the past six years, Sean had been shocked almost daily by the brutality of seemingly normal people.

When he pulled up to the Robinson house, he saw a moving van parked out front. A team of movers were streaming from the house like a line of ants emptying a cupboard. Sean went right in the open front door and looked around downstairs—most of the furniture except for a couch and a few small chairs was gone. Packing boxes were stacked by the doors and on the kitchen table. He went upstairs calling out Carter's name but found no one. He looked in all the bedrooms and then went downstairs again.

Excusing his way past the movers, he went out the kitchen door to the backyard. Carter's wife, Sharon, was standing next to a storage shed attached to the house. She was a good-looking blonde, twenty years younger than her husband, who spent a lot of time in hair salons and health spas.

She was packing a box with books that were in the shed when Sean walked up. "Hi, Sharon."

"Oh, hello, Sean." She stood up and slapped the dust off her hands.

"Sorry I missed you at the boat parade."

"Oh, I was out of town," she said. "What are you doing here?"

"Actually, I was looking for Carter."

"Carter's not here."

A clutch of gulls were gathered on pilings in the sun, squawking at one another.

"I didn't know you and Carter were moving," Sean said. "What did you do? Sell the place?"

Sharon was bent over at the waist, stuffing books into the box. She straightened and looked at Sean. "I guess you're the only one left in Newport who doesn't know."

Sean smiled in embarrassment.

"Carter and I are separating," she said and blew dust off the spine of a book, idly reading the title. "That's why I didn't see you the night of the boat parade."

"I'm sorry, Sharon," Sean said.

"Oh, don't be." She waved her hand nonchalantly. "I'm lucky to be rid of the bastard," she said. "Help me tape this box, would you?"

"Sure," he said and put his knee on the flaps after she closed them. She pulled off a long strip of packing tape and smoothed it down on the top. She put two more strips down to hold it tightly.

"You know," she said, "in a way, I guess I should be grateful to you and your client. What's his name? Curtis."

"Why is that?" he said and held another box top down for her.

"Because if your client hadn't killed Carter's little bimbo," she said, "I probably would have. And you'd be defending me right now."

"You mean Robin Penrose and . . ."

"And Carter. Yes," Sharon said, finishing his thought. "Don't look so surprised. He was an old hand at feeling up his secretaries," she laughed. She pushed her platinum hair back with a forearm. "How do you think Carter and I met? I was his secretary when he was married to Carrie's mother. I should have known the same thing was going to happen to me. But, you know, love is blind, tra-la-la."

A motorboat went by too fast, and its wake made the dock bob. A few gulls decided they'd had enough and flew off.

She stood up with an old book in her hand, fanned the pages, and threw it on a pile destined for the trash can. "Carter can't help himself. He never stopped gambling and he never stopped sleeping with his secretaries. He's working on a new one right now," she said and began rummaging through a box of kitchen tools. "At least he won't be able to take her here. That's one consolation."

"What happened?" Sean asked, wanting to get as much as he could. An irate wife often tells an attorney most of what he needs to know about her husband.

"He's lost the whole thing. And his big-deal boat," she said, waving her hand back at the yacht parked behind them. "And when my lawyers and I get through with him, he won't have a dinghy to paddle around in."

It appeared that Carter was another victim of the collapsing economy and his own addictions. He probably got buried in debt, Sean thought, or gambled himself into an inescapable hole and couldn't climb out. Then he got desperate and started betting on rigged games in the market.

"Can I ask you one thing?" he said, piecing the mystery together very rapidly.

"Sure." She pulled her hair back in a ponytail, fixing it with a rubber band she'd found among the kitchen bric-a-brac.

"Did Carrie know about Carter and Robin?"

Sharon sat on one of the taped boxes and grabbed a soda sitting on the wall. "I heard you and Carrie were seeing each other," she said and reached over and touched his hand. "I'm sorry, Sean. You know how close she is to Carter. Plus, Carrie and that bimbo were best friends," she said. "She had to have known."

Sean drove straight to Carrie's without really realizing what he was doing. She'd be coming home about this time, pulling her Porsche into her sweep-around driveway, dressed in a tailored suit. Everything in its place. All that style and all that grace. A lovely veneer disguising something heartless. *Of course she knew.*

Carter Robinson had been having an affair with Robin Penrose. He had been on the board of directors of Medtech when it merged with Kaufmann, and as their attorney he had been privy to the Laramie Homes deal that made its stock shoot up. Only someone with knowledge of the stock market could have set up this elaborate insider scheme. Carter was obviously the money and the know-how behind it. On top of that, only an attorney—a former criminal lawyer like Carter, for instance—could have directed the Jamaican in assisting Sean's defense of Chad Curtis. An attorney would know that supplying witnesses who could swear they'd seen Robin was the best help for the defense, short of supplying Robin Penrose herself. Which brought up the old, still unanswered question. Who *was* the woman Sean had seen in Bakersfield flying down the highway in Shabba's red Corvette? A lookalike? An actress between gigs? Or Robin Penrose herself?

He wound up the cliffs of the Back Bay and turned onto the manicured street where Carrie lived. She'd known the way to get to him, all right. Just hike her skirt up a few inches, let those long legs mesmerize, stare at him with those ever changing eyes. As Mac would put it, he'd been a Class-A sap. He still didn't know how deeply Carrie was involved—only that she knew of her father's affair with Robin—but he was going to find out.

She was in the shower when he let himself in. "That you, darling?" she said, sticking her head out the frosted door. "I'll just be a minute. Unless you want to join me," she said with a mischievous smile.

"No, thanks," he said.

He sat on the sink as she stepped out and began dry off. She didn't bother to hide anything. They were beyond that stage of the game. Her breasts lifted as she reached above to towel off her hair, the droplets streaming over them, down her belly, and into the dark between her thighs.

He was so goddamn in love with her. He could understand how murders of passion happened. All that desire fuels the anger and the mind gets overrun in one enormous rush and it's back to the jungle —a blunt instrument in hand, rage in the heart, and the object of all that overflowing hatred is standing right there, laughing.

Carrie put one leg on her vanity stool and wiped the length of it dry. The sweep of her long calves caught his eye. "I was just thinking about our trip to San Francisco," she said.

"I can't go anywhere during the trial."

"I know that," she said. "I meant afterward."

"All right," he said, feigning a smile. He was going to get her to tell him as much as possible before she realized he was on to her.

She was dusting bath powder across her shoulders when she suddenly looked at him. "What's wrong, sweetheart?"

"Nothing," he said and shrugged. "You know, just the trial."

"The trial? Well, I've got the remedy for trial nerves." She walked over and kissed him hungrily. As he kissed her back, she reached down for his zipper and pulled him out. He was stiff already. It was pure madness. One of God's little jokes that someone so poisonous could turn him on so completely. Reaching between her legs, he slid his fingers into her roughly and she groaned. She was already drenched inside.

That's the way he wanted her, softened up like a pussy cat, those green eyes out of focus, her mouth crushed into a longing expression. A little off balance, a little out of control. Even she couldn't fake that.

He grabbed her by the hair and pulled her head back. As he kissed her roughly, she pushed her tongue into his mouth. Then he pushed her down to her knees, and when he shoved himself toward her, she took him into her mouth with a sweet, satisfied groan.

He knew how to handle her. He picked her up, carried her into her bedroom, and threw her roughly onto the bed. He was on her and then in her before she knew it, her arms pinned against the bed.

"Oh, Sean," she cried, a little surprised, a little frightened. That was the way she liked it sometimes. She was full of grace and propriety. Except when it came to sex. The moment he began to touch her lips, she would unravel, all decorum gone.

She pushed him to get on top, but he forced her down, made her move to his tempo, made her imagination grow under his lead. This time when she lost control, he was in command. He brought her up slowly from that point, higher and higher up the cliff until he got her to the edge. Then he backed her off while she begged him not to stop. Then up again and again, drove her to the edge over and over until she was exhausted.

She was lying on the pillow, her hair still wet, her eyes awash with sex when he started gently questioning her. "You think Robin loved Chad?" he said next to her ear.

"Maybe," she said. "But more important, do you love me?"

"Of course, can't you tell?" he said and lifted his head so he could see her eyes. "It's impossible to fake anything that passionate, right?"

She kissed him as an answer.

"I've got this feeling Robin was seeing someone besides Chad," he whispered.

"You do?"

"She wasn't really interested in Chad, was she? She was using him. What they had was over a long time ago."

He slipped out of her and rolled over on the bed and sat up. She lay back dreamy-eyed beside him, only half aware of what he was saying.

"Robin was a big girl," he went on, "and she played in the big leagues. Coming back to Newport, Chad was small-time stuff for her. Of course, it didn't take her long to find somebody in her league again, did it?"

His hand was stroking the vulnerable underside of her neck.

"Why don't we talk about this later, darling?" she said. "I've got some things I want to explain anyway. But not now," she said and slid her leg over so she could rub it against his thigh. "Come back here, will you?"

He slid off the bed and knelt on the floor, his elbows resting on the mattress. "Carrie, I've got to know some things about your father."

He could see in her eyes the alarm go off. Her vision began to clear, the sentry awakening. "What do you want to know?" she said. The dreamy voice had thickened.

"How long had Carter been sleeping with Robin?"

Like a good lawyer caught off guard, she didn't answer. He could see her mind whirling, trying to find its balance again.

"Sean, I didn't know . . ." she finally began to explain.

That's all he really needed from her. But he kept hammering to see what came out. She was naked on the bed, vulnerable as she'd ever be, looking at him as he put his pants on.

"Sure you did," he said, coaxing her. "How about Laramie Homes? Did you know about that?"

"What do you mean?"

"I mean the insider stock trading you and Daddy and Robin pulled off," he said calmly.

"I didn't know anything about my dad and Robin until after you were appointed to represent Chad. That day you asked me if I thought Chad loved Robin. I knew he did, and that's what got me thinking. I remembered Robin and my father fighting that night. I confronted him and he finally told me he'd had an affair with her and all about their stock scam in Vegas. That's the first I knew about it." She was on her elbow, the sheet pulled over her breasts as if it were a shield.

He didn't believe a word of it.

"Did he kill her for the money?" he asked. "Or is she still alive and all three of you are in on it?"

"I don't . . . understand," she stumbled.

Their eyes met for the first time since he'd turned on her. She could see how cold his eyes became when he thought a witness was lying.

"Well, can you follow this?" he said, and his tone matched his eyes. "You're lying. You've been lying to me all along. In and out of bed."

"What are you talking about?" She sat upright, the sheet in place, her hair a mess from the sex, the mouth pouty as in one of those boudoir poses. He loved the way she could lie with that straight face.

"I think your father killed Robin, and he probably had an accomplice," he said.

"No, Sean!" she cried. An overtone of anger had entered her voice. The sex he'd drugged her with had completely worn off. "I was with him that whole night."

"That's what I mean, baby!"

"Please don't call me baby!"

"Sure," he said, "what should I call you? What do you call someone who sleeps with you to get information?" he said.

"That's what you think?" She was crying. "I never slept with you to get you to talk, if that's what you think." She reached for his hand as he buckled his pants. "I slept with you because I felt something for you. And I kept sleeping with you because I fell in love with you." She looked up at him, her eyes pleading. "Don't you believe me?"

No, he didn't believe her. He had never been able to quite figure out why a woman like Carrie, from the other side of the Bay, would want him anyway. "Of course, if I did happen to say something useful, you went to Daddy with it," Sean said.

When she didn't answer, he knew he was right.

"Maybe you could see your father go to prison and not do whatever you could to save him. But I couldn't," she finally said.

Sean didn't reply. She knew exactly how he felt about his own father.

"I didn't know what to do," she said. "I just hoped, I guess, that if you found out, you'd love me enough to understand." She stood up and locked her hands around his neck. "And if you couldn't understand," she said, "I was hoping you loved me enough to forgive me."

"Oh, don't worry. I understand," he said and pulled her arms away and grabbed his coat off the floor where he'd thrown it. She knew about the insider trading scam. She knew her father had been screwing Robin, scheming with her to defraud millions. What else did she know? The Jamaican? The killings? Had she known he was walking into a butcher shop when he went to find Shabba at the Fun Zone?

She began wiping tears off her cheeks, and the sheet had dropped to the floor.

"Sure, I understand," he said, his face close to hers. "You're just a very high-priced hooker."

"Get out of here!" she screamed.

"Don't worry," he said and yanked the bedroom door open. "I can't wait to get out of your sight. Tell me this, though. Who was it that actually killed her? Your old man? Or was it Chad? Or maybe it was you? That's all I'd really like to know. Just exactly what are you capable of?"

chapter

thirty-one

Early the next morning an old woman stepped off the bus in front of the county jail and looked up at the eight-story concrete fortress a moment. She slumped her shoulders, pulled her shawl tightly around her, and shuffled up the steps and through the glass doors. She hugged a wall of the long hallway and slowly made her way past a dozen cops and sheriff's deputies until she came to a long counter. The sign on the wall read: VISITORS MUST SHOW IDENTIFICATION.

The old lady fumbled around inside her handbag and pulled out a plastic wallet and carefully extracted her identification. It looked exactly like a driver's license, with the color photo and address, but she couldn't operate a motor vehicle with it. Many seniors who couldn't drive anymore got one.

She reached over and took a visitor's request form from a stack on the counter and slowly filled in each line.

Inmate you wish to visit: *Chad Curtis*, she printed.

Visitor name: *Emily Curtis*.

Relationship: *Mother*.

When she was done, she handed it to one of the deputies.

"ID," he demanded without looking up.

She slid her ID across the counter. He looked at it to find the expiration date, flipping it over once or twice. "When's your license expire?"

"It's not a license," she said.

"Huh?"

"It's only a California ID. They don't expire."

"Oh," the deputy said and tossed it back at her. "Sit down. We'll call you."

After twenty minutes, a jailor came out. "Chad Curtis."

"Yes," she said and followed him through a metal door, down a small, narrow hall to a steel door with bars. The jailor inside unlocked the door, and once the old lady walked through, he banged the door shut behind her. Then he pointed at a seat along the long horseshoe-shaped counter. "Take number eighteen."

After a few minutes, a jailor led Chad out and pointed him to a seat on the other side of the glass from where she was sitting. When she saw him, she smiled.

"Jesus!" he said and sat down. "Where the hell have you been? I haven't seen you for almost a month!"

"I wanted to come, but it's so dangerous right now," she said, almost whispering, "with everybody in the state out looking for me."

"Isn't that what you wanted?"

"Sure. It's working too. Your attorney must have at least a half-dozen witnesses lined up who will say they've seen me. They can't convict you if they think I'm alive."

"Barrett doesn't know if it's going to be enough."

"Barrett's the damn problem!" she snapped at him. "He's screwing everything up. Can't you control him, for God's sake?"

He looked at her in surprise.

"Look, Chad, he's on to the stock deals."

"I know," he said. "What good is all this? Why am I rotting away in here?" He stood, leaning toward her, almost shaking. A guard was watching closely.

"Chad, sit down, will you?" she said through her teeth. "Sit down, baby." He began to sink again to his seat. "Chad," she said, "you know I love you."

He shrugged.

"You know I'd never let anything happen to you, don't you?"

He didn't say anything. After sitting in jail the past four months, he didn't know what he believed anymore.

"This Barrett is supposed to be the best there is. But just in case something happens and you get convicted, I'll come forward. You know that," she said. "They can't put you away if I walk into the courtroom. And that's what I'll do, Chad, if I have to."

He looked up. She was beautiful even in that granny getup. Her blue eyes were luminous, her smile as sexy as ever. "No," he said, "I guess not." And he smiled for her.

"That's my lover," she said. "I'm going to win this one for you just like you won all those ball games for me. Remember, honey? Remember what your reward was if you won?"

He forced a smile, and a little of the sparkle came back into his eyes. "I love you, Robin," he said.

"I love you too, Chad," she said with that sweet smile which played so well on her angelic face. "But you've got to tell Barrett to back off."

Chad shook his head. He was sinking deeper into something he knew nothing about.

She kept at him. "He doesn't have to blow the lid on our stock deals in order to get you out of here. He's got eyewitnesses who'll swear they saw me in San Francisco and Bakersfield," she said. "That's all he needs."

Her shawl had slipped off her shoulder, and Chad could see the creamy skin of her arms that revealed her age.

"You have to get him to leave the stock deals alone." She broke off and began to cry quietly into her shawl. He could never stand to see her cry. Even in high school when they had had their little fights, he'd always given in.

"I'll talk to Barrett," he said.

"All right, good," she said and started to pick up her purse to leave.

"Are you going?"

"I think I better."

"Well, is the money still safe?" Chad asked, wanting to keep her as long as he could. All that awaited him was that concrete cell and hours of boredom.

"It's safe," she said.

"Still, you better be careful."

"Just make sure Barrett keeps his nose out of it."

"Don't worry," Chad said. Then he reached his hand out to her. "Robin, don't let me die in here."

She could see she still had a little work to do. "Oh, Chad, you know I could never do that. I want to see you every day. I miss you so much," she said and put her hand against the glass as if to touch him.

"I miss you too," he said, placing his hand on the glass opposite hers.

"I wish I could jump over this partition right now and crawl into your arms, Chad," she said, smiling. Then she looked away. "I miss you at night the most."

That broke him. "Oh, sweetheart, I love you so much," he said.

"I love you too," she said and kissed the air in front of her inconspicuously. "Just a little while longer, honey, and we'll be together." She got up and walked out the barred door without looking back. That would hold him for a while. At least until the trial was over.

Since Macklin had a morning dental appointment, court didn't convene until one-thirty. When Sean arrived at the courthouse, he picked up that day's investigative reports. The file was thin, only four or five pages. That was a relief. He tucked the report into his briefcase and walked over to the courtroom. It was still empty except for the bailiff, who gave him a perfunctory wave and went back to the sports section.

Sean sat down and began to glance quickly through the report. The first page or so was the usual dead-end leads Gamboa was investigating. Then he stopped and read carefully the testimony of an inmate who claimed that Chad had confessed to him.

Sean couldn't believe it. Lowenstein had found a snitch. The alleged confession was very specific, detailing the two most important aspects of the crime that the prosecution had been unable so far to substantiate—namely, Chad's motive for killing Robin and what he had done with her body after he killed her.

Sean read on, rapidly checking for inconsistencies, contradictions, anything that he could use to discredit this testimony. The witness, Jake Bigelow, gave a version exactly the same as the kids on the beach and Frank Johnson, but—and this was a crucial but—he also said that Chad had confessed that he had killed her because Robin wanted to break off their relationship. This was a claim the prosecution had been making all along but could never back up. Chad had supposedly told Bigelow he knocked Robin out at the beach and loaded her body into the car. Before she regained consciousness, he cut her throat. Then he drove out into the Mojave Desert and dumped her body in an abandoned mine shaft in the hills near the Calico Gold Mine outside Barstow.

Sean let the report drop into his lap. All the new evidence he had about Carter and the stock scheme wouldn't be enough to outweigh this. Whether or not Bigelow was lying made little difference. He knew details nobody else except Sean and Chad and Lowenstein and Gamboa knew. Nobody could have told him those things except those four people. Even if Sean thought Lowenstein or Gamboa had fed the snitch this information, he'd have an impossible time proving it. Every defense attorney confronted by a snitch tried to prove the cops put him up to it, but juries almost never believed the cops would commit such a drastic act just to get someone convicted.

Bigelow was all the prosecution needed to put Chad away for life. Sean knew he had to talk to Chad before the trial resumed. He wasn't sure what the stock scam had to do with it. But it was too late to try to piece it together without Chad's help. His client was going to have to cop to a plea immediately. Then he was going to have to crawl to Lowenstein and beg him to honor the murder-two deal he'd offered before.

"Bill," Sean called to the bailiff, who looked up from the paper. "I need to talk to Curtis. Tell the judge I'm in lockup, will you?"

Seelicke blew some air out of his mouth. "You know the judge, Barrett. He likes to start on time."

"Yeah, I know, but this affects the whole trial," Sean said and waved the report. "If he has any questions, tell him to ask Lowenstein about the contents of this new report. I'm sure he'll be happy to explain to the judge what my problem is."

Sean was fuming as he rushed over to lockup. Why would the damn fool tell a cellmate more than he was telling his own attorney? It didn't make any sense.

"I need to see Curtis," Sean told the jailor.

"No problem. He's already had a visitor earlier, so he's still in Visiting."

"Yeah, who was it?"

The jailor picked up the sign-in and ran his finger down the log. "Let's see. Emily Curtis. His mother."

"Is she still here?"

"Nah. Left a few minutes ago," he said, waving toward the door.

When Sean walked into Visiting, Chad was still standing at the window of his cubicle.

"I hear your mother came by to visit today," Sean said.

"Yeah?" Chad said, looking worried.

"That's real considerate of her, considering she died seven years ago."

Chad pushed his chair back, and it made a loud chirp on the floor.

"Want to tell me who it was?"

"Just an old friend who doesn't want to get involved. It's not important."

Sean let it pass. There were much more important matters now. He looked at Chad for a long time before he exploded. "Who's this guy Jake Bigelow?" The jailor looked over at them and raised his eyebrows.

Chad was suddenly scared. "He was in my cell for a few days. What's the problem?"

"Did you two talk?"

"Of course."

"What about?" He was forcing questions quickly down Chad's throat.

"Nothing special." Chad shrugged.

"Did you talk about what you were in for?"

"I probably told him. That's the first thing anybody asks you."

"What else?" asked Sean.

"Nothing. Why?"

"Because he says you confessed to him. That's why."

"Confessed what?"

"The whole damn thing," Sean said. Then he began to read back Bigelow's entire statement.

"No way I told him all that," Chad protested when Sean was through. "It's just one big lie."

"Why couldn't you just keep your mouth shut?" Sean said, disgusted. "He couldn't possibly know this much about the case unless you talked to him."

"I couldn't have cut her throat and dumped her down a mine shaft, because she isn't dead."

"Can you prove that in a court of law for me?"

Chad didn't answer.

"I didn't think you could," Sean said. "Look, I'm going to see if Lowenstein will still take that murder-two plea. But first you have to agree to tell them where the body is. They're going to want to know that before they cut a deal."

Chad shook his head. "I can't."

"Chad, goddamn it!" Sean said, losing what little he had left of his patience. "It's all over. You're going to prison for twenty, twenty-five years at least. Get that through your head! I'm just trying now to make sure you serve as little time as possible."

"Do you really think they'll convict me?" Chad asked as if it was the most absurd of notions.

"I don't think there's any doubt of that now," Sean said.

"Damn," Chad said quietly to himself. "I never thought it would come to this."

He sat on his stool for a long time with his face buried in his hands, then lifted his eyes slowly to Sean. "I lied to you," he said.

"That's not news."

Chad took a deep breath. "Robin is alive," he said.

"Right," Sean said.

"Really. She's not dead. She's in hiding in Palm Desert."

Sean shook his head. "It's too late for this crap, Chad. This won't even get a delay in the trial, if that's what you're hoping for."

"I'm not lying. Robin is alive. She's the one who visited me today posing as my mother."

"Then why hasn't she come forward?"

"She's afraid."

"Of what?"

Chad took a deep breath again. It all had to come out now. "You were right about the stock scam. Carter sent her to Vegas to buy stock on insider tips."

"And you went with her?"

"Only the last time. Carter got her involved in these illegal stock deals because she was so good at changing her looks. He got her the fake ID's to go with the makeup. Then he gave her the cash and had her set up an account at a bank somewhere and use the money to buy a designated stock. When that stock reached a certain price, he'd have her sell it. Then she'd close out the account and disappear."

"Another thing she's good at," Sean said.

"Yes."

He was tempted to mention Robin's affair with Carter Robinson, but thought better of it. "So when the SEC got wind of the deal, Robin decided to disappear for good rather than go to jail. Is that it?"

"That. And she was afraid of Carter. She was the only one who could connect him," Chad said. He was checking Sean's eyes to see if he believed him.

"And you helped her?" Sean asked.

Chad dropped his head. "I'd do anything for Robin."

Sean was beginning to believe that. Chad had already been willing to sit in jail for four months. "What happened the night she disappeared, Chad?"

"When the guy from Laramie Homes told Carter about the SEC catching on, Robin ran out of the meeting. Carter caught up with her and they started to fight. He slapped her around, threatened to kill her, until Carrie showed up. That's when Robin got out of there and came looking for me. She was hysterical when she came by my work. She'd been drinking a lot and she was scared."

"That's when the kids saw you at the beach?"

Chad nodded. "I slapped her like they said, but it was only to calm her down. She was drunk out of her mind by then. She got so drunk she couldn't walk, so I carried her back to her car. She didn't want to go back to her place, though. She was afraid the cops would arrest her there. So I took her to Huntington Beach and we rented a room. The next morning I put her and the money on a bus for Palm Desert. She said a friend had a place there she could use. All I had to do is ditch the car and she could vanish."

"Only you didn't plan on getting arrested, is that it?"

"Exactly. But the funny thing is, it turned out to be a lucky break because everyone thought she was dead."

Now Sean understood. Robin had been running from the SEC and Carter. When Chad had been arrested for her murder, all she had to do was have the Jamaican plant some witnesses. Then Chad gets acquitted and the two of them ride off with the money. At least that's the way Chad saw the ending.

"We never thought I'd be convicted without her body." He shrugged his shoulders at his own naiveté. "Once I was free, Robin and I were going to go get lost somewhere. But I just don't give a damn anymore, Mr. Barrett," he said. "Look, here's her address." He wrote something on a piece of paper and slipped it under the grating. "Go find her. I don't care about the money. I want to get the hell out of here."

Sean read the slip of paper. "Valley Drive, Palm Desert? You're sure she's there?"

"Positive."

"All right, Chad. I just hope you're not wasting what little time we have left."

Sean gathered his things and left in a hurry. Chad might not care about the money anymore. But there were a couple of other people who did. And they would probably do everything they could to stop Sean from bringing Robin back to save Chad's life.

On his way to Macklin's chambers, Sean stopped at a pay phone outside the courthouse. He dialed his own number and left a message on the answer phone, so Mac could pick it up when he called in.

"Mac," Sean said, "Chad just told me that Robin is alive. She's hiding out at a place in Palm Desert. The address is one-seven-four-six-nine Valley Drive. I have to talk to Macklin and stall for time by interviewing a snitch that Lowenstein's thrown at us. Hopefully, he will give me a continuance until Monday. I need you to go out there as soon as possible and bring her back. If you find her and she won't come, tell her Chad is going to be convicted. If that doesn't do it, kidnap her. Remember, she's a master at disguise, so keep your eyes open for anyone who comes near the place. Mac, be sure to call me as soon as you've got her."

chapter

thirty-two

Robin knew she had to make a move and it had to be now. Barrett was getting close. But she was even more afraid of the Jamaican. Where was he? She hadn't seen him for days. He had kept Barrett dancing like a marionette. Every time the Jamaican pulled a string, he or that investigator of his would jump. First to Hollywood, then Bakersfield, now why don't you try San Francisco? She knew the whole mad game was over now, though. Somehow, by dumb luck, Barrett's investigator had stumbled into Vegas and made the connection, and the whole scheme was falling apart.

She had always kept control of the situation. Mr. Big Deal Attorney had been clever and ruthless when it came to their scam, but he was really just a fool like the rest of them. Tell an older man he's a stud, moan in all the right places, beg to be released from the agonizing beauty of his lovemaking, then come for him, and the gray-haired fool would be mesmerized by the whole glorious show. That was before, though. Now that Barrett had found them out, he was leading the cops right to them.

"Besides that," she muttered, "I've had enough of this stinking desert!" She'd been stuck in this glorified old-folks home of a town for months, puttering along the streets in a golf cart with the rest of the old farts. Chad thought he had it bad in jail. Try standing in line at the supermarket checkout listening to them argue over which blue rinse highlights the gray best, or which denture adhesive kept their plates from slipping, or how their bowels were moving—described in painstaking detail.

She had thought of taking a chance more than once lately. Just rip off the gummy makeup that blocked her pores and made her face feel as though bacon grease were sliding around on it. Put on a dark wig and dress up and actually do something for a change, instead of rotting in front of the TV every night like the rest of these walking corpses.

Absolutely nothing happened in this town, except Mr. Big Deal Attorney came by about once a week and stayed a few hours. She was actually beginning to look forward to their sex. That's how she knew she was really going crazy—waiting breathlessly for someone who did it like he was taking care of another item at a meeting.

She'd had enough. This was it. The only reason she was still even here was to try to help Chad. She was going to go right home and pack up and get the hell out. She couldn't help it if Chad was still in jail. Maybe they weren't going to go away and live in Shangrila together like he thought, but he had to grow up sometime, didn't he? She'd go off with him to Tahiti or Bali or one of his other childish dreams of them living together in paradise. Then she'd leave him some money and she'd disappear. Hop the first jet to Europe. That was her dream—not dying of Polynesian paralysis in some sweat box on the equator with someone who wanted to spend the rest of his life with her.

She knew by heart exactly how her dream would go. She'd dreamed it many times while she was starving as an actress, sucking up to some third-rate producer for some crummy part. The Concorde left from Montreal once a week to Paris. She'd shake off the jet lag at the Internationale for a week—lounge around, buy a new wardrobe, eat at bistros, flirt with dark-haired Parisians. Then she'd fly to Stuttgart and pick up a Porsche, the big one that'll do three hundred klicks, and wind through the Black Forest until she got to the Autobahn near Munich. Then she'd take that monster all the way up

to two hundred miles an hour. That's when she'd finally feel free—
a hundred thousand in the luggage boot, the rest in an offshore bank,
her past far behind her, flying down the Autobahn, headed for Rome
or Monte Carlo, looking for the life she had always known she
deserved.

As soon as she arrived at the condo, she knew this was the time
to leave. She got in the golf cart and putted down to the store to pick
up some cold cream and cotton swabs and a few other things she
would need for her trip.

The desert wind was blowing hard as she putted back to the
condo, so the shawl wrapped around her shoulders billowed full and
flapped behind her. She bowed her head into the wind while she
clutched the shopping bag to her chest. When she got to her place,
she took a single key out of her purse, unlocked the door, and went
inside. She threw the shopping bag on the kitchen table and removed
the cotton balls and cold cream from the paper bag and went into
the bedroom.

First she pulled off the gray wig and threw it on the bed. Then
she removed the bobby pins that fastened her hair to the top of her
head, and her long, beautiful blond mane cascaded down her shoulders. In one practiced motion she took an elastic bow and pulled her
hair back into a ponytail.

Next she unbuttoned the rayon print blouse and took it off, revealing her lithe shoulders and delicate arms. In just her French-cut
bra she sat at the stool in front of the dressing table mirror and began
to peel the rubberized makeup off her face, the wrinkles around her
eyes, the creases on her forehead, the sagging jowls. Strip by strip the
years were peeled back until the image of a beautiful young woman
appeared in the mirror in front of her.

She unscrewed the top off the bottle of cold cream and started
applying it to her face. Then she began to scrub away the excess bits
of gummy makeup that stuck to her eyebrows and the down of her
cheeks and neck. This was always the painful part, like tweezering
her whole face.

There was a TV on a stand in one corner, and below it was a
VCR. Robin grabbed a screwdriver from the desk and sat in front of
the TV. She pulled it forward and turned it around. Then she took
the screwdriver and turned a screw in each corner until it fell into

her palm. Finally she removed the back plate. And there was the money—neat stacks of bills filling the gutless television.

Robin had a small suitcase next to the TV, and she started stacking the money neatly in it. The cash was in thin bundles of hundred-dollar bills bound together with paper rings that read $5,000. The packets of bills covered the entire bottom of the suitcase stacked three deep. There was one million, two hundred twenty-one thousand dollars left in all. No one except Robin knew she had that much.

She pulled one of the packets out and tucked it into a black straw purse sitting on her bedside table and put the suitcase lid down. Then she shut the snaps and spun the combination wheels next to the snaps so that the suitcase locked.

By the bed she had two more, packed suitcases. She strained as she lifted them onto the bed. She opened the first one and threw her wig and blouse and skirt inside. Then she opened the second and rummaged around but didn't find what she was looking for. She walked back to the dresser and pulled the drawers open, but they were already empty. Then she walked over to the closet, dressed in only her black bra and pink bikini panties. When she swung open the closet door, she looked directly into his eyes. Held at his side was the largest knife she'd ever seen. She knew he was there for only one reason—to kill her.

As he reached out and grabbed her by the hair on the back of her head, she stepped forward and brought her other foot up full force into his crotch. He let out a resounding whoosh of air and let go of her.

She was stumbling out of the closet on her hands and knees when his big hand caught her by an ankle. He lunged forward flat on his stomach, holding her foot with his outstretched arm, and she rolled over onto her back and thrust her heel into his scalp. She kicked him again, this time in the nose, and blood erupted from it. But he still wouldn't let go of her foot. She struggled, twisting onto her stomach again, but he began to pull her slowly toward him across the rug. Her bra hooked on the threshold of the closet door and was ripped off and caught around her neck. Three of her fingernails broke when she dug them into the rug as he dragged her to him. Then he reached up and caught her by the back of the thigh. Looking over her shoulder, she began to scream at the sight of the knife held above his head.

He drove the long, broad blade into her back and directly through her heart. She let out a groan and died, her hand still reaching for her money on the bed.

chapter

thirty-three

Sean fell asleep by the phone sometime after midnight on Thursday and was awoken early Friday morning when Mac finally called. He was in the bedroom of the condo at the Palm Desert address that Sean had given him.

"Mac, that you?" Sean asked. The last he'd heard from Mac was the message he had left on the recorder saying he was leaving immediately for the desert. "Jesus, I was about ready to get in the car and drive down there to look for you."

"It always takes longer when you don't find anything," Mac said.

"Dead end, huh?" Sean didn't bother to hide his disappointment.

"Found an empty condo with an old pizza in the fridge, a bunch of empty closets and a lot of dust," Mac said. "There's nobody here. Curtis is jacking you off again."

Mac heard something behind him and looked over his shoulder. He slowly dropped the receiver onto the bed. A man was standing in the doorway with a gun pointing at him.

"What the hell are you doing in here?" Sean could hear a man say.

"I'm looking for a girl who's supposed to live here," Mac said.

"I'll bet. What's her name?"

"Robin Penrose."

"No Robin Penrose here, smartass," he said. He was a tall, wiry man with a Semper Fi tattoo on his forearm and a dirty white cowboy hat on his head. He walked over to the bed with the barrel still pointing at Mac and hung up the phone. "Why don't you tell this story to the cops?"

"We don't need any official heat coming in on this," Mac said in his best imitation of a TV private eye. "I'm a P.I. investigating a case," Mac said and reached for his wallet.

The man pointed the gun at Mac's head. "Slow and easy there, pardner," he said, like he was in a Western.

"Just gonna show you my ID."

"All right." He nodded with a sneer. "But don't make any false moves."

Mac slipped his card out of his wallet and handed it to the guy, who snatched it and took a step back.

"I had information that my key witness lived in this apartment," Mac explained.

"A P.I., huh?" the man said and lowered the gun. "This a murder case?"

"Yeah, it is," Mac said. He thought he'd recognized a cop nut. This was the kind of guy who had a police-band radio and bragged to his friends about busts he was in on.

"No kiddin'!" he said and pushed the cowboy hat back on his head. "Who's your client?"

"I'm not at liberty—"

"Yeah, yeah, of course not," the man said. "Privileged info, right?"

"Yeah, that's right," Mac said casually, but he kept an eye on the gun.

"Who'd you say you were lookin' for?" he asked.

"A young lady about twenty-seven named Robin Penrose."

"Look, mister," he said and scratched his arm with the barrel of the gun, "the young ladies in this town are *fifty*-seven. I manage these units. Nothing but old folks around here."

"Here's a photo of her." Mac reached inside his coat pocket and pulled out the shot of Robin in a bikini. That was the one he usually showed to men because the sight of those long legs and bulging breasts always got their attention. "Have you seen her around here?"

"No," he said, fingering the photo as though checking a bill to see if it was a phony. "I wish I had. Hell of a set of lungs there."

"Yeah," Mac agreed, looking at the photo again. "Say, would you know who owns this place?"

"Some damn lawyer," he said and shook his head disapprovingly. Mac gave him a disgusted look back to let him know he felt the same way about lawyers.

"Know his name?"

"Can't tell you that. It's privileged," he said proudly. "But I can tell you he's the kind that uses it maybe three, four times a year. The rest of the time it sits vacant, except when he lets some of his big-deal friends use it."

"How 'bout lately?" Mac asked.

"Only one I saw lately was an older woman. She's been in and out. Looked like his mother. I don't like to be nosy, of course," he said and waved the gun around the room again. "I'm just here to make sure no one wrecks the place. Like with you. I seen the busted window out back and I figure you broke in."

"Nah, that wasn't me," Mac said. "A P.I.'s got those special keys. We can break into Fort Knox if we want to."

"Yeah, you gotta have 'em," the guy said with that tincture of awe in his voice that a fellow pro has for a good cop.

Mac put his hand out to shake. "Well, thanks, you been a great help, ah . . ."

"Floyd," the man said and shifted the gun to his left hand so he could shake. "Floyd McCracken."

Mac left and called Sean back and told him what had happened. Sean wanted him to stay in Palm Desert through the weekend to see what he could find. As far as the jury was concerned, until they saw Robin in the flesh, she was missing and probably dead.

Sean arrived at the courthouse early on Monday and was a little surprised to see Lowenstein already there. Usually the D.A. liked to wait until just before the judge came in so the cameras could catch his determined charge into the courtroom. Sean took a seat at the defense table next to Chad, and as soon as he had, Lowenstein walked over. He was smiling broadly. "I want to show you the Valentine Gamboa found pinned to his door this morning," the D.A. said.

Sean saw a flash of red as Lowenstein tossed an eight-by-ten photo on the table in front of him. It was Robin. She was naked from the waist up except for the locket lying between her breasts as though it had been lovingly placed there. Her throat was cut open well past each ear, her mouth agape, her eyes staring. The blood had been wiped away from the neck to show the wound better. This was not a quick snapshot in an adrenally charged moment. Robin had been posed. The locket was placed directly between her breasts, a fleck of blood on its gold facing. Her hair was pulled back and tucked under her head. The chin was forced up so the gash in the neck was spread wide, a chasm of bloody flesh cut back to the neck bone. Even her eyes seemed to be pinned open—bloodshot and stunned.

The photo was meant to leave no doubt that it was Robin Penrose and she was dead. This wasn't just one of her disguises. She'd been murdered and brutally mutilated.

Chad picked up the photo and stared numbly at it. He mumbled something that Sean couldn't understand, then he screamed, "Noooo!"

Suddenly everything broke loose in Chad. The girl he'd loved his whole life was gone. The months he'd spent in jail, months when he couldn't be with her, trusting her, not trusting her. They would never be together as she said, sailing off to some tropical island with only their dreams and a suitcase full of money. Now that it had all gone wrong, now that the noose Lowenstein had him fitted for was drawing tight around his neck, she would never come forward to save him.

Lowenstein saw the look on Chad's face and backed away. Then Chad suddenly broke for the door at the back of the court. Sean dived for him, but he missed and watched from his hands and knees as Seelicke drew his gun. Chad lowered his shoulders at the two bailiffs that stood in the way of the door and hit them hard enough so all three of them tumbled to the floor together. Chad tried to get to his feet, but the knees of three deputies held him down. He wrestled with them for a few minutes before Seelicke got the handcuffs on him.

Sean was in among them when Chad was pulled to his feet. He

took ahold of Chad by the back of the neck and started shouting in his face, "Chad, don't worry. It's going to be all right. We don't even know if that's her," he lied.

Four deputies crowded around Chad and lifted him, his feet barely touching the ground, through the door back to lockup. Sean followed them the whole way, talking to Chad.

Sean came back into the courtroom a minute later and charged up to the D.A. "Where the hell did you get that?"

Lowenstein winked his brows. "Anonymous," he said. "Probably just a concerned citizen."

"You know this isn't conclusive," Sean said. "How do we know it's Robin or that she's even dead?" He was flapping the photo in front of the D.A. "It could be a fake."

Lowenstein gave a short laugh. "You're going to have to convince a jury of that," he said. "And I don't think you can."

"This isn't evidence until I get it checked by a competent expert," Sean said, bluffing for time until he could think of something. But what? Robin Penrose had been brutally murdered. Chad was going to be convicted.

"Don't bother. I've already taken it to the coroner," Lowenstein said and handed Sean a path report. "In his opinion you can't fake what you see there," Lowenstein said, pointing at Robin's throat. "It's not as good as the actual body, but it's the next best thing. When the jury gets a look at that photo, I'd bet my Mercedes they'll only be out five minutes before they convict your boy. And you know how much I love my Mercedes," he said and grinned.

Sean knew Lowenstein was right. All he could do now was fight for more time. He turned to the judge. "Your Honor," Sean said, "the prosecution has just handed me this photo that they allege is the victim in this trial."

"I've seen the photo."

"Well, then, as you can see, this new evidence, if it can be considered evidence, makes it impossible for the defense to proceed at this time."

"Why is that?" Macklin snapped. Sean could see that he was still upset about the disturbance Sean's client had made in his courtroom. He was not in a generous mood. "Both sides in a no-body case have to expect that a body can be produced at any time."

"But, Your Honor, there still is no body. I'll need time to determine the authenticity of this photo—when and where it was taken." Sean knew with the coroner's statement already in his hands, the judge wasn't going to allow him a lot of room. "This is the prosecution's most damaging evidence," he pleaded. "I need more time."

"Mr. Barrett, I gave you two days last week. This case has already dragged on much too long. Unless you can show further cause, you will be ready to proceed tomorrow at nine o'clock."

Sean knew he had to take a chance if he was going to convince the judge to grant him more time. It would be disastrous for the defense to continue without investigating the photo and further developing what Mac had found out in Vegas. He didn't really want to be forced to show Lowenstein where he was headed with his investigation into Carter's stock scam. But he had to do something quickly. Macklin had to grant him a delay, and as unconfirmed as this new evidence was, he had to use what he had.

"Your Honor, there is, in fact, quite a lot of new evidence that has only recently come to my attention."

Macklin looked heavenward. How many times had he heard the promise of new evidence from a drowning attorney? "Go on, Mr. Barrett," he said.

Lowenstein had his arms folded across his chest, almost grinning. He was enjoying the whole show. Technically he could still have his no-body conviction, but now with this photo the jury wouldn't have to be worried about whether or not a death had taken place.

"It has recently come to my attention that the alleged victim, Robin Penrose, was involved in a complicated scheme of insider trading and money laundering that the IRS and the SEC are at this moment actively investigating. It is my belief that if she was killed, her death was related to that investigation. And I believe if she was killed, it could have only happened in the last two or three days."

As Lowenstein and Gamboa sat and listened, Sean went on to tell the judge everything he knew about Las Vegas, Carter Robinson and his relationship with Robin. When he was through, Macklin leaned back in his chair, tapping a pen against one of his desert boots propped on his knee.

"Mr. Barrett, nothing you've just said convinces me you deserve a lengthy continuance. From what I've seen of that photograph, there is a strong argument that Robin Penrose is dead, all right. Nothing except that photo alters the facts of this trial so far. Whether or not she was involved in some illegal stock dealings is not relevant to that photo unless you can connect the two, which so far you haven't," Macklin said. "The notion that she was hiding with the full knowledge of your client and that she was only murdered in the last few days seems a little too convenient for your purposes. All I'm willing to do based upon what you just told me is give you one additional day," Macklin said and swung his gavel hard against the wood block. "This court is adjourned until Wednesday."

chapter

thirty-four

"That was some yarn Barrett tried to sell Macklin." Lowenstein laughed and took a drink of his margarita. A few flakes of salt stuck to his upper lip. He was seated at a front table in El Ranchito with Gamboa and Knox, celebrating his imminent victory. They were surrounded by plates of Mexican chichis—nachos, chips and salsa, and guacamole. Lowenstein was the only one eating.

"Can you believe he'd try that smoke screen about the girl being alive until a few days ago? Here, have another drink, Sergeant," Lowenstein said and hailed a waiter.

"I've had enough," Gamboa grunted.

"How about you?"

Knox looked over at his partner's scowl. "Nah, I'm all right," he said.

"I got a problem with this investigation," Gamboa said.

Knox rolled his eyes. Here goes, he thought.

"There's no problem, Sergeant," Lowenstein said gaily. "It's all over. Have a drink. It's time to celebrate."

"I ain't buyin' it," Gamboa said.

Lowenstein lowered his margarita to the table and looked incredulously at the cop.

"This is what you always wanted, isn't it?" Knox said. "The guilty to get what they have coming. That's what you always told me. Curtis is guilty, isn't he?"

"I'm not so sure now."

"What do you mean, you're not sure?" Lowenstein said. His face was beginning to turn red with alcohol and anger.

"I mean that fuckin' photo."

"That fucking photo, as you refer to it, seals the conviction," Lowenstein said, his voice rising. He didn't want any trouble from some dumbshit cop.

"It's just too easy," Gamboa said. "Where did it come from? Who took it? Who sent it? The whole thing just doesn't feel right."

"Goddamn it, Gamboa, you've been with the department long enough to know that tips and other pieces of evidence arrive at the station anonymously all the time. People don't want to get involved, but they still want to see the bastard get nailed."

Gamboa put both forearms on the table and looked squarely at the D.A. "Okay," he said, "then why did Curtis take that photo?"

"Who says it had to be Curtis?"

"If it wasn't Curtis, then we've got an accomplice or, at the very least, an accessory after the fact."

"You're overthinking this case, Sergeant," Lowenstein said, trying to be patient. "That's a dangerous practice."

"Maybe. But I'm going to spend a day or two checking out Barrett's story."

Lowenstein slammed his glass down on the table, and the salt flew in all directions. "Who the hell do you think you're working for—the damned defense?" he said. "Now, listen to me carefully, Sergeant." His eyes narrowed for an attack. "You're my chief investigator on this case. You do exactly what I say. If you don't do exactly what I say, I'll take you before the review board and nail your sorry ass for insubordination and ten other things." He stabbed a finger toward Gamboa. "And, believe me, you'll find yourself in some very serious shit when I'm the one pressing the beef."

Gamboa didn't answer. He just stared back at Lowenstein. Knox knew that look, and it scared the hell out of him. Gamboa was like a pit bull. If he got something between his teeth, he could be rapped over the head with a two-by-four and he wouldn't let go.

"Now listen up, Sergeant," Lowenstein said. Gamboa's stare was locked on the D.A. "Don't spend one minute investigating Curtis's bullshit, on or off duty. I want you to get ahold of the coroner and have his ass in court Wednesday along with the photography expert from downtown. There's a guy there named Watanabe who will tap dance all over that photo for us. He's a little flaky, though, so send a unit down to pick him up in the morning so I know he'll be in court on time. Then show the photo to that woman—what's her name—at the firm where the Penrose girl worked . . . ?"

"Carrie Robinson," Knox threw in to help out.

"Right. Get her to ID the picture," Lowenstein said. Then he threw back the rest of his drink. "All right, you two have a lot to do by Wednesday. You better get going," he said and dismissed the two cops with the back of his hand.

"Sure thing," Knox said and pulled at his partner's arm. Gamboa still hadn't said anything. He just kept staring at Lowenstein.

"We're absolutely clear on all this, aren't we, Sergeant?" Lowenstein said, staring right back.

Gamboa nodded slowly and got up. Knox nudged him toward the door. He knew he had to hustle if he was going to get everything done. And he knew he'd have to do it all by himself because Gamboa hadn't heard a word the D.A. said.

Sean was sitting at his desk, trying to find some escape for Chad. If he was telling the truth, then Robin had to have been killed in the past three or four days. She'd visited Chad on Thursday at the jail, and Gamboa had received the photo on Monday. The only problem was, Sean couldn't prove any of it. Even the photo didn't help. The coroner's report had stated that there was no way to tell when the photo was taken. The batch of paper it was printed from was over six months old, so the photo could have been snapped any time since then. That meant Chad could have killed her, photographed her mutilated body, and been arrested the next day. The photo just proved that Robin was dead. And proof of her death was all the prosecution had ever needed to ensure a conviction.

But if Chad was telling the truth, then who killed her? Shabba would have been the most likely one, but he was at the hospital in a coma. It had to be Carter. With Robin dead, his crime was now untraceable. And what about Carrie? How was she involved?

A knock at the door interrupted his thoughts. He was reading the coroner's report for the umpteenth time as he made his way to the door. When he opened it, Carrie was standing in the doorway.

"Can I come in?" It was a question she'd never asked. Before when he opened the door, she'd step into his arms, and a lot of times they'd just kiss their way right into the bedroom.

He hesitated a moment. Then he noticed that her eyes were red and her mascara smeared. "They showed you the photograph, didn't they?" he said and opened the door for her.

He had a copy of that photo on his desk. Robin's blood gave a sepia hue to the whole frame, and her eyes had a pitiful, agonized look. It had to have been tough for Carrie to look at. She walked across the living room to the sliding glass door and gazed at the sea.

"Sean, will you answer me one question?" she said, turning away from the window to look at him. The late afternoon sun silhouetted her hair and turned her eyes green.

"Probably not," he said. "But you can ask it anyway." He walked to the desk and sat on it. Beside him were photos of Robin: the glamour shot in the bikini, the aged photo, and the last one she'd ever posed for.

"When was that photo taken?"

He knew which one she meant. "You mean, when do I think it was taken?"

"Yes, of course," she said. Her face had suddenly taken on a lawyer's probing expression.

"Sometime in the last three or four days."

She moved away from the window into the dusk of the room, and everything about her seemed to soften, even her voice.

"Are you sure of that?" She put a hand on the back of the sofa.

"I'm sure," he said, even though he wasn't. All he had to go on was Chad's word, and he knew how reliable that was. He was just betting that Chad no longer had any reason to lie.

"Can I ask you how you know?"

He hesitated.

"Please, Sean," she said and began moving toward him, "this is very important. My knowing can't hurt your client now."

She was right, of course. At one time he couldn't have waited to tell her everything that was on his mind. Even though it wouldn't matter, telling her anything now felt like a betrayal.

"Robin visited Chad in jail last Thursday disguised as an old woman," he said. "And four days later Gamboa gets the photo."

"How do you know it was Robin at the jail?"

"Chad told me."

She looked at him doubtfully. "That's not enough for a court of law." They were doing what they had done for so many hours in the past few months—discussing law.

"I know that. So I took this computer-aged photo of Robin and showed it to the jailor on duty at the time and he identified her." He took the photo off his desk and handed it to her. "Plus," Sean said, "she signed in as his mother."

"Chad's mother died years ago," she said, studying the photo.

"Exactly," Sean said. "Besides, who else could pull off a disguise like that?" He pointed over at the photo. "It had to be someone very close to Chad who would have a motive for not wanting anyone to know who she was. Nobody I know of fits that description except Robin Penrose." He hesitated as he realized he was using Carrie to sound out his ideas again. He wasn't sure that pastime was safe to indulge in anymore. "It's not conclusive, of course," he said. "But it's enough for me to be convinced."

"Me too," Carrie said. She sank onto the sofa. "Then who killed her?" she finally said without looking up. "Who could have done *that* to her?"

Sean got up from the desk. No matter how much she'd betrayed him, he still didn't like hurting her. "I'm sorry to say this, Carrie, but your father had every reason to want her dead."

She swung around on him. "My father could never have done that!" she screamed and pointed toward the bloody photo on his desk.

"You never know what someone will do when they're backed in a corner."

Carrie began to cry again. Sean went to get a drink for her. He poured a glass of bourbon and water and threw in two cubes. He handed it to her, and just holding it seemed to steady her.

"I think I may have killed her," she said without looking up.

He stood looking down at her, and all he could think to say was "What?"

When she finally looked up at him, he could see by her face that it would be many nights before she would sleep again unhaunted. "I came here last Thursday," she said, "to pick up my things when I knew you wouldn't be here. I couldn't really handle seeing you. . . ." She hesitated for a second and looked at him.

He nodded. "I knew you'd been here. All your things were gone."

"But . . . Sean," she said, struggling with how to say what was coming, "I replayed the message you left for Mac that day telling him where he could find Robin."

"And you told your father?"

"Yes."

Sean knew he didn't want to hear the rest. But, of course, he had to know. "Then what happened?"

She took a sip of the bourbon, her face reflecting the burn in her throat as it went down. "I should have known something was wrong," she said. "He just sat there staring at me. Then he told me he had to go to the office and we'd talk about it later." She turned and put her hand on the armrest. "I haven't seen him since. He's been gone all weekend!"

Sean sat down heavily on the edge of his desk. "Didn't you stop to think that your father had a very strong motive for wanting to see Robin disappear permanently? She's the only one who could tie him to insider trading."

She shook her head. Sean could see the confusion and horror mixed on her face. Her father had murdered, or ordered that butcher to murder, her best friend. "That photo of Robin . . ." she said. "She was . . . mutilated, for God's sake. He almost cut her head off. . . . How could he do it?"

"Because if she came back," Sean said, "he knew he'd spend the rest of his life in prison."

"But why the photo? Why did he have to cut her up so brutally? And then to photograph her that way." Her voice cracked. "It's horrible, Sean."

"That photo is going to convict Chad and he knows it. With a photo the time of death can't be pinpointed," he said. "So the prosecution has the next best thing to the body, and I have no way to contest when she was killed."

"So Chad will be convicted and sent to prison for life for my father's crime," Carrie said.

Sean just nodded.

"That lousy bastard," she said, and her head sank to her chest.

When Carrie finally looked up, her expression was resolute. She went on to tell Sean everything she knew about her father's involvement in the stock scheme. She knew nothing about the Jamaican or Berger, though.

When she was through, she reached up and put her hand on his arm. He turned away from her. "You used me," he said.

"It wasn't really like that. Sure, at first I thought if we had dinner I might be able to find out some things. I thought Chad had killed Robin when she tried to break their relationship off. Sure, I wanted to help my father. But I had no idea he would become involved in murder," she said and took his hand. "And I didn't know I was going to fall in love with you."

Sean didn't say anything. He could feel his anger slipping away. He wanted this whole nightmare to be a fantasy. He wanted to believe everything she said. But he held on to his anger. It was the only protection he had from her.

He walked to the window and looked out at the sea. It had always been his refuge. Out in the ocean he was untouched by anything on land. All the smells were of the sea, all the sounds were the thousand different sounds water made. Even the feeling of land was replaced by the roll, bob, and rise of the sea.

Carrie watched his back for a while, then picked up the aged photo of Robin and began to inspect it. "Sean, I think I've seen this woman before," she said.

Gulls were filling the sand in front of his cottage. "Of course you have," he said. "That's Robin."

"No," she said, slowly shaking her head. "I mean I've seen this old woman before. The clothes and the hair are different, of course. But I've seen her somewhere."

He turned toward her. "When did you see her?" he said.

She looked at the photo again, trying to piece it together. "Just the other day," she said. "But I can't remember where exactly."

If Carrie had really seen Robin in the past few days, it would verify everything Chad had told him. "You sure it's not just Robin's likeness that's familiar to you?"

She looked at him as if to say, "Come on, this is Carrie." The truth was, it was hard for them not to communicate perfectly. Their minds worked so well together. Despite himself, he smiled at her.

"You know how it is?" she said. "When you know you've seen someone but you can't place where?"

"Sure. I know what you mean."

He moved close to her and put his hands on her shoulders. "Look, Carrie," he said, "this is very important. If you can remember where you saw her, will you let me know immediately?"

"Don't worry," she said. "It'll come to me."

Within an hour after Carrie left, Carter called Sean. He'd just talked to Carrie. "Can you come by the office?"

"All right," Sean said and looked at his watch. It was just two. "How about six o'clock?"

"Fine."

Before Sean confronted Carter, though, he wanted to confer with Spann. He had phoned him several times during the trial to go over some of the details of Chad's defense, and at this point there was no one else he could go to for advice. Besides that, Spann had known Carter for years, and he might have some insight into what Carter was thinking.

He tracked Spann down in the bar at the Santa Ana Country Club. He was sitting with his foursome, giving their beery postmortems on the round when Sean walked in.

"Sean, how are you?" Spann said, standing up. "You know Ted Slater and Bob Bruenig and that's Bob's brother Ken." After he'd shaken hands all around, Spann said, "Join us for a drink."

"Thanks. Some other time," Sean said. "I need to talk to you."

"All right," Spann said, turning off the smile. By the look on Sean's face, Spann knew it was urgent. "Will you fellows excuse me? Sean and I have to talk. He's got that big trial going, you know."

Spann took him by the arm and led him over to a corner table that overlooked the eighteenth green. "Now, what's the problem?" he said. It was the way he'd started so many of their meetings at the firm.

"I think Carter and Robin were engaged in insider trading," Sean began. "He was obtaining information from his own clients, and then they were using that information to buy and sell stock," said Sean.

"And you have proof of that?" Spann asked.

"He admitted most of it to Carrie, and there are witnesses who can identify Robin in Vegas trading the stock of one of his biggest clients. Plus, his wife told me he was having an affair with Robin."

"So far I haven't heard enough to get Carter indicted for any securities wrongdoing."

"Well, it's obvious Robin Penrose can't testify. Carter made sure of that. I believe he was hiding Robin out in Palm Desert. And when he found out I was on to their stock scam and she was the only one who could connect him to it, he killed her."

Spann whistled. "That's a very serious allegation," he said. "Can you prove that the girl was in Palm Desert?"

Sean shrugged. "I think so," he said, exaggerating what he had. In any case, that wasn't the point he was most worried about. "Last Thursday," he went on, "someone who strongly resembled the same old lady who was in Vegas with Chad visited him in County lockup. As a matter of fact, I nearly ran into her myself."

Spann shook his head as if those facts were of little value. Sean had to have the kind of goods that would sell in a courtroom. "Do you know for sure it was her?"

"The jailor on duty at the time identified this photo." Sean pulled the computer-aged photo of Robin out of his briefcase and laid it on the table. "This woman signed in as Chad's mother, who's been dead for years."

Spann looked at the photo for several long seconds before he spoke. "In my experience, juries don't like these newfangled techniques," he sniffed. "Anything else?"

"Yes," Sean said, trying to surmount, one by one, the obstacles Spann was throwing in his way. "I just showed Carrie the photo, and she's sure she recently saw the woman."

"Really? Did she say where?"

"Well, she doesn't recall exactly right now," Sean said. "But you know Carrie, she'll come up with it."

"Yes," Spann said, still eyeing the photo. "I'm sure she will."

"So with my eyewitnesses in San Francisco and Bakersfield and the hotel and bank employees who saw the old lady in Vegas and what we know about Carter, I think we've got a strong defense."

Spann frowned at Sean's confidence. "Frankly, I'm a little surprised at you," he said. "You're not going to be able to prove Carter did it without more."

"I know. You taught me better than that," Sean said, cuffing Spann on the arm. "All I'm trying to do is place as much doubt as possible in the jurors' minds. And even if I can't prove it, there's enough to at least establish doubt."

Spann sat a moment thinking it over. "Sean, you're right about one thing. It could place doubt in the jurors' minds. But this strategy could very easily backfire on you too."

Sean was surprised. "How do you figure that?"

"You're going to give the prosecution a perfect motive for Chad to kill her."

"You mean the money?"

"And jealousy," Spann said. "You're going to have to prove that Carter and Robin were lovers. If Chad loved her, he wouldn't like that, would he?" He put his hand on Sean's shoulder. "If you introduce this whole idea of insider trading, which the jury knows nothing about, you will be supplying the prosecution with all the ammunition they will need to bury your client."

Sean sat back. He didn't agree, but he couldn't afford to ignore what he had to say. Spann's instincts for criminal law had proved many times to be uncanny.

"It's best if you stay completely away from that stock angle," Spann said, waving it away with his hand. "I think your lookalikes in Bakersfield and San Francisco are all you need to place sufficient doubt in the jurors' minds. All of that stuff about Carter is overkill. I wouldn't risk it."

Sean sat and watched a hacker in a green-side sand trap take three wild swings to get free. After he trudged out of the sand, he slammed the club down.

"I'd hate to depend on just the lookalikes," Sean said. "Lowenstein might easily convince this jury that there are any number of young blondes who could be mistaken for Robin. To me the odds are still too high that he'll be convicted."

"I'm telling you," Spann said, "if you put Carter up on the stand, you're taking a very big gamble."

Sean respected Spann's opinion. But he'd come to trust his own judgment. It was his career on the line, not Spann's. Sean got up and shook hands. "I think I'm going to have to take that gamble," he said.

chapter

thirty-five

Carrie turned her car onto the private lane that ran behind the homes lining Doheny Beach, pulled into Sean's carport, and used her key to unlock his back door. Sean was bound to be along soon, and since she was in Capistrano already, she figured she'd just wait for him at his house. A light was on in Sean's back bedroom-office, so she went in and read a magazine while she waited. She had remembered where she'd seen Robin disguised as the old lady. But more important, she'd remembered who Robin had been with.

A minute after she pulled into Sean's place, a silver Mercedes drove into the public parking lot and motored slowly to the north end, farthest away from Sean's house. The driver turned into a dark corner near a snack bar and quietly got out of his car. Opening the trunk, he reached in under a blanket and pulled out a long leather case. Then he opened the back door and got back into the car. When he emerged a few minutes later, he was carrying a loaded safari rifle with a night scope.

Since it was a weeknight, there was no one on the beach that he could see. He checked the lifeguard tower and behind the snack bar for any signs of teenage sex rituals, but there was no one there. He made his way down to the shore, shuffling awkwardly in the sand with the rifle held against his side. When he got to a jetty a hundred yards from Sean's place, he crouched behind one of the larger boulders. He made sure he was hidden from the parking lot and most of the beach. He laid the rifle across his lap and waited for the lights in Sean's front room to go on. That way he would get a clear shot at her. If she stayed in the back too long, though, he'd have to go in after her. He couldn't let her live to tell Sean what she knew.

After a while Carrie went out the kitchen door, down the side of the house to the back patio, and stretched out on the lounger. It was in a shadow near a trellis of geraniums that Sean had grown to give a little privacy from the beer-drinking rappers who liked to cruise the lot. It had always been her favorite place to sit in the evenings and watch the cold, clear winter sky—the Bear, the Dippers, and Venus some nights as bright as the strike of a match.

The man crouched behind the rocks, unable to see Carrie as she lay motionless in the lounger, looking at the stars, safe as long as she didn't move.

By the time Sean arrived at Carter's office, the last pink hues of a winter sunset had dissolved into the blue ink of evening. He parked his car down the block and trotted across the busy street to the high-rise where Robinson, Racine and Robinson was located. Everyone else in the office had gone home for the day, and Carter greeted Sean at the door.

"Come in. Let's go back to my office," he said, pointing down a darkened corridor. Sean stiffened, realizing he was alone in an empty building with a man he suspected of murdering four people. And he was here to accuse him of those murders.

Carter poured them both a bourbon and sat behind his desk. He skipped the frat-boy chitchat for once and got right to the point. "I talked to Carrie," he said without preface. "You really upset her." He took an easy swallow of the whiskey. It was not his first of the day, Sean could see that. "She said you think I had something to do with Robin's death. So why don't you at least do me the courtesy of telling me what you think you've got on me?"

Sean threw the aged photo of Robin on the desk. "I can prove this woman was in Vegas with Chad. I can prove she bought at least a million dollars of Laramie Homes stock the day before it skyrocketed. And I can prove she visited my client last Thursday in lockup."

Carter glanced at the photo, then back at Sean, and took another mouthful of his drink.

"What's this photograph have to do with Robin?" he asked, waving it.

"This is a computer-aged photo of her," Sean said.

Carter looked at the photo again. This time he put together what Sean suspected. "I see," he said. "You think you can connect me to insider trading. And since Robin was alive until a few days ago, according to your theory, I was probably the one who killed her." He took another drink. "And if the jury buys your story, your boy Chad gets cut loose."

"I don't think a jury would convict him," Sean said.

"All right," Carter said, "but what about motive? What reason would I have for killing her?"

"Come on, Carter. That's the easy part," Sean said. "So that she wouldn't connect you to your stock and money-laundering scheme. I understand the SEC and IRS are both very anxious to hear about that. Robin was the only one who could hang you."

Sean put down his glass still half full, and Carter reached over and filled it. "That's probably true," Carter said, filling his own glass. "Now, you say this woman, allegedly Robin in disguise, was seen as recently as last Thursday?"

"Right," Sean said.

"And when did the D.A. first come into possession of the photo of Robin's body?"

"Early Monday."

"So your theory is I killed her sometime between Thursday and late Sunday or early Monday. Is that it?"

"I'm afraid so," Sean said.

Carter stood up and hurled his glass against the wall. The crystal shattered into a thousand shards at Sean's feet. "You little punk," he yelled. "You've turned my own daughter against me."

Sean got up and walked toward the door. "Hey, we're not going to do it this way, Carter," he said.

"Hold it," Carter said, calming quickly. "I have something to show you first."

Sean stood with his hand on the doorknob.

"You think you have a neat little package, don't you, Sean?" Carter reached down and opened the bottom drawer of his desk. Sean froze and looked at the door.

"Don't worry, Counselor." Carter pulled out a file and held it up for Sean to see. "It's not loaded."

Sean stayed by the door but let go of the knob.

"Last Thursday when Carrie told me Robin was alive and your investigator was bringing her in, I called the SEC and met with them in Los Angeles that afternoon. That's where I was until late yesterday. I knew as soon as you found Robin, the whole mess would be exposed."

Carter held the file out toward Sean, who walked over to get it, then sat down again.

"As you can see by these documents, I've been in SEC custody since last Thursday," he said. "I'm out on bail now."

Sean thumbed through the papers as Carter continued. "That little move probably saved me a minimum of ten years in the clink. They like it when you can put a ribbon on their case for them. I'll probably spend some time in jail, but it'll be at some country club. And they won't insist on wiping me out financially to prove their point either."

"What you're saying is, you no longer had a reason to kill Robin," Sean said as he leafed through the file.

"I had nothing to gain by seeing her dead."

Sean knew he was right, of course. Why would he confess and then kill the person who was going to turn him in?

"It was smart to go to the SEC," Sean said.

"If I were really smart, I never would have tried a stunt like that in the first place."

Sean's drink hit his empty stomach and began to spread through his body. Carter filled both glasses again.

"I wanted to see you before you made me prove in open court that I didn't kill anybody," Carter said. "It's going to be tough enough on my family and friends without the whole mess being dragged into a murder trial."

He sunk heavily in his swivel chair and put one foot on the top of his desk. The knot of his tie was already pulled loose at the collar. "Something I want you to understand is that Carrie had nothing to do with any of this—the stocks, the money laundering, Robin. None of it," he said and emphasized it with a bottoms-up swig. "The only mistake she made was trying to protect her father. And loving you, of course."

"Me?" Sean laughed.

"Yeah, you!" Carter said. "What the hell are you made of anyway? Stone, for God's sake?" he scolded. "When I told her everything, I handcuffed her. She fell in love with you, but she had to protect me. It had to be damn rough on her, don't you think?"

Sean looked down at his drink. The mirrored surface bounced with light. It had hurt to break it off with Carrie. As soon as the rage had eased in a day or so, he had started to ache for her. "I guess so," he said.

"If you weren't so damn proud, you'd have realized she had nothing to do with all this," Carter said, disgusted. "You'd have trusted her."

"That's exactly what I did. That's how I let her get so close." His anger flared a moment, and he looked Carter in the eye. "Tell me, how could Robin be involved in such a complicated scam and yet Carrie, her best friend, have no idea about it? It's hard to swallow."

"Look, Sean," he said, "Robin was a first-class manipulator. She used me, your client, and everybody else she ran into, including Carrie," he said, punctuating his daughter's name. "Robin went after me with a battle plan. One minute she's telling me how no man had ever made love to her like that before, and the next she was asking me about stocks." Carter laughed at his own blindness.

"It was all her design," he went on. "The disguises, the fake ID. She sat in on most of my client meetings anyway, so she knew who was hot and who wasn't." He pointed down at a chair where Robin had sat, taking notes and scheming. "She knew exactly when a stock was going to jump. She wasn't just beautiful and smart, she was clever too. The only thing she really needed me for was the capital to pull it off."

"And you gave it to her," Sean said, only half accusing, the rest curiosity. A lot of mayhem had been unleashed because of her, and he wanted to know the how and why.

"Sure, I gave it to her," Carter said. "Gladly. Remember, she was a damned beautiful girl. A face like that can make a man dream maybe a little more than he should." He sat back in his chair and stared at the night sky out his window. "But, hey," he said, looking back at Sean, "I don't want to make it sound like I was completely innocent here. I needed the money and she had what seemed like a good way to get a lot of it fast. It was a beauty of a plan too. All we had to do was not get greedy."

"But she did," Sean prompted.

Carter shook his head. "Greed was her middle name. I thought Spann loved money. This bitch worshiped it. I gave her five hundred grand, and she was supposed to buy Laramie issues with it. Only this time she's got another five hundred grand, or maybe more, and she buys another chunk of Laramie stock with that money." Carter laughed again. "She'd found another sucker."

"You mean Chad?"

"No, someone besides that poor sap," Carter said, dismissing the idea with a wave of his hand. "Chad was just her convenient little fool. She needed someone to escort her around Vegas with all that loot. Up until then she'd treated him like a stray dog. He's the real tragedy in all this. She dangled that pussy in front of him, told him it was going to be just like before, and she had him walking up walls for her."

"That's the way I always had it figured," Sean said. Draining his glass, he stood up and put his fists on Carter's desk. "So who killed her?"

"It's simple, really," Carter said. "As soon as you find out who gave her the other half mil, you'll know."

"It looks that way, doesn't it?" Sean said and flopped back down in his chair. He'd made an ass of himself charging up here like a TV detective. "I'm sorry, Carter. I guess I jumped a little too quickly to accuse you."

"Forget it, Sean," he said, waving. "What the hell. I got myself into some pretty deep shit. Why wouldn't you think I'd be capable of murder too? I'll tell you, I'd like to have murdered her," he said, a little drunk. "I bet there's a couple dozen other jerks just like me that would like to help. She was something on a stick, let me tell you."

Sean slowly sipped the bourbon while he pieced it together. Carter had nothing to do with Robin's death, but what about the Berger case? What was his part in all that? "Something just doesn't make sense to me, though," Sean said. "You're on the board of Medtech, right?"

"Yeah."

"And you knew about the upcoming merger with Kaufmann?"

"Yes, but I didn't use that information to buy stock."

"Why not?"

"Because a member of a board of directors is the first person the SEC suspects. And they were already sniffing around about the Laramie Homes deal. They'd be all over me. I didn't want to take that kind of chance." Both feet were resting on the top of his desk. Sean had scooted his chair closer so he could prop his feet up too.

"You knew about the break-in, though?"

"Sure. What about it?"

"The president at Medtech told Scott the break-in involved insider trading."

Carter took a few seconds to realize what that meant. "I see," he said disgustedly. "So naturally you thought that I was involved in that break-in too. Shit, Sean, just because I was involved once with insider trading doesn't mean I'm responsible for every dirty deal on Wall Street. Three people were murdered in that case, including Scott."

"There's a connection between the two cases besides you," Sean said calmly.

"What's that?"

"The Jamaican that I believe murdered those three people in the Berger case called me several times about the Chad Curtis case, and I'm certain I saw him with Robin in Bakersfield after her disappearance."

"So you thought I hired this muscle to kill, what? Four people?" Carter was growing angry again.

"I knew you were involved in the Laramie Homes deal," Sean said. "Then I found out you were on the board of Medtech. And I already knew this Jamaican was involved with both cases. So, of course, I thought you were behind both scams."

"Hey, who is this Jamaican?" Carter asked. "What's his name?"

"Shabba St. James."

"Christ, I know that asshole! He's an old client of Spann's. In fact, he was on Spann's payroll at one time as a street informant," Carter said. "Oh, he's a lovely boy. Ran a major drug gang called the Cane Cutters. Shabba used to keep his animals in line with a machete, I remember that."

"That's the guy," Sean said, not sure if he was being bluffed. "How long ago was that?"

"Just before you were hired. When Spann was still handling the criminal cases for the firm."

The phone rang then on Carter's private line, and he picked it up. "Yeah . . . everything's fine. . . . Yeah, he's here. . . . Hold on, I'll put you through on the speaker phone."

Carter pushed a button on the phone and put the receiver back in the cradle. "Go ahead, Carrie."

"Sean," Carrie said, "I'm sorry to interrupt. But this is very important. I've been at your house for a while now waiting for you. Then I figured out you were probably at my father's office."

"Yes, what about it?" Sean said.

"That old lady who you suspect was Robin in disguise? I remember where I saw her."

"Great! Where?" Carter leaned toward the speaker with Sean.

"She was talking with Jonathan Spann last Thursday in the parking garage next to his office," she said. "I went over there on business. When I was walking toward the elevator, they were standing next to his car together. I noticed they were arguing. She was crying and I asked Jonathan if I could help. He said everything was all right, and he practically shoved her into his car and drove away."

"What happened?" Carter and Sean said together.

"Nothing. I took the elevator down to the office and forgot all about it. What threw me off was her clothes. They were completely different than in the photo. But I'm sure that was her."

"Wait a second, Sean," Carter said, grabbing his arm across the desk and speaking toward the phone so Carrie could hear. "Do you know the address where Robin was hiding out in Palm Desert? Carrie never told me."

"I thought you knew."

"Hell, no. As soon as she told me Robin was alive, I knew I had to get to the SEC before she did. I didn't bother to find out exactly where she was," Carter said. "It wasn't on Valley Drive, was it?"

"Yes, it was, as a matter of fact," Sean said as he pulled a piece of paper from his wallet. "One-seven-four-six-nine," he read.

"That's Jonathan's place," Carter said and stood up. "Jesus, what the hell was he up to?"

"I'll tell you what he was up to. He had to be the one who financed the rest of the stock purchases," Sean said. "And that means he probably had something to do with those murders."

"Do you really think Jonathan is capable of murder?"

"That's obviously where Shabba comes in." Sean took a long drink of his bourbon and set the glass down on Carter's desk.

"What about Robin's murder?" Carrie asked, her voice crackling with static.

"Don't you see?" Sean said. His mind was racing toward an answer. "He had to kill Robin too. He knew I was about to blow the whistle on the stock deal, so they had to make sure that the only person who could connect them was out of the picture."

"I just have a hard time believing Jonathan would be capable of that," Carter said. "The sex and the money part I could see, maybe. Hell, I went for those myself. But to kill her too? That's a stretch, isn't it, Sean?"

"Not if Spann thought she was going to take off with the money all by herself and leave him to take the fall. He'd be ruined."

Carter sat there, shaking his head. "You know," he finally said, "you might be right."

"Why's that?"

"See, what really clinched my guilt for you, Sean, was when you saw I was on the board of Medtech."

Sean remembered that feeling of utter certainty he'd had that night after he'd broken into Spann, McGraw. It's what had made him come up here and make an ass of himself.

"But what you didn't know," Carter said and leaned across the desk, "was that Spann is special counsel for Kaufmann."

That was the missing piece.

"The break-in at Medtech had to be ordered by someone who suspected a merger," Carter said. "But only Schwitters and the two top guys at Kaufmann knew for sure when and how. That was part of the strategy to prevent just such a leak."

"What does it mean?" Carrie said, still on the speaker.

"I think it means your life could be in danger, Carrie."

"Why, for heaven's sake?"

"I met with Spann earlier and told him you recognized the photo. Spann knows now that you can connect Robin to him as late as last week."

Sean could hear Carrie plunk down in the creaking old wicker chair by his phone.

"You said you're at my place?" Sean interrupted.

She found herself trembling too violently to answer.

"Carrie?" they both said.

"Yes," she finally said, "I'm at your cottage."

"Stay there," Sean said. "I'm on my way."

Running to his car, Sean fishtailed out of Carter's lot and sped down MacArthur Boulevard to PCH. Depending on traffic, he was at least thirty minutes from Capistrano. There was nothing to suggest that Carrie was in any immediate danger, nothing to call the cops about really. But something was searing in his gut, telling him he had to get to Carrie as soon as he could.

That's why Spann has been so generous with his advice throughout the trial, Sean thought. I kept him up to date on every aspect of the case, every clue, every fact, every piece of evidence that could lead to him. That's why, in the beginning, Spann had wanted him off the case. Who knew better Sean's reputation for relentlessness? Then, when he had seen he couldn't stop Sean from taking the case, Spann did a turnabout and graciously offered his help. *Feel free to drop by and discuss the case anytime.*

After her call to Sean and Carter, Carrie walked back out onto the deck, where he had a clear shot at her. The swells were breaking four to six feet, and the roar of the waves was considerable. When a huge breaker hit the beach, it muffled the sound of everything else—a semi going by on PCH, a jumbo winging toward John Wayne, a gunshot.

He rested the rifle against the boulder and steadied the stock against his shoulder. As Carrie walked across the patio and down the steps to the sand, the man trained the scope on her. He settled down and put the calibrated hairs across her chest, where it would do the most damage, and followed her down the beach, waiting. The next big wave would hide the blast and the scream.

He followed her in the green hue of the night scope as she bare-footed down toward the shore, the swells rolling in, a big wave mounting higher, bobbing into the rhythm of its exploding finale, his target sighted, his finger sweating against the steel trigger.

But there was something there. Yes, *there*. Farther down the beach. The man shifted the scope off Carrie and zeroed in on a couple strolling hand in hand toward her in the dark. He lowered the rifle and watched them while Carrie made her way down to the water. She found a spot on the rocks of the jetty in front of Sean's house and sat down.

The man waited. Since no other cars were in the parking lot, the couple had to have come from one of the houses back down the beach. As soon as they reached their house, they would probably turn and disappear inside.

He slid back down in the sand and waited.

As Sean came up over the rise at Dana Point, he could see that his place was still dark. He sped down PCH, turned onto Beach Road, and pulled up behind Carrie's car. He started calling out her name as soon as he opened the back door. A light was on in the bedroom and he went in.

"Carrie," he shouted, but she wasn't there. Flipping on a light in the living room, he opened the sliding glass door and stepped out onto the patio. He saw her sitting on the jetty and called her name, but the waves obscured his voice.

The strolling couple had gone inside, and the man rose to one knee, put the scope on Carrie, and waited for the next wave to crash. Sean started running across the sand toward her, calling out her name.

She didn't see Sean, but the man did. He switched the scope onto Sean, saw who it was, and immediately went back to Carrie. As he squeezed off a round, she finally heard Sean calling and turned around. The bullet slammed off the rocks.

Sean grabbed her as he fired again, and the impact of the high-velocity bullet catapulted both of them onto the rocks below. They lay motionless as blood stained the sand beneath them.

From where the man was crouched, he couldn't see where they'd fallen. He scanned with his night scope and spotted the couple emerging from their house up the beach. He couldn't afford to check to see if he'd killed them both. His rifle could bring down a five-hundred-pound cat, though. If he'd hit them—and he knew by the way their bodies had been blown off the jetty that he had—it had probably done the job.

The man ran up the beach, got in his car, and peeled out of the lot onto PCH. Now all he had to do was get rid of the weapon.

thirty-six

The neon flash of Whiskey Pete's a few yards beyond the California–Nevada border meant to Knox that he could nap another twenty minutes while Gamboa pushed the Buick hard toward Vegas. He laid his head back, listening to the drone of tires on pavement, and dozed off. When he lifted his head again, they were already winding past the last outcropping of hills before the highway dropped into the technicolor lights of Vegas.

"Gamboa," he moaned, "what are we doing in this godforsaken place?" He hated these out-of-county investigations, especially if they were unauthorized.

Knox could see the frayed shoulders of Gamboa's old brown suit as he hunched forward over the wheel, pressing the unmarked to do ninety. "We're going to find out who really killed Robin Penrose," Gamboa said.

"Boy, for someone who was so convinced we had our killer, you sure did a one-eighty."

"Look, college boy, unlike someone else we know who only wants to ring up another conviction so he can look like a big shot to his buddies at the TV stations, I want to nail the asshole who killed that girl."

"Yeah," Knox groaned, "but did we have to go off on an unauthorized trip that could get us both suspended to do it? Christ, why couldn't we just stay in town and investigate the leads around there?"

"Because, hay brains, that's not where the leads are in this case."

Knox pulled a cigarette out of Gamboa's shirt pocket and lit it. He hadn't smoked since college, but somehow it seemed like a good idea now. "So this means we have to call the station every hour and pretend we're at Dunkin fucking Donuts so they don't catch on that we've just crossed a state line."

"Relax, you big pussy, I've had my nuts in tighter vices than this plenty of times."

"Oh, sure," Knox said, taking a big drag, then coughing most of it out when it seared his throat. "But did you have to go and put my nuts in there next to yours?" He moaned again. "Hey, it's all right for you to ruin your life. But I've got a family. I've actually got something to live for."

"Aw, fuck you." Gamboa reached over and ripped the cigarette out of Knox's hand and took it over.

Knox slid down into the seat farther and closed his eyes again.

When they got into town, they headed directly for the Desert Sands. That's where Barrett had said MacDuff first picked up the trail of Robin Penrose. They asked around for Terwilliger and found out he didn't come on for a couple of hours, so Knox went looking for a phone to call his wife.

Gamboa was standing against one of the booths outside the card lounge when he spotted MacDuff at a blackjack table. The dumbshit, Gamboa thought, he's addicted to Vegas. MacDuff had lost everything because of this town. His wife, his career, every nickel he had. And here he was back again with that same look every addict had— the buggy, riveted eyes and the dry lips.

To Gamboa all addicts were the same. They never realized it's the drug that's the problem. They blamed everything and everybody else. MacDuff was addicted to Vegas—to the money-grubbing show girls, to the snapping of all that neon, to the upside-down hours everyone kept, and to the narcotic of gambling. He didn't understand that his empty bank account, his suspension from the force, his divorce, driving around town in a dented tin can—that wasn't all the result of bad luck. There he was sitting with that swoony look they all had, happy as hell, just pissing his life away.

Knox came back with a disgusted look.

"What'd your wife say?" Gamboa asked.

"Wants me to bring something home for her. If I go to El Monte, I gotta bring back a souvenir, for chrissake."

Gamboa grinned. "Hang on," he said, "I want to see what they're getting for a room here."

"See if you can get me a king, will you?" Knox asked hopefully.

Gamboa came back a few minutes later. "Come on, let's go."

"They full?"

"No, they're eighty-eight bucks a night for a double bed," he said and kept walking toward the door.

Knox nearly had to trot to keep up. "So?" he said. "The department'll pay for overnights on investigations."

"Yeah, if it's authorized," Gamboa said over his shoulder. The electronic door buzzed open and he strode through it. "You wanna be the one to hand the req sheet to Lowenstein for his signature?"

"Christ, what now?" Knox said. "Gamboa, I am definitely not shelling out of my own pocket for this little cruise of yours."

Gamboa stopped and turned around to Knox. They were standing in the middle of the Desert Sands driveway, and two cars lined up waiting for them. "Don't worry. I'm covering it. I know a good place."

"What about dinner?" Knox asked. "I haven't eaten since lunch."

One of the waiting cars honked, and Gamboa reached into his pocket and held the badge in the headlights without looking toward the car. "Oh, this place has a great restaurant."

"Good," Knox said, brightening. "Maybe we can get some room service. I'd like to put my feet up on the bed for a few hours if we're going to be up all night interviewing."

"Hey, whatever you want, partner. It's on me," Gamboa said cheerfully, and they crossed the street to one more long blast from a car horn.

Gamboa drove back up the strip and out of town. After a few miles he pulled into a place called the 18 Wheeler Cafe. It had a sign pole two hundred feet high that winked DIESEL and a parking lot as big as a football stadium's. It was full of semis and RVs. The restaurant was lit up bright as a classroom, curtainless and devoid of all females except for the waitresses. Next to the restaurant was the Wagon Wheel Motel. It had a sign out front in green neon: ROOMS $14—TRUCKERS WELCOME. Half the dark brown doors had numbers stenciled in white paint, the rest had metal numbers nailed up.

"I'll get the rooms," Gamboa said to Knox as he pulled in. "You check out the menu. If you can find anything on there that don't say 'chicken fried,' order two."

When Terwilliger came on at two, Gamboa and Knox were in the lobby belching. Terwilliger recognized them right away as cops and tipped his head at them. Since he was the man of this house, any cops on business would see him first. That was common courtesy. "Can I talk to you?" Gamboa asked as Terwilliger came up.

"What's it about?"

Gamboa took his badge out and let him look at it. "Like to talk to you about a murder investigation in Orange County."

"Gamboa? Yeah," he said, recognizing the name. "I worked L.A. Sheriff's for twenty-two years."

Gamboa nodded. He wasn't surprised.

"This the one about the missing girl?" Terwilliger asked.

"She's not missing anymore," Gamboa said. "She's dead."

"No kidding?" Terwilliger said, pursing his lips to show surprise. "Let me get somebody to cover for me." He walked over to a young bodybuilder in a dark suit jacket that was straining to hold his outsized torso.

"Let's go in the lounge," he said, pointing through a doorway. "It's quieter."

"You go ahead. I'm going to call the station," Knox said, and he took off for the phones again.

"Look, just a few questions," Gamboa said as they sat down. He took out a mug shot of Chad and showed it to Terwilliger. "Did you identify this person as someone who spent a week or so here three or four months ago?"

Terwilliger took the picture and looked it over for a few seconds before he recognized Chad. "Yeah," he said, handing the photo back.

"Was he here with an older woman?"

"Yeah, a lot older, though. Sixty-five, seventy."

"Got any ideas what they were doing here?"

"They weren't doing a damn thing," Terwilliger said, scratching his sideburn. "That's why I remember them. An old lady and a young guy that ain't gambling, you notice."

Gamboa grunted, "Mmmm."

"You should talk to one of our drivers named Felipe, if you want to know exactly what she was up to. He drove them around town while they were here."

"What time does he come on?"

"In the morning about eight."

Gamboa looked at his watch. "All right," he said. "Let me talk to him and then I'll get back to you."

"No problem," Terwilliger said. "I'll be here until ten, or you can get me at home." He shoved a card across the table.

Mac walked into the lounge then and called to Gamboa, "I just saw Knox. Did Lowenstein let his two doggies off the leash for the night?"

Gamboa looked around and frowned when he saw who it was. "Does Barrett know this is the way you interview witnesses?"

Mac was going to insult Gamboa again, but Knox came running into the lounge. "Barrett's at St. John's in ICU," he shouted.

"Jesus! What the hell happened?" Mac said, spinning Knox around by the arm.

"Somebody shot him. They don't know if he's going to make it."

Gamboa looked down at the photos of Chad and the dead girl again. Barrett was probably right about the whole damned thing after all.

chapter

thirty-seven

Carrie shouldered her way through the door of the hospital lobby, carrying some of Sean's things. After she had seen the gunman run down the beach in the dark, she had dragged Sean up the sand and hidden him under the deck of the house two doors down. She hadn't known if the man would come back to see if he'd done the job properly. Then she crawled down the beach to the side door of Sean's cottage and, still on her hands and knees, crossed the living room to the phone and dialed 911.

She rode with him in the ambulance, and that's where he told her he loved her. "I love you too," she said and held him. He was still lucid then, but by the time they arrived at the hospital he was unconscious. Getting out of the ambulance in the bright lights of the emergency room, she saw for the first time the bullet hole in the flap of her sweater and the blackened hole in his chest.

The first morning, she went home for a change of clothes, and he took a turn for the worse. When she came back, he was on the respirator again. So she hadn't left his side for two days. Yesterday he had rallied and the doctors had moved him out of ICU. Most of his color was back. When she'd leaned over him on the bed, his hands roamed her rear sinfully and they both smiled.

She came down the long corridor and looked into his room. Dr. Bergman was still at his bedside.

"You were lucky," the physician said. He was a tall, stringy Swede with a ski burn. "The bullet passed through the lower chest and missed every major organ except your lung, which collapsed. There is a very real chance of severe complications, especially pneumonia. We have to be very careful of infection."

"So what's this mean, Doctor?" Sean said impatiently. He'd been in the hospital for two days already, and he wanted to know when he was getting out. He knew that Macklin was going to want to know when and if he could continue with the trial.

Bergman put the clipboard under his arm and looked at Sean sternly. "It means you need to stay right here for two to three weeks," he said, "while we continue to pump heavy doses of antibiotics into you and keep a close eye on that lung."

A monitor was beeping monotonously at Sean's ear, and he scowled. He was certain of one thing. He wasn't going to be spending two or three weeks in this sterilized prison.

"Look, Doctor, I'm in trial," he started off. "I have a client who I'm sure is innocent of murder, and I think I can prove it." Bergman nodded slowly. Sean could tell he wasn't listening. "I can't prove it from this bed, though."

"I see," Bergman said, writing something on the clipboard.

"Look, Doctor, if I don't get out of here in the next couple of days, the judge will declare a mistrial and that'll be it. My client will spend at least another couple of months in jail, and who knows how his next trial will go?"

The tubes on Sean's arm were jerking about as he talked, and Bergman eyed them. "If you try to check out of here before it's safe," he said, "you won't have to worry about the retrial because there's a good chance you won't be around for it. If I release you any sooner than ten to fourteen days, you'd be in a life-threatening situation." He held Sean's chart up in front of him for emphasis. "There's no way I can give my consent to release you."

He hung the clipboard on the end of the bed with a clang. "You're not the only attorney in Orange County," he said and walked out of the room.

Carrie entered as Bergman was leaving.

"I guess that's it, Carrie," Sean said. "If I'm stuck here for anything more than a few more days, Macklin will have no choice but to shut this case down."

She put her things on a chair. "Well, maybe it's for the best, Sean."

"Not you too," Sean said, suddenly depressed. It wasn't just the trial he wanted anymore. Someone had shot at him. He wanted to get Spann and the Jamaican and hang them by their testicles in open court.

"It will be all you can do to recuperate from this, let alone battle Lowenstein," she said and sat on the bed next to Sean.

He groaned and rolled away from her.

"Sean, get this through your head," she said. "A foreign object passed through your chest at supersonic speed, missing your aorta by a couple of centimeters and nicking your lung, which promptly deflated like a flat tire. A couple days ago I watched you lying on the beach literally drowning in your own blood." She shuddered at the memory. "How you lived is a mystery to me. I just thank God you didn't die. And I'll be damned if I'm going to let you do anything to jeopardize your life."

"I want Spann," Sean said, ignoring everything she had just said.

Carrie sighed. She knew he wanted to talk it out now that he finally could. "If it *was* Spann who shot you," she said.

"Who else could it be?" he said, rolling over to face her. She could see his eyes were alive again.

"I just have a hard time believing Jonathan is responsible for all this."

"Maybe, but I'm still going to get him up on that stand and barbeque him."

"You're not going to do anything but lie here and get better," she scolded. "Besides, you've got to consider what's best for Chad."

"The best thing for Chad is if I walk into that courtroom next week. We've taken the jury all this way. This started as a no-body case. Now they have a body, or at least a photo of the body. So even though they can see it's her and the coroner and photo experts will say she's dead, there is still some room for doubt. Who sent it? When was it taken? And ten other questions," Sean said, sitting up in bed.

Carrie pushed him back down with a hand on his shoulder. He was too weak to resist.

"Plus," he went on, "if Macklin asks for a new trial, that gives Gamboa three or four more months to shoot holes in our theory. And what's Chad doing all this time but rotting in jail? If we can just go on with the trial, we've got a mile-high stack of circumstantial evidence going for us. All of it corroborated by the eyewitnesses who claim they saw Robin in Bakersfield and San Francisco."

"Who Lowenstein can tear to shreds," she objected.

"Maybe," he said, unconvinced. "That whole stock scam means there are at least two or three people who had a very profitable motive for killing her."

"Including Chad."

"Maybe," Sean said. "But now there's a wider cast of characters to choose from."

"So at the very least, the jury would be divided?"

"Exactly," Sean said, picking up momentum. He sat up again and this time Carrie let him. She was smiling. Only three days ago it had been fifty-fifty whether he'd live. Today was the first time he'd recovered some of his passion. So she let him go.

"We have Spann on the run now. We can tie him to the condo in Palm Desert," he said. "Besides, the fact that I was shot will not go unnoticed by the jury."

He reached over for a cup of water, and Carrie poured it for him.

"Who, they'll ask, would try to kill the defendant's attorney?" Sean went on. "And that'll create more doubt. We just have to pile up enough doubt in the jurors' minds and Chad will walk out of there." He looked at her to see if she was buying it. "With everything that's happening, Lowenstein has to know his case is hanging by a thread. And all we have to do is let Spann tell his tale and I think that will do it."

He took her hand. "But you have to corner him or he'll wiggle free, Carrie," he said. "Can you do it?"

"What do you mean, can *I* do it?" she asked and pulled her hand away.

"Well, let me ask you this," he said, looking into her eyes. "Do you believe Chad is innocent?"

"Of course I do. Spann's your boy."

"Then there's only one thing to do," he said. "You have to represent Chad in court as my co-counsel."

"I can't do that!" she said, shaking her head, wondering if the trauma had made him delirious.

He took her hand and pulled her back. "Yes, you can."

"I don't have the experience to pull off something like that."

"You know as much about this case as I do. You helped me develop it. I think Chad would agree to it and, besides, I'll be holding your hand all the way," he said.

"Yes, flat on your back in a hospital ward." She stood and started pacing the room, back and forth in front of his bed. "But even if I could do it and Chad goes along with it and I'm brilliant—"

"You will be," he said, smiling at her. He followed her with his eyes around the room.

"Well, suppose that's all true. There's one problem with this little fantasy."

"Which is?"

"Macklin," she said and stopped.

He put his hand on hers. "Macklin's not the real problem. Not if we do it right. The last thing he wants is a mistrial," Sean said. "The problem is Lowenstein."

"Lowenstein?" she asked, clearly baffled. "I'd think he'd love to have some minor leaguer like me filling in."

Sean waved the wrong arm again, and the I.V. bounced against the metal rail of the bed. The monitor began to beep frantically. He reached over and snapped the toggle to Off, and the thing went dead.

"Sean?" she said, frowning.

"When we're through talking, I'll turn it back on. Promise."

She nodded her head slowly.

"Lowenstein's not dumb enough to think he can win now, especially when he learns from the SEC what your father will testify to," he said. "He's going to be pushing for a mistrial to avoid a bad loss. He can't wait to pass this lemon off to another D.A. He's already lost the no-body aspect. And he's going to end up losing the case entirely. Trust me, Lowenstein will want to bail out at the first opportunity. That's all he's got left. Sabotage the case. And we have to do everything we can to make sure that doesn't happen."

chapter

thirty-eight

Gamboa and Knox entered the secured wing of County Hospital, where Shabba St. James was still recuperating from his gunshot wound. They waved at the jailor at the nurses' desk and walked down to Room 7, where Shabba took up most of the double bed wedged against the wall. The caged window threw a checkered shadow across the bed.

"Well, well, if it ain't Shabba St. James, the slimiest fucking nigger in Orange County," Gamboa said as they came in. "What's wrong, still feeling a little weak from the hole I put in you?"

The Jamaican turned to the cops. He'd been in a coma for over a week, and both his arms were still hooked up to I.V.'s.

"Don't pay any attention to my partner," Knox smiled. "The guy's a bigot."

Shabba slowly nodded his head at Knox.

"Yeah, forget the crack," Gamboa said. "Why don't you and I become friends?"

"Whatchu want, mon? Shabba need his rest."

"You'll have plenty of time for rest. Right up until the time they gas you for murder," Gamboa said.

Shabba lifted his head off the pillow. "Murder? Whatchu mean? You keep talkin' like dat, Shabba goan get his lawyer."

"Should we call an attorney for him, Sarge?" Knox asked.

Gamboa looked up at Knox with disgust. He motioned Knox to the corner of the room and spoke softly to him. But not so softly that Shabba couldn't hear everything he was saying.

"Emory, I know how you like to do things by the book and I can appreciate that," Gamboa said, his voice starting to rise. "But someone's been making us look like a couple of damn fools and I'm fucking tired of it. We've been playing by the book and look where it's got us. Berger, Romero, and Powers are all dead, and this son of a bitch did them." Gamboa grabbed Knox by the arm and pulled him to where Shabba was lying. "See this piece of shit? Not only is he responsible for those murders, but he's involved up to his ass in the murder of Robin Penrose. There's some kind of a connection between all these crimes, and I'm going to find out what that connection is, with or without your help. Now, if you don't like what I'm going to do, then go get us both a fucking cup of coffee." Gamboa was almost shouting now, and Shabba's eyes followed him warily.

"Sarge, come on," Knox said, playing along. "I know all that, but maybe we should let him talk to his attorney first."

"Says who, college boy?" Gamboa snapped back.

"Miranda, that's who!"

They were standing next to the Jamaican, arguing back and forth. Shabba's heart monitor was starting to blip dizzily behind them.

"Miranda, fuck Miranda! We're going to do this my way! And this piece of shit better understand that." Gamboa nodded down at Shabba. "Now go get yourself a fucking Danish if you don't like what I'm going to do!"

Knox's eyes darted nervously back and forth from Gamboa to St. James.

"Look, Emory," Gamboa said in a softer voice, "as much as I'd like to, I won't lay a hand on the guy. I'll tell you what. I'll turn on this tape and record everything for his protection." Gamboa reached into his inside coat pocket and pulled out a small tape recorder. "Then if I do lose my temper again, it will all be right here on the tape."

Knox looked warily at Gamboa.

"Hey, don't worry, partner," Gamboa said. "I'm not going to hurt him."

Knox shook his head. "Sarge, that's what you say every time. And you know what happens. That goddamn temper gets the best of you, and somebody always ends up in the hospital."

"That's what the recorder's for," Gamboa said. "If I get out of hand, it's all on tape."

Shabba was motionless, as if unaware of what the two intruders were saying, but he had his ear leaning toward them.

"I know this guy wants to talk. He doesn't want to take the fall for all those murders," Gamboa said. "Go on. Take a break."

Knox stood with one hand on the doorknob and the other on his chin, as though thinking it over.

"Nah," Knox said at last. "I'm coffee'd out. Let's get on with this."

The sheet over Shabba's chest rose and fell as he took a deep breath. Knox nodded at Gamboa. This turkey was fully basted.

"Now, Shabba, we're gonna have a little chat, you and I," Gamboa said.

"Fuck bof of you," Shabba said. "I ain't sayin' shit until I talk to my lawyer."

Gamboa looked at the recorder, then at Knox. "All right, asshole," Gamboa said. "Who do you want us to call? Who's your attorney?"

Shabba didn't answer.

"Come on, if you want to talk to your attorney, you gotta tell us who he is."

"Jonathan Spann," St. James finally said.

Gamboa and Knox looked at each other and nodded simultaneously.

"How does a lowlife like you happen to retain some big-money corporate attorney like Spann?"

Shabba gave Gamboa a cold stare. "You two jokers just wastin' your time. I don't have to tell you shit."

"Oh, yeah?" Gamboa said. "I know a few things that should interest you."

"Like what?"

"Like you just so happened to be in custody on February twenty-second of this year during a stabbing at the Orange County Jail."

"Yeah, me and three hundred other suckers."

"Maybe so. But you were on the rooftop right next to a guy named Theodore Berger as he was lining up to go back to his cell. And guess what happened to him?"

St. James smiled and said, "Let's see. He slip and fall off dee roof," Shabba laughed. "I tell you one thing, mon, I never know dis Mr. Ham-Berger you talkin' 'bout."

"Yeah, you know who the hell he was," Gamboa said. "You also knew he was on trial for a murder you committed. The murder of a security guard at Medtech. Let me refresh your memory. You sent Eddie Romero and Berger into Medtech to steal files on Kaufmann Industries."

"Like to see you prove dat," Shabba said. "Dat would be really somethin'."

Gamboa got up real close to the big Jamaican and spoke right into his ear. "I'll tell you what I can prove, scumbag. I can prove that you killed Berger on the rooftop that afternoon."

"I think you been smokin' some bad weed," Shabba laughed. "You want Shabba to get you some better stuff?"

"I know you not only killed Berger, but you also killed Eddie Romero and Berger's attorney, Scott Powers."

"You think so, huh? Sound like all you got is a bunch of dead witnesses. You don't know shit. Now get me my attorney," Shabba cried.

"Look, St. James," Gamboa said. "I have a hunch that you wanted to kill Barrett that night at the Fun Zone because he was close to something. What were you afraid of? It has to do with Robin Penrose, doesn't it?"

"Hey, dat was self-defense. I was just protecting myself. He was attacking *me*," Shabba said.

"Yeah, sure. With what? His fucking briefcase? Give me a break, huh?" Gamboa snorted. "I don't want to hear any of your bullshit. Don't deny trying to kill Barrett. I was there that night, asshole, remember? Who in the hell do you think put the slug in you? But that's not what I'm after. What I want you to tell me is what you know about the murder of Robin Penrose. And if you can help, I'll see what I can do for you."

"Whatchu offerin'?" the Jamaican asked.

"Tell me what you know and then I'll talk to the D.A. to see what kind of deal we can make," Gamboa said.

"Fuck you. We make dee deal first. Record it," he said, pointing at the machine in the cop's hand. "Den I goan tell you what I know 'bout dee girl."

"*And* the murders," Knox interrupted.

"Fuck dee murders. Just what I know 'bout dee girl. Dat's dee deal. Now whatchu offerin'?"

"We can't make a deal unless we know your information can help us," Knox said.

The Jamaican lifted himself up on his elbow. "I goan tell you who killed dat little bird."

Gamboa stepped in again. "All right, damn it. I'll settle for probation on the attempted murder of Barrett."

"Just probation?" Knox said. "We can't do that!"

Gamboa waved Knox off. "What do you say? Probation for the attempted murder of an attorney. Sounds pretty good to me."

Shabba's eyes narrowed as he saw his way out. "All right, but get me a lawyer. I know better than to make a deal without any lawyer."

"Look, Shabba, I'm making you this offer now. I don't have the time to try to locate Spann."

"Forget Spann. I don't need Spann anymore. Get me dee public defender."

"I don't have time to get a P.D. over here, and you can't afford to turn this deal down."

Shabba slumped back on the pillow. "Is dat thing still on?" he said, pointing at the recorder.

Gamboa nodded.

"If I tell you about dee girl, Shabba goan get probation?"

"That's what I said."

"What about dose murders?"

Gamboa shook his head. "I don't have enough to keep you on those."

"Sarge," Knox said, exasperated, "what the hell are you doing? Probation for attempted murder? You're giving away the farm to this asshole."

"Hey, partner, the guy's going to cooperate. I gotta give him something decent."

Shabba was nodding his head in agreement.

"Decent? Hell, that's the deal of the century," Knox said.

"Let me handle this, college boy," Gamboa said and turned to the Jamaican. "We got a deal?"

"So Shabba goan walk outa here when we're done?"

"As long as you help me on the Penrose murder."

A smile spread across Shabba's face. "Spann killed her."

Gamboa and Knox looked at each other, then back at Shabba.

"Jonathan Spann?" Gamboa said. "Can you prove that?"

"Listen to me," Shabba said, sitting up. He went on to tell how he had been represented by Spann several years before. Afterward he had helped Spann locate witnesses. When Spann switched his practice to corporate law, he hadn't heard from Spann for years until late last fall. Spann had asked him to help him hide a girl from the authorities at a place in Palm Desert. The girl's name was Robin Penrose.

"Who was after her?" Gamboa asked.

"You know, dose stock market police."

"The Security and Exchange Commission?" Knox asked.

"Yeah," Shabba said. "Dee girl was gettin' rich doin' somethin' funny with dee stocks."

"You mean like insider trading?" Knox asked.

Shabba shrugged.

"So you were the girl's bodyguard?" Knox asked.

"And chauffeur."

"What?" Gamboa asked.

"Spann had me drive her all over California to help Curtis."

"You mean so Barrett could find witnesses who'd say they'd seen her?"

Shabba nodded. "I call dis Barrett plenty times to tell him where to find dee girl."

"I don't get it," Gamboa said. "Why would Spann want to help Curtis?"

"Dat was her idea. Dat little bird got Spann wrap around her little finger. She wave dat cute Robin tail and she get anything she want."

"Spann loved her?" Knox asked.

Shabba frowned. "Fool gone crazy for her."

"Now, how about this stock scam?" Gamboa asked.

"Hey, mon, I tell you who killed dee girl. Dat's the deal."

"Wrong," Gamboa said. "The deal was you tell us everything you know."

"Dat's all Shabba knows. Now get me out of here."

"Look, asshole, you haven't told me why you think Spann killed her," Gamboa said.

"Because, mon, he was dee only one who knew where she was."

"Except for you."

"Hey, last time I saw her she was in Palm Desert dressin' like an old lady. That was dee night before you decided to use me for target practice. I couldn't have killed her."

"Why would Spann want to kill her if he loved her so much?" Gamboa asked.

"Maybe dee little bird was goan sing to get her boyfriend out of jail?"

"Okay, just one more thing," Gamboa said. "What's Medtech got to do with all this?"

"I don't know nothin' about no Medtech."

"I think you do. And you're not going to get any kind of deal until you tell me what the connection is."

"You never say nothin' 'bout no Medtech."

"Come on, Shabba," Gamboa coaxed, "you can walk out of here as soon as you're on your feet. Now tell me about Medtech."

The Jamaican eyed the cop. "Only thing I know is Spann asks Shabba to find someone who works at Medtech."

"Why?" Gamboa said impatiently.

"Another stock thing. First one he and Robin pulled off in Vegas went so well, dey figure dey goan do it again."

"But the guard got killed and that screwed everything up, right?" Knox asked.

"How dee hell I goan know dat if I wasn't dere?" Shabba said.

"Sure," Knox said. "So what happened to the Medtech deal?"

"Dat was the same time dose SEC guys come lookin' for Robin," Shabba said. "Spann got scared and hide Robin in dee desert."

"You still haven't told us who killed the security guard," Gamboa said.

Shabba raised his eyebrows. "I told you, I don't know nothin' 'bout no murders."

"You're lying, Shabba. We both know that. I want to know how the guard and the others got murdered."

Shabba shook his head.

"Are you sure you don't want to help us with those murders?" Gamboa pressed.

"Dat ain't part of dee deal, mon."

"The deal's canceled, asshole, unless you tell me what happened to the others. What did Spann have to do with their murders?"

"I ain't tellin' you nothin' else."

"What you've told me ain't worth a shit. It's just your word."

"We made a deal. It's on dee tape," Shabba said.

"What tape?" Gamboa picked up the recorder, ripped out the cassette, and threw it on the ground. He looked at the Jamaican and grinned; then he stomped the cassette with his shoe and it shattered, the exposed brown ribbon crushed beneath the detective's foot.

Shabba's mouth fell open. "Fuck bof you assholes," he screamed. "You only fuckin' yourself. Without dee tape you can't prove shit."

"You know what, dickwad, you're right," Gamboa said. "But I never planned on using anything you told me anyway. No D.A. worth a shit would make a deal with you. I just needed to be sure Barrett wasn't blowing smoke. I'm going to nail you *and* Spann. Your good buddy Hoops wants to talk to me."

"Dat's bullshit, mon," Shabba shouted as the detectives turned to go.

"No, *mon*. Dat's gospel," Gamboa laughed and shut the door.

chapter

thirty-nine

Gamboa barged into the hospital room, where Carrie was sitting on the bed talking to Sean. "The court asked me to see if you're physically able to continue," he said without bothering with hello, how you feeling?

Carrie stood up as if to keep him away from Sean. Anytime these two got together, they ended up shouting at each other. "I suppose you've read the doctor's report too," she said to Gamboa.

"I hear you're out for two weeks minimum. That right?"

"Dr. Bergman told you that?" Carrie asked in disbelief.

"Nah," Gamboa said and walked to the end of the bed, "I scared it out of an LVN. How 'bout it? You gonna go on with the trial?"

Sean was watching the detective cautiously. Despite all their differences, he had a feeling about Gamboa, and he figured he'd take a gamble on that feeling right now.

"Look, Gamboa, can I talk to you straight?"

Gamboa gripped the metal rail of the bed with both hands and leaned forward. "Go ahead," he said.

"I'm going to win this case," Sean said. "I think you know that, don't you?"

"You mean because of that story you told Macklin in court about some stock scam. Come on! Even the judge didn't think much of it."

"But you did," Sean pinned him. "MacDuff said you were in Vegas checking out the story."

Gamboa shrugged and his lips flattened into a thin smile. "Yeah?"

Sean knew he had him, so he took a chance and gave him a crucial piece. "Carter Robinson confessed the whole thing to the SEC."

Gamboa eyed Sean as he lay in bed: an attorney flat on his back still fighting like hell for his client. "Then I think you're probably right about this whole thing," Gamboa said and gave him a piece back. "You'll probably be interested to know that St. James corroborated that the girl was alive in Palm Desert all along. Curtis couldn't have hacked her up. I believe that now."

"When did you talk to St. James?" Sean asked excitedly.

"He's been out of his coma a couple of days."

"And he agreed to talk to you?"

"Until I got a little greedy," Gamboa said.

"What do you mean?"

"Since he was in custody when you got shot, I knew somebody else pulled the trigger. So I went to him with a deal, and he told me he'd been hiding Robin Penrose in Palm Desert for Spann."

"He admitted it was Spann? What else did he say?"

"Well, that's where I made my mistake. Before I had time to get any details, I decided to push my luck and ask him about the Romero, Berger, and Powers murders and he shut up on me. He didn't mind hanging Spann, but if he admitted to the killings, he knew he was going to be looking at death row."

"But he did convince you she had been alive all this time?"

"Convinced me but . . ."

"Let me guess. Lowenstein won't dismiss the case."

"You got it. Says he's not going to believe anything that dirtbag has to say."

"So I take it Lowenstein wants the case to proceed?"

"Only long enough so the judge will have to declare a mistrial because you're going to be laid up so long here."

"That's just his way to avoid a big loss, right?"

Gamboa shrugged.

"Damn. Chad's not the only reason we have to continue with the trial. We have to get the s.o.b. that killed Robin. Since you took care of Shabba, if Spann wanted Robin and me dead, he had to do it himself. Not only do I think he was responsible for Robin's death, but I think he orchestrated the murders of Teddy Berger, Scott Powers, and Eddie Romero." Sean fell back onto his pillow. "I want to get Spann worse than ever, and I think I know how. But I need your help."

"I'm listening," Gamboa said.

"I don't want a mistrial. I want to get that son of a bitch now. He's on the run. That's why he killed Robin. If a mistrial is declared, the pressure is off and it gives him time to regroup."

Carrie put her hand on Sean's shoulder to calm him down. He took her hand and went on.

"The trial has to go on without delay," Sean continued. "But as long as Lowenstein objects, there's no way the judge will allow the defense to proceed with me in here lying on my back. Carrie has to take my place. The problem is if Lowenstein objects too strenuously, Macklin will have to declare a mistrial."

Gamboa stood with his big arms folded across his chest. He looked at Carrie, then back at Sean.

"Can I talk to you alone?" Gamboa said.

"Carrie is my co-counsel on this case now," Sean said. Carrie stood, as if assuming her role. "It's all right to speak in front of her."

"I'm sure it is. But what I've got to say I'd prefer to say to you alone, if you don't mind," Gamboa said and looked at Carrie.

"I'll get some coffee," she said and walked out.

"You really think that broad can pull this off?" Gamboa said, jerking his thumb over his shoulder at the door.

"That *broad*," Sean said, "can out-lawyer all of us."

"Maybe, but Spann's an old family friend, isn't he?"

"Yes, but Robin was her best friend. He killed Robin in cold blood and then he tried to kill Carrie but messed it up and got me instead. That's who the bullet was meant for, you know."

"That right?" Gamboa said.

"Yeah, that's right."

Gamboa looked back at the door to make sure no one could overhear and stepped around the bed closer to Sean. "Let's say I buy all that. What have you got in mind?"

"Look," Sean said, "you want exactly what I want, and that's to get whoever killed Robin Penrose. And I'm sure you wouldn't mind solving three or four other murders along the way. You know Lowenstein could give a damn about anything except what's good for Lowenstein. Will you help me?"

Gamboa thought about it for a moment. If he was going to stick his neck out, he wanted to make sure the payoff was guaranteed. "Say I help. Are you going to be able to get enough on Spann to nail him? Or are we just jerking off here?"

"Don't worry about that," Sean said. "The problem is Lowenstein. He's not going to want to take this loss."

"Don't worry," Gamboa said. "I think I know how to take care of Lowenstein."

Carrie and Lowenstein were seated in chairs flanking Macklin's desk, while Gamboa paced about the chambers, inspecting the chaos of the room—the stacks of law books tumbling across his desk, an old half-rolled map leaning against a broken couch, a ripped-in-half Lakers' ticket on the floor next to the waste basket. Gamboa ran his finger across the dusty shelf of a bookcase and shook his head in disgust. Gamboa's office was as big a mess as Macklin's, but a judge wasn't a cop. He was supposed to keep some order.

A few minutes later, Macklin rushed into the room with his robe unbuttoned, flapping behind him. He was wearing a pink shirt, cords, and desert boots.

"All right, Miss Robinson," the judge said as he sat behind his desk, "how does Barrett wish to proceed?"

"Well, Your Honor," Carrie said, "I've been asked to be co-counsel for Mr. Curtis, and since Mr. Barrett is unable to make a court appearance as of yet, I will now be handling the trial duties for the defense."

Lowenstein almost leapt from his chair. "If Curtis is convicted, an appellate court would have an easy time overturning the verdict for inadequate representation," he said and looked over at Carrie. "No offense, miss."

"Mr. Lowenstein," Carrie said, "I think if we take adequate waivers from Mr. Curtis, that he completely understands the risks, then I don't feel an appellate court will second-guess anyone for that reason alone. You've been into this trial for almost two months now, and it would be a shame to abort it when it's gone this far."

"What's your response to that?" Macklin asked Lowenstein.

The D.A. tucked his chartreuse tie inside his creme suede jacket. "I think it's an automatic reversal," he said. "She's not an experienced criminal lawyer, and although it's true we've been in trial quite a while, she hasn't been here for any part of it. I would strenuously object to this trial going forward. Our only recourse is a mistrial and then start all over again." This time he didn't bother to apologize for the insult. If she was going to stand up and try to argue against him, he had every right to slap her down.

"And will you be the one retrying the case, Mr. Lowenstein?" Macklin asked, even though he knew the answer.

The D.A. shook his head almost forlornly. "Regrettably not, Your Honor. My calendar just won't permit it."

"Of course not," Macklin said. "It's no longer a no-body case, so now you want out."

Lowenstein didn't answer. Carrie knew the judge was on her side. If he could find a way, he would make Lowenstein go on with the trial. But there was only so much he could do.

Macklin stood up and started pacing about the room. He didn't want to order Lowenstein to continue. "This is a real tough call," he said finally. "If you two can't come to an agreement, I guess I'll have to rule on it."

Gamboa, a few steps behind Lowenstein, stepped forward. "I think maybe I can help."

Macklin didn't like the interruption. He looked around the D.A. at Gamboa and frowned. "What is it, Sergeant?"

"Can I have a word with Mr. Lowenstein?"

The D.A., who had been staring at Gamboa ever since he'd opened his mouth, turned to Macklin and shrugged as if a trained dog had just crapped on the rug.

"Only if it will help us get this damned trial over with," Macklin said. He was getting desperate. A retrial would clog his calendar for months.

Lowenstein followed Gamboa out into the hallway.

"Okay, what's this all about, Sergeant?"

Gamboa nudged up close to Lowenstein to keep their conversation out of earshot of passing deputies. "What's the problem with letting her take over?"

Lowenstein's mouth dropped open, his eyes disbelieving. He just stared at the detective for a moment. "Well, absolutely nothing, Sergeant," he said finally. "Except the way things look now, if we proceed, we'll lose this fucking thing."

"Why's that?"

Lowenstein took a deep breath. "Because they've got enough doubt for even the dumbest goddamn jury to acquit," he said.

"So instead of letting an innocent man go, you want to get a mistrial and retry the guy just so you won't have to be hung with a big loss, is that the story?"

"Yeah, that's exactly the story," Lowenstein said. "As soon as I get that mistrial, I'm bailing out of this piece of shit."

"And leaving me with your fucking mess. Is that it?"

"We've all got our crosses."

"Yeah, except there ain't going to be a mistrial," Gamboa said.

Lowenstein pushed him aside and started back for Macklin's chambers. "Fortunately, Sergeant, you have nothing to say about it."

"Yeah, well, listen to this, peckerwood," Gamboa said, clutching the D.A.'s arm. "If you don't go along with what she wants, I'm going to tell everybody, including your precious fucking press out there, that you were going to use perjured testimony to convict Curtis."

Lowenstein's mouth fell open. "You mean . . . our snitch?"

Gamboa grabbed Lowenstein's tie with one hand and poked his chest with the other. "You're fucking right I mean our snitch."

Lowenstein stood staring at the cop, frantically cataloging his ways out of this catastrophe. "Are you fucking nuts, Gamboa?" he said. "You do that and you'll go to prison right along with me."

Gamboa pulled the D.A. toward him by his tie as if it were a leash—which was exactly where he intended to keep him until this trial was over. "That's right, asshole, but I'll survive in there," he said and looked venomously into Lowenstein's panicked eyes. "Will you?"

Lowenstein looked around nervously. Everybody had warned

him about this maniac. He knew now he should have listened. He had too much to lose for a scandal like that to get out. If the press started running with it and the judicial system felt public pressure, they'd turn on him like so many jackals. This half-ass no-body case that wasn't even a no-body anymore wasn't worth the gamble.

"Ah, who gives a fuck about this piece of shit case anymore?" he said finally and pushed past Gamboa. "I'll give her what she wants."

Mac and Carrie gathered in Sean's hospital room the next afternoon to decide their strategy. The trial was set to continue on Monday, and they had a lot to do.

"Have you figured out yet how I'm going to pull this off?" Carrie asked.

"I think so," Sean said. He was out of bed now, his face no longer drawn, the tubes out of his arm, eating real food again.

"Okay, let's hear it, Counselor." She sat on the bed and watched him pacing as he always did when he was thinking out a problem.

"Wednesday, after the prosecution rests, you're going to call Chad to the stand. And he's going to tell everything."

"Aren't you afraid of Lowenstein on cross?" Carrie asked. The D.A. had a well-deserved reputation for skewering witnesses.

Sean shook his head. "Not if Chad's telling the truth," he said. "And at this point I have absolutely no doubt he is."

Mac and Carrie both nodded. Mac was sitting in the corner in the only chair big enough for him. He was twirling his handlebar mustache, which had grown well below his chin.

"After Chad, I want to put Spann on the stand and hit him with the whole battalion."

"Wouldn't it be best to lay a foundation first with the lookalikes and Vegas witnesses?" Carrie asked.

Sean stopped pacing and rested his arm on a machine. "Normally I'd go along with you on that, Carrie. But I don't want to give Spann time to cook up an escape," he said. "If he denies everything and we feel the jury's not buying our story, then we'll follow it up with our other witnesses. So that means," he said, turning to Mac, "this is what we're going to have to do. Mac, you arrange transportation and housing for the Bakersfield, San Francisco, and Vegas witnesses. That means all the flights, all the hotel rooms, the airport pickups, the works. In the meantime, I'll talk to as many of them by phone as I can to prepare them for their testimony."

Sean checked his watch. Dr. Bergman was due to check in on him in a few minutes, and Sean didn't want to be caught at work. The doctor's orders were for him to rest.

"That should do it, except for one last thing, Mac. This damned thing," he said, looking at the photo of the dead girl. "Get ahold of Dennis Carson for me, will you? He's that attorney who's in to photography. Here's his number and address. Take this photo over to him and have him blow it up."

Mac took the card, looked at it, and stuffed it into his coat pocket.

Carrie looked at Sean curiously. "What are you up to?" she asked.

"I don't know exactly. But take a look at this photo."

Carrie grimaced. It would never get easier, looking at that picture of her friend with her throat cut.

"See in the corner of her left eye," Sean said, pointing at the photo. Mac and Carrie looked over either shoulder at the photo. "There's something there. Maybe it's nothing, but I want to see what it is," Sean said and handed it to Mac. "Get on it right away, will you?"

"All right." Mac grabbed the photo and walked out.

"Now, Carrie," Sean said, "let's figure out how we're going to corner him."

Several hours later, after Carrie had gone home to get some needed sleep, Dennis Carson came in with the blowups of the photo. "You getting any sleep with all the racket?" Dennis said as he stuck his head in the door.

"Not a lot," Sean said. "Every time I fall asleep, a nurse wakes me up to give me a sleeping pill."

"Mac said Carrie's going to have to finish up the trial for you. That's too bad," Dennis said.

Sean shrugged. "Hey, I'll live to fight another day, right?" he said, and they both laughed. Then Sean pointed at the envelope under Carson's arm. "Did you bring the blowups?"

Carson laid the accordion file on the bed, and Sean grabbed it and pulled out the photos.

"What are you looking for?" Dennis asked.

"I'm not sure," Sean said, studying the pictures. "It looked like there was something near the corner of her left eye. Did Mac mention it to you?"

"Yeah, he did, in fact," Dennis said. "I went ahead and enlarged that area four or five times. You can see it pretty clearly now."

Dennis snapped on the light above Sean's bed and pointed at a photo. "Looks like some kind of fake skin or something."

"My bet is theatrical makeup," Sean said.

"She didn't do a very good job of removing it."

"Or someone else didn't do a very good job," Sean said. "According to Chad, Robin was made up to look like an old lady when she visited him last Thursday. That's about when we figured she was killed."

Dennis looked at him, then at the photo again. Like everyone else, he'd read the papers. "I thought she was killed on the beach months ago."

"Well, if she was, this picture makes no sense. Because she was at work all day before she was seen with Chad. She wasn't wearing theatrical makeup on the beach that night." He inspected the photo again, squinting as he brought it close to his face. "Look at this, Dennis," he said and angled the photo so Carson could see. "Is there any way you can blow up just this area?" he said as his finger drew a circle on the photo.

"Sure," he said and pulled a grease pen out of his pants pocket and marked the spot. "I'll get to work on it first thing in the morning."

Sean put his arm around Dennis's shoulder. "I need it before that. The trial's almost over."

"You mean tonight?" he said. "It's two in the blessed morning."

"I know," Sean said, smiling.

Dennis slowly shook his head. "This'll cost you dinner at the Stuffed Shirt as soon as you're on your feet."

"Bring a date," Sean said.

chapter

forty

Carrie was carrying Sean's old briefcase for luck. She'd had it re-stitched and restained for him, and it was quite handsome, the age deepening the burgundy of the leather. Under her other arm were several thick files. Dressed in an autumn gray suit with her black hair long and full, and a red hankie tucked smartly into her front pocket, Carrie backed through the side door and entered the rear corridor to the courthouse. A throng was building around the place. *Time* magazine, the *New York Times*, the London *Times*, AP, Reuters—they all wanted the story. The press would still instantly fall on her when she turned the corner. But by coming in the back way, she could at least avoid the half-dozen minicam crews and the out-of-town press that didn't know their way around the labyrinth of the county building. They waited on the front steps for her, setting up cameras, lights, the wires snaking hazardously across the steps.

Shep Milligan from the *L.A. Times* got the scoop: "The Chad Curtis no-body case has taken another bizarre turn. After the nearly fatal shooting of Curtis's attorney, Sean Barrett, it seemed that nothing could trump the dramatics this case has already delivered. And now comes this. Barrett's girlfriend, Carrie Robinson, a prominent corporate attorney in her own right and the victim's best friend, is going to take the reins from Barrett, who is still in the hospital unable to continue." That's how Milligan began his piece. It contained just enough facts to hold all the hot air.

Carrie increased her stride as she rounded the corner, and before the media could swarm her, she was past them and into the courtroom. Seelicke stepped in front to keep them from pursuing her into the court. "No cameras in the courtroom, gentlemen," he said and pushed the door shut in their faces.

Lowenstein was nettled by her sweeping entrance, stealing the attention from him. She smiled at him, and he nodded curtly back at her as she sat next to Chad.

"How do you feel this morning, Chad?" she said, taking his hand. "We're going to do this thing together, you and I."

"Yeah, okay," he said. He wore the blue suit that Sean had first brought to him from his closet. His dark hair was slicked back tightly against his head, as if he'd just showered. It made him look even younger than he was.

"Good," Carrie said. "Lowenstein is going to call Robin's mother, so prepare yourself for a lot of crying."

"I don't blame her."

"I know," she said. "But don't let it shake you. Keep your face toward her while she testifies. We don't want the jury to get the impression that you're afraid of what she has to say. She still thinks you did it, so don't make eye contact with her either. She could get hysterical."

"I understand," he said. They had gone over and over his instructions. Sean had been calling the past several days on the phone, and Carrie had followed up.

"Now, when you get up there, remember what Sean said."

"I know," he said, "just tell the truth. If Lowenstein trips me up, just get right back to the truth."

She patted his arm. "Exactly."

Macklin hurried into the courtroom still buttoning his robe and immediately started the proceedings. Lowenstein called Robin's mother to the stand. The courtroom had to be adjourned several times while she broke down sobbing, trying to identify Robin from the photograph of the mutilated girl. It was a long, sad hour in which several of the jurors cried as well. An old woman with a photo of her own daughter's grisly death scene in front of her. Despite Carrie's admonitions, Chad broke down too, but Carrie thought it might help the defense. The jury could see he had loved her too.

Lowenstein then called the coroner, who testified that based upon his evaluation of the photo, Robin Penrose was indeed dead. Carrie didn't cross-examine either witness, and Lowenstein rested his case.

Macklin turned to Carrie then and said, "Miss Robinson, are you ready to call your first witness?"

Carrie rose to her full height, adjusted her belt waist, and advanced a couple of steps. "Your Honor," she said in a poised tone, "the defense would like to call to the stand Mr. Chad Curtis."

This long-awaited announcement caused a loud stir in the audience. A buzz went through the crowd, and several reporters slipped out the door. Any time a defendant in a murder case takes the stand, it's news.

Macklin rapped the gavel once. He'd been waiting for just such an opportunity to lay down his rules. "Gentlemen and ladies of the press. I know you've got a hot story here, but this is still my courtroom. If any of you jump up like that again and disrupt these proceedings, Deputy Seelicke will see that you get free room and board on the county tonight."

Chad stood. Nearly everything that can befall a man, short of death, had happened to him in the past six months. He'd lost his career, his lover had been murdered, and he had sat in jail for months, wrongly accused. But he held his shoulders squared as he walked to the stand.

Carrie led him through his whole story systematically. He explained in detail everything he knew about Robin's scheme, including their trip to Las Vegas. He told the jury that she had never explained to him exactly what was taking place. What little he did know he had learned from her afterward during her many visits to him in jail.

"And you don't know who gave Robin the money or hid her in Palm Desert?" Carrie said.

"No, she wouldn't tell me," he said. "And I really didn't want to know."

"Chad, I would like to ask you one last question," she said and stood close to him. "Did you love Robin Penrose?"

"Yes," Chad said. "I've always loved her."

"Thank you," Carrie said and turned to Lowenstein. "Your witness, Counselor."

Lowenstein rose very slowly from his seat. He had a broad, closed-mouthed smile and was shaking his head as if he'd just heard a whopping good tale.

"Now, Mr. Curtis, do you really expect us to believe that you sat quietly in jail for almost five months while your girlfriend ran around some resort with over a million dollars in cash?" He looked at the jury and let a little chuckle play off his lips. "Come on."

Almost every question Lowenstein asked Chad after that was couched the same way. "Do you really expect us to believe . . . ?"

Chad withstood the barrage of sarcastic questions. He came off as a gullible, lovestruck young man caught in a web of deceit and greed of which he was little more than a dupe.

When Lowenstein finished, Macklin recessed. During the break Carrie asked Mac if her next witness was in court.

"Sure is," Mac said. He'd stuffed himself into a buttoned collar for his court appearance. Since he'd left the force, his weight had piled up, and he left his jacket unbuttoned because he had to. "He's out in the hall squirming right now."

"Is he alone?"

"Yeah, he's alone," he said. "He laughed when I served him the subpoena, like it was no big deal."

Carrie spotted her father for the first time in the second row behind Lowenstein. He'd come to cheer her on. She waved with her fingertips and he smiled back.

Macklin rushed back in after ten minutes, and while he was still ascending the bench he said, "Call your next witness, Miss Robinson."

Carrie stood and turned to the back of the room. "Jonathan Spann," she said.

Seelicke went into the hall and held the door open as Spann

walked through and approached the witness stand. As always, he was impeccably dressed. This time he was wearing a dark blue Italian suit. One of Spann's strongest assets was that he looked like everybody's idea of a lawyer: tall, thin, and gray at the temples.

Carrie had tried to prepare herself mentally for this moment. But now she had second thoughts. Spann had always been such a good family friend that it was going to be painful accusing him of such a gruesome crime. She looked at the photo of Robin in her death pose, stood up, and began her assault.

"Mr. Spann, what is your occupation?" Carrie asked after he'd been sworn in.

"I am the managing partner of the law firm Spann, McGraw and Newsome."

"You are an attorney?"

"Yes," said Spann.

"Do you know the subject matter of this trial?"

"I'm familiar with it," Spann said. He had his hand on his hip as if he were still standing. "Mr. Barrett was on my staff when he was asked to represent Mr. Curtis. When Mr. Barrett left the firm, he continued to consult me on occasion concerning some of the idiosyncrasies of the case."

There was an arrogance to his tone that irked Carrie. She knew what he was going to try to do. He'd make sure everyone knew who the experienced attorney was.

"In case you're not aware," he went on, "this is a very complicated legal case."

Carrie just looked at him for a moment. She was going to enjoy the spanking she was about to give him.

"Do you know Robin Penrose?" she asked. She had moved to the center of the courtroom, questioning Spann without referring to notes.

"Only what Mr. Barrett has told me about her."

"So to your knowledge you have never met Robin Penrose?"

"I may have," he said with a casual lift of his shoulders. "I understand she worked for your father. I might have met her at his office or a social function, or maybe when the two of you were just kids," he said and smiled benignly at her. "But to answer your question, no, I don't specifically recall meeting her."

"Are you familiar with a company named Laramie Homes?" she asked, moving in another direction.

"I know it's some sort of real estate development company. They have projects all up and down the state."

"Have you ever purchased any of their stock or had anyone buy their stock for you?"

"No, I invest in real estate mostly," Spann said. "I find it less risky than the market. At least until recently." He smiled at the jury. One of the old hardcases grunted.

"Now, you stated, Mr. Spann, that you discussed this case on several occasions with Sean Barrett. Is that correct?"

"Yes."

"And some of those discussions have been as recent as the last few days. Is that right?"

"We discussed a few things about the case recently, yes."

"Would I be correct in stating that during the last few years you have served as Mr. Barrett's legal mentor? That is, he has sought your opinion on certain matters pertaining to his criminal caseload?"

"In case you're not aware of it, that's not unusual, Counselor. Attorneys often consult each other. When he worked for me, we often conferred on cases he was handling. My career began in criminal law, as you know, and I'm familiar with the problems."

"Did Mr. Barrett ever tell you that his investigation in this case may have involved the illegal trading of Laramie Homes stock?"

"Miss Robinson," he said, taking another opportunity to belittle her, "you should know that by answering that question, I could be breaking a confidential communication between your client and his attorney."

"Well, thank you, Mr. Spann," she said in a cute tone that had a few of the jury members smiling. "Then let me rephrase the question."

"I think you'd better," Spann scolded.

"Were you having an affair with Robin Penrose?"

The question caught him flush. It froze him a moment, long enough to let the jury see perhaps he wasn't as cool and confident as he wanted them to believe. "Well . . ." he said, stuttering slightly, "that would be difficult since I didn't know her, now wouldn't it?"

She moved in. "Is that a no, Mr. Spann?" she asked, pushing harder.

"That's correct," he said. A bead of sweat had formed above his lip.

Carrie walked to the defense table and picked up the aged photo of Robin.

"Now, Mr. Spann," she asked as she walked back to the witness stand, "have you ever seen the person depicted in this photograph?"

Spann took it from her.

"This appears to be some kind of artificially generated photograph."

"I'm not really interested in your photographic expertise. I only want to know if you've seen anyone that resembles the person in that photo."

"I don't think so," he said. Then he made a show of inspecting the photo very closely. "No, I've never seen this woman."

"I will now show you another photograph of someone who has been identified as Robin Penrose," she said, handing him the publicity shot of Robin.

She was in control now, continually switching from subject to subject. Spann didn't know what was coming next. He kept trying to slow her down with little time wasters like pretending to really go over the photo, but she kept at him.

"Have you ever seen the person depicted in this photograph?"

"No, I don't think so."

"Mr. Spann, you own a place in Palm Desert, do you not?"

Spann paused for a moment. "Yes, I have a condo there."

"And have you ever taken Robin Penrose there?" Carrie asked.

"No, Counselor," he said, his voice louder than he wanted, "I have not."

"Sir, isn't it true that you and Robin Penrose have been to your place in Palm Desert on several occasions?"

"Absolutely not."

Lowenstein stood up slowly, making a racket with his chair as he did. "Your Honor, I'm going to have to object," he said. Carrie swung around as he rose. "I can't tell who's testifying here."

"Would you like to be a little more specific, Counselor?" Macklin said to the prosecutor.

"Yes, Your Honor—" Lowenstein started to say, but Gamboa grabbed his arm. Lowenstein looked down and saw Gamboa had scratched the word SNITCH in bold red letters across his yellow legal pad.

"Could I have a moment?" he said to the judge as he sat down.

"Look, dipshit," Gamboa whispered as he leaned toward the prosecutor, "this'll be the last time I'm going to say this. If you don't keep your ass planted in that chair and be as quiet as a fucking little church mouse from here on out, I'll blow the fucking whistle on you and your snitch. And, Counselor," he said, squeezing Lowenstein's forearm until it tightened the D.A.'s shoulders, "if you think I'm just jerking off here, just try to interrupt her one more time."

Lowenstein stared at the maniac beside him. Was this lost cause of a case worth risking his career over? He'd get this asshole sometime, someplace.

"Mr. Lowenstein, are you or are you not objecting?" Macklin said.

"Your Honor, I'll withdraw my objection," Lowenstein finally said.

"Then you may proceed, Miss Robinson," Macklin said.

She turned to Spann again. "Let me ask you again, Mr. Spann, isn't it true that you and Robin Penrose were having an affair at the time of her disappearance?"

"No. Never!"

"And you accompanied her on several occasions to your place in Palm Desert?"

"No!"

"Does someone look after your place in Palm Desert when you're not there?" Carrie asked.

Spann looked at her with narrowed eyes. They both knew she had him trapped. The manager could identify Robin and him.

"Well, someone manages the complex," Spann said quietly.

"And would that someone be a Mr. Floyd McCracken?"

"Yes," Spann finally said, slow and serious like a mourner answering the chant of a priest.

"Thank you. Now, did you or did you not take Robin Penrose to your condo in Palm Desert?"

Spann felt the nauseating panic he never thought he'd feel in court. When he got his stomach to stop racing, he looked up at Macklin.

"Mr. Spann?" the judge asked.

"Your Honor," Spann said, "in accordance with the laws of the State of California and the Constitution of the United States, I would like to invoke my constitutional rights and respectfully decline to answer that question on the grounds that it may tend to incriminate me."

The courtroom burst into a loud gasp. Then it exploded. Newsmen were shoving at one another to get through the back door. Macklin was pounding his gavel and shouting, trying to get order.

"Would Counsel approach side bar?" he shouted through the din.

Carrie and Lowenstein hurried to the side of the bench away from the jury. Macklin leaned down to talk to them.

"Is it your intention to continue along these same lines, Miss Robinson?" he said. "If it is, he's probably just going to take the Fifth again. I think it's best if I let him talk to an attorney first."

Carrie put her hand on the top of the bench. "Your Honor," she said, "I don't think that's necessary because, believe me, I'm going to pursue an entirely new line of questioning."

Macklin nodded. "All right, but be careful," he said. "You can be very sure I'll stop you if you stray anywhere near that area again."

Carrie and Lowenstein were returning to counsel table when Sean, using a cane, walked into the courtroom through the back door.

"Hey, it's Barrett," one of the reporters yelled.

The courtroom erupted again—the reporters risking jail rather than their bosses' blue-note salute the next day.

"Are you going to take over again?"

"Was Spann the one that shot you?"

"Do you think Spann killed her?"

They crowded him, pushing from behind, and Sean lost his cane in the shuffle. He'd forgotten about the press.

"Go help him!" Carrie yelled to Mac.

He leapt over the gallery railing and pushed his way through, pulling bodies away from Sean. When he got to him, he wrapped his arm around Sean and pushed the cameras out of his face.

"What the hell kind of stunt is this?" Mac asked him as they made their way to the defense table. "Carrie's doing just fine."

By now Carrie was next to him. "What do you think you're doing?" she scolded. "This is very dumb. Look, let's have Mac drive you back to the hospital."

"I feel fine," Sean said.

Macklin was still up on the bench with the gavel in his hand, but he'd finally given up and just sat there until the roar settled. He shook his head while he stared at Sean.

"Can I have a moment with my co-counsel, Your Honor?" Sean finally asked.

"Why not?" Macklin said.

"I see Spann's still up there," Sean said to Carrie. "What's happening?"

"He's taking the Fifth. Macklin won't let me ask any more questions about his relationship with Robin. I was just about to question him about the stock scam," she said and looked at him. "Do you want to take over?"

He shook his head quickly. "No, no. It sounds like you're doing just fine. Do you mind if I just sit here and watch for a while?" Sean said as he slowly eased himself down into a chair next to Chad. "I hear things are going pretty well," he said to Chad, patting his arm.

"Yeah, Carrie's doing a great job. I hope she can nail him," Chad said with his fist clenched.

Sean turned back to Carrie. "How's Lowenstein been?"

"Hardly a peep out of him, actually," Carrie said.

"Good," Sean said and looked over and nodded at Gamboa. The detective nodded back.

The judge gaveled several times, and the gallery slowly calmed down.

"I assume you have your doctor's clearance to be here," Macklin joked after it had quieted.

Sean smiled back at the judge. "He doesn't seem to have quite the same power over me that you do, Your Honor."

"Is Miss Robinson going to continue?" Macklin asked.

"Yes, she is."

Smiling at Sean, Carrie picked up a stack of papers and walked back to the witness stand, where Spann sat readying himself for the next onslaught of questions. The appearance of Sean in the court-room made him visibly uneasy.

"Mr. Spann, I asked you earlier if you were familiar with Laramie Homes, do you remember that?"

"Yes, and I believe I said I had heard of them but had never invested in any of their stock," Spann said, trying to regain control. The long disturbance had settled him somewhat. But he knew he was in deep. He was certain now they had most of it figured out.

"How about Medtech Corporation? Have you ever heard of them?"

"Yes, I have. They manufacture medical supplies."

"And what about Kaufmann Industries, have you heard of them?"

"Yes, I have been their special counsel for approximately eight years."

"Then you must know that Kaufmann purchased Medtech just a few weeks ago?"

"Of course," he said agreeably.

"Then let me ask you. When Kaufmann purchased Medtech, did their stock increase in value?"

"I believe it did. Yes."

"As a matter of fact, the stock almost doubled within three or four days."

"I guess."

"You guess," Carrie said. There was acid in her tone. He'd fallen back on the Fifth, so the jury wouldn't mind now if she got testy. "Aren't you Kaufmann's attorney? Don't you know?"

"Yes, Counselor, the stock doubled in value."

"And couldn't someone in those companies who knew the purchase was going to take place have made a lot of money?"

"Yes. But that would be illegal."

"Weren't you aware beforehand that the purchase was going to take place?"

"No, I wasn't. I am only one of Kaufmann's attorneys. I didn't represent them on that particular transaction."

"But you were aware of it?" she said. She was standing by the jury.

"I may have known it was going to happen, but I didn't know

when," Spann said. "I believe only the top management at Medtech and Kaufmann were privy to that."

"I see," Carrie said and walked over slowly to Spann. She knew she had strayed into a completely irrelevant area and kept expecting Lowenstein to object. But the prosecutor was nestled comfortably in his seat with Gamboa at his elbow. Carrie intended to keep right on digging until Lowenstein tried to stop her.

"Well then, do you know a Mr. Shabba St. James?"

Spann, appearing unsettled by the question, sat up straight in his chair. "No, I don't believe so," he said.

Carrie stepped directly in front of him and continued her attack. "Have you not, Mr. Spann, represented Mr. St. James in the past and even used him as an investigator?"

Spann hesitated a moment before he answered. Now they were on to Shabba. "Now I remember, Miss Robinson," he said. "As you well know, it has been quite a while since I practiced criminal law. Yes, I believe I did represent a Mr. St. James and later used him on several occasions to locate witnesses for me. He was quite useful."

"And when was the last time you saw him?"

"Oh, I don't know. I'd guess six or seven years ago."

"So then you haven't had any dealings with him in the last several months?"

"No." He was shaking his head. "No reason to."

"The break-in of Medtech wasn't reason enough?"

"I don't know what you mean by that," he said quickly and sharply in defense.

"You do know that a few months ago Medtech was burglarized and a guard was shot and killed," she said.

"Of course I do. My firm was handling the defense of the employee accused of committing those crimes, a Mr. Theodore Berger."

"And who at your firm represented Mr. Berger?"

"Originally Sean Barrett, and after he left us a Mr. Scott Powers."

Carrie hesitated a moment and turned to the jury. "By the way, Mr. Spann, where are Mr. Berger and Mr. Powers today?"

"They're both dead."

"In fact, they were both *murdered*, isn't that correct, Mr. Spann?" She was coming at him again.

"Yes," he said.

"Would you know if Mr. Shabba St. James had anything to do with those murders?"

"No, I don't," he said. He looked around the courtroom, checking for the Jamaican.

"You know Mr. Gamboa, do you not?" Carrie said as she pointed in the direction of the prosecution's table.

"It has been some time, but yes, I have worked against him on several cases in the past." Spann nodded to Gamboa.

"Well, would it surprise you to learn, Mr. Spann, that the sergeant over there had quite a lengthy discussion with Mr. St. James just recently? And Mr. St. James admitted to the killing of both Berger and Powers?" Carrie bluffed, knowing that Shabba had admitted nothing of the sort.

Spann didn't answer.

"And that he also said that you hired him to break into Medtech to find out when the purchase by Kaufmann was to take place."

"That's preposterous," Spann finally said.

"Let me change the subject a little, Mr. Spann," Carrie said, stepping back a few feet. "Didn't you orchestrate the killings of not only Ted Berger and Scott Powers but also of a Mr. Eddie Romero?"

"How is any of this relevant to Ms. Penrose's murder?" Spann said. Then he glared at Lowenstein. "Why aren't you objecting?"

The D.A. glared back. It was nothing but a big loss for him now.

"Miss Robinson," Macklin finally said while looking at Lowenstein, "I guess I'll have to interrupt. Would you please ask only relevant questions? And remember, Mr. Spann is the one testifying, not you."

"Thank you, Your Honor, I will," she said and went right after him again. "Mr. Spann, didn't you pay Mr. St. James to hide Robin Penrose from the SEC?"

Spann didn't answer immediately. For the first time he saw an opening, at least a partial way out. It was obvious that the Jamaican would tell Gamboa everything to try to save himself from the gas chamber. If Spann could make it look like all the killings were Shabba's doing, then he might slip through the noose Carrie was neatly knotting for him. It was time for damage control. That's what he would advise his clients. Admit to what you know you can't get out of and deny the rest. That way your denial will seem more credible.

"Miss Robinson," he said, reaching toward her, "could I see those photographs again, especially the one of the old woman?"

Carrie walked back to the counsel table and then handed the computer-aged photograph to Spann.

"I was wrong, Miss Robinson," Spann said after he'd pretended to reassess the photo. "I do know this young lady."

Macklin immediately jumped on Spann's turnaround. "Are you withdrawing your right to assert the Fifth Amendment, Mr. Spann?"

"Yes, Your Honor," Spann said, turning to the judge, "I was just confused. I'll retract what I said earlier."

The courtroom erupted again. Reporters poured out the door and Macklin started banging. "Bailiff, anyone who goes out this time doesn't get back in!"

When they heard this, there was an immediate backwash of media. When they'd found a place to sit or crouch, Macklin turned to Carrie. "You may proceed, Counsel," he said.

"Could you tell me the name of the person depicted in these photos?"

"Yes, it's Robin Penrose," Spann said. "And, if I may, Counsel, I could save a lot of time by saying at the time of her disappearance Miss Penrose and I were having an affair."

Spann spent the next thirty minutes telling of his involvement in the stock scam, how Robin and he had split the profits, and when the SEC got wind of it, how he had Shabba hide her in his Palm Desert condo.

"But everything fell apart when Mr. Curtis was arrested?" Carrie asked.

"Well, Ms. Robinson, I must admit it would appear that way at first, but actually it was a blessing." Spann looked at Chad and smiled.

"A blessing, sir?"

"You see, after she was missing for several weeks everyone began to think she was dead. When Chad was arrested, that clinched it. The SEC did exactly what everyone else did: they concluded the same thing. Now there was no one to prosecute for the illegal trading, so they closed their file."

"But there was one problem, wasn't there, Mr. Spann?"

"Of course. Chad Curtis. But Robin was able to handle him. It didn't take her long to understand how perfect his being a suspect was. And he was blindly in love with Robin. So he agreed to go along—with the understanding, of course, that if he was ever convicted, Robin would come forward."

"And Mr. Shabba St. James helped you and Robin make sure Chad would not be convicted?"

"That's correct," Spann said.

"But weren't you afraid that if Chad was acquitted, the SEC would start up their investigation again?"

Spann laughed. "That was the least of my concerns. The SEC would think Chad was acquitted not because Robin was alive but because twelve gullible jurors were fooled by a clever lawyer."

"And what if your plan didn't work? What if Chad was convicted?" Carrie asked.

"The thought never occurred to me."

"Come on now, Mr. Spann. Isn't it true that if Chad was convicted, you were going to have St. James take care of him the same way he took care of Ted Berger?"

"I don't know what you are talking about," Spann said, waving the back of his hand at her as if dismissing the thought.

"Mr. Spann, you know exactly what I am talking about," Carrie shot back. Then she suddenly shifted to another subject. "You and Robin Penrose made a great deal of money on the Laramie Homes deal, didn't you?"

"I guess," Spann said.

"You made so much money with such little effort that you were going to have Robin Penrose do the same thing with Kaufmann Industries stock."

"That's incorrect."

"Incorrect, Mr. Spann? Well, would it surprise you to learn that's exactly what Shabba St. James told Sergeant Gamboa?" Carrie turned and walked toward Gamboa.

"Shabba St. James is not credible, and you and Mr. Gamboa know it. He will say anything to save his own neck. I have admitted to my wrongdoings with Ms. Penrose. That was the end of it. The last thing Robin or I wanted was another scam. Besides, we were too busy trying to help Chad Curtis."

"But, Mr. Spann, didn't at least five weeks elapse after the Laramie Homes deal before the SEC became suspicious?"

"Approximately."

"And would it surprise you to learn that sometime during those five weeks is when Shabba St. James helped burglarize Medtech and kill the guard?"

"Nothing Shabba St. James does or says would surprise me."

Carrie paced the courtroom a moment. Spann was still hiding the worst of it. With Shabba in the hospital, Spann would have to have butchered Robin himself.

"I appreciate your candor, Mr. Spann," she said. "But you've left out a few things, haven't you?"

"Oh, really," he said.

The jury turned to her. What else was there?

"When Carter Robinson went to the SEC and confessed to insider trading, you knew you would be found out for your involvement in *both* stock purchases, unless you destroyed the one person who could connect you to your crime—Robin Penrose." She was shouting as she charged at him. "You killed Robin Penrose because she was going to turn herself in and expose you."

Spann looked up at Carrie and smiled. Then he looked over at Sean and said, "Am I correct in assuming that the defense feels Robin Penrose had to have been killed sometime between Thursday of last week and Monday?"

"That's correct," Carrie said.

"Then I couldn't have killed her," Spann said smugly.

"And why would that be?" Carrie asked, afraid that Spann had found an escape.

"I was at your father's side as his attorney when he was being interviewed by the SEC from last Thursday through the weekend. I couldn't have killed her," he said and pointed into the gallery at Carter. "Ask your father."

Carrie turned to look at her father, who nodded his head.

"Now maybe someone will believe me when I say that Shabba was out of control!" Spann cried. "I had nothing to do with any of it. I didn't order the break-in. And I never ordered Shabba to kill anyone."

Carrie walked to the lectern and fumbled with some papers to stall for time. It suddenly struck her that she no longer knew who had killed Robin. Until this minute she was sure it had been Spann. She knew it couldn't have been Shabba because Gamboa had had the

Jamaican in custody when Robin was killed. But she was certain of one thing. Spann had shot Sean. She turned back to Spann and began to question him again.

"Did you have a discussion with Mr. Barrett at the Santa Ana Country Club last Tuesday night?" she asked.

"Yes, I believe so," Spann said.

"After this discussion with Mr. Barrett," Carrie stated, "do you recall what you did the rest of that evening?"

"I believe I went right home," Spann said.

"So your wife could confirm that?"

"My wife was out of town."

"I see," Carrie said. "So you went right home?"

"Correct."

"You didn't take a drive out to Capistrano?"

"Well, you seem to know everything I did that night, Counsel. Suppose you tell me," Spann snapped.

"You know better than that, Mr. Spann," Macklin said, irritated. "Just answer the question."

"No, I didn't take a drive out to Capistrano."

"You are aware that Mr. Barrett was shot that night, are you not?"

Lowenstein rolled his eyes. He would normally have jumped out of his seat and objected. Sean's shooting had no bearing on the murder of Robin Penrose. But the no-body victory was lost, so he sat disinterested while the trial proceeded to its conclusion without him.

Macklin looked at Spann. "You can answer the question."

"That's what I read in the papers."

"Well, weren't you there that night?" Carrie asked.

"I already answered that question."

"So you did, sir. Let me ask another question, then. How many cars do you own?"

Spann hesitated as if he had to think about it. "Two. My wife drives a new Jaguar, and I drive a Mercedes."

"What model is your Mercedes?"

"One of the big ones," he said proudly. "A 560 SEL."

"What color is it?"

"Silver."

"Tinted windows?"

"Smoked."

Carrie began to pace in front of Spann while she raced through the next series of questions. "You said your wife was out of town. Is she still out of town?"

"Yes, she is."

"Then she couldn't have been driving your car that night, is that correct?"

Spann shook his head. "It doesn't seem likely, does it?"

"And your Mercedes wasn't reported stolen?"

"No."

"And you're not aware of anyone else driving your car that night?"

"It was locked in the garage," he said. He was watching her closely as she paced back and forth.

"Oh, by the way, Mr. Spann," Carrie said, "can you tell me what the license plate on your Mercedes reads?"

"TP ATRNY," he said with a smile.

"Are you aware, sir, that the date and time that Sean Barrett was shot was March 22 at approximately eight-thirty p.m.?"

"Yes. That sounds correct."

She stepped forward and put her hand on the rail of the witness stand. "Then let me ask you this," she said. "Could you explain to me why your car was parked at Doheny Beach at eight-sixteen p.m. on March 22?"

"I assume you're going somewhere with this line of questioning," Spann asked as if he were the prosecution. Then he looked up at Macklin. "Your Honor, do I have to answer these questions? What relevancy does all this have with Robin Penrose's death?"

"Mr. Spann," Macklin said, "as you are aware, this court decides relevancy, not the witness. Answer the question."

Spann turned to Carrie. The last of his arrogance was gone. He knew she had something that could hurt him. "Could you please repeat the question?" he said.

"Let me ask you this, Mr. Spann. Have you been to Mr. Barrett's beach house on prior occasions?"

He nodded. "Yes, two or three times."

"Was that during the day or the night?"

"I don't recall ever being there in the evening."

"Where did you normally park your car?"

"The parking lot right down from his house."

"Are you referring to the public parking lot?" she asked, still standing in front of him.

"Yes, that's the one."

"Do you know if it's open at night?"

"I don't know. I assume it is."

She backed away from him as from an attack dog.

"Are you aware that there is a one-hour parking limit at Doheny Beach until ten p.m.?"

"No," Spann said slowly. "I'm not."

Carrie walked over to counsel table and pulled a slip of yellow paper from a file folder.

"Your Honor," she said, "I would like to have marked for iden-tification, 'Defendant E.' May I approach the witness, Your Honor?"

"Go ahead," Macklin said.

"Mr. Spann, would you please look at this slip of paper marked 'Defendant E' and tell us what it is."

Spann took the paper and looked at both sides. "It appears to be a parking citation issued by the Capistrano Police Department."

"Let's quit playing games, Mr. Spann," she said. "Look at this citation and let me ask you, isn't it a fact that a 1992 Mercedes with the license plate TP ATRNY was issued a parking citation, *this* ci-tation, at eight-sixteen on the night Sean Barrett was shot?"

Spann didn't answer.

"Can you tell me," Carrie went on, "how this citation could have been issued if your car was locked in your garage that entire night?"

"I can't," Spann said, barely audible.

"Come on, Mr. Spann, explain to this court, if you can, why your car was parked in that lot at approximately the same time Sean Barrett was shot."

After a long pause, Spann looked up at Macklin once again. "Your Honor," he said, "in accordance with the laws of the State of California and the Constitution of the United States, I would like to invoke my constitutional rights and respectfully decline to answer that question on the grounds that it may tend to incriminate me."

"Miss Robinson," the judge said, "it is obvious to me by now that anything Mr. Spann has to say about his involvement with the shooting of Mr. Barrett would not only tend to incriminate him, but is also irrelevant to this murder trial. Now, unless you want to question Mr. Spann in a different area, I will let Mr. Lowenstein begin his cross-examination."

"No, I think I'm finished with the witness," Carrie said and sat down.

"Mr. Lowenstein?" Macklin asked, "cross-exam?"

Lowenstein had been sitting expressionlessly during the past hour as if nothing of great import had occurred. He looked at Macklin. This piece of shit was lost, he thought. He might as well do what he could to get out of it as gracefully as possible.

"No questions," Lowenstein finally said.

"Mr. Spann, you can step down, but it's my understanding that you are to remain in the courtroom. There are some gentlemen who would like to talk to you," Macklin said and pointed at the chair next to Seelicke's desk. "Just take a seat right there."

The courtroom exploded once again. Reporters fighting their way to the phones, minicams rolling for an update, the gallery awash with what had happened. Spann would eventually go to jail for a long time, that was certain. But neither he nor Shabba nor Carter could have killed the girl. And that was what this trial was all about. Who had killed Robin Penrose?

chapter

forty-one

"Miss Robinson, call your next witness," Macklin said as the court-room returned to order.

Carrie looked over at Sean. She knew the best thing to do now was to call the witnesses from Bakersfield and San Francisco and then rest their case. Surely no jury would convict in light of what Chad had said and Spann's testimony that Robin had been alive until some time last week.

Sean leaned toward Carrie and whispered, "If you don't mind, I found out something early this morning. Can I take it from here?"

"Of course. It's still your case." Carrie smiled and rested her hand on his. "Are you sure you're all right?" she said.

"I'm fine," Sean said, grabbing his cane and pulling himself to his feet. He still was in some pain, but there was no place he would rather be at this moment than in the eye of this legal storm.

"Glad to see you're up and about, Mr. Barrett," Macklin dead-panned. "That's all this circus needed was another act."

"Thank you, Your Honor," Sean smiled. "I certainly appreciate your concern."

Macklin smiled back.

"With the court's permission I would like to take over the defense now," Sean said.

Macklin waved his hand. "Go ahead."

"I'd like to call Mr. Craig MacDuff."

Mac stood up and walked to the stand to let the court swear him in. He knew where Sean was going with this. He needed Mac to confirm the existence of the witnesses who had seen Robin alive since her disappearance and explain to the jury what he'd gotten from the witnesses in Vegas.

"What's your occupation and assignment, Mr. MacDuff?" Sean started.

"I'm a licensed private investigator currently working for the defense on this case," Mac said and pulled his tie tight to hide his unbuttoned collar.

"On March 17 were you instructed by me to go to an address in Palm Desert to locate Robin Penrose?" Sean said. He was a few feet from Mac, half resting on the cane.

"Yes," Mac said, readjusting his seat. The chair was too small for him. "I went there, but I couldn't find her at the address you gave me."

"Did you find any evidence that Robin Penrose had been at that address?"

"No," Mac said, shaking his head.

"What did you do after you learned no one was there?" Sean walked over to the jury box and leaned against it.

"I spent the next couple of days on surveillance around the condo waiting for her to show up, talking to neighbors to see if they knew anything about the missing girl."

"Did you obtain any information that someone else had seen her at that location?"

"No."

Sean crossed his arms. He was wearing a coat that was a size large for him to accommodate the bandages around his chest. It was Dr. Bergman's coat. Sean had finally talked him into letting him go if he promised to return in a few hours.

"How long did you continue your surveillance?"

"From Thursday, the day you sent me, until, let's see, Sunday."

"So you continued to look for Robin Penrose in Palm Desert that entire weekend?"

Mac hesitated for a second, wondering where Sean was headed. "Yes," he said.

Sean turned and motioned to Carrie, who walked up to him. "Your Honor, can I have just one second?" Sean said a few words to her, and she walked out of the courtroom. A minute later she returned escorting Terwilliger. She seated him in the front row in plain view of Mac.

When Sean turned back to Mac the two old friends stared for a moment into each other's eyes. There was a clear understanding between them. Sean wasn't going to settle for anything but the truth.

"Now, Mr. MacDuff," Sean continued, "do you recognize the person that was just seated?"

"Yes, that's Pete Terwilliger. We were both with the Sheriff's Department together years ago."

"And more recently?"

"I saw him in Vegas," Mac said. "He's a pit boss at the Desert Sands Hotel, where I stayed while investigating this case."

Sean took a few steps toward Mac, leaning more heavily on the cane now. Dr. Bergman had been right. He wasn't going to last long. "Do you know the dates you were at the Desert Sands?"

"Not exactly. The first time was about three weeks ago when Terwilliger first identified Curtis's photo. But I'd have to check my notes for the exact date," Mac said and reached for his coat pocket where he kept his pad.

"That's all right," Sean said and waved him off. "Have you seen Mr. Terwilliger at the hotel since then?"

"Yes. I went back a couple days later to interview witnesses at the banks."

"And have you been back to the Desert Sands since?"

"I was there the night you were shot," Mac said. "Interviewing more witnesses," he added.

Sean stepped up closer. "Mr. MacDuff, do you recall the weekend I sent you to Palm Desert to look for Robin Penrose?"

"Yes."

"Weren't you in Las Vegas that weekend as well?"

Mac looked over at Terwilliger as if he could help him. He suddenly knew what Sean was getting at. "Oh, yeah, I forgot about that," he said. "I went back and played a little blackjack that weekend. Sorry, Sean. I meant to tell you." He smiled, a little embarrassed.

"Then why did you just tell this court you were in Palm Desert that entire weekend?"

"I didn't want you to find out about it because I didn't want you to think I wasn't doing my job. But I got bored sitting around waiting for some chick to show up who we all knew was already dead. So I drove up to Vegas later that Saturday night."

"And you did a little gambling?" Sean asked.

"Yeah, you know, I like to play blackjack," Mac said.

"How much cash did you have with you?"

"I had a hot hand," Mac said. "So I had a few bucks."

"Like maybe a million of them?"

"No way," Mac said.

Sean walked slowly toward the witness stand. "You knew when you went to look for Robin Penrose in Palm Desert that she probably had at least a million in cash with her, didn't you?" Sean said.

"Yeah," Mac said warily, "I was aware of that."

"So we can assume that since you didn't find Robin Penrose in Palm Desert, you also didn't find the money she had with her."

"Hey," Mac said, moving around in the old chair, "it was a few bucks I had put aside. Don't make such a big deal of it, Sean."

"All right," Sean said and changed direction on him. "Let me ask you something else, then. While performing your duties as a private investigator, do you have occasion to use a camera?"

"Sure, all the time," Mac said, relaxing again.

"Do you recall taking any photos concerning this case in the last week or two?"

"This case?" Mac screwed his face up, thinking it over. "No, not that I can recall."

Sean approached Mac and showed him the photo of Robin with her throat cut open.

"For the record, I am showing you a photo admitted into evidence as 'People's number 74' for identification. Do you recognize it?"

"Yes," Mac said without looking at the photo.

"Did you take this photo?" Sean said.

"How could I do that?"

"Did you take the picture?" Sean asked. The cane was shaking at his side.

"Absolutely not!" Mac said, looking over at Terwilliger for help.

"All right, then. Could you tell us what Robin Penrose is wearing around her neck in this picture?"

Mac looked down at the photo. "A locket."

"Is it your understanding from interviews with her mother and close friends that she never took that locket off even to shower?"

"That's what they all told me," Mac said.

"Have you ever seen a close-up of that locket?"

"A close-up?" Mac asked. "No."

"Your Honor," Sean said, "would you allow the bailiff to set up the slide projector on the counsel table and put the screen next to the witness, so Mr. MacDuff and the jury have a clear view of it?"

"Go ahead."

When Seelicke was finished setting up the projector and screen, Sean continued, "Now, Mr. MacDuff, let's see if we can get a close-up of that locket."

Sean pushed a button on the projector, and the picture of the dead girl flashed on the screen.

"As you can see, this is a duplicate of the photo marked 'People's 74.' Now, I am going to show you an enlargement of just this area here," Sean said and pointed at the girl's neck and chest where the locket lay.

He pushed the projector button, and a close-up of the locket appeared on the screen. "As you can see, from this enlargement every detail of the locket is shown, including an inscription at the bottom. Can you make out what it says, Mr. MacDuff?"

Mac leaned forward to get a better look. "It says, 'Denmark.' Must of been made in Denmark."

"Now, how about the reflection in the locket? Can you make that out?"

"No, looks like somebody's shadow or something. I can't make it out."

"Well, then let's look at a further enlargement of the photo, shall we?"

Sean reached over to the projector again. But before he pushed

357

the button, he asked, "Before I do, is there any part of your testimony that you would like to change, Mr. MacDuff?"

Mac shrugged. "Like what?"

"Come on, Mac. Let's quit playing games," Sean said. His tone was harsh. "When you arrived in Palm Desert on the night of March 17, didn't you find Robin Penrose alive?"

"No!"

"And didn't you find approximately a million dollars in cash that she had there with her?" he asked, waving the cane at Mac.

"No."

"And all that money was just too much for you, wasn't it, Mr. MacDuff?"

"What are you getting at?"

"I'll tell you what I'm getting at," Sean thundered. "Did you kill Robin Penrose?"

"No," Mac said, looking at the judge, the jury, Carrie, Chad, all of them. The bailiffs stood ready.

"And after you killed her, didn't you take the million in cash and then photograph her and send the photograph, *this* photograph," Sean said, pointing at the screen, "to the district attorney's office to make it easier for them to convict Chad Curtis?"

"That's crazy!"

"It was perfect, wasn't it, Mac? Chad was already on trial for her death, and with that photo you knew he would be convicted and that would be the end of it. And you'd be a million dollars richer with no one even bothering to look for the money because they thought it had disappeared along with the dead girl."

Sean pushed the button on the projector.

"The locket. Look at the locket, Mac! And tell us all what you see!"

Mac looked up at the screen and then bowed his head while Sean continued to yell at him, "I said, tell us what you see! Tell us what you see!"

The courtroom erupted again—the press running out into the hall and the spectators screaming and yelling.

Even Macklin was stunned. He sat back in his chair and mumbled, "I'll be damned!" as he stared at the image reflected in the locket. It was a fuzzy image of Mac and his unmistakable handlebar mustache, with what looked like a camera poised in front of his face.

Mac grabbed Sean's arm and said under the din of the courtroom, "Damn it, Sean. There was just so much money."

"Your Honor," Sean said, "I think Mr. MacDuff needs to consult with an attorney. I have no further questions."

Mac started to get up, but Macklin pointed at him. "Mr. MacDuff, stay right there. I believe someone will want to talk to you too."

Then Macklin turned to Lowenstein. "Do you have any motions to make?"

"Your Honor, move to dismiss all charges against Mr. Curtis," Lowenstein said without even bothering to get up.

"And I take it there will be no objection to this motion, Mr. Barrett?"

"Not a chance, Your Honor," Sean said smiling.

"Case dismissed!" Macklin said and slammed the gavel down for the last time. "Mr. Curtis, you are free to go. This court is adjourned!"

Carrie and Sean came out of the courtroom arm in arm with Chad and answered the media's questions for several minutes until Carrie broke them off. "Mr. Barrett has to get back to the hospital. Can we do this later?"

Sean gave Chad the keys to the SL, and he hurried off to start his life again.

"You amazed me back in there, Sean," Carrie said. "How did you do that?"

Gamboa was right behind them by now. "Yeah," he said, grabbing Sean's shoulder, "how the hell *did* you do that? I thought I saw something on that locket too. So I had the lab boys blow that photo up until it was bigger than Arizona. We got it so we could see somebody with what looked like a camera but never clear enough to make out who it was."

"I had the same problem," Sean said. "I was pretty sure Mac was guilty before I blew it up, though. I was preparing Terwilliger to testify when he told me that Mac was in Vegas that weekend. That's when I knew Mac had to have killed her."

"Why?" Carrie asked.

"He was blowing money in Vegas like a drug dealer. And not just at the Desert Sands," Sean said. "Where did he get all that money? The rest was easy after that."

A few cameras started to gather around them again. "Come on, let's keep walking," Sean said. They went through the front doors and down the steps. Sean was feeling weaker. He leaned against the railing at the bottom of the steps.

"You still haven't told me how you got such a clear blowup," Gamboa said.

"Well, that was just a little creative evidence-gathering."

"What's that mean?" Gamboa asked.

"I had an old photo of Mac at the racetrack looking through binoculars. So I had a photographer superimpose it onto the locket," Sean said.

Gamboa couldn't believe what he was hearing. "That's dishonest!"

"Maybe," Sean said. "But I figured that photo was never going to be admitted as evidence. Even if it costs me my license and a criminal charge or two, it would be worth it. It was the only way to nail him. So I went for the bluff. If he didn't kill her, that blowup would never have caused him to confess."

"That's true," Gamboa said. "But that means I probably can't use the confession."

"That wouldn't be the first confession you weren't able to use," Sean kidded.

"But to risk your license?" Carrie said.

"I know. I thought that over a lot. But I had to get him."

"Ah, who cares anyway?" Gamboa said. "How they going to know you faked the evidence?"

"Hey, all they need is that slide."

"Come on, Counselor! You mean the slide that you gave me and I seemed to have misplaced?" Gamboa said and slipped the slide into his top pocket. "You know," the detective said, "my life was a lot simpler when we were enemies."